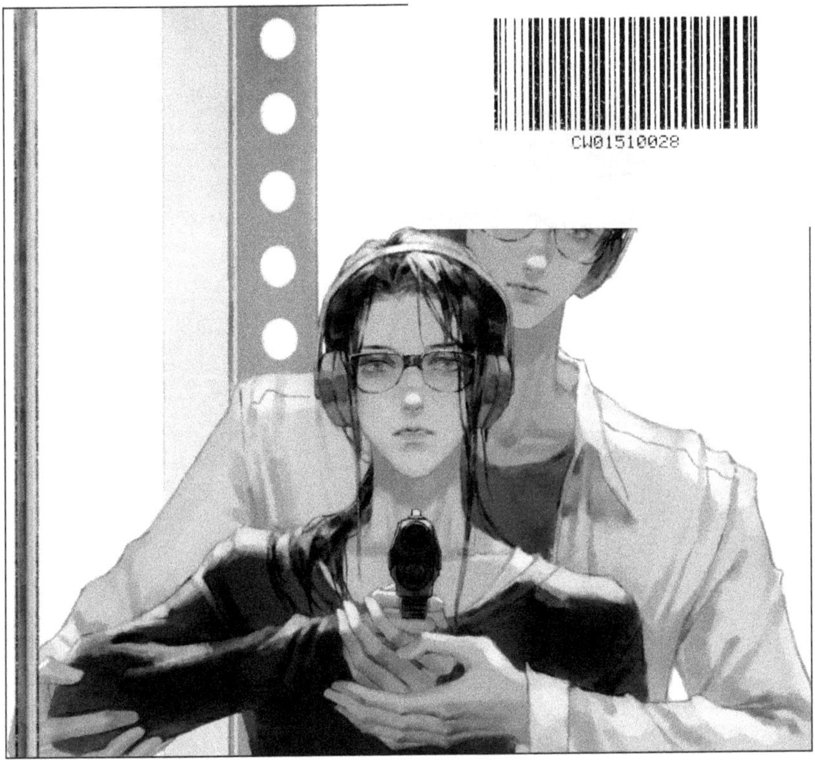

CW01510028

kids make choices, adults make love.

Via Lactea

VOL.02

ROSE
AND
RENAISSANCE

STARRING XIA XIQING	STARRING ZHOU ZHENG	AUTHOR ZHI CHU	

Born to be Loved.
Compared to the boundless night sky, the light of one star is very faint.
But as long as the star continues to shine, it is not pure darkness.

Rose and Renaissance

An imprint of Via Lactea Ltd.

Author: Zhi Chu
Translator: MS; XiA; Meiling
Editor: Michaela M

CONTACT:
Customer Support: info@vialactea.ca
Wholesale & Distribution: market@vialactea.ca
Other Cooperation: https://vialactea.ca/pages/cooperation
Discord Channel: https://discord.gg/vialactea

Follow us on Twitter/Instagram/Facebook: @ViaLactea_Ltd
Official Website: www.vialactea.ca

ISBN: 978-1-77408-359-8(pbk)
Printed in Canada

LOCATION:
Shops At Waterloo Town Square
#27, 75 King Street South, Waterloo, ON
Canada
N2J 1P2

Rose
and
Renaissance

His gift is the most beautiful rose in the universe,
nourished by the stars and the milky way.
It will never wither and die. It will be among the stars,
blooming forever.

"The romance of the universe is what I want to give you."

Only roses match you.

ROSE AND RENAISSANCE

CONTENT

THE MOVIE STARTS ◎ ◎ ◎

◎ ◎ ◎

Butterfly Memory

When they land at the airport, Xia Xiqing can palpably feel Zhou Ziheng's rising popularity. He was already a lethal weapon in the entertainment industry, and now with the blessings of a reality show and this pairing, he's unstoppable compared to the other celebrities of his generation.

Xiao-Luo and a few bodyguards surround Zhou Ziheng, enclosing his tall form and creating a wall in front of the fans to make way for him.

Zhou Ziheng alone would not be difficult to protect. But now he's traveling with a popular boy band member, a very pretty lady, and his "other half." Shang Sirui, being the gentleman, asks his bodyguards to protect Ruan Xiao while he follows behind.

Xia Xiqing is walking behind Zhou Ziheng when a fan suddenly pulls on his sleeve, exposing a portion of his shoulder. He quickly regains composure and pulls his shirt back up.

"Don't pull Xiqing's clothes!"

"Xiqing's clothes!"

"Who's pulling? Let go!"

Xia Xiqing can't help but frown. The life of a star is difficult; no matter how angry he is, he must not lose his temper. Thus, he endures it.

Looking back, he can't see which fan was tugging on his shirt in the crowd of people. Feeling helpless, he says, "No need to tear my shirt."

The scene is chaotic. Zhou Ziheng suddenly stops walking and reaches out to a girl's wrist. "Let go."

The girl lets go of Xia Xiqing and looks up blankly at Zhou Ziheng.

"Don't do that, it's dangerous." Zhou Ziheng turns and adjusts Xia Xiqing's torn shirt, then walks on his other side to block his torn clothes from the crowd.

The fans are getting more and more excited, and the bodyguards are starting to lose patience. They reach out to push for more room, but Zhou Ziheng stops them.

"Don't push them," he says sternly. "Pushing can cause a stampede." His voice grows louder. "Don't block us, please. There are plenty of opportunities to see us. Be careful. Don't fall and stay safe."

Xia Xiqing, still quite irritated, can't help but find this situation amusing—Zhou Ziheng; magnificent saint that he is. Any other person would have cursed hundreds of times.

He tilts his head to look at the hand supporting his shoulder. A sudden sense of envy rushes through him. Not quite envy, but jealousy. Regardless of the situation, Zhou Ziheng is always able to respond positively.

A natural gentleman.

Despite all that Xia Xiqing has done to him, he still offers a helping hand. Following the morals in his heart, he always offers protection to those who are in need even if they aren't worthy.

Xia Xiqing can't stand that type of person. Their existence makes him feel more despicable than he already is.

The crew takes them to the recording location of the next episode. The schedule is tight this time around, so meals are casual between filming sessions. Zhou Ziheng, Xia Xiqing, and Shang Sirui share a large dressing room and Xiao-Luo and Shang Sirui's assistant bring takeout to them.

"Xia Xiqing," Xiao-Luo calls out. "Try this; it's a well-known place around here, you'll like it. It's the perfect meal for you."

Xia Xiqing responds with a smile. He's not expecting much—the last few times he's eaten with Zhou Ziheng, he found that the man didn't eat a single bite of spicy food. However, he's met with surprise when he walks toward the table. As Xiao-Luo is unpacking the food, he notices that while half the dishes look plain, the other half are bright red with chili peppers.

It is clear which half is Zhou Ziheng's meal.

"Zhou Ziheng ordered it all; I just picked them up," Xiao-Luo explains while covering his mouth, then chuckles. "If you don't like it, blame Zhou Ziheng."

Zhou Ziheng walks in, having just changed clothes. He now sports a simple outfit that closely matches Xia Xiqing's, with a dark blue hoodie and light blue jeans. Xia Xiqing lowers his head and looks at himself, confirming that despite a few subtle differences, they almost look like twins. He smiles, thinking the shippers will go crazy once they see the upcoming episode.

"Hey, you're back, Zhou Ziheng. Wow, you two look alike."

Xiao-Luo scratches his head. "The crew did that on purpose?"

Zhou Ziheng's expression immediately becomes unnatural. He pretends to kick Xiao-Luo. "What? Nah, shut up."

Xia Xiqing chuckles slightly and sits on the couch. "You ordered this?"

"Me?" Zhou Ziheng also sits down while pointing at Xiao-Luo's innocent face. "Xiao-Luo, did you do this? Are you trying to kill me with spiciness?"

Xiao-Luo and Xia Xiqing lock eyes with each other, trying not to laugh.

Zhou Ziheng combs a hand through his hair, looking like a teenager, and says awkwardly, "This is too spicy for me; you eat it. I'll eat the half that's not spicy."

"Hmm..." Xia Xiqing looks at him with a faint smile.

Zhou Ziheng is afraid of him when he talks like that, but he's happy to have the old Xia Xiqing back. The person on the plane gave him a strange and sad feeling. He lowers his head, grabs a pair of chopsticks, and buries his head into the food.

"Dig in."

"Thanks. This is my favorite; what a coincidence." Xia Xiqing picks up a pair of chopsticks and begins eating.

Hearing those words, Zhou Ziheng feels happier inside. In order to maintain the lie, he can only remain silent and carry on eating his food.

Soon, Shang Sirui shows up, humming a song. Xia Xiqing glances at him.

"You look happy."

"It's our title song for the new album. What do you think?"

His assistant shakes his head helplessly. "Alright, calm down, king of spoilers."

Shang Sirui doesn't seem bothered by the comment and jumps on the side of the couch. "Wow, smells good. And you two really look alike." He pulls down his dark red coat and sits next to Xia Xiqing. "You know, red and blue have been good buddies since the beginning of time." Putting his chin on Xia Xiqing's shoulder, he asks, "I want to eat too. I like that type of spicy chicken."

"Okay." Xia Xiqing picks up a piece of chicken and feeds it to Shang Sirui. "Open wide!"

This kind of intimate behavior happens quite frequently between these two, and Zhou Ziheng thought he was used to it. However, he was wrong. He quietly eats a few bites of rice. His chest feels like a lemon being squeezed for every last drop of juice.

Finally, he gets up in preparation for styling. Shang Sirui comments in surprise, "Zhou Ziheng, you ate so little."

"Have to manage my weight, might need to audition next week."

It's not completely a lie, Zhou Ziheng comforts himself.

Shang Sirui's assistant opens a box of fried chicken and places it in front of Shang Sirui, who takes a large piece and stuffs into his mouth. "Must be one of those tragedy films again, right? If you're doing a TV drama, maybe I can try for a supporting role."

Zhou Ziheng, sitting in front of the styling mirror, replies, "Yeah, sure, when I have a script about a man and his pet."

Shang Sirui has no response to this small slight, so he turns his pique into appetite and eats more chicken.

Before the filming session begins, the guests gather together. Some crew members bring in blindfolds and escort them to their initial rooms. Xia Xiqing discovers that Ruan Xiao's clothes arc very similar to Shang Sirui's; a red denim jacket with black jeans. Is it possible that they're grouped like this for a reason? Just like the last episode, the clothing probably means something.

If it's true, then it's quite obvious.

If this episode has the same screenwriter, they'll know the story when they're fully immersed in it.

Xia Xiqing is intrigued and indulges himself in deep thoughts. He raises his head and sees Zhou Ziheng looking back at him. There seems to be worry in his eyes, but before they can react, the blindfolds are put in place.

Fuck. He almost forgot about this part.

From the darkness, he feels his arms being grabbed by someone leading him to walk forward. Not long after, he is instructed to sit down.

Sitting in the chair, Xia Xiqing hears footsteps get further and further away until they disappear. The darkness inevitably causes discomfort, but fortunately, it does not last long. He hears the familiar voice of the announcer.

"Hello everyone! Welcome once more to *Survive and Escape*. First, everyone please remove your blindfolds."

I can just take it off this time? Xia Xiqing thinks, pleasantly surprised. He quickly rescues himself from the darkness and begins to scan the room. It appears to be an ordinary bedroom, with dark blue wallpaper and gray bedding. Some video games are scattered on the table. It looks like a teenage boy's room.

The biggest difference this time is that he has spawned here by himself. He feels empty. Maybe he's just not used to it.

"Before we begin, I would like to outline the structure of this game. Please note that you are each trapped in different rooms. If you wish to emerge victorious, you must escape your room by solving various puzzles and eventually crack the puzzle of the final outer door. Just like last episode, there is a Killer among you, and they can choose to kill one of the other players. If the Killer wins, all regular players will gain no points this round. You will again be using your phones to vote anonymously. Those who are killed or voted out will not be able to continue the game.

"You should also note that there is a radio in each of your rooms. While you are in separate rooms, you are able to communicate with other players through this radio.

"Three... Two... One...

"The game begins now!"

Radio? Xia Xiqing stands up and walks around. He finds the cameras that have been strategically placed around the room by the crew. In the center of the room, there is a table with a small rug beneath it. On the table, there is a radio.

The layout of the room is very realistic, like someone actually lives here. Beside the bed there is a desk with a chair tucked into it, and a laptop rests on the desk next to some stacked books and a lamp.

What's strange is that many items in this room are arranged in circles—for example, the cup on the desk is set in a circular indent. Xia Xiqing picks up the cup and gently knocks the circle with his knuckle.

Hollow.

This is only one of many circles around the room. Xia Xiqing finds it odd, but is unable to offer a reasonable explanation.

"Right, the radio," Xia Xiqing deliberately says to himself, knowing he is being recorded. He walks to the rug and lifts it up. There are no objects beneath, but there are a similar circle of indents as seen on the desk.

He tries the radio, but hears only noise. This technology was slightly before his time. There are three knobs on it, one blue and two red. The red knobs are different from each other. One has a "o" under it, while the other one is blank.

Blue?

He remembers Zhou Ziheng's clothes and makes a reasonable guess that they are related. However, nothing interesting happens when he tries to turn it in either direction. Nothing but noise.

Knowing the difficulty level of the puzzles in this show, this is not going to be easy. He puts the radio down without turning it off and begins to search for other clues while listening to its noise.

He goes back to the desk and opens one of the books. A bookmark falls out.

It's made from a butterfly specimen.

Xia Xiqing picks it up and stares at the insect trapped in transparent film, thinking about his days in elementary school.

In science class, the teacher had asked everyone to go home and catch some kind of insect with their parents, then bring it back to class next week for show and tell.

Xia Xiqing was not a fan of hard-shelled bugs that live in the soil. Butterflies with beautiful wings were more his thing.

But neither of his parents wanted to help him with bug hunting.

"I don't have time to catch bugs with you, I need to work."

Xia Xiqing was a stubborn child. When his parents rejected him, he went to the garden by himself grimly.

Occasionally, he would see a blue butterfly flashing its wings on some roses. His little heart quivered for it, and the third-grader spent all night making a net in order to attempt to catch it.

After much perseverance, a sprained ankle, and multiple scratches on his skin, he finally managed to lock his butterfly into a small cage.

There were four days before the show and tell. Xia Xiqing woke up early every day to feed his new pet. Indulging in the beauty of his prize, he often forgot how difficult it had been to obtain it.

Finally, the day came for him to bring his little butterfly to show his class. He found a piece of blue velvet that perfectly matched the butterfly, which he used to bring the insect in.

Some of his classmates brought ladybugs, beetles, and scarabs. None were on the same level as his butterfly.

"This is mine." He smiled proudly as he lifted the velvet.

But unlike what he had in mind, the butterfly was still. He expected it to be dancing and flapping, but it never flew again. He never again saw its beautiful wings in motion.

If only I didn't catch him in the first place.

If only I never found him and tried to lock him up. Then he would still be alive.

I wouldn't have lost him.

"Xia Xiqing."

"Xia Xiqing."

Xia Xiqing suddenly snaps back to reality. He puts down the specimen and looks at the radio, which is making a scratchy sound.

"Can you hear me? It's Zhou Ziheng."

Xia Xiqing clears his mind and moves toward the radio. As he had guessed, the blue button knob was indeed Zhou Ziheng.

"I hear you." Xia Xiqing immediately asks, "Did you turn a blue knob?"

"Yeah." Zhou Ziheng's affirmative answer comes in from the speaker. "You also have three knobs? Two red and one blue?"

"Yes," Xia Xiqing replies. "They're like walkie-talkies, but they'll only work if both ends turn the same knob. I left mine there for some time now, waiting for you."

Zhou Ziheng's heart pounds as he listens to those words. Xia Xiqing quickly diverts the topic.

"What's your room like? Mine is a boy's bedroom."

"Mine looks like a bedroom, too," Zhou Ziheng replies as he looks around the room.

Both are bedrooms? Such a coincidence.

Xia Xiqing fiddles with the radio. "Are there anything written under the knobs on your end?"

"There's an 'o' on one of the reds."

Is it the same for everyone? Xia Xiqing turns one of the red knobs and immediately loses Zhou Ziheng's voice. Nothing but static comes from the radio.

Maybe it's broken?

Immediately turning off the red knob and turning on the blue, Xia Xiqing hears Zhou Ziheng's voice return. "What happened? There was suddenly no sound."

"I turned one of the other knobs. Seems like you can only connect to one other room at a time."

"Has to be a mutual choice..." Zhou Ziheng jokes.

"Yeah, exactly, like a committed relationship."

Zhou Ziheng remains silent. Xia Xiqing immediately regrets saying it, unsure if it was appropriate after the kiss they shared.

But in reality, Zhou Ziheng is actually quite happy to hear

"committed." Feeling embarrassed, he remains silent.

The atmosphere becomes slightly awkward. Xia Xiqing stands and walks around the room to give each other some space.

The strange thing is, there's no lock on the door—instead, there's a square pasted there with a small puzzle piece embedded inside. The rest of the door is blank. Xia Xiqing attempts to remove the puzzle piece, but finds that it is fixed to the surface. The puzzle piece is edged with that same ring pattern found in other areas of the room.

"Should be some jigsaw puzzles around. Probably need them to open the door," Xia Xiqing mumbles to himself.

Hearing this from the other room, Zhou Ziheng replies, "Jigsaw puzzles? I have some in my room."

"Really?" Xia Xiqing is slightly surprised. Previously, each room had its own theme and was independent from the others. But this time, the rooms share so many similarities.

"Well, I just found a piece inside a book. Just one piece, though. I don't have any suitable place to put it."

The more Xia Xiqing hears, the stranger it feels. He walks toward the books in his own room. "What else?"

"There's a blank square on the door. The puzzle piece has two edges, so I tried putting it there; that happened to be the correct option. They appear to be magnetic, too; it stuck quite well."

Door?

His door already has a piece on it, but Zhou Ziheng had to place his by himself.

Why is that?

"Where on the square? Upper left corner?"

"Yeah. Upper left."

"Does your puzzle area have a ring of grooves?"

"Yeah! How did you know?"

"Mine, too."

Xia Xiqing stops asking questions. He feels that clues are beginning to reveal themselves, and he must remain calm to uncover them layer by layer. Zhou Ziheng had mentioned his desk, so Xia Xiqing feels there must be more around that area. He walks closer and finds another butterfly specimen attached to the drawer.

A second butterfly. This is not a coincidence.

"Are there butterflies in your room?"

"Butterfly?" Zhou Ziheng's voice sounds puzzled. "No butterflies here."

"Does your desk have drawers? Anything that resembles a butterfly near there?"

Zhou Ziheng lowers his head and carefully examines his desk. "Drawers, yes, but no butterflies. There's a four-digit padlock, though."

Lock? Xia Xiqing checks his drawer and notices no locks. He attempts to open it, but it is indeed locked. There's no visible keyhole or passcode dials. He looks at the butterfly specimen, hoping that something is under it, but discovers no lock mechanism after removing it. There is, however, a phrase written on the wood:

The last one

Xia Xiqing looks down at his blue shirt and thinks of the idea he rejected previously. Maybe he is indeed grouped with Zhou Ziheng. Their rooms share similarities, so they must work together to solve puzzles.

He tries to verify his theory.

"Do you have books on your desk?"

"I've got three."

Xia Xiqing counts his books and derives the same number.

"What's the name of the first book?"

"Chaos Theory." Zhou Ziheng also realizes something. "Yours too?"

"Yes, that's right." This is the book that contained the butterfly specimen. Fortunately, Xia Xiqing is still able to find the page where the bookmark was placed. "I also have that book. There was a butterfly bookmark in it."

"Bookmark?" Zhou Ziheng flips through his book and finds nothing. "I don't have any bookmarks. Which page was it on?"

"377."

Zhou Ziheng turns to page 377, but there is no bookmark. However, he notices the name of the chapter that starts on that page: *The Butterfly Effect.*

"Butterfly Effect?"

"Yes, it's about the butterfly effect. We have the same book." Xia Xiqing feels a little strange. "What do you know about the butterfly effect? It's physics, right?"

Zhou Ziheng gives an affirmative answer. "It's about a deterministic nonlinear system. One whose outcome is nearly impossible to predict due to its high sensitivity to initial conditions."

Xia Xiqing is decent with mathematics, but he's still an artist. He flips through the book and teases, "And what's that in Chinese?"

Zhou Ziheng laughs and patiently explains, "Let's take an example sequence of time. This morning, you make the choice of wearing a white shirt instead of a black one. Afraid of staining it, you skip your morning routine of buying a coffee on your way to work. Instead, you drive directly to the office.

"By skipping this cup of coffee, all traffic lights are in your favor and you arrive at the office earlier than usual. Your boss happens to be in an important meeting and chooses you to go on a business trip since you're the only one there. You take a plane to Brazil. That plane crashes and kills everyone on board, including you. All this began with your choice of a white shirt over black."

Xia Xiqing laughs. "Great, I died. Must be a good story for you."

Zhou Ziheng also laughs. "It's an analogy. Have you considered what would have happened if you chose the black shirt instead?"

If I had chosen the black shirt...

Xia Xiqing follows Zhou Ziheng's thoughts. "Black shirt, coffee, stuck in traffic, no promotion, no travel, and I would still be alive."

"That's part of chaos theory. The butterfly effect states that tiny disturbances in initial conditions eventually yield significant changes in outcome. A butterfly flaps its wings in the Amazon forest, which in turn causes a hurricane in Florida."

They both freeze for a moment and begin to laugh.

Zhou Ziheng says with a sigh, "So, small choices you make in life can make irreversible changes to the future."

Hearing this, Xia Xiqing suddenly remembers something. If Xu Qichen hadn't given him a VIP ticket, he wouldn't even be here talking to Zhou Ziheng at this moment.

Why am I thinking about that...?

"Xia Xiqing?"

Xia Xiqing returns to his senses. "Yeah. I just don't think there's any need to be thinking about all this."

Without knowing Xia Xiqing's attempt to cover up his distraction, Zhou Ziheng replies, "Of course there is; chaos theory is one of the most important aspects of physics. It helps to explain many unpredictable phenomena, such as the weather."

Hearing this, Xia Xiqing finds Zhou Ziheng extraordinarily charming right now—his explanations and how he defends the science he believes in.

Smart is the new sexy. Lots of people say it, very few have witnessed it.

"You're right."

Xia Xiqing's voice is suffused with a soft smile. Although the weight of his emotions are weakened by the archaic radio, it still falls heavily on Zhou Ziheng.

Zhou Ziheng tries to convince himself that his joy originates from the recognition of his knowledge.

"Let's get back on topic."

Xia Xiqing continues to flip through the books, forgetting their situation. It feels like he's chatting with Zhou Ziheng on the phone in the comfort of their own homes. After he fetches the other two books, he finds another small butterfly in one of them.

"I found another butterfly in the second book."

"Still no butterflies here. Which book and which page?"

"Page 610, *Big Bang Theory*." Xia Xiqing picks up the third book immediately after responding to Zhou Ziheng.

As he predicted, another butterfly.

"The last book too. Another butterfly on page 987. This one is about...well...hypoplastic heart syndrome...and theoretical physics, cosmology, and...medicine? Quite a wide range of reading material here."

Zhou Ziheng notes all three page numbers. "Anything else? Any more butterflies?"

Xia Xiqing looks around, but there are no more books.

"Butterfly... butterfly..."

He suddenly remembers the butterfly specimen hanging from the drawer.

"The last butterfly is hanging from my drawer. Didn't you say there's a lock on yours?"

"Yeah, there is."

That's it!

Each butterfly corresponds to a book he owns, and the butterfly marked with "the last one" corresponds to his drawer. Could the last butterfly represent the four-digit code Zhou Ziheng is looking for?

"The code you need may be derived from the other three butterflies in my room."

If they hadn't connected their radios, this puzzle would be impossible. It's a new way for the directors to hype up their pairing—as long as they choose each other, they have the opportunity to escape. It forces a new level of cooperation.

The directing team always has something up their sleeves.

"Anything else apart from the butterfly bookmarks?" Zhou Ziheng's voice comes from the radio. "We only have three-digit numbers, and we only have three of them. This might not be correct."

That's right. Xia Xiqing looks around the room and finds a beautiful, delicate conch next to the book. On the wall above the desk, there are several paintings. One is a close-up shot of a sunflower. The other is *The Vitruvian Man* by Da Vinci, which Xia Xiqing is familiar with.

These seemingly unrelated things catch Xia Xiqing's attention. He stares at the wall, thinking, when he suddenly hears Zhou Ziheng's voice.

"What are you doing? I can't hear you."

"Looking at a naked guy," Xia Xiqing replies seriously with

his eyes fixed on the portrait.

Hearing this, Zhou Ziheng almost chokes. He finally coughs up some words. "Oh, there's one on my wall, too."

Surprised, Xia Xiqing tries to describe the painting to Zhou Ziheng. "It's a man with long curly hair, standing with his legs together. His hands and feet are in a square, and his arms and legs are circumscribed in a circle. Is that what you have?"

"Correct."

This is not accidental; the two rooms are too similar.

"Does it mean anything?" Zhou Ziheng has seen this painting many times before, but he does not know much about it. Thus, he consults the expert.

Xia Xiqing touches the tip of his chin. "Oh, the meaning is vast. It's a sketch by Da Vinci, made to illustrate the ancient Roman architect Vitruvius's work, *The Ten Books on Architecture*. Vitruvius praised the golden ratio in his book, which inspired Da Vinci to sketch the human body to those exact proportions. The man depicted is considered by the world to be perfectly proportional."

Something important flashes past Xia Xiqing as he speaks, and he suddenly stops. "Wait a minute."

He looks at the conch, then at the sunflower. The distribution of the seeds captures his attention.

That's it.

"It's the golden ratio." Xia Xiqing sits back on the chair. "The spiral of the conch, the arrangement of the sunflower seeds, and the Da Vinci painting. They all reference the golden ratio."

Zhou Ziheng calculates the next number in the sequence. "The golden ratio sequence is the Fibonacci sequence, right? 987 is exactly 377 plus 610. The next number should be 987 plus 610, which makes 1597. That's my guess."

"So, the other clues are just hints." Xia Xiqing puts down the conch. "Try the password."

After so much time, they finally unlock something. Xia Xiqing sits while waiting for good news.

"The password is correct but the drawer won't open," Zhou Ziheng replies.

"How is that possible...?" Xia Xiqing questions. He knows they're in different rooms, but he decides to try to open the drawer in his own room instead.

And surprisingly, it opens...

This is too weird. Xia Xiqing's tone is one of total disbelief. "Umm, your password unlocked my drawer."

The strange events don't stop there.

Zhou Ziheng suddenly replies, "Now my drawer can be opened too. Weird."

Hearing his reply, Xia Xiqing thinks of the helpless expression on Zhou Ziheng's face and begins to laugh. "Maybe you were too weak earlier."

"Impossible. It really wouldn't open."

Maybe something's broken. The artificial props might have malfunctioned.

"Don't worry, let's see what's inside."

Xia Xiqing looks into his drawer and finds a photo. In it, a couple are holding hands with their backs turned to the camera. The photo is in a very beautiful frame.

According to this, the owner of this room probably has a girlfriend. But why is this kind of photo stuffed in a drawer, instead of being displayed on the desk? Xia Xiqing thinks it unreasonable, and also knows that he does not have a lot of time to think. He casually puts the picture on the desk and begins to look for other things.

"What did you find?" Zhou Ziheng asks.

Xia Xiqing mentions the picture while digging for more clues. "I found a notebook. It seems to be a..." He flips through a few pages. "A journal, I think."

"I also found a journal, but no pictures." Zhou Ziheng continues to exchange information. "There's also a birthday card with a few things written on it."

As Zhou Ziheng organizes the stuff he found, Xia Xiqing has already opened the birthday card he found on his side.

"The moment I met you was the Big Bang. Every particle left me and flew toward you. After that smallest instant, the universe was truly born."

After reading it in one breath, Xia Xiqing suddenly realizes this is a love story between two people. The atmosphere becomes embarrassing. He does not know what to say; he only regrets reading it out loud.

"Umm, romantic. Is this normal for you STEM majors?" Xia Xiqing tries to ease the tension with some jokes.

Panic often causes people to say the wrong thing. As it turns out, this is very true. Xia Xiqing, just finishing his question, thinks of the photo of the Tyndall Effect that Zhou Ziheng took on the plane.

Crap. Zhou Ziheng must have thought that Xia Xiqing was teasing him. Which is not Xia Xiqing's actual intention...

He didn't think Zhou Ziheng would reply, but he does.

"It depends who you're talking to."

Zhou Ziheng doesn't sound awkward at all—he seems rather calm. Xia Xiqing doesn't realize which "who" Zhou Ziheng is referring to; his nervousness gets the best of him.

"The birth date on this card is October 23rd. That might be useful later." Xia Xiqing quickly changes the subject to protect his dignity.

Zhou Ziheng notices Xia Xiqing's nervousness, but he thinks it's due to the pressure he put on him. Changing the subject is Xia Xiqing's way of rejecting him.

They are on different wavelengths without knowing it.

As he puts down the birthday card, Xia Xiqing's attention shifts back to the journal. This notebook is aged, with frayed edges and bent corners. Xia Xiqing takes it and turns to the first page.

"Let me take a look at this journal."

November 11, 2014. Sunny.

I think this was my hardest day. The young man who broke his leg spent the day alone in the hospital. Unexpectedly, a new guest arrived in the double ward. She's a super cute girl. When she smiles, her pair of buck teeth make her like a bunny; so cute.

This is a boy's journal... Xia Xiqing quickly flips through more pages.

"Huh, can't believe it took this guy six months to succeed..." he mutters to himself, looking at the page dated May 20, 2015.

"Succeed?"

Xia Xiqing hears Zhou Ziheng's question and the sound of him turning pages. "You read too slow."

She was hospitalized again. I hope the operation will go smoothly and there will be no more problems.

The girl was hospitalized multiple times. Must be a serious illness.

He suddenly remembers the book on the desk.

"His girlfriend's disease must be related to the third book—hypoplastic heart syndrome. She must have some sort of heart disease." Xia Xiqing flips through the book, hoping to find some useful information.

"The radio is a gift from the girl," Zhou Ziheng says

suddenly. "Did you see it?"

"Let me see." Xia Xiqing turns to another page.

May 20, 2016. Clear Skies.

She gave me an antique today! A radio! She said it was bought by her grandfather as a gift to her grandmother. When she was a child, she listened to it every day for stories. I can only imagine the small and cute bunny look on her. Ah, it would be nice to be able to time travel, to see what she looked like as a kid.

"Turns out the radio is actually part of the story." Xia Xiqing smiles. "This old antique might be there for their wedding."

"No." Zhou Ziheng calmly vetoes Xia Xiqing's joke. "There's a problem with their relationship."

"What?"

"Go to the last few pages of the journal."

Xia Xiqing follows Zhou Ziheng's prompts.

May 13, 2019. Overcast.

We fought today. It feels like we haven't communicated with each other in a while. How did we get to this point? I really don't understand, does time really change everything?

Seeing this page, Xia Xiqing suddenly falls silent. The stories of idiotic men and women are endless. They always begin so beautifully, but as time goes on, friction builds and negative emotions begin to swallow what was once perfect.

So why even start?

The most stable and harmless relationship in the world is none at all.

This kind of love story brings Xia Xiqing's mood down, and he flips through a few more pages.

May 20, 2019. Heavy rain.

Why did I turn off my phone? No matter how misunderstood and angry I felt, I shouldn't have turned off my phone. If I hadn't, she wouldn't have gotten worried and fainted. Emergency contact...must be a joke. The one time that feature was activated, I had my phone off. I should be the one who's dead.

"The girl is dead..." Xia Xiqing did not expect the story to end like this. "Died from a heart attack."

"Died..." Zhou Ziheng seems to have something to say, but pauses. "Died because she didn't get to the hospital in time?"

"Yeah." Xia Xiqing has passed the age when he would have been touched by such a story. Now, his only focus is how this ties into the room. There must be something around that can offer a clue. *We've already found an unlock code; the rest of these items must be useful for something.*

These items might also help lead to the Killer. Nothing seems to indicate as much thus far; the love story has no resemblance to the suspenseful murder in the first episode.

So what kind of identity would the Killer have in this story?

Xia Xiqing frowns as he finds nothing else in the drawer. He closes it and begins to look at the photo he put on the desk, and discovers a sentence written on the back that he hadn't seen before.

Return it to its rightful place.

Its rightful place?

The coincidence is that Xia Xiqing has thought of this since the beginning. A photo like this has no place in a drawer. It makes sense linking this to the fight they had. It just makes sense.

He picks up the photo. Where should it be placed?

"Is there really no photo frame on your side? Anywhere?" With all the similarities between their rooms, Xia Xiqing has to confirm with Zhou Ziheng. Maybe, just maybe, he missed something useful.

"No, no photo here," Zhou Ziheng replies confidently.

At that moment, Xia Xiqing sees a small rectangular groove in the upper right corner of the desk. He looks at the photo frame in his hand and suddenly has an idea.

Could it be...?

He tries the placement and it fits perfectly!

"I found the rightful place." Xia Xiqing lets out a sigh of relief.

Suddenly, the desk lamp turns on without warning. And what happens next is even more shocking. Zhou Ziheng's voice crackles from the radio.

"Hey, a photo appeared," he exclaims, surprised. "You won't believe this. The desk just opened, and some mechanism pushed up a photo frame. Now it's standing there perfectly!"

"What did you say?"

What Zhou Ziheng just said makes Xia Xiqing rethink his conclusions. He thought they were in the same group given the similarities between their rooms, but now he is doubtful.

"Does your room have blue wallpaper, a bed, a black wardrobe, a small round table on a square rug, a radio on the round table, and a walnut desk?

"Yeah," Zhou Ziheng offers an affirmative answer. "There's a laptop on the desk, along with a lamp and those books we talked about earlier. There was some empty space until that photo came up."

Xia Xiqing stares at the exact same desk Zhou Ziheng just described. "Let's try the laptop," he says, turning on the computer. After a short boot-up, a line of text appears on the screen.

Password: _ _ _ _ _ _ _ _ _ _

Zhou Ziheng sees the same prompt.

"What's the username you see?" Xia Xiqing stares at the screen.

"Love1023."

The same...

Facing endless doubts, Xia Xiqing sits back on the chair. As he stares at the photo, he notices something. The couple's clothes are blue and red.

He looks down at his shirt and suddenly remembers their costumes. Okay, blue team is the boy and red team is the girl. But why are there two instances of each? As he thinks on this, all sorts of doubts begin to surface.

Their drawers are somehow connected, and the photo triggered something else in the other room. The sequence of actions must be important between the two rooms.

"Zhou Ziheng, what time is it on your laptop?"

"One-ten PM."

Xia Xiqing stares at his screen...

13:00

"I'm ten minutes behind you."

Something to do with time travel? Xia Xiqing suddenly recalls the book on chaos theory and the journal.

He traveled through time to save the girl? Big assumption there, but not completely unreasonable. Xia Xiqing picks up the journal once again but discovers nothing new apart from a big "1" written on the cover.

He decides to discuss the existing clues with Zhou Ziheng.

"Zhou Ziheng, this is my guess. We're both acting as the male protagonist. He feels guilty for the death of his girlfriend, so he time travels with some unknown method to save her. That's why there's a time difference between you and I."

"So you're the version that went back in time to save the

girl? Then why is her death documented in the journal?"

That's a good question. As the situation clearly states, 13:00 is after the time of death.

Xia Xiqing thinks for a bit and walks to the radio. "We need to hear from the female protagonist. We need to find a way to communicate with those two."

"Okay, let's disconnect first and make an appointment to reconnect later in case there are new clues?"

Zhou Ziheng does not want to hang up on Xia Xiqing, but he knows that is the only way to make progress in the game.

"Sure. Thirty minutes."

Xia Xiqing turns off the blue knob. Not knowing the difference between the two red knobs, he decides to turn on the one labeled with an "o." He hears nothing but noise; he had no expectations for anything more. He just hopes Shang Sirui and Ruan Xiao have figured out that they need to communicate with their "boyfriend."

He returns to the desk to look for more clues. Staring at the familiar desk, he notices an odd-looking shadow cast by the recently-lit lamp. The shadow is in the shape of a jigsaw puzzle. Unable to remove the lampshade, he reaches his hand inside and removes a puzzle piece from the bulb. On the back, there's something written.

The writing is tiny. Xia Xiqing peers at it closely to identify the words.

Are you eager to log into my computer? I wrote the password on the birthday card.

The password is on the card? Xia Xiqing opens it and reads it again.

The moment I met you was the Big Bang. Every particle left me and flew toward you. After that smallest instant, the universe was truly born.

Apart from this text, the only number on the card is October 23rd. Considering this number already appeared as the username, Xia Xiqing has no hope for it being the correct password, but tries regardless. As predicted, it is incorrect.

Suddenly, a voice comes on the radio. It's a girl's voice.

"Xia Xiqing? Zhou Ziheng?"

"This is Xia Xiqing. Ruan Xiao, you probably know you're acting as the girlfriend, right?"

"Yeah, so does Shang Sirui."

"So you've talked to Shang Sirui." Xia Xiqing grabs a pen and prepares to write down any useful information. "Have you found anything? Identity differences? Time differences?"

"Umm, how do I put this...?" Ruan Xiao seems troubled. "There's a calendar with many events written on it. I have no idea which ones are real and which ones are fake."

Xia Xiqing is quite surprised to hear Ruan Xiao in such a panic; she's very smart and usually thinks clearly. Something must be bothering her. "Tell me, what makes you think some are fake?"

"Because Shang Sirui's calendar has different events. If we're the same person, shouldn't the chain of events be identical?"

Xia Xiqing asks, "What if you're girlfriends from different timelines?"

Ruan Xiao is silent.

"I have a book here on chaos theory and the butterfly effect. Maybe the small change in the past has caused completely different future outcomes? That actually kinda makes sense."

Speaking of this, Xia Xiqing suddenly realizes that if Ruan Xiao is on the same timeline as him, their chain of events should overlap. This can help him identify which timeline he belongs to.

"Ruan Xiao, what events do you have on your calendar?" Remembering that there's a Killer in the game, Xia Xiqing must gain Ruan Xiao's trust. "I have a journal with a few events. I'll spare you the love story; let's talk about May 20th, 2019. They had a fight and she wanted to go back to her parents. His phone was off and she died of a heart attack at the train station."

"Sudden heart attack..."

"Yeah, it's in my journal. What do you have? What are your events?"

Ruan Xiao remains silent for a while, then replies, "Similar to you, the girl eventually dies."

Xia Xiqing senses something weird in Ruan Xiao's voice, but he can't pinpoint the problem.

Ruan Xiao continues, "From the clues you have, did the boyfriend leave his house that day?"

Not a question that Xia Xiqing had anticipated. "Not sure. I don't have any evidence to suggest anything. All I know is that he decided to turn off his phone."

"Okay. There are two blue knobs on my radio, and one red. I assume yours look different?"

"Yeah. I got two red knobs and you're labeled with an 'o.'"

"So are you. We're supposed to be a match."

"That means the other pair must be between Zhou Ziheng and Shang Sirui."

Xia Xiqing senses some doubt in Ruan Xiao. Why did she say "supposed to"?

"What time is it in your room?" As soon as these words leave Xia Xiqing's mouth, he hears the radio crackle and Ruan Xiao's signal has disappeared.

Why is she doing this?

Maybe something I said caused her to doubt me? The real Killer wouldn't reveal a lot of information; they couldn't be sure what might expose them. Ruan Xiao knows this, so why does she distrust him so much?

Xia Xiqing tries the knob corresponding to Shang Sirui and gets nothing but noise. He then returns to Zhou Ziheng.

"You there?" he asks, not expecting a response.

"Yes."

"Have you just been waiting for me this whole time?"

"Half an hour has passed. What do you have?"

"Nothing useful."

Xia Xiqing is not inclined to share Ruan Xiao's anomalies with Zhou Ziheng. The Killer could be anyone, including him. He's lost, and if he's not careful, the consequences could be fatal.

"Were you able to unlock your laptop?"

When Zhou Ziheng mentions that, Xia Xiqing suddenly remembers his half-solved password. "No, but the password should be on the birthday card."

"Try 1043."

If anyone else said it, Xia Xiqing would have had his doubts. But coming from Zhou Ziheng, he feels confident that the password has been verified. Upon the final stroke of the Enter key, the laptop unlocks.

"You calculated that based on the contents of the card?"

"Yeah." Zhou Ziheng explains, "I felt there was something there. He first compares their encounter to the Big Bang, then the universe was born. Which made me think of the book."

Xia Xiqing picks up the second book and turns to page 610. "So, want to explain?"

Hearing Xia Xiqing ask like an entitled child, Zhou

Ziheng clears his throat and begins to do so.

"There are many theories regarding the origins of the universe. The Big Bang Theory is the most accepted one. Scientists divided the Big Bang into many stages; at one special stage, the universe is considered to be 'born.' This happened at ten to the power of negative forty-three seconds."

So that's how the number came about. As Zhou Ziheng explains, Xia Xiqing has already found the page on the Big Bang Theory. Listening to him speak, Xia Xiqing can't help but bite his lips. He's is a totally different person when talking about high-level sciences. He's not a regular movie star—instead, he becomes a sophisticated, logical, and gentle person who people involuntarily worship. Science is in his nature.

If they weren't on camera, Xia Xiqing would have said many things to Zhou Ziheng. *I'm imagining us having sex while you explain physics to me.*

Something as far as light years away, and something as close as the touch of skin on skin. When these two collide, a beautiful nebula forms from the explosion.

People always say artistic men are sexy. Why does Xia Xiqing feel men of science are the truly sexy ones? Perhaps intellect and sex appeal are on the same level.

"What's wrong? Have you unlocked it?"

"Oh, it's good," Xia Xiqing replies. Thinking about his daydream just now, he laughs at himself. The computer boots up with a background of the same photo he found earlier. Looking around the screen, he finds a folder named "2 Memory Archive." Opening the folder, he finds an executable. He double-clicks on it and the screen turns black.

"My screen turned black."

Xia Xiqing subconsciously presses the power button.

Receiving no feedback, he closes the laptop, and by doing so he notices a number attached to the outer shell of the laptop—"2." He quickly remembers the journal had a "1" on its cover. The numbers must be related.

"Is it alright? How come the screen went black?"

Xia Xiqing opens up the laptop again and finds that it has restarted.

"Wait a minute, I'll log on again."

Just as he is about to press Enter after the number 3, he notices something odd.

The time on the laptop lock screen has changed—it now shows 12:30.

This is strange. What does it mean? Why did time go backward? Xia Xiqing logs into the computer and clicks on the same folder. This time, there's a text file in it.

We've been together for so long, yet she still doesn't trust me. The bombardment of phone calls is simply unreasonable. I want to be alone, with no one bothering me.

The cursor remains at the last word. Xia Xiqing suddenly realizes that at this time, the boy doesn't know about his girlfriend's death.

He stares at the name of the folder silently. The clue marked "1" and the clue marked "2" are different events.

Remembering what Ruan Xiao said, she and Shang Sirui have different chains of events as well. They must also have different clue numbers.

"Are there numbers on your journal?" Xia Xiqing asks.

"As well as the laptop," Zhou Ziheng confirms.

Of course.

According to this, clues with the same number must be from the same timeline.

But Ruan Xiao's attitude was not clear; Xia Xiqing is

unwilling to risk revealing his clues in case she is the Killer. Shang Sirui has yet to establish contact. The chances of him being the Killer again might seem low, since he had that role last round, but there is no certainty in that claim.

In any case, he must try to communicate with Shang Sirui. "Zhou Ziheng."

Every time Xia Xiqing calls his name, Zhou Ziheng seems surprised but undoubtedly happy. "What's wrong?"

"I need to disconnect and try to talk to Shang Sirui, is that okay?" Xia Xiqing does not need to ask Zhou Ziheng's permission; he could simply turn off the radio. But that would affect his performance in the show, and he also feels mildly sorry for him.

Zhou Ziheng's voice becomes dull. "Sure; won't be the first time."

Xia Xiqing smirks hearing him. People who don't know better might think he has a thing for Shang Sirui... He's not sure if QingSi or Self-Study shippers would be happy, but the ones that root for the OT3 would definitely be over the moon.

"I will be back for you in a bit," Xia Xiqing says, feeling like he has to leave his wife behind to accomplish a mission.

"Do you think I'll be waiting for you?"

Xia Xiqing chuckles. "I don't care. I'll wait for you to show up."

He turns off the blue knob and rotates the red knob with no label, trying to establish communication with Shang Sirui. Then, he stands and picks up the puzzle piece he found earlier. As Zhou Ziheng said before, it fits perfectly into the spot on the door. The magnetic attraction is in impeccable alignment. Judging by the remaining space, there should be two more pieces.

Suddenly, Xia Xiqing hears a voice. He looks behind him and sees the closet door opening by itself. A red laser shines straight to the wall on the opposite side.

"Shit... scared me," Xia Xiqing says to himself. "They really went all out on the props."

He subconsciously associates bouncing lasers with escape rooms and attempts to move the closet door. As he predicted, the angle of the laser changes with the opening and closing of the door.

There are no mirrors in the room. Xia Xiqing tries various angles with no interesting results. Suddenly, the laser turns to a different direction and hits the wall on the right side of the bed. The light gathers on a single point on the blue wallpaper. He waits for a bit, but nothing new appears.

Looks like a position indicator.

He walks over to the dot and palpates the wall. Under it, he finds a small bump.

It is a position indicator indeed.

Xia Xiqing tears a small hole in the wallpaper and a third puzzle piece falls out. Some strange characters are written on the wall.

He stares at the sentence and immediately recognizes that it is mirrored. It is, in fact, two lines of mirrored characters superimposed on each other.

This wouldn't be hard to handle with a mirror, but he doesn't have one.

"Well, it's stupid, but it's not stupid if it works..." Xia Xiqing murmurs as he rips a blank page from the journal. He flattens this against the wall and begins to rub.

At this point, he has no idea what is happening with the plot. The identity of the Killer is totally unknown. He suspects they gave him the most difficult bits.

Finally, a human voice appears.

"Xia Xiqing?"

"Finally," Xia Xiqing replies while continuing to rub the paper against the wall. Last episode, he underestimated Shang Sirui's intelligence, but he will not make that mistake again. "What do you have over there? Any clues?"

"You probably know that we've assumed the identity of the room's owner."

Playing dumb only works once, and he already used that last episode. This time, Shang Sirui dives straight to the point. "I talked to Ruan Xiao. There are very few clues in my room."

Sounds like Shang Sirui's typical strategy of pretending to know nothing.

"How so?"

"I figured out most of the plots that could be concluded from my room, but when I talked to Ruan Xiao, she had a completely different plot. I thought maybe one of us is a fake girlfriend. The next time I talked to Ruan Xiao, her plot changed, but it still doesn't match mine."

Xia Xiqing remembers how Ruan Xiao suddenly disappeared when they were talking. Shang Sirui now informs him that Ruan Xiao has two plots, just like Xia Xiqing himself.

"Are there any numbers or labels on your clues?" Xia Xiqing asks.

"You too, eh? All of my clues have some sort of label."

Shang Sirui gives no explicit numbers, clearly still having doubts about Xia Xiqing. At least it's better to have no clue than a false clue; the former isn't disruptive.

"I got numbers, too. My room is like Ruan Xiao's, with two plot lines. They're not completely different, though."

"What's the difference, then?" Shang Sirui asks.

"I have two different times. At one in the afternoon, the boy already knows that his girlfriend is dead. Another plot happens earlier, before he discovers her death. So in the second plot, he doesn't know the fate of the female protagonist."

Shang Sirui is silent for a while. "Nothing more?" he finally asks.

"She had a fight with him and decided to go to her parents'. The boy turned off his phone angrily. They're the same up to this point."

Xia Xiqing walks to the small table and sits down.

Shang Sirui's tone changes. "Well, ours are quite different. Your plot is consistent with Ruan Xiao's."

Ruan Xiao really does have something that matches Xia Xiqing. He feels a slight relief, knowing that at least some things make sense.

"Wait, how come you and Ruan Xiao have different plots? You two are the same character. Zhou Ziheng and I have the same character, and our rooms interact with each other. When I move something, it causes things to happen in his room. The rooms are related."

"Maybe Ruan Xiao and I were on different timelines when we connected."

Shang Sirui's words inspire Xia Xiqing. Everything he's done assumes they're on the same timeline where events have a causal effect. If they're on different timelines, the plots will happen independently of each other.

Shang Sirui continues, "When I first entered the room, my first contact attempt on the radio was Zhou Ziheng, but he didn't answer. By the time I connected to Ruan Xiao, we both had numerous clues already."

Xia Xiqing understands. If none of them found numbered clues, they would all be on the same timeline, or no timeline at all.

"So you're saying that your room has no effect on Ruan Xiao's because she hasn't found any clues that match your timeline?"

Getting clues apparently means switching timelines.

"Yes. I was waiting for Zhou Ziheng to connect, so I missed my chance with Ruan Xiao before she found any clues. Turns out that Zhou Ziheng was talking to you the whole time! For almost half an hour!"

It feels like he's playing with two kids.

Xia Xiqing suddenly remembers his laptop. The time displayed is not important; what's important is that he's entered a new timeline—from the journal's timeline 1, to laptop's timeline 2.

Shang Sirui is currently in a timeline that Ruan Xiao hasn't found.

Xia Xiqing clears his thoughts. "How does your plot progress? Death from heart attack?"

"Seems like the ending is all we have in common." Shang Sirui's smile can be felt over the radio. "In my timeline, the girlfriend attempts to save the boyfriend. She goes back to the boyfriend, who locked himself in his house with the gas turned on in an attempt to kill himself."

"What?"

Suicide?

The new plot shocks Xia Xiqing. He read about him contemplating suicide in the journal after learning about her death, but he did not think much of it.

"Wait a minute; that's quite different from my plot. Did she go to save him?"

"She's already at the train station. She knows the boy will commit suicide in half an hour, so she took the 420 bus back to him. But there was an accident on the road, and the bus was blocked. She tries to get a cab, but can't find any, so she runs to the nearest intersection hoping to find one there. The intense exercise overloaded her heart."

This overthrows everything Xia Xiqing knows, but he seems to have come to understand something. "Are all your clues labeled '3'?"

"Yes."

There are three different plots, then. Xia Xiqing looks at the radio and the 'o' over Ruan Xiao's name. What does that mean, exactly? Is it just to differentiate the knobs? If so, there are so many better ways it could have been done.

"Do you have any clues that are labeled '3'?" Shang Sirui asks.

"No, not so far."

"Really?" Shang Sirui's tone becomes suspicious. "Why are your clues so similar to each other? Ruan Xiao has two completely different versions, but yours are really similar."

Xia Xiqing laughs. "Seriously, I find that weird too. We're all working with the same butterfly effect, but why is Ruan Xiao the most affected?"

Unsure whether Shang Sirui accepted his explanation, he offers an idea to him. "You're missing too much information. If you're not the Killer, you have two ways to leave. The preferred one is by escaping your room, but you can try to connect with Zhou Ziheng and see if he has any information for you. Neither of you two have a number marked on the radio knob, so you must be related somehow."

Shang Sirui is silent for a while, then lets out a sigh and tells the truth as if he is giving up. "To tell you the truth, I've already unlocked my door. But the setup is crazy; the clues I got after escaping are incomplete. It tells me that I have to combine my clues with my partner to get the final password, but I don't even know who my partner is."

Hearing what he had to say, Xia Xiqing is dubious. The "I'll be honest with you" trick seems like Shang Sirui's tactic to gain trust.

"So, you're hiding in your room now?"

"Yeah." Shang Sirui lets out a breath of relief. "Okay, I won't take up more of your time. I'll try your method to confront Zhou Ziheng."

Xia Xiqing laughs. "Do you even hear yourself? You're talking like he's the Killer."

Shang Sirui fights back with his lovely tone. "How come you don't suspect him at all in this episode?"

Huh?

Xia Xiqing, feeling slightly guilty, hides his emotions and asks, "What do you mean? You think I should doubt him?"

"You're smart. Shouldn't you doubt everyone?"

His statement is full of implication. Shang Sirui must have discovered the ambiguous relationship between him and Zhou Ziheng, and is now making jokes about it.

"Okay, go talk to him. If you find that he's the Killer, don't forget to tell me."

"Nah, I now think you're the Killer. I'm going to tell him."

Xia Xiqing replies with a smile and a sinister voice, "Then I should just kill you right now to hide my secret."

"I don't think you will," Shang Sirui replies before he disconnects his radio.

Shang Sirui didn't get the impression that Xia Xiqing doubts Zhou Ziheng, but he truly is the person Xia Xiqing doubts the most. He simply lacks evidence. Besides, he's still alive—if Zhou Ziheng was the Killer, he would have killed Xia Xiqing before the first voting phase to avoid trouble.

Xia Xiqing takes the puzzle piece and sticks it on the door. This time, nothing happens.

Maybe this one isn't supposed to trigger anything.

He stares at the butterfly pattern on the puzzle and thinks about the book. *If this is the theme, why are my plots so similar?*

Suddenly, the laptop on the desk beeps—there's a new email.

Excuse me, what does the zero on the radio mean? Please reply when you get the answer.

"If only I knew..." Xia Xiqing walks toward the wall and continues to rub the piece of paper against it.

Under the light, the tracing on the paper becomes translucent. There are only two overlapping lines, barely recognizable.

"When you...close all the news from the outside world..." Xia Xiqing attempts to read the words. "The other you appears, trying to save everything."

Another me?

At the end of the first line, his gaze returns to the beginning.

"You are...the initiator of the timelines...not the savior... whether it is one, two, or three."

Xia Xiqing slowly puts down the paper, losing himself in deep thoughts.

I am the initiator, not the savior. Regardless of which timeline.

He suddenly remembers how Ruan Xiao hesitated when she questioned him.

Did the boyfriend leave his house that day?

Xia Xiqing finally understands. He is the original male protagonist in every timeline. He does the same thing in all plots. Time travel does not happen to him, and the butterfly effect does not affect him.

Then Ruan Xiao is the original female protagonist. She does not time travel, but her events are heavily affected by the butterfly effect. That's why she has so many different plot lines.

It is all clear now. He finally recognizes the significance of the "o" on the radio. "o" represents the number of times they time travel. They are the original, they are omnipresent in all timelines.

He quickly stands and walks to the laptop.

The number of time travels is o

Xia Xiqing immediately receives a reply.

Congratulations! The answer is correct. Here is a small reward.

The bed that Xia Xiqing has checked many times suddenly pops out a hidden drawer from its side. Xia Xiqing walks over to inspect the content. It is a fax machine with a "3" on it.

Shang Sirui's plot!

There are many cameras set up around the desk to facilitate the show's filming. Xia Xiqing puts the machine on the desk and stares at it. This one doesn't look like the fax machines he had in mind; instead of a dialing pad, there's a touch screen.

How do I use a fax machine?

At that moment, a line of text shows up on the screen.

Excuse me, how many deaths has the girlfriend been through? You have one chance. Please choose wisely.

"That can only be answered by Ruan Xiao once she's collected all three plots..."

Xia Xiqing walks over to the radio and turns the knob

belonging to Ruan Xiao.

A voice comes on the PA, "Attention platers, voting will begin in five minutes."

There's no response from Ruan Xiao. Xia Xiqing looks at the laptop. Three minutes until voting.

This one-sided mode is torture.

In the last two minutes, Xia Xiqing turns off the red knob and turns on the blue one. To his surprise, the noise stops.

"Zhou Ziheng?"

"I'm here."

His voice soothes Xia Xiqing's irritation of being unable to reach Ruan Xiao. "The voting phase is coming."

"Yeah," Zhou Ziheng replies calmly. "I hope no one's voted out. We barely know anything."

He's right; the rational thing to do is to vote for no one. However, if he discards his vote and someone votes for him, he won't stand a chance.

"Don't discard your vote." Zhou Ziheng is seemingly able to read Xia Xiqing's mind.

Xia Xiqing frowns and asks, "Why not?"

"I just talked to Ruan Xiao. I know you're eagerly trying to reach her to complete your third plot line, but she won't connect with you right now."

"Why?"

From his first interaction with Ruan Xiao, he found her very hesitant. Trying to connect with everyone is how you should play; there should be no reason to avoid contact.

"She thinks you're the Killer," Zhou Ziheng says calmly. "We all know who we are now, but the identity of the Killer is still vague. There's no murder this time. From her perspective, someone has to be responsible."

Xia Xiqing immediately understands. "So she thinks it

was me in the original timeline that caused all this? If I hadn't turned off my phone and didn't attempt suicide, none of this would've happened. That makes sense. Nothing wrong with that explanation." Xia Xiqing's tone changes. "But why should I believe you?"

Zhou Ziheng remains silent.

"What if you're just trying to gain my trust so I'll help you vote her out?"

"Why would I do such a stupid thing? If neither of you leave, then you'll find out I'm lying."

Still doubting Zhou Ziheng, Xia Xiqing does not say a word. Like Zhou Ziheng said, it is not a logical play for the Killer.

"I assure you; I will discard my vote. Shang Sirui will discard his. If you do the same, you'll be voted out."

"What if you're the Killer?" Xia Xiqing can't let go of his suspicion. "Then I can't believe anything you say."

Zhou Ziheng raises his voice slightly. "Even if I were, I wouldn't lie to you." He pauses and continues, "Never mind, it's all a matter of risk. If you don't want to give me a chance, then I have nothing else to say."

The last sentence is quite flirty. Xia Xiqing's heart beats loudly. He lets out a sigh and moves on.

The countdown ends.

"Attention players, the first round of voting begins now. Please select the player you wish to vote for."

Zhou Ziheng says nothing to interfere with Xia Xiqing's choice. Xia Xiqing stares down at his phone and clicks a button.

If Zhou Ziheng isn't lying, his current decision might result in his own elimination. But if he was, Ruan Xiao might be innocently thrown out.

"Please confirm your choice."

"Three... Two... One..."

Xia Xiqing clicks send.

"Votes have been submitted, please stand by."

The world suddenly becomes quiet. The wait appears long and difficult for Xia Xiqing.

"Results are in. The one voted out is..."

Xia Xiqing takes a deep breath.

"No one! Ballots resulted in a tie. The next voting phase will begin in thirty minutes. Hurry and find the Killer."

Xia Xiqing looks down at his phone, which is still displaying his vote—Ruan Xiao.

Zhou Ziheng was telling the truth. Ruan Xiao did attempt to vote Xia Xiqing out.

"Let's discuss the plot of time and space now." Zhou Ziheng does not mention anything about the vote. "I've only found two plot lines so far. One of them is related to Ruan Xiao, so if you want, I can tell you more about her plot."

Xia Xiqing smiles and cracks a cunning joke. "You saved my life and gave me clues. Don't you think you might be too biased?"

The Zhou Ziheng Xia Xiqing had in mind would retaliate. Instead, he admits it.

"Of course I'm biased."

Zhou Ziheng pulls a fast one and catches Xia Xiqing off-guard. "We're on the same team," he adds to make everything more subtle.

"Same team..." Xia Xiqing smiles. "Then let me ask you: what is your plot line? Don't lie to me or I won't team up with you anymore."

Zhou Ziheng laughs at Xia Xiqing's threat. "I won't lie. My first plot is the time travel, which began after you committed suicide. By the way, Shang Sirui should have mentioned your suicide."

"Yeah." But Xia Xiqing corrects him, "The male protagonist committed suicide, not me. You're a professional actor, you know that."

"It's just easier to say 'you,'" Zhou Ziheng continues. "My time travel was intended to save Ruan Xiao from dying at the train station. At the time and location of my arrival, she was already on the 420 bus.

"I drove really fast to the station. I almost ran into a truck full of oranges, which fell everywhere. I helped pick them up and had to wait to get to the station. I later heard the news that the 420 bus collided with that orange truck, injuring ten people and killing two."

Zhou Ziheng takes a deep breath. "Ruan Xiao was one of them."

Sure enough, it really is a butterfly effect.

"Which of Ruan Xiao's clues is this one?" Xia Xiqing asks.

"Two."

Two? In plot line two, Xia Xiqing stayed home. He shut his phone off and did absolutely nothing... Zhou Ziheng traveled into plot line two attempting to save the girl. Shang Sirui doesn't have any clues associated with the number 2, so he doesn't exist there.

What happened to Zhou Ziheng after he failed?

"Where did you go after?" Xia Xiqing asks quickly.

"I committed suicide. I wanted to try again. This time, I stopped the truck from passing, hence stopping it from encountering the bus."

"So, you entered timeline three?" Xia Xiqing is getting excited. "What happened in three?"

"We are both alive," Zhou Ziheng says with a flat tone.

"Happy ending."

Ruan Xiao is not dead in the third plot line. This information gives Xia Xiqing the solution to the puzzle on the fax machine. He walks over and types the answer:

Twice

As the initial girlfriend, Ruan Xiao experienced death twice.

Congratulations, that is correct.

The fax machine delivers a piece of paper.

"Any new clues?" Zhou Ziheng asks.

"Yeah." Xia Xiqing waits for the piece of paper to print. "Are you going to get out soon? You only have two plot lines. You have everything you need to complete the puzzle."

"Soon..."

Xia Xiqing takes the paper from the fax machine and frowns. It's blank. Apparently, he will not be finding out more about his role.

He was so immersed in his thoughts that he did not hear Zhou Ziheng. "What did you say?"

"I said 'soon.'"

Xia Xiqing remembers that Shang Sirui needs a partner, since he only has half the clues. Could it be that Zhou Ziheng is being nice because he needs something from Xia Xiqing's room?

But that's illogical; if anything, the male and female protagonists should pair off.

He should find out if his clues match Shang Sirui's, then attempt to eliminate Shang Sirui's doubts.

Zhou Ziheng described the ending of the third plot line without much detail. From what Shang Sirui said, the ending of the third plot line is far more than just a happy ending—the time traveler Shang Sirui dies in that timeline.

Although everyone appears calm, the facts are building up.

"I'm behind, then. I need to catch up." Xia Xiqing laughs. "I'll turn off the radio for now."

"Are you looking for Shang Sirui again?"

"Smart!" Xia Xiqing replies. Just as he's about to turn the blue knob, Zhou Ziheng suddenly speaks.

"Wait."

"What?"

"After you get clue three, you need to switch plots."

Xia Xiqing, confused, asks, "Why?"

Zhou Ziheng turns off his radio without answering, leaving Xia Xiqing pondering.

What does he mean? Is the third plot line bad for him?

Without the luxury of time, Xia Xiqing immediately turns the radio to Shang Sirui's channel.

Suddenly, he notices something he missed. The fax paper is blank, but a reminder is showing on the screen of the fax machine.

How can I see the words without light?

It seems like nonsense, but Xia Xiqing knows it means something.

"Xia Xiqing?"

"That was quick." Xia Xiqing is surprised to hear from Shang Sirui so soon. "Are you still in your room?"

"Yes. I got a message saying that if I leave, the door will close and I won't be able to return."

"There is no medicine for regret." Xia Xiqing touches the fax paper and feels something is wrong. "What's your plan?"

"I don't know. I don't want to go out alone. Not with only half the clues. That'll only make me a target."

Xia Xiqing cannot judge from Shang Sirui's tone who he

suspects. "Is there anything on your clue that might hint to where the rest of the clues are?"

Shang Sirui is silent for a while. "You ask that so directly; it makes me wonder whether you know something."

Xia Xiqing did not expect this reply. "If I knew something, I wouldn't be stuck on the third plot line now."

"You still haven't found anything on the third plot?"

Shang Sirui's rhetorical question makes Xia Xiqing slightly speechless. It's not easy playing the original; all the plot lines are very similar and none are affected by the butterfly effect.

"No, but hopefully soon. Zhou Ziheng said the ending to plot three is a happy one; he saves Ruan Xiao and no one dies. But how come you did?"

Xia Xiqing holds the piece of fax paper in his hand. He wants to get more lighting but notices a smell instead.

The smell is quite familiar.

"I died trying to save you! If you didn't commit suicide, I wouldn't need to come back to save your ass," Shang Sirui complains in a childish voice. "A car accident would have been an easier death. Instead, I died from running because I couldn't get a cab."

Xia Xiqing is amused by Shang Sirui. A car accident, apparently, is a better way to die.

Car accident?

"Wait a minute. You took the 420 bus and encountered an accident that caused a traffic jam?"

"Yeah, I told you that."

Zhou Ziheng traveled to plot three in an attempt to change the collision of the 420 bus in plot two. That successfully changed the ending. Why is Shang Sirui...?

"I see... The 420 bus you were on was headed to my place,

the one going the opposite way. You were going to save me, but he changed the route of the truck somehow. Instead of colliding with the bus, the truck collided with another vehicle, which caused a traffic jam that blocked the 420 you were on," Xia Xiqing mutters to himself about his missing information.

"Have you contacted Zhou Ziheng recently?" Shang Sirui hears Xia Xiqing talking to himself and feels concerned. "What are you saying?"

Xia Xiqing has yet to complete his clues, and replies with the only answer he can give, "Well, I just finished talking to him."

"The last round of voting was a draw. It's probably between you and Ruan Xiao."

Suddenly, the topic is about voting. Xia Xiqing, who is under Shang Sirui's suspicion, asks, "You already know, so why ask me?"

"I guessed. Zhou Ziheng said we should discard our votes if we're unsure."

Xia Xiqing laughs. "Why would he go through all the trouble trying to persuade everyone?"

Shang Sirui replies with a grin, "You really don't know? If it weren't for him, who among us would have died?"

Xia Xiqing is astounded by Shang Sirui. He laughs. "Well, maybe he just wants what's best for the game, and to not kill innocent players."

"Are you an innocent player?"

As soon as Shang Sirui finishes, Xia Xiqing knows that he also believes Ruan Xiao to an extent. After all, it's very unclear who the Killer is, so her theory does make sense.

"You're asking someone who almost died." Xia Xiqing sighs. "Maybe I ought to vote for you next round."

Shang Sirui keeps laughing on the other side. Xia Xiqing stares at the words on the screen and ponders. Something is odd.

How can I see the words without light?

Lamps, invisible words, sourness on the paper, he does not know what to do. The smell keeps lingering in his mind.

Xia Xiqing sniffs the paper again.

Lemon.

So, something is written in lemon juice.

He finally knows what needs to be done. He brings the paper to the lamp and places it right on the bulb. Citric acid makes paper easier to carbonize; it'll leave marks.

While waiting for the paper to cook, Shang Sirui suddenly speaks up, "I decided to go out."

"Why all of a sudden...?" Xia Xiqing interrupts himself upon seeing what has appeared on the white paper—a few lines of charred handwriting. It's not what Xia Xiqing had expected.

Do you believe in so-called destiny?

The condensed world line, the inescapable fatalism, the karma. What does it make you? The savior or the executioner?

Remember, there cannot be two of "me" in the same plot line. It must end in life or death.

The mysterious words immediately provoke all the doubts Xia Xiqing had previously.

What is my ending in each plot line? Why am I unaffected by the butterfly effect? What happens to me in the third plot?

Why is Zhou Ziheng so obsessed with getting him to switch plot lines?

"Hello? Xia Xiqing? Are you okay?"

Along with Shang Sirui's voice, the fax machine beeps.

"Just a minute."

A sentence appears on the screen.

What's the final ending of the male protagonist who originally existed in the third timeline?

With no hesitation, Xia Xiqing enters the answer that's in his heart.

Congratulations, that answer is correct. Please claim your reward.

A square lid opens in the upper corner of the fax machine, revealing a small box. There's a four-digit code lock. He knows it must be the last puzzle piece. If it was anyone else, they would celebrate.

But not Xia Xiqing. He knows he will lose this round.

Such a pity. He assumed a difficult role, and others even tried to help him escape death.

These acts of charity are clear to Xia Xiqing. But to him, they're nothing but shameful and pathetic.

Zhou Ziheng is definitely something.

The sound of the fax machine fills the empty room. Another piece of paper ejects, and on it there's a single sentence.

He who is defeated in the same time and space will sleep in eternal darkness.

Xia Xiqing chuckles slightly.

Nothing is lost yet.

Removing fuel from the fire is always a good tactic.

"I can go out soon," Xia Xiqing says to Shang Sirui.

"Really? Are you planning to..."

"I won't go out," Xia Xiqing interrupts. "Shang Sirui, if you want to win this round, there's only one way to go. Vote Zhou Ziheng out. He's the Killer."

"How do you know?" Shang Sirui asks with suspicion. "Even if you have evidence, I can't see it. You have to show me first outside."

"It's too late." Xia Xiqing squeezes the jigsaw puzzle and puts it back in the fax machine. "I have only one way to verify that he is the Killer, and it's also the only way to win. I will describe the situation; if it happens, we win."

Xia Xiqing tells Shang Sirui his plan. Although Shang Sirui is unsure why Xia Xiqing is so confident, he still agrees to it. "So, another kamikaze-style move? You seem to like doing that."

"It's a gamble. If I lose…"

If I lose, I can only say that I take myself too seriously. What I'm really gambling on is Zhou Ziheng valuing morality more than winning.

Or, whether he cares about…

"If what I said doesn't happen, you can vote me out." Xia Xiqing smiles. "But be quick."

He turns off the signal to Shang Sirui and makes an attempt to communicate with Zhou Ziheng. Strangely, communication is established almost immediately.

"Zhou Ziheng, have you gathered all your puzzle pieces?" Xia Xiqing asks in a calm tone.

"Yep, I'm going out."

"Guess you can't chat with me anymore. You can hang up now."

"Wait." Zhou Ziheng hesitates. "What plot line are you in now?"

Xia Xiqing looks at the fax machine and the black screen of the laptop.

"Two."

The PA announcement interrupts them. "Fifteen minutes until the next voting phase. Please hurry and find the Killer."

Zhou Ziheng is silent. Xia Xiqing speculates that he is

wondering whether he's been lied to.

"You should go out now."

"Okay."

A few seconds later, the radio signal shuts off.

Xia Xiqing stares at the ceiling. He begins to count time. One second, two seconds, three seconds...

The darkness in his vision is endless, crashing into him like a mountain, leaving him breathless.

The PA once again comes on.

"Players Shang Sirui, Zhou Ziheng, and Ruan Xiao have successfully escaped from their rooms. Player Xia Xiqing is now trapped in the third timeline and has lost the qualification to escape. The room is now locked. Waiting for other players to clear the level."

The familiar response to darkness comes quickly. His brain begins to feel dizzy.

Desperate memories await him in the dark. His younger self is locked in the darkness, his soul swallowed by fear.

No one knows or cares that he is scared.

They cannot know about his fear of darkness. They will use his weakness to tame him.

Every second in the dark is extremely difficult. The infrared camera is rolling. Xia Xiqing can only endure it to the best of his ability.

Knowing this would happen, he still had to gamble.

In a room without power, there's no way to tell time. Ever since he met Zhou Ziheng, he was always there to lend a helping hand in darkness. This time, that's not going to happen.

However, the darkness isn't like anything before. It's more like bait, tempting him and the person he's expecting to see. But no matter how he prepares himself, the bait still takes his breath away.

His expectations are slowly eroded by the darkness. In this illusion, Xia Xiqing approaches closer and closer to the dark abyss.

"Player, Xia Xiqing, dead.

"Player, Xia Xiqing, dead."

What he awaited for finally came to pass.

The door opens with a click and a beam of light enters the room.

"Player, Xia Xiqing, is asked to wait in the elimination zone."

Xia Xiqing restrains his pounding heart and walks out the door. Unsurprisingly, he sees Zhou Ziheng standing outside, brow furrowed.

He wants to speak, but he knows he is no longer allowed to. Sweat runs down his forehead. With such a pale face, he looks rather ill. He looks around at Zhou Ziheng, Shang Sirui, and Ruan Xiao.

Shang Sirui is unable to make sense of what happened. "It's like you said..."

Although he sees the confusion in their eyes, Xia Xiqing cannot explain more. He smiles and tilts his head to indicate that they should forget about him and then proceeds to the elimination zone.

A countdown begins. Once the beeping stops, the floor opens up and Xia Xiqing falls through.

Zhou Ziheng is still staring into the dark room. He finally turns and licks the corner of his lips. He leans against a wall and looks at the others.

The ending couldn't have been clearer.

"When you vote me out, you will get my half of the clues," he says aggressively.

"So you really are the Killer," Ruan Xiao states.

"Yes. I represent the boy who saved the girl in plot line three, who is Ruan Xiao. I also caused Shang Sirui's death by accident. But that's insufficient to prove that I am the Killer." Zhou Ziheng lets out a crooked smile like a real Killer. "After I get the ending I want, I kill the original me, who is Xia Xiqing.

"There cannot be multiple versions of me in the same time and space.

"My plan was going well," Zhou Ziheng continues. "I gained your trust and escaped my room. I was about to get his clues by killing him. I almost won."

But Xia Xiqing, who was subject to so many restrictions, still solved everything.

His desire to win is so strong that he traded himself in to prevent me from winning.

Shang Sirui does not know that Xia Xiqing is gravely afraid of the dark, so he had no clue. However, to him it seems Zhou Ziheng saw through Xia Xiqing's trap. So why did he still do this?

The next round of voting proceeds without any surprises. Ruan Xiao and Shang Sirui promptly eliminate Zhou Ziheng and take his clues.

"I lost this round. Nothing to do with my ability. No regrets." Zhou Ziheng willingly walks into the elimination zone and falls through the floor.

The victor of the last episode becomes the Killer this time. He thought he could continue winning, but he was opposed by Xia Xiqing.

Shang Sirui still hasn't figured out why Xia Xiqing was so confident when telling him of his plan.

"When Zhou Ziheng comes out, I'll be killed within ten minutes.

If everything goes well, you'll vote Zhou Ziheng out next and win."

Why did Zhou Ziheng have to kill Xia Xiqing? He was locked in his room. He posed no threat whatsoever. Why did he risk exposing himself to kill someone who had no chance to contribute anything?

Those two are so strange.

The first person Zhou Ziheng sees after falling into the basement is Xia Xiqing. Whether he wins or he loses, the first person to greet him is Xia Xiqing.

This man blew himself up in order to help Zhou Ziheng escape last episode, and now, he brought harm upon himself in order to reveal his identity.

Xia Xiqing hasn't yet recovered. His lips are still pale. There's no welcoming hug this time; instead, he just stands a few yards away, grinning like a kid who just succeeded in a prank.

Zhou Ziheng takes off his mic with a gloomy face. "What you grinning at?"

Xia Xiqing, who was murdered by Zhou Ziheng, replies, "You died with me."

"If you do this again, I won't help you."

Zhou Ziheng lowers his eyes, not wanting to look at Xia Xiqing. Xia Xiqing has no idea how worried he was; he asked him again and again to change his plot line. But in the end, it became a weapon.

Zhou Ziheng does not like this method of attack.

Seeing Zhou Ziheng upset, Xia Xiqing gently kicks him on the calf. "How old are you? Why you so upset over a game?"

Zhou Ziheng nods at a few staff members passing by and then turns back to Xia Xiqing. "It's not about the game. It's about you using me."

It's because you didn't care about yourself.

Xia Xiqing turns and looks at Zhou Ziheng. "I just..."

"Don't deny it."

Xia Xiqing pauses. "Okay, I used you. But you didn't have to let yourself get used."

He regrets saying that. He doesn't want to admit it, but he regrets it.

Zhou Ziheng turns and walks quickly toward him. He grabs his collar and speaks in a low and angry voice.

"I'm willing to be threatened by you, but that doesn't mean you can purposely hurt yourself."

His heart is lit by fire, burning hot and beating violently. With his neckline loosened, Xia Xiqing stands blankly, consumed by Zhou Ziheng's power.

The furious Zhou Ziheng sighs. He looks around and finds the area is unpopulated. Seeing Xia Xiqing stunned, he uses his superb acting skills to play friends.

He hugs Xia Xiqing. Their chests touch and their hearts pound wildly.

A soft voice fills the space between them.

"Don't do it again. I mean it."

C.08

:

Intimate Wars

During the twenty-five years of Xia Xiqing's life, he's lived very peculiarly. He stripped his heart out of his body, leaving nothing but his shiny skin. He's done everything possible to get love-like feelings from others in order to desperately fill the empty void inside him, but nothing can fill that bloody hole.

He channels his emotions into art. He must empty his body and mind to be able to produce work that moves others.

The Xia Xiqing that others worship is safe; at least, he considers himself safe. If everyone loves him, how can he be miserable?

But now, with the appearance of a strange person that's ignored his empty body, he is defenseless. They're going straight for his fragile heart.

The alarm bells in his head are ringing.

His self-protective nature makes him afraid.

"Won't happen again. I promise." Xia Xiqing withdraws from the hug and presents Zhou Ziheng a cynical smile.

Everything he feels is a response to stress.

Zhou Ziheng is slightly startled. He thought this hug would last longer.

Xia Xiqing pats him on the shoulder. "We should go."

"Okay."

Was I too obvious just now? Zhou Ziheng thinks to himself in anger and worry.

Maybe his feelings are too obvious.

The basement is quite isolated. The air quality is terrible. Zhou Ziheng follows Xia Xiqing out of the underground passage.

Just like before, the guests are supposed to go shoot some bonus content, so Zhou Ziheng proactively asks for a camera and walks over to Ruan Xiao.

"Let's go as a group."

"Us?" Ruan Xiao looks around suspiciously. "Are you sure?"

"Yeah."

"Why me though? Xia—"

Zhou Ziheng quickly interrupts, "Well, I had to travel through time on multiple occasions to save you."

Ruan Xiao looks at Zhou Ziheng with a confused look. "Uh, is that a reason?"

Zhou Ziheng thinks about it for a moment. "It's okay, I can go with Shang Sirui."

"Wait! I'll go with you." Ruan Xiao grabs Zhou Ziheng and bumps his arm. "What's wrong? Why not go with Xia Xiqing?"

"Nothing."

"You two fighting? Is it because he made you lose the

game?"

Zhou Ziheng, feeling slightly irritated, raises his eyebrow and replies, "Yes, he cost me the game."

In a sense, that was a sufficient reason.

"Is that so...?" Ruan Xiao teases. "Not a fan of losing, I see. I thought at first your relationship with Xia Xiqing was pretty strained, but then it seemed you guys were pretty tight. It's confusing; why can't you stay friendly?"

Seeing the direction of this conversation, Zhou Ziheng frowns and stares at Ruan Xiao. "Why do you care if we're friendly?"

Ruan Xiao nudges Zhou Ziheng's elbow. "Because I'm a Self-Study girl, silly."

Out of the four guests here, one is a fake fan who wants to sleep with him, one is a shipper who wants them to sleep together, and the last one is a competitor ship for his fake fan... Excellent.

What a mess.

"You're kidding, right?"

"No, for real."

"Don't. Can I expel you from the fan group?"

"You wish. I need more shippable moments, please..."

Zhou Ziheng and Ruan Xiao joke as they walk. Suddenly, Zhou Ziheng bumps into someone else while holding the camera.

"Sorry!" he says on reflex, but he didn't expect the person to be Xia Xiqing.

"It's okay..." Xia Xiqing replies while covering his chest. He lets out a smile with his peachy cheeks. "What were you guys talking about? What's so funny?"

Ruan Xiao, knowing Zhou Ziheng did not want to be grouped with Xia Xiqing, decides to help him keep the secret. "I was saying how Zhou Ziheng should post more selfies for his fans."

"Right." Xia Xiqing brushes the long hair covering his forehead. "You haven't posted anything in a while, big star."

Zhou Ziheng already has Xia Xiqing figured out. The way he emphasized the words "big star" is quite unpleasant to his ears. He does not understand where the hostility comes from.

As if he's so certain that Zhou Ziheng won't be mad at him.

Zhou Ziheng turns around and hands the camera to Ruan Xiao. Then, he pulls his phone out of his pocket and forcefully grabs Xia Xiqing by the shoulder.

Xia Xiqing raises his head and stares at the screen that is in front of him. "What are you doing?"

"Taking a selfie."

The shutter sound clicks and Zhou Ziheng releases Xia Xiqing.

"Don't post on Weibo."

"It's for the fans."

Xia Xiqing is angry, but he maintains a smile and looks at Ruan Xiao. "See? This hotshot actor is the one who's baiting our ship. I was forced to take this photo unwillingly."

"I'm sure now." Ruan Xiao clicks her tongue at them. "You two definitely fought."

Zhou Ziheng is too lazy to respond. He just puts his phone back into his pocket.

"Will you post that photo?" Ruan Xiao asks. "Or you can send it to me."

"Let's keep on shooting." Zhou Ziheng clenches the phone tightly in his pocket.

It's almost midnight by the time they finally wrap up the bonus content.

Shang Sirui runs up to the group and announces, "I asked my assistant to order from the most famous sushi place around here. There's sake, too. You guys should come to my room later."

Ruan Xiao shakes her head. "I'm so tired and sleepy." She looks at her watch. "If I eat now, I'm going to gain so much weight."

She is unmoved despite Shang Sirui's persuasion, so he turns his focus to Zhou Ziheng. "Don't run away from me! We haven't had a hangout in a long time. Let's drink! Don't you care about me anymore?"

"I have an audition in Beijing..."

"I asked Xiao-Luo and your audition is in two days. A little sake won't hurt."

Arms seized by Shang Sirui, Zhou Ziheng somehow still hears the conversation between Xia Xiqing and Ruan Xiao.

"Xia Xiqing, is that a new cologne? It smells good. I wanted to ask you about it at the airport."

"Oh, me? This is actually my friend's."

"What brand?"

"Super Cedar? I don't really remember. It's some stupid label."

"Haha, is it okay to call your friend's cologne stupid?"

Zhou Ziheng suddenly realizes that Xia Xiqing's fragile side aroused his desire to protect, making him forget about the man's addictive nature.

Friend? Probably with benefits.

It started again. His heart is suddenly sour with jealousy.

"Okay." Zhou Ziheng raises his head and agrees to Shang Sirui's request.

Seeing Zhou Ziheng surrender, Shang Sirui gives him a big hug. "Really? Cool! Let's do it!"

After Ruan Xiao leaves, Shang Sirui drags Zhou Ziheng and Xia Xiqing downstairs. There are a lot of fans gathered around, all of them girls. They start to shriek as soon as they see Shang Sirui.

"Aaaaah!"

"Holy—Xia Xiqing, Zhou Ziheng, and Shang Sirui!"

"Aaah! Self-Study!"

"Heng-Heng! Mama loves you!"

Xia Xiqing put on a mask prior to coming out. He waves amicably at the fans, showing his soft side. However, Shang Sirui is different. He's been an idol to many fans for a long time, and greets them generously.

The only one that's not so friendly is Zhou Ziheng. He starts to lecture them, "Thank you for coming out, but it's late. It's dangerous to be out here at night. Do you all have a safe way to get home?"

The fans shriek. "We know! We want to see you!"

The crew gets into Shang Sirui's car while Zhou Ziheng continues to calm the crowd.

"Don't do this next time."

"We promise!"

That normally means "there won't be a next time," Xia Xiqing thinks to himself.

Apparently, Zhou Ziheng is just a good and kind guy who shows a bit too much affection to someone dangerous and unstable like Xia Xiqing.

It's stupid to take his words seriously.

Xia Xiqing sits next to Shang Sirui in the car and rests his head on Shang Sirui's shoulder.

"What's the matter?" Shang Sirui turns to Xia Xiqing.

"Tired and hungry."

Shang Sirui smiles like a sunflower and pats Xia Xiqing.

"You'll be fine soon. This sushi is the best. And the wine at this hotel—simply amazing."

"Let's take a selfie," Xia Xiqing suddenly interrupts Shang Sirui.

"Huh?"

"Take a selfie and post it on Weibo. We just finished recording the show. Fans have been waiting," Xia Xiqing replies softly.

"Hey, you're right! For our shippers!"

As a member of a famous male idol group, Shang Sirui is quite familiar with this procedure. He takes out his phone and poses for a picture. He raises his eyebrow and gestures a peace sign.

Xia Xiqing raises his head and takes off his mask before the shutter sounds.

Zhou Ziheng, who hasn't noticed anything, sits down by himself in the car after he finishes educating his fans. As he lowers his head and buckles his seatbelt, Shang Sirui yells out with excitement.

"Hey Zhou Ziheng, go like my Weibo post, will you? I just posted."

Zhou Ziheng hums agreeably in acknowledgment and pulls out his phone. Sure enough, there's a new post from Shang Sirui.

@HighFiveShangSirui: Just finished recording and I'm so tired... Check out this suicidal player next to me.

The post is the selfie they just took.

What is this? Zhou Ziheng accidentally exits the app. He opens the photo album and stares at the photo he took with Xia Xiqing earlier. He clicks the photo out of anger and hovers his finger over the delete button.

He grits his teeth and taps it.

Zhou Ziheng, who does not feel cheered up, returns to Weibo and likes Shang Sirui's post.

Tilting his head, he is met by Xia Xiqing's eyes. He lies lazily on the seat with a smile on his face. Zhou Ziheng almost sneers when he sticks out his tongue at him and raises his chin like a snobby toddler.

Simply unbelievable.

Zhou Ziheng doesn't want to speak, and he also doesn't want to hear Xia Xiqing talk with Shang Sirui. He takes out his earbuds and plugs himself in.

Shuffle.

Danger's what we're doing.

We lock lips to ruin.

Don't you trust love?

Never trust love.

What a trash song. Zhou Ziheng irritably presses next. The music changes from the psychedelic female voice to the simpler sound of acoustic guitar.

We all know how to play, looking for fun with the lowest risk

Confession is not an option, it doesn't matter if things go against your wishes

The topic should jump intelligently, the distance should be ambiguous and light

No matter who crossed the line first, you should forget it tomorrow

Excuse me?

Who wrote the algorithm for daily recommendations? The devil himself?

Zhou Ziheng scrolls down the list to see what the devil has planned for him today. Coincidently, he gets a message from Zhao Ke, his best friend.

Ke-zi[1]**:** Heng-ge, when are you going back to Beijing? Old Four came back a few days ago, let's go hang out.

Old Four grew up with them in the same neighborhood in the military district. Zhou Ziheng is not that close with him, but they've known each other for many years.

Heng-Heng: I'm going back for an audition. I don't have time.

Ke-zi: Can we not work so hard for the money? Look at you, flying around all the time like you're Superman. You don't even have a personal life, you're 20 and have never been in a relationship. That's strange for a guy with your qualifications.

Heng-Heng: You're starting to sound like my mom.

Ke-zi: I'm going to ignore that. But seriously, you're not still thinking about her right? She's probably married with kids by now. You need to move on and find someone else.

Zhou Ziheng was going to fight back, but he feels guilty seeing the words "find someone else." Although he's only twenty, he's been an actor for fourteen years. Being in this business for so long, there have been plenty of people chasing him. It's just that he's never moved on. He simply can't.

Truth be told, he's almost forgotten what that girl looked like.

He always thought he'd wait for her forever. But then someone else showed up—not just someone else. A man, an utter scumbag.

Zhou Ziheng doesn't want to admit it, but he is indeed tempted. He feels guilty for shifting his feelings toward another person.

Ke-zi: Hello? Are you upset?

Heng-Heng: You wish.

---

1 In this context, "-zi" is being used to make a diminutive nickname.

Ke-zi: If you're not upset, then change your profile picture. That little flower has been there for years. It's way too gay.

Heng-Heng: Die.

Zhou Ziheng exits the chat window and clicks on his profile photo.

"We're here." Shang Sirui stretches and puts on his hat. He pushes Xia Xiqing to get out of the car, who catches a glimpse of the profile picture on Zhou Ziheng's phone as he gets up.

Zhou Ziheng nods and puts the phone back into his pocket.

Their rooms are on the same floor, with their assistants one floor below them. In the elevator, they come to the agreement that they'll shower in their respective rooms and then meet in Shang Sirui's room for food. Shang Sirui is at the end of the hallway, Xia Xiqing is beside him, and Zhou Ziheng is across the hall.

Halfway through his bath, Xia Xiqing realizes he doesn't have a change of clothing, since he came directly from Zhixu's place. He's also reluctant to wear the hotel bathrobe.

Shang Sirui is shorter than him, his clothes won't fit. Zhou Ziheng is probably a better choice, so he sits down and quickly sends a message to him.

Zhou Ziheng, who is drying his hair, notices his phone has rung.

Terrorist: Hey handsome, can you lend me some of your clothes?

Does this guy make a habit of wearing others' clothes?

Moral Role Model: No.

Terrorist: Okay, I'll just come naked then.

...

Moral Role Model: What clothes do you need?

Xia Xiqing looks at his phone and laughs.

Terrorist: Anything will do. I didn't bring any.

Zhou Ziheng stares at his suitcase. Everything in there has already been worn.

Moral Role Model: I'll ask Luo to buy you some.

Terrorist: Where is he going to find clothes at 1am? Hurry, I'm not picky. Oh, and underwear too.

Zhou Ziheng can imagine Xia Xiqing's cynical smile.

Moral Role Model: I have nothing that hasn't been worn.

Terrorist: That's fine. I'll wear whatever you bring.

Sitting on the bed, Xia Xiqing waits for about ten minutes. Zhou Ziheng comes knocking on the door with wet hair, gray pants, and a black long sleeve shirt. Typical college kid.

His face only looks more and more attractive. Xia Xiqing appreciates his high standards for aesthetics.

"Finally." He smiles at Zhou Ziheng while leaning against the door.

Zhou Ziheng hasn't finished drying his hair. Small beads of water drip from his head. Before he came, he mentally prepared himself to find Xia Xiqing hiding in the bathroom like a little girl, reaching one hand out for clothes. To his surprise, he's walking around wearing nothing but a towel.

"Come in." Xia Xiqing bumps his shoulder trying to close the door.

Zhou Ziheng realizes that he could have just dropped off the clothes and left.

What's going on with him?

Xia Xiqing walks back to the bed bare-footed. Zhou Ziheng can't help but check out his ankles and calves. Feeling dizzy, he walks over and throws the clothes at him, then turns and finishes what he wanted to say.

"I found these relatively new ones. They probably don't fit you exactly, but that's the best I can do. I also don't need them back after..."

"Yeah, they don't fit me very well. You really aren't at all small."

Xia Xiqing's words cut in and Zhou Ziheng turns around, looking surprised. He sees his black underwear in Xia Xiqing's hands.

"I mean, nutrition just keeps getting better for you in the younger generations." Xia Xiqing smirks.

Zhou Ziheng feels his ears burning. He quickly grabs his underwear from Xia Xiqing's hands. "Fine. Don't wear them, then."

Xia Xiqing, who's still wearing a towel, smiles innocently at him. "You want me naked down there? I don't think so. I can't let my family jewels hang in the cold."

"You're shameless." Zhou Ziheng storms out, but immediately comes back and drops the underwear on the bed.

He doesn't forget to slam the door behind him this time.

Xia Xiqing feels like he is watching a lion show at the zoo. Both pleased and amused, he begins to hum. The size turns out to fit quite well.

Zhou Ziheng only had time to drink some water before getting a text from Shang Sirui. When he finds Shang Sirui in his room, he's sitting on his bed with a face mask on. The table is laid out with sushi, sashimi, and sake.

Seeing Zhou Ziheng walk in, Shang Sirui jumps off the bed in excitement and starts to praise the sushi place to Zhou Ziheng.

He'd make a good salesman. Who knew? Zhou Ziheng thinks. He stares at the icy vodka bottle on the table. "Wait, you ordered this too?"

"Yeah."

"That's crazy." He frowns. "How are you going to get anything done tomorrow?"

"I'm all good. Didn't I tell you I have nothing to do tomorrow? I'm gonna sleep in." Shang Sirui pouts and throws himself onto Zhou Ziheng. "I haven't had a good night's sleep in a whole week."

Zhou Ziheng pushes him off, pretending to be disgusted. "Suit yourself, then. I'm flying back to Beijing tomorrow. I'll pass."

"You can mix it with sake if you want." Shang Sirui nudges his elbow. "Just a few shots. Are you a man or not?"

Zhou Ziheng rolls his eyes.

"Xia Xiqing? Come on in." Hearing the footsteps, Shang Sirui takes off his mask, patting his cheeks cheerfully. A few drops splash on Zhou Ziheng, and, disgusted, he silently stands up and moves away.

And then in comes Xia Xiqing.

Zhou Ziheng shifts his gaze to the person wearing a long-sleeved blue hoodie and a pair of black sweatpants. Wrapped in that oversized clothing, his whole body looks smaller than it really is, especially with his hair tied up into a little curved tail at the top of his head.

He feels a strangeness gathering inside him at the sight of Xia Xiqing wearing his clothes. They're completely normal on him, but on Xia Xiqing, it just seems...

"Hey, you know you don't have stand up to welcome my arrival."

That shuts down whatever he's feeling right now. He sits back and stuffs a piece of sushi into his mouth uneasily.

Xia Xiqing walks to Zhou Ziheng, who planted himself on

the sofa, clearly suggesting he moves over. Shang Sirui's eyes shift between the two of them and he quietly retreats to the only chair in the room. Feeling a slight kick to his feet, Zhou Ziheng unenthusiastically moves over a bit to make room for Xia Xiqing.

Shang Sirui hands a pair of chopsticks to Xia Xiqing. "Your hoodie is cool. What brand is that?"

"It's actually..." Before he can say anything, a piece of sashimi flies into his mouth. Choked with fury and sushi, he glares at the culprit, who is pouring himself a glass of sake like nothing happened.

Shang Sirui puts on a knowing smile. "Finally, you're no longer fighting."

"Fighting? Who's fighting?" Zhou Ziheng takes a sip and puts the glass down.

"Whoever is fighting knows who they are. It's not like I'm blind to these things," Shang Sirui mumbles before changing the subject. "Guys, dig in. I'm starving."

Xia Xiqing carelessly picks up the half-empty glass in front of Zhou Ziheng and gulps down the rest of it.

"There's a new one over there." Zhou Ziheng takes his glass back, looking shocked.

"What? I thought you didn't mind me using your stuff." Xia Xiqing licks the corner of his mouth. "I mean, I don't mind how much it's been used."

Zhou Ziheng can only play dumb at the double entendre and buries himself in food.

"Holy shit. They comment so fast my eyes can't keep up." Shang Sirui wants to share with them the comments under his newest post.

"What did they say?" Xia Xiqing asks halfheartedly.

"'Oh wow San-San feels suddenly a bit dommy!' and

'Xiqing is so adorable I wanna fuck him so bad…'"

Shang Sirui can't contain a snort of laughter.

Xia Xiqing shrugs, fixing Shang Sirui with an unimpressed look. "I'm totally used to it. They say the same things under my posts."

That's because they don't know what an asshole you are, Zhou Ziheng retorts in his head.

"I can see why; you just look too good. Your face is beautiful in the way that reveals a sense of history." Shang Sirui opens the vodka bottle and pours himself some. "It's time for a drinking game."

Zhou Ziheng protests, showing a frown of disapproval, "I don't think I can handle another game so soon."

"You're telling *me*." Shang Sirui huffs a long-suffering sigh. "When I was the Killer, I swear I thought I was gonna have a heart attack." He finishes the last bit of sake and places the bottle horizontally on the table. "How about Truth or Dare? We have no cards."

"Objection." Zhou Ziheng looks unimpressed.

"Overruled, on the grounds of me paying for dinner," Shang Sirui retorts cheerfully.

"I have no objections whatsoever." Xia Xiqing smiles lazily.

Yeah, I'll bet. 'Cause you don't tell the truth, Zhou Ziheng responds in his head.

Moments later, the three of them agree to play a modified version of the game, since they're public figures.

"Whoever it points to will have to answer a question truthfully."

"What if I refuse to answer?" Zhou Ziheng wonders. "What if there are questions I can't answer?"

Shang Sirui nods thoughtfully. "The price to pay for not answering is a shot of vodka."

The game starts as dull as could be. Zhou Ziheng doesn't get chosen at all, rendering him the luckiest of the three. Shang Sirui has had three shots, and his cheeks are flushed. Zhou Ziheng catches a glimpse of Xia Xiqing, who's had one shot and shows no signs of intoxication.

"Well, I gotta say, this is not working." Shang Sirui waves his fingers wildly and changes the rules again. "We only get three chances for not answering a question."

Upon agreeing on the new rules, Shang Sirui spins the bottle, and it stops whirling in front of Zhou Ziheng. He flounders about whether he should uphold his privacy or be on a flight tomorrow with a hangover. After he's given it some thought, he picks up a shot and instantly begins coughing after having it.

"Are you that bad at drinking?" Xia Xiqing gently pats Zhou Ziheng on the back.

His heart is pounding out of his chest. It must be the influence of alcohol, he tells himself. He sits up, wiping his lips with the back of his hand.

"A little bird told me that bad luck will follow those who can't drink." Xia Xiqing dazzles him with a radiant and blooming smile.

Are all southerners as pale as him? Zhou Ziheng feels the liquor burning in his stomach.

"Come on, let's do it again. Xia Xiqing, your turn."

Xia Xiqing places his fingers on the bottle, wrapping it inside his palm. Zhou Ziheng shifts his gaze somewhere else, away from those graceful fingers he's always found attractive.

"Ha, ha, ha. Zhou Ziheng again. Xia Xiqing, didn't you say something about bad luck?"

"What?" Zhou Ziheng looks like he's been struck by lightning. "I quit."

"Yeah, if you're a coward," Shang Sirui retorts sluggishly, not letting Zhou Ziheng off the hook that easily. "No more evading questions for you! I gotta think... Hmm... Yes... When was your first romance?"

"It was..." Zhou Ziheng abandons dignity. "Never. I've always been single."

"No way. Seriously?" Shang Sirui covers his mouth, pretending to be utterly shocked. "Even I've had a girlfriend before."

"And you, Shang Sirui, get drunk too easily." Xia Xiqing's voice is soft and fluffy. He shoots Zhou Ziheng a flirtatious look and pushes the question further on behalf of Shang Sirui. "What about crushes? When was your first crush?"

Shang Sirui excitedly agrees, "That's right. Your first...first crush. Who and when? You have to drink double if you don't answer."

Zhou Ziheng recalls what he talked about with Zhao Ke in the car earlier. If Xia Xiqing wasn't here, maybe he could share his story as a joke and Shang Sirui would be too drunk to remember any of it in the morning. But Xia Xiqing is here, and he chokes on the words before he even opens his mouth.

Seriously, what's there to be afraid of? It's just a crush, right?

It's not like he's afraid of Xia Xiqing or anything...

"Come on!"

"Six."

"Jeez, that's young. You hit puberty early or something?" Shang Sirui howls in disbelief.

Zhou Ziheng scratches the back of his head. "I don't even know if it was a crush or not. So, yeah, I was shooting a scene at a park full of people and I got nervous. It was my first time as an actor. I ran off at lunch break and met a little jiejie. She was kind to me and even made me a...” He hesitates. “She encouraged me, and if it wasn’t for her, I wouldn’t even have a career as an actor.”

Xia Xiqing suddenly smiles halfheartedly. “Girl? How old was she?”

“That’s K-drama worthy! Boy and girl and love at first sight.” Shang Sirui giggles.

Zhou Ziheng kicks Shang Sirui’s feet. “She was taller than me, and probably older too.”

“Older?” Shang Sirui is more cheered up. “Ahahaha, so your type is older girls, I see, I see.”

“Oh, shut up.” Not intending to dwell on this subject any longer, he quickly adds, “Is it my turn now?”

Surprisingly, Xia Xiqing didn’t laugh at him like Zhou Ziheng thought he would. He just sat there quietly eating sushi.

He spins the bottle and it ends up pointing at Xia Xiqing.

“Xia Xiqing! Xia Xiqing! Xia Xiqing...” Shang Sirui cheers.

“What’s the question?” Xia Xiqing puts his hands up, surrendering to the four-year-old, who happily repeats the question after Xia Xiqing.

“What’s the question?”

Zhou Ziheng taps Shang Sirui’s head with his chopsticks.

“Ouch!”

No one remembers to ask Xia Xiqing a question.

In fact, a lot of questions are on the tip of Zhou Ziheng’s tongue. He’s known nothing about Xia Xiqing’s past for so long.

But he couldn’t ask even a single one.

“Okay, since I don’t get a question, here’s my shot.” Xia Xiqing raises a glass, lips pressing against it.

"Why are you afraid of the dark?"

His hand pauses, not expecting this line of questioning. He takes the shot, grinning. "You're too late."

Fully aware of the sign of rejection, Zhou Ziheng has no intention of getting turned down again tonight. Truth be told, he doesn't even know if he could bear the truth.

Shang Sirui is half asleep at this point. "Uhh? Who's next..."

"Shang Sirui, time for bed." Zhou Ziheng chuckles and shakes his head wordlessly.

He spins the bottle and it points at Xia Xiqing again.

"Eh? Xia Xiqing, you're here." Shang Sirui half-opens his eyes and giggles.

The smile-like expression on Xia Xiqing's face disappears. He whispers into Zhou Ziheng's ear in a warning tone, sounding like a wounded animal protecting his territory, "No more questions."

Before Zhou Ziheng can react, Xia Xiqing quickly takes another shot.

"I-I didn't even ask anything yet," Shang Sirui moans.

"Too late." Xia Xiqing beams at Shang Sirui.

The burning liquor stimulating his throat makes him cough non-stop. Zhou Ziheng reaches out a hand, trying to help, but the one on the receiving end carefully evades, making him feel even guiltier than he already is.

Shang Sirui's hand is in the air reaching for the bottle, but in the next second, he passes out in his chair.

"Hey." Zhou Ziheng gently shakes Shang Sirui, who is completely out of it. "That's just great."

He stands and helps Shang Sirui walk to the bed, then puts him down.

"My legs hurt... I don't want to dance anymore..."

Their idol training must be hard. Zhou Ziheng sighs, putting a comforter over him.

"I'm going back." Xia Xiqing lowers his head, leaning on the armrest to get up, and then takes a few steady steps toward the door.

Zhou Ziheng knows he just stepped into Xia Xiqing's minefield, but doesn't know what to say or do. He watches him leave the room and thinks he will do the same after he makes sure Shang Sirui is okay.

Not long after, he hears a loud bang coming from the hallway and bolts out of the room. He sees Xia Xiqing kneeling on the floor with his back facing him, gasping heavily.

"Are you okay?" He immediately grabs Xia Xiqing's arm and places it on his shoulder, trying to help him stand up, but Xia Xiqing is too weak to do so with his trembling legs.

It seems like Xia Xiqing is trying to talk. He parts his lips, but no words come out. His eyes are slightly squinted, and his ears and neck are flushed.

This is different from the last time he saw this man drunk. *Fortunately, his room is just across from here,* Zhou Ziheng thinks to himself while gently closing Shang Sirui's door with his foot.

So that's the aftertaste of vodka... Even though he only had one shot, he feels a slight dizziness and everything seems a lot brighter and funnier. Xia Xiqing leans on him, more radiant than ever.

Zhou Ziheng has to open the door for him. He first props up Xia Xiqing by putting one hand on his shoulder and reaching for the door with the other, but it's too far. He then props him against the wall, but after he lets go of his hand, Xia Xiqing's body slips away and he has to catch him before his head hits the floor.

He sighs. He has one hand crossing under Xia Xiqing's arm, letting the drunk person face and lean on him, and another reaching for the key card in his pocket. There seems to be a tiny bit of consciousness left in Xia Xiqing's body, because he also reaches into Zhou Ziheng's pocket and grabs his finger.

"Hey..."

"Catch you." Xia Xiqing smiles mindlessly.

Zhou Ziheng looks a bit dazed, feeling an abnormal heat rushing down his spine.

When he finally gets the key card out, he has to hold Xia Xiqing by the arms while kicking the door open and dragging him into his room. The hand that grabbed his finger is now on his neck, and is unwilling to let go.

Zhou Ziheng puts him on the bed and wants to get him a comforter as he had with Shang Sirui, but as soon as he lets go of his hand, Xia Xiqing attempts to follow.

"What are you doing?"

"Need...shower." He sounds as hoarse as the hard liquor he's been drinking all night.

Seeing him fall to the bed again, Zhou Ziheng feels his irritation growing. "Can't you just do it tomorrow?"

"I...have to..."

He must have owned this guy a lot of money in his past life to deserve this. Zhou Ziheng reluctantly picks up Xia Xiqing and leads him toward the bathroom as he clings to him like a wounded animal. Zhou Ziheng's heart is beating fast.

"Shower."

He puts Xia Xiqing on the bathroom floor. Xia Xiqing opens his eyelids and checks the surroundings, as if to make sure this is indeed his bathroom, and then he begins to take his shirt off. The liquor numbs his senses, making the simplest task seemingly impossible to perform. Zhou Ziheng stands aside, watching Xia Xiqing get his head stuck in his shirt.

This is fun. It turns out that even the most cunning person can be clumsy at times like this.

Squatting, Zhou Ziheng helps pull up his shirt like he's helping a young child, and throws it out of the bathroom.

This is the first time he's ever undressed someone, and he doesn't even dare to look him in the eyes. Even though they're both men.

Xia Xiqing slowly blinks in response to the cold air. He looks down at himself confusedly, and then at Zhou Ziheng beside him.

"Why...why are you taking my clothes off...?"

Zhou Ziheng rolls his eyes at the ungrateful drunk.

"Okay. I'm going now. You be good."

Before he can stand, Xia Xiqing tugs his shirt forcefully, causing him to sit back down on the floor.

"Too cold..." Xia Xiqing shoots him a sad look.

The soft side of Xia Xiqing is always hidden under his cynical skin, but this time he looks at Zhou Ziheng with nothing but his beautiful eyes seeking help.

There's just no way to say no.

"You really are a piece of work, you know that?" Zhou Ziheng turns around, grabbing the shirt he threw away. "So no shower then?"

No response is given, but he feels something sneaking under his shirt. He turns, startled, and sees two arms around his waist.

"Hey!" Zhou Ziheng holds Xia Xiqing's waist and pushes him away. "Don't go full drunk on me now."

But Xia Xiqing just won't let go. His burning cheek presses against Zhou Ziheng's throbbing chest.

"Cold..." A whimper slips out of Xia Xiqing's lips.

Feeling speechless at the situation, Zhou Ziheng wants to help Xia Xiqing walk to bed. But Xia Xiqing's grip on his waist is too strong for him to stand, so the only method he can think of is to carry him like a child.

The human-shaped koala is thus carried from the bathroom to the bed. The second he lands on the bedsheets, he panics and grabs whatever he can reach—which is Zhou Ziheng's pants—and won't let go.

Zhou Ziheng feels like he's going insane. He wasn't trying to leave, but now he can't. He tries to free himself from Xia Xiqing's hands, but once he touches them, they crawl their way to his waist.

"Don't go..."

First shower, then no shower, and now he doesn't want him to leave. Zhou Ziheng sits on the bed with all kinds of mixed feelings in his mind as he sweeps those hands away.

"Come on, you're drunk."

Nothing functions in Xia Xiqing's body right now. His eyelids are heavy; eyes wet and unable to focus. His lips are stained red, pursed but recovered a second after. His voice is shaking.

"Can you not go? I don't want to be alone."

His head is lowered. Merely speaking the words seemingly drained him of all his strength. Zhou Ziheng's mind is a total blank until a dripping sound breaks the awkward silence that lingers between them.

"What, what's wrong?" Zhou Ziheng feels panic rising from the bottom of his stomach. He wouldn't have dreamed he'd see Xia Xiqing cry in front of him—not in a million years. When he outstretches a hand to hold his chin, he sees the tears trickling down his cheek—as soft as silk, as thin as a cicada's wings.

The small beads between his lashes shine under the lights.

Xia Xiqing buries himself in Zhou Ziheng's neck, letting out soundless cries. Feeling his shoulder becoming soaked, Zhou Ziheng props a hand on his back.

"Hey. It's okay." Zhou Ziheng strokes his back and gives his neck a gentle pinch. Being the youngest child in his family, he doesn't have much experience when it comes to comforting others. He has to go with his gut on this one.

Needless to say, seeing Xia Xiqing like this makes every fiber of his being scream.

"Don't leave me alone here..." Xia Xiqing mumbles, making a nasal sound. His sniffling reminds Zhou Ziheng of a scared little kid waking up from a nightmare. "It's so dark in here. I'm scared..."

Zhou Ziheng feels as if Xia Xiqing isn't just grasping and clinging to a part of his skin, but his own heart—a vital organ bearing the essence of life and death.

"But it's not. You see? You can see the light."

Head down, Xia Xiqing acts like a kid refusing to see reason.

"You lied! There's no light... No one... I'm locked up and I'm gonna die..." Gasping for breath, Xia Xiqing escapes from Zhou Ziheng's chest and pulls his right hand toward his waist. He looks up at him with reddened eyes filled with tears. "It hurts here..."

In that instant, a wave of sadness sweeps over Zhou Ziheng's body unlike anything he's felt before in his entire twenty years of existence.

"Where?"

He frantically shifts his eyes to the spot his hand was led, and feels a raised scar under his palm—from a knife, if he were to guess. The cut seems deep and terrifying against the pale skin.

Xia Xiqing gasps painfully for more air like a fish suffering a loss of water. A few strands of hair are stuck to his face.

"Help me... I don't want to die..." He hisses. "So much blood... I just need a shower... I don't want to go to the hospital..."

Zhou Ziheng regrets acting on his stupid curiosity tonight—so much that he feels like crap. It feels like he peeled off a scab on Xia Xiqing and there's nothing he can do to stop the bleeding.

"You won't die." Zhou Ziheng tugs him even deeper into his arms. "I'm here. You're not alone."

"Mom..."

Zhou Ziheng thinks he must've misheard him.

"Don't lock me in here... please..." Xia Xiqing begs like a kid who made a mistake. "I promise I'll be good... Please don't kill me..."

Kill me?

The scar on his waist.

How is this possible?

Zhou Ziheng's blood runs cold. The waves of shock run through his body, leaving him paralyzed and incapable of wondering what this man went through in his childhood. He begs for forgiveness over and over; he begs to not be left alone in a cold dark room.

Zhou Ziheng's eyes are red as holds him and whispers into his ear again and again, "Don't be afraid. I'm here."

He continues until Xia Xiqing's eyes run dry, until he has no more strength in him to beg for mercy, until he falls silent in Zhou Ziheng's arms.

After checking Xia Xiqing's pulse, Zhou Ziheng can finally breathe again.

He just fell asleep.

He finally fell asleep.

Zhou Ziheng gently lays him on the bed, watching him curl up into the soft white sheets with a frown on his face, like a weak kitten that might not make it through the night.

Xia Xiqing's weeping is still echoing in his ears: *"Don't leave me here alone."*

Zhou Ziheng decides to stay.

He lays down beside him, but doesn't want to shut his eyes. He tilts his head to get a better look at the sleeping figure resting just an inch away from him and runs a hand up into his hair.

Those eyelids are swollen and bulging and almost transparent in a way that he can see the veins under the shadows of those incredibly long lashes. They're longer than anyone else's he's ever seen, he thinks.

His fingers continue to run down from his hair to his forehead to the corners of his eyes, causing the sleeping person to frown slightly and shift toward Zhou Ziheng's warm body.

Their bodies become closer, arms brushing against each other. Xia Xiqing adjusts his head slightly in his sleep to ease the air going in. Zhou Ziheng's gaze trails along his facial features before finding a place to land—his nose. He raises a finger and touches the tip, causing ripples like a dragonfly landing on water. But those ripples are spreading across his heart and every one of his nerves, until he finds himself leaning forward and pressing his lips to Xia Xiqing's nose.

Zhou Ziheng kissed him, and Xia Xiqing doesn't even

know.

It feels amazing and satisfying to steal a kiss from him, leaving him wonder if he could just have Xia Xiqing to himself for one night.

Just one night. He'll give him back in the morning.

Xia Xiqing feels like he's stuck in a nightmare where someone pressed the replay button on his shitty childhood and he's forced to relive everything again.

He never falls fully asleep or is completely knocked out when others are around, because he's terrified at the thought of accidentally revealing the pathetic side of him when he loses consciousness.

He must have had too much to drink last night...

A haunting pain cracks through his skull before he even opens his eyelids. Something's wrong. Why does he feel like someone is holding him?

He opens his eyes, waking up to discover that he's indeed being held in someone's arms—and the owner of those arms seems to be his long-term target...

Is this a joke? Did he violate this poor guy?

Sensing a slight shift in his arms, Zhou Ziheng tugs Xia Xiqing in closer and rests his chin on his forehead. He mutters while stroking Xia Xiqing's back, "Don't be afraid..."

"Me? Afraid?"

Breathlessly angry, Xia Xiqing bites him on the shoulder to escape from his grip of death.

"Hey..." Zhou Ziheng squints and presses on his newly wounded shoulder. "What are you doing?"

"What did you do?" Xia Xiqing flips over the comforter, exposing his naked chest to the air. "What exactly did you do to me?"

"Nothing." Zhou Ziheng rubs his eyes with the back of his

hands. His loss for words quickly turns into a shiver down his spine when his eyes meet Xia Xiqing's grinning face.

"Then why did you hug me in your sleep?"

He gives Zhou Ziheng a gentle pinch on the chin. Zhou Ziheng grabs the comforter to cover his head, turns over, and pretends to be deaf.

Seriously, is this the same person as last night? Zhou Ziheng moans. He must still be dreaming...or could it be that *he* was the one who got drunk last night and this is all a dream? If that's the case, then everything will be back to normal when he wakes up again.

"Hey, are you turning your back on me to avoid my question?" Realizing he is pushing an immovable object, Xia Xiqing wraps his legs around Zhou Ziheng's waist and straddles him. He outstretches his hands to turn Zhou Ziheng's face toward him and asks, "Tell me, what happened last night?"

Zhou Ziheng refuses to open his eyes. When Xia Xiqing was pulled out of his dream on the plane, he had the same defensive expression on his face as he does right now—it's his self-defense mechanism. If he shares the truth with him about last night, he may never want to see him again.

Zhou Ziheng feels sad all of a sudden. Despite not liking to lie to get what he wants, he desperately wants to do so at this moment. He needs to.

"Believe me, nothing. I got you back in your room and I was tired so I spent the night here."

He puts on a sincere face to make his story convincing. *I am a good actor*, Zhou Ziheng reminds himself as he meets Xia Xiqing's skeptical stare.

"Is that true?" Xia Xiqing shoots him an accusing look, thumb rubbing against Zhou Ziheng's lower lip. "What's the matter with me? You sure we did nothing?"

Would I even dare when you were crying like a little girl? Zhou Ziheng retorts in his head. *That's definitely not a kink of mine.*

Feeling embarrassed at his own thoughts, he tilts his head a bit. "Get off. I need my sleep."

Xia Xiqing's inner mischievousness resurfaces seeing Zhou Ziheng's lack of interest in anything except for going back to sleep.

"Is that a request...?" Xia Xiqing leans in, soft lips pressing against Zhou Ziheng's ear, breathing out the steamy words. "We can do something else instead..."

Zhou Ziheng can handle the words, but not the lips trickling down his neck; pressing kisses and rubbing against his legs through the bedsheets.

"Stop that..." Zhou Ziheng grabs Xia Xiqing's knee to make him stop, but only lets Xia Xiqing in on another secret.

"Your neck is red," Xia Xiqing continues teasing him.

Zhou Ziheng's anger is building up inside; every shred of compassion he's given Xia Xiqing since last night is being thrown out of the window. He sweeps Xia Xiqing down and climbs on top of him easily; he's less muscular and still hasn't recovered from the hangover.

"I told you to stop."

Zhou Ziheng's anger brings out something else in Xia Xiqing: a hunger for the sweet, exciting taste of conquest. With his head held high, Xia Xiqing whispers into his ear, "Kiss me and I'll stop." He then shoots him a wicked look. "Or don't, and you'll lose everything.

"Just a kiss..."

Xia Xiqing's words trickle out, casting a spell on Zhou Ziheng's heart.

"Please..."

It seems Zhou Ziheng must have a hangover too, for he finds that Xia Xiqing's image is starting to overlap with the man in tears last night. He looks into those wet eyes dancing in front of him and his world starts whirling.

He has no intention of giving in, but he wants to return what he stole from him last night.

That must be the lamest excuse in history. Zhou Ziheng thinks something along those lines as he lowers his head and presses a gentle kiss to Xia Xiqing's lips.

As he's pulling back, he finds surprise written all over Xia Xiqing's face. His pupils are dilated and his lips parted. Zhou Ziheng's heart skips a beat.

Based on his past experiences with him, Xia Xiqing didn't expect his tricks to ever work on Zhou Ziheng. But this time, it worked. Zhou Ziheng kissed him.

The uncomfortable silence lingers and the space between them seems absolutely still. Just thinking about the way Xia Xiqing reacted to the kiss makes Zhou Ziheng want to disappear.

"One more?" Xia Xiqing blinks, seemingly recovered from his state of shock.

"What did you say?" Zhou Ziheng thinks he must have heard him wrong.

"One more kiss." Xia Xiqing's eyes are alight. He wraps his arms around Zhou Ziheng's neck, giving him a sincere look. "Just one more, I promise."

What's going on?

He actually is kind of tempted, but...

But.

No "but." He wants to.

The second he lowers his head, he feels himself yanked forward by a hand on the back of his head and their lips collide at full force.

Xia Xiqing captures Zhou Ziheng's lower lip between his teeth and holds it there until they part in pain and invite his tongue in. He doesn't quite understand it yet, but when Zhou Ziheng agreed to the kiss, an image popped into his head—one of Zhou Ziheng holding him in his arms, in a hug so affectionate that he'd be willing to drown in it a thousand times over just to prove it's where he's supposed to be.

This must be a dream. Let this be a dream. He greedily maps the inside of Zhou Ziheng's mouth and takes whatever he can find to sustain his own life. He's a man proud of his skill in trickery, but the only thing that makes sense to him right now is licking and biting. No tricks, no rules, just pure instinct to release the simple urge to touch. To his luck, Zhou Ziheng hasn't pushed him away.

What Xia Xiqing doesn't know is that Zhou Ziheng has been at the breaking point for so long that he's done making excuses for his excessive affections. Compassion is a good explanation for his feelings, but it's another pitiful excuse.

All of his struggles were to cover up the fact that he *felt* something.

Xia Xiqing tugs on the back of his nec and pauses for a moment before trickling down the lines of muscle on those arms, fingers exhaustively tracing as though they're one of the most important discoveries of mankind. He presses their flushed chests together only when the urge to do so is too strong to ignore.

Zhou Ziheng shugs off the protectiveness he feels toward Xia Xiqing; it feels more like conditioning he has no control over than actually an effort to protect himself from physical harm. He tips himself sideways off Xia Xiqing, who uses his position to try to wriggle his way between his legs while pressing further kisses.

Zhou Ziheng frowns and tries to pull on Xia Xiqing's leg, which is causing unwanted heat, but instead Xia Xiqing groans louder against his mouth—a sound that just makes the situation worse. Being a pleasure-seeker, Xia Xiqing won't deny himself a single moment of it; especially with someone he's craved for so long.

This is neither the right time nor place, but Xia Xiqing doesn't care about that. Every nerve inside Zhou Ziheng's body is ignited in demand for more—they know he can't put out the fire alone. Zhou Ziheng bites Xia Xiqing on the lips and lifts him by the neck, and that's when he sees his long eyelashes and his closed eyes underneath.

A wicked idea crosses his mind.

Will he cry?

Knowing nothing of Zhou Ziheng's thoughts, Xia Xiqing feels his senses burning away; his face and body are ablaze. He bites Zhou Ziheng's lower lip again, holds it there, and then lets it go—but not before he makes sure to give a thorough lick to that piece of wet flesh under Zhou Ziheng's full attention. He presses his lips against Zhou Ziheng's ear, tongue and hot breath tracing the lines and relishing every bit of skin he brushes against.

And then, all he has to say is, "Zhou Ziheng, look how hard you are."

Before the last syllable disappears into the thin air, Xia Xiqing lets out a sharp exhale when he feels an unexpected thrust against his legs. The sound he makes tears apart whatever sense is still left in Zhou Ziheng's body. Zhou Ziheng caresses Xia Xiqing's back with one hand and strokes his waist with the other, sending a current of electricity down to the stiff part of him that screams for attention.

Zhou Ziheng's pants are surprisingly difficult to pull off. Before Xia Xiqing even succeeds in doing so, his cock is wrapped inside Zhou Ziheng's palm.

Knowing Zhou Ziheng still has his worries, he kisses the words into his mouth. "A hand job is enough. I'll help you." He parts his lips and kisses him again on the chin. "Come on. I'm hard..."

Zhou Ziheng pulls Xia Xiqing's pants off, along with his underwear, and presses a kiss to his ear.

"Can't believe how quickly you got my pants off..." Xia Xiqing is gasping for breath. He squeezes his hand into Zhou Ziheng's pants and grabs his stiff, warm cock in his hand.

Zhou Ziheng exhales sharply. "My pants. Don't ruin them."

"What if I did?" Xia Xiqing grins and gives a few gentle strokes. "It's not like I'll get pregnant."

Zhou Ziheng feels a pleasant moan stuck in his throat but he refuses to surrender to his enemy. He pinches Xia Xiqing's chin before stuffing a finger into his mouth.

"Um..."

Zhou Ziheng coughs, pretending to be cool. "What's the matter? Didn't you do this for me before?"

Reacting to the deliberate provocation, Xia Xiqing sucks on his finger like it's a lollipop; licking and pushing it in and out with his lips, swirling around the tip a bit, all while gazing at Zhou Ziheng erotically with his dazzling brown eyes. In response, Zhou Ziheng takes his finger back and grips him hard around his dick, jacking him off with rough urgency and forcing a satisfying moan out of Xia Xiqing.

"Fuck... Slow down..."

Xia Xiqing takes a shaky breath in and out as Zhou Ziheng's tight fist works harder and faster. He gasps, moans, and squeezes his eyes shut as his head jerks back, hips lurching forward, pushing his cock into Zhou Ziheng's fist, sobbing and on the verge of orgasm. Zhou Ziheng props him up in his arms, fingers wrapping around his cock, slick with pre-come, and thumb tightly pressing on the dripping tip.

"Fuck. Let me come." Xia Xiqing grits his teeth, body shivering. "Pervert."

"You can if you beg me." Having already accepted himself for who he is, Zhou Ziheng whispers, "Beg me if you want to come."

"Fuck." Xia Xiqing lets out a moaned curse, leaning toward Zhou Ziheng's ear. "Let me come... I'll make it up to you."

When he looks into those eyes, Zhou Ziheng gives up making fun of him and watches Xia Xiqing come into his hand with a loud sob.

Zhou Ziheng presses his lips to his forehead gently and grins. "I see I overestimated how long you last."

Xia Xiqing buries his head between Zhou Ziheng's neck and shoulder and retorts in a shaky voice, "You try lasting when you've been dry for two months straight."

Zhou Ziheng is confused. What does he mean?

Two months?

"You didn't do it with...?"

Before Zhou Ziheng can finish his sentence, the other person present slips beneath the sheets. Sucking and licking and extreme pleasure follows, setting his toes shivering.

"Zhou Ziheng... The duvet..."

Xia Xiqing's low voice comes from under the comforter, reminding Zhou Ziheng of the fact that it must be too dark for him down there. He immediately flips back the comforter, revealing the scene of Xia Xiqing gently stroking the base of his cock with one hand and cupping his balls in another while his mouth sucks on its swollen head back and forth. Xia Xiqing looks sexy as hell, with a long lock of wet hair falling over his face and swaying as his mouth moves. The scene could not look more pornographic, and the urge to come in his mouth is too overwhelming to delay any longer.

"You're a bit too big..." Xia Xiqing's jaw muscles are quivering and aching, so he decides to take it out and rest a little before going at it again, but the next thing he knows, he's got cum all over his face.

"Fuck." Xia Xiqing shoots him an accusing look. "Did you do this on purpose?"

Seeing Xia Xiqing's face covered in white fluid, Zhou Ziheng coughs and quickly grabs a tissue from the bedside table. He sits up, wanting to wipe off Xia Xiqing's face.

"Hold on." Xia Xiqing is not as embarrassed as he thought he'd be. "Look at this. Look how quick you came, you utter virgin."

Zhou Ziheng wipes his face while apologizing in a low voice, "You were too good."

"I was too good? No it's just that you're a virgin." Xia Xiqing lays on top of him, lips gently rubbing against Zhou Ziheng's nose. "My first blowjob can't possibly be that good..."

"I don't believe you."

Xia Xiqing nips at the tip of his nose. "Fine, don't believe me." He runs a smooth hand up and down Zhou Ziheng's chest, indulging in the ecstasy of getting what he wanted; in dragging an angel down to hell.

Zhou Ziheng's senses are coming back to him, including the long lost sense of embarrassment for what he just did with Xia Xiqing. He runs a hand up to cover Xia Xiqing's teasing eyes, but quickly takes his hand back, worrying it'd be too dark for him.

"Can you not look at me?"

"What are you embarrassed about?" Xia Xiqing shifts an inch toward him and presses a kiss on his palm. The feeling that's curled inside Xia Xiqing's chest confuses him. It's a satisfaction so strong that it makes him forget he's only gotten a taste of Zhou Ziheng—not even dessert.

Xia Xiqing's fingertips trickle down Zhou Ziheng's neck. "Feel those calluses? Are you satisfied?" He whispers, "They were born when I drew you. Now I can return them to you..."

Zhou Ziheng feels his heart defenseless against such loving words; his face is burning hot. "Stop that."

"If you really mean that, you should kiss me." Xia Xiqing wraps his arms around him, breathing against his mouth, ready to slip his tongue in.

Until they both run out of breath and fall back into the sheets.

Xia Xiqing feels like Zhou Ziheng must be the equivalent to a shot of adrenaline straight to his heart, and enough of that would kill him eventually.

"I need to sleep a bit more." Feeling embarrassed, Zhou Ziheng pretends to be tired and sleepy.

"My eyes are sore..." Xia Xiqing calmly opens his mouth, gazing at the white ceiling. "Maybe I drank too much last night. And my head still hurts."

Zhou Ziheng feels his heart ache upon hearing those words. He grabs him and locks him in his arms, resting his head on top of his forehead. He asks gently, "Can I cuddle you to sleep?"

"No, because I am not a girl, nor am I your childhood crush." Xia Xiqing tries to push him away, but Zhou Ziheng is immovable.

"I don't mean that. And I don't have feelings for her anymore."

"So you say." Xia Xiqing chuckles. "But I thought you were the never-gives-up type of guy."

"My type?" Zhou Ziheng gives a self-deprecating laugh. He thought so too, and that's why he felt so horribly guilty when he found his feelings had shifted toward someone else.

Someone he saw through from the beginning, but still fell for.

"Well, maybe I wasn't really into her. I just thought it'd be nice to see her again."

Feeling he's in no position to comment on Zhou Ziheng's childhood crush, Xia Xiqing keeps his silence and secretly admits to himself that being held in warm arms is quite comfortable.

The silence lingers for a long while. Xia Xiqing opens up when he is almost certain Zhou Ziheng has fallen asleep. "If you're okay with it, we can keep our relationship as-is."

Xia Xiqing instantly considers himself the stupidest guy in the universe. What did he just ask for? It sounds a lot like exclusive, long-term friends with benefits.

"You know what? Never mind. I know how easily I get bored..." He deliberately adds, "Let's just..."

"You aren't afraid that I'd fall for you?"

Xia Xiqing pauses, then laughs heartily. "No. You know what kind of person I am. I can't fool you, and I know you don't like me that way." His tone sounds certain. "That's why our arrangement will be safe."

He takes Zhou Ziheng's silence as a yes, although he feels weird at the thought that he doesn't think of it as a onetime thing. After a while, Zhou Ziheng opens up without emotion.

"If I find out you're messing around with others, I will ruin you."

The implications behind those words are amplified a hundred times coming from an idealist who has done nothing immoral in his entire life. It sends Xia Xiqing into a state of shock. He tries to comfort himself by thinking something along the lines of: *It's okay, he just doesn't trust my chaotic personal life. It's totally understandable, since this is a big commitment for him.*

As a way to comfort the younger guy, he caresses his neck like it's a perfect art piece. "I haven't laid eyes on anyone else since I met you. I won't deny that sometimes I lie, but I'm being honest with you right now."

Zhou Ziheng hopes Xia Xiqing is telling the truth. He even has a despicable wish that he'll be the only one Xia Xiqing lays his eyes on from now on. Maybe he has a heart of a collector, too. At this moment, all his heart desires is to magically turn the person in his arms into an inanimate object whose sole purpose is showing off its beauty to its owner.

I must be an awful person, Zhou Ziheng thinks, trying to shake off these unhealthy thoughts.

Feeling exhausted, Xia Xiqing quickly falls asleep in those warm arms before Zhou Ziheng can form a response.

The sleep is nice.

The next time Xia Xiqing opens his eyes, he finds that Zhou Ziheng is already gone. To his surprise, he is fully dressed in a dark red hoodie, a pair of denim jeans, and even a pair of socks.

Xia Xiqing is awed by the kindness and thoughtfulness that flows from Zhou Ziheng's naturally-grown body, like a sun radiating an inexhaustible supply of energy. He must be born out of pure love, Xia Xiqing thinks. That warm feeling must run through his veins each day.

Not like himself. He only gets to forge that kind of feeling.

The clothes on him smell like Zhou Ziheng's usual cologne: a bitter grapefruit fragrance that lingers on every inch of his skin.

He sits up, arms crossed in front of his chest, seemingly in a daze.

After his mind is back in place, he walks to the bathroom. When he's back, he finds a single-serve box of milk and a sandwich on the table. A note is placed neatly under the milk.

I have to leave early to catch a flight. No need to return this set.

Xia Xiqing chuckles, casually turning the note over. There's something on the back, too.

Don't argue with my choices. Just doing the best I can.

Well, his taste is childish as ever. Even the bright color...

Xia Xiqing looks down and a few printed letters catch his eyes.

Born to be loved.

C.09

Guns and Roses

Xia Xiqing says frankly to Xia Xiuze on the phone, "I don't want to."

The kid wants Xia Xiqing to show up on his birthday, and he's been bombarding him with texts.

"Who else will be there besides you?" Xia Xiuze mumbles his answer.

"You know they'll be there. And you still want me to come? Are you trying to ruin your own birthday?" Xia Xiqing retorts as he walks into the elevator, frowning at the childish tantrum being thrown at him.

"Come on, we can still celebrate together." The elevator door slowly opens and he walks out. "Just us. You can bring your friends and I'll get us a table..."

When he's pushed back into the elevator and pinned against the wall, he loses his train of thought.

"Fucking—"

But then he realizes that the person pinning him is Zhou

Ziheng.

Xia Xiuze screams like a scared girl. "What happened? Are you okay, brother? Brother!"

Xia Xiqing's ears hurt. After taking off an earbud, he reaches out to grab Zhou Ziheng's chin, rubbing it between his thumb and index finger while mouthing to him, "What do you want?"

Zhou Ziheng is in dark gray athleisure today. His face is covered under a hood and a black mask like a typical college boy. It reminds Xia Xiqing that looking fashionable depends more on a pretty face than on pretty clothes.

Zhou Ziheng lowers his head and asks in a low voice, "Can I kiss you?"

If his question had been framed as "I'm going to kiss you," or "I want to kiss you," Xia Xiqing would have pulled him into a kiss without hesitation. But instead, Zhou Ziheng wears a nervous look of expectation on his face, like a kid who just asked for a Christmas present.

Xia Xiuze is still yelling his concern into the phone, and Xia Xiqing's heart won't stop fluttering. Having decided to steal his present rather than wait, Zhou Ziheng tugs on a strand of hair and leans forward to press their lips together through the mask. His eyes are bright and cheerful, like he just pulled a trick on Xia Xiqing.

It hits Xia Xiqing right in his weak spot.

Zhou Ziheng grabs the earbud hanging around Xia Xiqing's neck and holds it near his mouth.

"Happy birthday, *Xiao-Ze*[2]."

The poor kid goes quiet for a second, then begins stutter-

---

2 "Xiao-" is a prefix used for making diminutive nicknames, often used affectionately for children or for someone who's younger than whoever is speaking. Literally, it means "little" or "young."

ing until Xia Xiqing takes the mic back. "Who else could it be? It's your Ziheng-*gege*[3]."

Even though it's just Xia Xiqing's usual teasing, Zhou Ziheng finds his heart buzzing with so much joy that he has to bite back on a grin under his mask.

Xia Xiqing has his hands full with his brother, so he gives Zhou Ziheng a warning pat on the arm. "I'm home."

"Wait." Zhou Ziheng reaches into his pocket and produces a bag of candies.

"What?"

"My treat," Zhou Ziheng says in a casual way. He likes to have some candies in his pocket as emergency food for when he has no time for a full meal, but it seems that he won't need them today. He already feels recharged.

"Childish," Xia Xiqing scoffs, but he collects them from Zhou Ziheng's hand anyway, faking a cold glare at him as he walks away.

He pops one into his mouth as he approaches the door. Orange, milky, and sweet—he can see why Zhou Ziheng likes it.

Xia Xiuze hasn't hung up yet. Half-listening to his sad pleading, Xia Xiqing walks to the end of his living room and draws all curtains open, embracing the warmth of sunlight.

It's getting hotter every second.

Summer is Xia Xiqing's least favorite season, but it doesn't seem so bad this year. For just a fleeting moment, he wonders what it would be like to spend it with Zhou Ziheng.

"Fine, but just one meal." As it turns out, sweets do bring

---

3 "Ge(ge)" is an honorific title or suffix that is used any boy or man of the same nominal generation as the speaker, occasionally even for those who are slightly younger than the speaker, especially if they have some other form of seniority over the speaker. Literally, it means "older brother," but it is used regardless of familial relation and also sometimes regardless of relative age.

out the softness in him. "Don't cry this year, I'm warning you."

Xia Xiqing has been dying to hold his own art exhibition in the country for a long time now, but it seems whatever he draws recently feels wrong, lacking the sharpness that used to be his signature. Like melted shards of glass, every single one of his strokes have gone sticky and soft. It makes him restless and wary—for better or for worse, he's never liked change.

His thoughts drift to the magazine cover he did with Zhou Ziheng. Thinking that issue ought to be out by now, he logs onto Weibo and scrolls through the comments under the official channel. Unsurprisingly, their shippers are ecstatic over the magazine release; it's a veritable record-breaker for the magazine.

Something else has happened recently. In a small town down south, a teenage boy experiencing gender dysphoria committed suicide after getting bullied at school, causing LGBTQ social movements to spring up in his wake. And of course, those movements have caused counter-movements. A video of Zhou Ziheng's speech on normality was somehow dug up by a major press outlet, and then the LGBTQ community.

@everything21: This guy isn't just a pretty face. I like him.

@YouAreDelicious: He threw out some good points there. Who can ever be certain that they are normal and others aren't? Instead of judging each other, we should mind our own business and respect diversity.

@EightFeetHengHeng: Zhou Ziheng is a real treasure, always true to himself.

@NotDumb: Color blindness paradox is not common knowledge, is it?

@XiXi: I doubt most stars know what a paradox is.

@Wennie: I like his "we were born to be ourselves."

@3444122: Stereotypes like boys can't wear makeup or have long hair are just stupid.

@MyShipMarriedToday: I've heard this from my friend that Zhou Ziheng chose philosophy as one of his electives in first year and you can still find his final presentation on "what is a good moral system" on Bilibili.

"What is a good moral system"...? Xia Xiqing wonders what a younger Zhou Ziheng looked like in class, so he turns on his laptop and manages to track down this video from two years ago. It was a forty-minute slideshow presentation, and he completed it clean and off-script, answering courteously every time someone threw him a question.

He finds himself charmed that the enthusiastic, dedicated speaker on stage is the same guy who just ambushed him with a pocket full of candies. Zhou Ziheng's charm is a mixture of innocence and intelligence, pivoting on his good nature and kindness. At this thought, Xia Xiqing starts to sketch. This new piece depicts Zhou Ziheng standing at the front of a lecture hall, elbows on the podium, fixing the audience with a glamorous smile. He uploads it onto Weibo, where it is quickly acknowledged by a group of fans.

@xxx1: Another masterpiece!

@INeedCandy: Quick question **@ZhouZiheng** What's it like to be in love with an amazing artist?

@BestHeng: Is this Ziheng's freshman year presentation? I was just watching it. *Taitai*'s[4] drawing is too good, I'm wordless.

---

4 On the internet, "taitai" is an honorific title or suffix given to artists and writers who operate primarily online. It means "grand-grand," and is similar to another suffix, "dada," which means "big-big." Some people believe this to be a somewhat feminine title as there exists a homonymous "taitai" in offline speech, which is an honorific title or suffix used for married women—or, in

@SelfStudyEveryDay: So rude! He's not just any random taitai, he's Zhou-taitai

@SelfStudyGirlsUnite: zhou-taitai hehehe mrs zhou rofl

@DoYouSelfStudy: Mrs. Zhou? Ahahahaha this is the best!

The comment section veers more and more off-topic as the shippers take over. It seems that the Self-Study fandom has already decided Xia Xiqing would be the wife in this relationship. How naïve. They must've made that decision based purely on physical appearances. Xia Xiqing finds himself increasingly irritated by the misconception.

As the sun goes down, he gets more and more reminder texts from Xia Xiuze. Eventually, knowing that resistance is futile, he changes into a dark blue shirt and leaves home with the newest version of an AR console in his hands.

The place he's heading toward is a private joint near the outskirts of the city—a beautifully designed, traditional courtyard-style restaurant. He's been there before once on Xu Qichen's birthday.

Before he leaves the car, Xia Xiqing lights himself a cigarette—it's his brother's birthday, after all; he doesn't want to cause trouble. He parks and walks toward the gate, where Xia Xiuze is jumping up and down and waving nervously at him.

"Brother! I'm here!"

His frown relaxes a bit. "Here. Take this."

"Aw, I asked Xia Zhixu for this before, but he didn't give me one," Xia Xiuze says, unable to hide the excitement in his voice upon receiving a new toy.

"Because you always call him by name." Xia Xiqing's lips curl into a smile. "Learn some manners. Try calling him gege

---

some parts of China, as a colloquial term of address for one's wife. Despite this, "taitai" is used regardless of gender in its online context.

and then maybe he'll be nicer."

"But you always call him by name; you even call him your nephew sometimes," Xia Xiuze says weakly, slightly petulant.

"Yeah, but you're not me."

Xia Xiuze squeezes Xia Xiqing's arm affectionately, walking him to their reservation area while telling him all about the recent happenings of his life, as if he'd saved up all the interesting things for Xia Xiqing.

Their reservation is in the most expensive section of the restaurant, in a separate little courtyard that's separated from the main dining area by a small wooded garden. This section has only two rooms: the east and the west dining hall. The Xia family have the east one.

He pushes the door open, and the first thing he sees is Xia Yunkai sitting at the head of the table. He looks older and weaker than the last time Xia Xiqing saw him—three years ago, when he'd returned to China for the Christmas holidays. Even then, it had been an accident—they both just happened to be at the same high-end bar, and they hadn't even spoken to each other.

"You're here. Come sit," Xia Yunkai says with a kind smile on his face.

To onlookers who don't know any better, he might really seem like a loving father. He's become weaker as he's grown older, as if he's lost very badly in his fight against time and is now just a breath away from being relegated to bedrest. At this thought, Xia Xiqing finds himself overcome not with pity, but with amusement.

This most recent time that Xia Xiqing has returned from abroad, Xia Yunkai had transferred a solid quarter of the company shares to him without any previous negotiation. What does he expect Xia Xiqing to do? Tend to him at his bedside as he becomes senile?

Wearing his best poker face, Xia Xiqing sits across from Yu Fangyue. She's all dolled up, trying but failing to bury her inherent vulgarity under exquisite makeup and flashy jewelry.

"Xiqing! It's been so long; you should come home so we can have a family dinner or something. Your father misses you, you know."

He has to admit that it's super fun to watch her little befriending act, knowing that all she wants to do is rip him apart. As he unbuttons his cuffs, he smiles up at her, giving her a meaningful look. "It has been a while. You looked younger the last time I saw you." He reaches for the tea, his words trickling out nice and slow, "You know, I've got a friend who's a plastic surgeon. Want me to book you a face-lift?"

For a woman whose biggest fear is losing her beauty, this comment is not one she can find a good response to. Xia Xiqing has many things to say to her, and none of them very kind. However, he decides to let her off the hook in front of Xia Xiuze. The kid starts to chatter about various inconsequential matters as if his life depends on it, trying not only to fill up the silence but also to make sure nobody else feels the need to say anything.

"Xiqing, you still need to come around to the office when you get some spare time," Xia Yunkai says as he adds some food to Xia Xiqing's plate.

Xia Xiqing lowers his head, feeling an instant loss of appetite. This is the exact kind of insincere gesture that's most repulsive to him.

"Your office? Why? You don't think you'll live long enough to see your younger son take over the company?"

Xia Yunkai doesn't seem offended by the hostility in Xia Xiqing's tone. Yu Fangyue wants to say something, but Yunkai beats her to it, and there's a hint of grace in his voice.

"The company is too big now, I can't rely on your brother alone to take care of in the future." After a pause, he adds, "I know your mom left you all her art galleries, and you could live off those for the rest of your life—"

"Why are you mentioning her?" Yu Fangyue objects resentfully.

"As an outsider, what place do you have in this sort of discussion?" Xia Xiqing retorts, fingers tapping against the side of a porcelain bowl. Eyes still on Yu Fangyue, he addresses Xia Xiuze, "Xiao-Ze, I ordered a cake for you. Could you go outside and see if it's here yet?"

Xia Xiuze nods amiably and stands up, but then his mother shouts, "Don't you move! Who does he think he is, to order you around like that?"

Hearing this, Xia Xiuze freezes. It's only when Xia Xiqing gives him a few encouraging pats on the leg that he leaves the room without hesitation.

"You! You come back right now!"

Xia Xiqing stares at her with false sympathy. "Too bad. Your kid only listens to me. The family fortune is mine, and the child you carried for nine months is also mine."

Lost in shame and rage, she yells, "You are exactly like your mother, a complete psycho—"

Before she can finish the word, Xia Xiqing splashes his tea in her face.

"I wanted to serve you this earlier, but I didn't want to do it in front of Xiuze." He twirls the cup playfully between his fingers. "Just because I play nice for him doesn't mean you're anything to me."

"Let it go, Xiqing. Enough is enough."

Xia Xiqing laughs bitterly. "You want to play the good father now? Why didn't you stop and think 'Enough is enough' back when you beat me so bad I had to go to the hospital?"

"That was a long time ago. I was young and..."

"Don't even." Xia Xiqing's eyes lower to his own fingers, and he sees a fleck of red paint on his fingertip; looking like blood. How offensive. "Scumbags will always remain scumbags. Even when they're old." Then he raises his head, lips curling up into a contemptuous smile. "No offense, though. I was only talking about myself."

Walking back into the room with his cake, Xia Xiuze grins when he sees Xia Xiqing. "Brother! You haven't left yet."

"Nah, I was waiting for you." He pats the kid's shoulder as he sits. "Today, you're officially one year older than you were yesterday. You need to act less childishly from now on."

"But I'm still just a kid compared to you."

Xia Xiuze sticks the candles on the cake, too busy getting excited for his birthday to notice that his mother's makeup has been damaged by water stains. The absurdity of the scene makes Xia Xiqing want to destroy something. This kid is the only good thing that came out of this messed-up family.

"I'm going for a smoke."

"Brother..."

"I'll be back. Leave me a piece of cake." Xia Xiqing walks out.

There's a guy coming out of the other room in this area. A complete douchebag; Xia Xiqing can tell by the way he walks. The guy spots him too, and eyes him up and down. Xia Xiqing would find it quite strange, but he's more or less used to it now that he's been on TV. He snags a cigarette from his pocket, body faintly swaying back and forth in the wind of the bamboo forest in the dark night. It takes him a few tries to light it, which only aggravates his irritation.

Listening to the rustling of the wind through the bamboo leaves, he looks ahead where there seems to be figure standing far away on the porch. It looks awfully like his friend Xu Qichen.

He tilts his head and squints. It really is him!

"Qichen?"

Xu Qichen turns and cracks a smile as soon as he sees Xia Xiqing. "Look who it is. I didn't expect to see you here."

It's always nice running into a friend. Xia Xiqing walks over. "Why are you here? What are the chances, right?"

"Work dinner. Just finished."

"Oh, so you are waiting for your ride?" Xia Xiqing looks innocently at him. "Is Zhixu late in picking you up?"

Bashful, Xu Qichen tries to explain, "I told him not to, but he insisted. He should be here any minute now."

"You guys..." Xia Xiqing prods at his waist. "...are inseparable."

Being a ticklish person, Xu Qichen catches hold of Xia Xiqing's hands even as he can't help but start laughing.

"What are you guys doing?"

Xia Xiqing freezes as Zhou Ziheng's voice comes from behind him, catching him red-handed. Wondering how he's always able to catch him when he's fooling around with his friends, Xia Xiqing turns around, ready to explain.

Xu Qichen beats him to it: "I think I can skip the introductions. You guys are already familiar enough with one another, no?"

"Who? Me and him?" Xia Xiqing quickly realizes. "Wait, are you saying that he was also at your work dinner?"

"Yeah." Xu Qichen smiles. "We were discussing a script."

"He's playing a role from another one of your novels?" Xia Xiqing sees a loose thread on Xu Qichen's sleeve, so he grabs his arm, ready to pull it taught and burn off the excess.

"Not quite, it was an original script."

Zhou Ziheng coughs. Seeing that he's being a bit of a third wheel, Xu Qichen grins and says, "Well, I've still got someone waiting for me outside, so I'll take my leave. See you two later."

"Wait…" But before Xia Xiqing can stop him, Xu Qichen pulls out of his grasp and walks off. He turns to Zhou Ziheng. "Look at that; we weren't even talking for two minutes, and now he's left. I'm blaming you."

"You two seem close." Zhou Ziheng leans in and plucks the limited-edition lighter from Xia Xiqing's grip.

Knowing that he's talking about the loose thread, Xia Xiqing smiles. "I was just trying to help him out."

"What kind of 'help'?"

Xia Xiqing taps Zhou Ziheng's chin. "You know, they say that fans take after their idols, but why do you seem to be taking after me more and more?"

Zhou Ziheng grabs Xia Xiqing's wrist. "It's contagious. I must've caught it from kissing you."

"Oh, piss off," Xia Xiqing says, but there's very little reproach behind his words. He reminds himself that they're in public, which means they need to be careful about kissing. So he makes to leave, flipping easily over the railing.

Zhou Ziheng reaches out, trying to catch his waist, but Xia Xiqing slips away, grinning.

"No touching."

Then it hits Zhou Ziheng—Xia Xiqing has a scar there; he doesn't want anyone to know about it.

"Where are you headed next?" Xia Xiqing asks.

"Home."

"Take me with you?"

Zhou Ziheng runs a hand through Xia Xiqing's hair. "Aren't you going back to your brother's birthday dinner?"

Xia Xiqing lowers his eyes. "I regretted coming here ages ago. I feel dirty." Sensing a grip on his wrist, he looks up, falling into Zhou Ziheng's dark brown eyes. He feels something in there pulling him in. "Where to?"

"Let's elope."

Sure, Xia Xiqing thinks. Elopement is too exciting for him to ever turn down, even though deep down he thought he'd be the one proposing it. But who cares? He wants to go with Zhou Ziheng right now, and leave his troubles behind.

"Let's go in my car. Xiao-Luo can drive yours back."

"What happened to your old car?"

Zhou Ziheng is driving a black Lexus LS that Xia Xiqing hasn't seen before, which is still incredibly low-key for someone of his status.

"That was the company car."

"I always hated that one." Xia Xiqing smiles when he sees Xiao-Luo and tosses his car key to him. When Xiao-Luo looks nervously at the label on the key, Xia Xiqing says, "Don't worry. I've got good insurance."

"Please crash it for him. It's so damn flashy." Zhou Ziheng smirks.

"Yeah, of course, this black one of yours fits the aesthetics of moderation *much* better."

Hand slippery with nervous sweat, Xiao-Luo waves off his two young masters.

Fans are typically interested in the family backgrounds of their idols, but rumors tend to get blown out of proportion. "Upper middle class" can easily be turned into "trust fund baby," just as anyone with a family member in a simple civil service position tends to get stuck with a label of "family in politics." Having come from an actual background of wealth and privilege, Xia Xiqing is of course utterly unimpressed by this sort of thing.

But the more he gets to know Zhou Ziheng on a personal level, the more he leans toward the assumption that his family background isn't anything ordinary. It's not because the kid errs on the side of extravagance in his daily spending—he's a celebrity, and they tend to be like that—rather, his mannerisms and worldly outlook point toward a relatively ideal family situation. He seems to have never wanted for anything, yet he seems also to understand the mundanities of life. His principles seem to be the result of strict moral teachings, but he maintains a great respect for the liberty of thought.

"What's wrong?" Zhou Ziheng asks, sensing Xia Xiqing's unusual silence. "Still annoyed by my sense of aesthetics? Or do you disagree that your Cayenne is too flashy?"

"You know what? You're kinda right. That Cayenne is the most low-key car I've got." Xia Xiqing grins. "See the office lady walking across the street? That car is to me like her black work bag is to her—spacious, handy, good for the wear and tear of day-to-day life."

Zhou Ziheng frowns, giving him an unconvinced look.

Xia Xiqing's fingers play with the drawstrings of Zhou Ziheng's hoodie. "If that lady is going to the club, she won't take that handbag. A truly flashy car is used for similar reasons: to attract potential partners and—" He lowers his voice. "—for car sex."

Zhou Ziheng almost hits the brakes. Amused at the reaction, Xia Xiqing shrugs, faking regret in his voice. "Well, don't get too excited. Considering your profession and this temporary gig of mine, I doubt we'll get to experience that."

Zhou Ziheng puts a lollipop into his mouth, which is soon stolen by Xia Xiqing. Because he has to pay attention to the road ahead, Zhou Ziheng simply chooses not to protest.

"Ugh, this is too sweet."

Xia Xiqing's muffled voice reminds Zhou Ziheng of that morning when he climbed on top of him, gasping. He shakes those thoughts out of his head.

Meanwhile, Xia Xiqing takes advantage of the current lull in conversation to pull out his phone and message Xia Xiuze.

I gotta leave early. Eat my cake for me, okay? I'll take you out for dinner next week. Happy birthday

As usual, he gets an instant reply.

Brother, do you really think my birthday is worth celebrating? Did my birth actually make anyone happy?

It's deleted almost immediately, but Xia Xiqing manages to read it before that happens. He takes a deep breath, then answers:

You know, I wasn't thrilled by it at first either.

But I've come to realize that you're the only thing in this family that makes me happy.

Before he can send out another message forbidding Xia Xiuze from replying to that last one, a call comes in, startling him, and he accidentally taps the speaker button.

"Waaaah, big brother, I love you so much, waaaaah..." Xia Xiuze wails incoherently.

Xia Xiqing keeps calm and responds, "Please chill. Don't call me." Then he hangs up in the middle of his brother's unbecoming display of affection, then breathes a slow breath out.

He's a pretty cold person, no? So why does he have a

brother as clingy as Xia Xiuze?

"Your brother is cute." Zhou Ziheng looks amused.

"So are you." Xia Xiqing reaches into Zhou Ziheng's hood tweaks his earlobe.

Zhou Ziheng purses his lips, palms sweating a little as he feels the touch on his ear linger warmly long after Xia Xiqing's hand has left. He tries to concentrate on driving.

You're not lovers, he tells himself, snapping back from the false sweetness of the dream that they're in a romantic relationship. It seems it's all he can do lately. He wonders if his more physical reactions will eventually fade away, too. After all, it's human nature to learn to let go.

He also knows letting go is easier said than done.

In the meantime, if he can keep Xia Xiqing from finding out about his feelings, their arrangement will remain intact. Besides, he's already started to like the intimacy.

Meanwhile, Xia Xiqing is on his phone checking his social media. He wades through a sea of jokes about him being Zhou Ziheng's wife.

"Literally..." he mutters to himself, but doesn't finish his complaint.

"What's wrong?" Zhou Ziheng asks.

"No—nothing." Xia Xiqing puts away his phone. When he realizes they're out of town, he asks in a teasing tone, "Why are we in the middle of nowhere? Wait, are you going to rape and murder me out here? Nobody would ever find my body."

Zhou Ziheng replies with a serious face, "Do you know the one role I've always wanted to play?"

"Psychopath!" Xia Xiqing answers instantly.

"Psychopathic murderer."

"That's weird." Xia Xiqing glances at the rear-view mirror and adds, "You don't seem worried about paparazzi following you."

"And you only just noticed?"

Xia Xiqing pouts, then notices a building appearing in the night. It's nothing special or fancy, but Xia Xiqing swears it looks like a government building.

"What is this place? I thought we were going to fly to an island on your private jet."

Zhou Ziheng rolls his eyes, slowing down the car. "You thought this would be like a movie, didn't you?"

"Isn't that what you do?" Xia Xiqing smiles, casting a look at the guard in uniform at the gate. Government badges—he finds his curiosity rising.

Then Zhou Ziheng greets the guard: "Evening, Meng-*shu*[5]."

"Oh, it's Ziheng. Come on in." The man sees Xia Xiqing and turns to Zhou Ziheng. "A friend of yours?"

"Yeah."

The guard lets them pass the gate.

Xia Xiqing knew Zhou Ziheng comes from a military family—his fans have known for years—but he's not clear on any details, nor does he know how high up they are in the chain of command.

After driving for a few more minutes, they step out of the car.

"Ziheng."

Hearing someone call his name, Zhou Ziheng turns and finds a guy in uniform in his early thirties.

"Cheng-ge," Zhou Ziheng greets.

"You brought a friend today." The man called Cheng-ge speaks with a heavy Beijing accent. "I'll drive you two."

---

5 "Shu(shu)" is an honorific title or suffix that is used for any man at least one nominal generation older than the speaker. Literally, it means "uncle," but is used regardless of familial relation. As a suffix, it can be abbreviated (as it has been in this case) to "-shu."

On their way, Cheng-ge nags Zhou Ziheng to visit his parents more, but doesn't chatter much beyond that. Once they stop, he tosses Zhou Ziheng a set of keys, then says, "Let me know when you're done. I'll drive you out, too."

Zhou Ziheng nods, leading Xia Xiqing into the large unassuming structure.

"Where are we, exactly?"

"A paparazzi-free zone."

Zhou Ziheng walks to a gate labeled 23 and unlocks it. The only thing they see inside is darkness. He lays a hand over Xia Xiqing before pressing a button on the wall.

A hall big enough to be a soccer field lights up in front of them.

"Is this a shooting range?" Xia Xiqing turns to Zhou Ziheng.

"If you ignore every qualifier that comes before the name of this place, then yes."

"Are these real?" Xia Xiqing asks skeptically after Zhou Ziheng pulls him into the gun room.

"Nothing in here is open to the public, so of course they're real." Zhou Ziheng passes an AUG rifle to Xia Xiqing, then picks up a Type 88 sniper rifle. "Try these two first."

Xia Xiqing's heart is pounding with an excitement that all men probably experience in the presence of firearms. He's been overseas often enough to have encountered a handgun or two, but he's never actually pulled the trigger before.

Zhou Ziheng puts on a dark blue tactical vest and a pair of yellow goggles. He walks to Xia Xiqing with a pair of earmuffs in his hand, looking more attractive than ever. Xia Xiqing gives himself a mental thumb up for his taste in men.

"It's gonna be loud." Zhou Ziheng puts on the earmuffs for him, receiving a head-tilt in return. "What's wrong?"

Actually, Xia Xiqing can't hear Zhou Ziheng's question very clearly through the earmuffs, but he reads his lips well.

"Nothing. Just wanna look at you."

Zhou Ziheng blushes and licks his lips nervously, eyes flitting over to somewhere else before landing on Xia Xiqing.

Xia Xiqing takes off the earmuffs and asks, "You come here often?"

Zhou Ziheng admits, "When I feel stressed, I come here."

"Like when?" Xia Xiqing can't think of anything Zhou Ziheng would be stressed about; he basically radiates positive energy all the time. Receiving silence, he presses, "When was the last time you came?"

He actually wanted to ask when was the last time Zhou Ziheng had brought someone here, but he changes his words at the last second.

"Last week."

"Last week?" Xia Xiqing frowns at the answer. Last week before their trip to Shanghai?

"Why? Exams?"

Zhou Ziheng shoots him a glare and picks up the sniper rifle. "If you say so."

What kind of answer is that? Xia Xiqing shrugs, quickly putting on the earmuffs.

Zhou Ziheng's aim is incredibly good. Now he gets why the fans beg him to play a cop; his body is built for the role. He grabs another tactical vest for Xia Xiqing and gives him some beginner notes.

"Do I have to wear this?"

"Yes, you do. It's for the good of your shoulders." Zhou Ziheng puts on the goggles for Xia Xiqing, then loads the AUG and passes it to him.

"Hey, why don't you coach me?"

"Sure." Zhou Ziheng stands behind him, adjusting his arms.

"Relax your shoulders, eyes forward, and concentrate." Zhou Ziheng wraps him in his arms. "Don't be afraid of the recoil. I'm here to hold you."

Tense and unable to concentrate, Xia Xiqing hears Zhou Ziheng say, "Take a deep breath." Those lips almost breathe into his ear. "Your heartbeat is going to affect the accuracy. So lower your heart rate as much as you can."

Xia Xiqing only feels his heart pounding faster.

"Let's try it once."

"Three..."

"Two..."

"One."

The moment Xia Xiqing pulls the trigger, he feels the recoil push him backward; his back hits Zhou Ziheng's chest like he's being nailed to a wall. In that split second, all his troubles cease to exist. The explosion takes away everything around him except for Zhou Ziheng's warm chest against him and his arms around him.

"What do you think? Is it stress relief?" Zhou Ziheng takes off his earmuffs and checks the target. "You did much better than my first time. You're good at this."

Xia Xiqing falls in love with shooting almost instantly, and he starts to indulge himself in it without Zhou Ziheng's assistance.

"You having fun?" After a while, feeling ignored, Zhou Ziheng strides toward Xia Xiqing.

Xia Xiqing looks up. "Of course, this is more fun than you are."

Zhou Ziheng grins. "Which part?"

Xia Xiqing imitates Zhou Ziheng's shooting position. "It

lets me do it, you don't."

This again. Zhou Ziheng snorts, "Come on, be reasonable."

Xia Xiqing points the gun at Zhou Ziheng's chest and says shamelessly, "Let me do it."

"That's some hardcore way of getting my consent." Zhou Ziheng doesn't even pretend to raise his hands. "But you're not getting it."

Xia Xiqing pushes the gun slightly against his chest. "Think again. I can always fuck you after you're dead."

"I don't need to think again."

"Any last words?" Xia Xiqing's lips curl into a wicked smile, just like a professional killer.

"My last words..." Zhou Ziheng seemingly takes a second to gather his thoughts. "Use half of my money to build elementary schools, donate a quarter toward the initiative to build more roads in mountainous regions, and as for the rest..."

He suddenly leans in. He couldn't care less about the gun pointed at his chest.

"Buy up all the art Xia Xiqing has ever made of me. I want to take it to the grave with me."

At the end of his statement, Zhou Ziheng gently kisses the dazed Xia Xiqing on the lips, stealing away his gun and his heart.

Xia Xiqing never imagined that he would ever fall in love with anyone.

He's always said that the greatest misstep people make in romance is that mistaking momentary pleasure for love; using their fluttering heartbeat to justify their entanglement in the spiderweb of romance. These moments are but ripples on the surface of a lake, coming and going with the wind.

He can't be sure that what he's experiencing isn't ripples

on the surface of a lake, but he can be sure that he enjoys the moment.

"Your grip is loosening." Zhou Ziheng grins, gesturing at the AUG he's holding.

Xia Xiqing watches Zhou Ziheng's face as he tries to tell if any of his earlier words were true. Coming from such a talented actor, it's hard to tell.

They have nothing real. They shouldn't.

Xia Xiqing reassures himself and purses his lips, eyes seductive. "Doesn't matter. You'll see that my other gun is steady enough."

How stubborn is this guy? Zhou Ziheng laughs. "I tried. Accidental discharge."

"Hey, watch your mouth!" Xia Xiqing pretends to kick Zhou Ziheng, who in turn pulls him into his arms.

"I'm just kidding."

"Don't hug me." Xia Xiqing pushes him away. "Don't hug me like I'm a fucking girl."

This is the second time Zhou Ziheng has heard Xia Xiqing say something like that. He wonders if it's because he previously had a crush on a girl, so Xia Xiqing is a bit insecure about it. But that explanation probably makes himself out to be too big of a deal—a better explanation is probably just that Xia Xiqing is more comfortable in a dominant position.

"Wanna hug me instead?" Zhou Ziheng opens his arms.

Xia Xiqing glances at him. With their height difference, he'll probably feel like a girl no matter how they hug.

"Go away. I don't want to hug you." He tries to take the gun back, but as soon as his hand touches it, he feels a tight grip around his wrist.

"Your hand is injured?" Zhou Ziheng sounds horrified.

Injured? Xia Xiqing is confused, but he soon gets it. "Oh,

you mean this? Just paint. Not blood."

Zhou Ziheng sighs in relief, but he still rubs at it, confirming that it is in fact paint. "You scared me. You painted today?"

"Huh? Yes..." Xia Xiqing is not used to being the subject of concern. Instead, he starts practicing his shots again.

Zhou Ziheng wanted to ask him more about what he painted today, but seeing Xia Xiqing go back to shooting, he decides not to bother him. He opens WeChat instead; he hasn't checked it all day, having been busy with various auditions and meetings, as well as that work dinner just earlier. As expected, he's got lots of unread messages. He replies to the few important work-related messages, then opens up his conversation with Shang Sirui.

Sirui: Ziheng! Did you see the new painting of you Xiqing did today?

Sirui: [image attachment]

It's a watercolor painting of him doing a presentation two years ago. The right corner of the PowerPoint slide is red. So that's where the red paint came from.

Ziheng: He sent you this?

Sirui: Nah, I downloaded it from his Weibo.

At this comment, Zhou Ziheng immediately opens Weibo, where he's flooded with notifications of people tagging him.

@SelfStudyGirlForLife: @ZhouZiheng, come see what your taitai painted for you!

@Study101: @ZhouZiheng, how does it feel to be in love with an artist?

@MyShipIsReal: @ZhouZiheng, I hereby announce that you and this beautiful artist have been locked together, and that I've swallowed the key!

"His" taitai? Is that how that word is used nowadays?

There are also some non-shipper comments under Xia Xiqing's original post.

@TheBestHengInTheUniverse: Thank you for posting, taitai!

@TheRealMrsZhou: Thanks for posting, taitai, but to the shippers out there please chill out. An overactive imagination is a symptom of psychosis.

@MyDearHeng: Come on, guys. Zhou Ziheng is totally straight.

...

Zhou Ziheng bites his lower lip. Is he straight? He certainly used to be pretty straight, but now...

As for the shipper's imaginations... Their fantasies are probably not that different from what they're doing in real life...no?

The discussion escalated pretty quickly; Xia Xiqing's solo-fans also got involved. They seem to have an attitude of "are you bullying our little artist just because he doesn't have a fanbase?" Really? Even if Xia Xiqing actually needed protection, it still shouldn't come from a gaggle of teenage girls.

Zhou Ziheng clicks on the share button and starts typing.

@ZhouZiheng: Thank you, taitai.

He doesn't think much of it—even though "taitai" is what people call their wives, that's a completely different context from this, and it's really common to use terms like "dada" and "taitai" to address artists online. Still, the shippers go crazy in response to it.

@ThinkIShouldSelfStudy: Ahhhhhhhh! I can't believe he said that! It's real!

@MyShipIsReal: Oh my god did he just call him taitai?

@GoSelfStudy: Protective!Ziheng is here!

@LovelySelfStudyGirls: I'm going to cry all day for Protective!Ziheng. Honestly these toxic solo fans deserve it for coming to start shit under Xiqing's post.

@LetsGoStudy: I feel like we have something new to celebrate every day...

"What are you doing?"

Zhou Ziheng looks up, finding Xia Xiqing walking toward him with earmuffs and goggles in hand.

"Just browsing Weibo."

Xia Xiqing stretches a little before he sits down next to Zhou Ziheng. "The bullseye is so hard to hit."

"You've had enough practice for one day. Your arms will be sore tomorrow." Zhou Ziheng rises to his feet. "Let's go home."

"I'm hungry." Xia Xiqing's eyes are full of delight, glistening under the light. Without his signature smile, he looks even more innocent.

Zhou Ziheng pulls him up. "My mom brought me some herbal chicken broth yesterday. We can make noodles when we go home."

Xia Xiqing follows Zhou Ziheng out of the shooting range, mood significantly improved. The last time he was at Zhou Ziheng's place, he'd forced himself on him. Thinking back to it, he still feels a bit embarrassed about it. But it's strange—Zhou Ziheng had been so angry back then, and now he's inviting him over?

"You can wear my slippers." Zhou Ziheng pulls out a pair of blue slippers and puts them in front of Xia Xiqing.

"Oh, okay," Xia Xiqing says, then realizes something. "Or I can just go home and get my own."

Zhou Ziheng is getting out a pair of single-use slippers, the kind usually used for guests. He doesn't even look up when he says, "If you're averse to using mine, feel free."

How passive-aggressive! Xia Xiqing almost chuckles. "That's not what I meant! I just didn't want you to be uncomfortable."

He then steps into Zhou Ziheng's slippers. They're nice and soft, but they're a bit big on him.

"Your feet are huge."

"I'm six-four."

"Wow, impressive."

"I know."

They exchange looks of amusement. Xia Xiqing's stomach starts to rumble, and he starts wandering around. When he goes further into the living area, he finds that it's taken up by a sizable pool.

"Hey, not bad." Xia Xiqing squats and glances his fingers over the surface of the water. "Now I kind of want this layout in my place."

"Isn't that bit unnecessary?" Zhou Ziheng walks to the kitchen and pulls the fridge door open. "You can always come here for a swim."

The moment those words leave his mouth, he begins to regret them. What's wrong with him? Xia Xiqing must have plenty of places he can go to when he wants to swim.

Xia Xiqing remains quiet. He was going to say, *"But then what would I do if we break up?"* It's not like he's kept contact with any of his exes. It's a good thing he kept his mouth shut, though; that's a very awkward thing to say when he and Zhou Ziheng don't even have a proper relationship.

"And that's the permission I was looking for." For want of things to do, Xia Xiqing bounces a little on the balls of his feet.

"Wait, I haven't turned on the temperature control," Zhou

Ziheng says, assuming that Xia Xiqing is preparing to jump right in.

"What? No, I'm not gonna try to swim right now. I'm starving." Xia Xiqing lays down on the sofa, sighing in comfort. Worried that he might get bored, Zhou Ziheng turns on the television and passes him the remote. Some boring love drama is on, and he watches with the background noise of Zhou Ziheng cooking in the kitchen.

Xia Xiqing lays there, thinking it's been a long time since he felt like this.

Like he has a home.

He doesn't let the idea grow. He shifts his focus to something else, not wanting those pathetic feelings to take over.

"Hey, look at the special effects... They need to tone down the saturation. I feel like I'm going blind here.

"What kind of dress is that? Ugh. Don't ever do teen shows, please, or you'll lose me as a fan.

"The scene... Newton's rolling over in his grave.

"Actually, that guy looks alright. His eyes are nice. Not so much his nose, though."

He's not even close to Zhou Ziheng's level.

Zhou Ziheng walks in carrying a bowl of noodles to deliver to the coffee table, face stony all the while.

"Wow, that's fast." Xia Xiqing pulls himself up from the sofa. "Why are you looking at me like that?"

"You done ogling that poor guy? Is he your food?" Zhou Ziheng says, walking back to the kitchen for his bowl.

Xia Xiqing smiles, hands cupping around his bowl. "Of course not, you are. If you let me, you know..."

Zhou Ziheng walks over with another bowl. "Then you should continue watching."

"I don't think so." Xia Xiqing picks up a pair of chopsticks, sitting straight. "You know I have high standards. Only you passed my minimum requirements."

"Minimum requirements?" Zhou Ziheng raises an eyebrow at him.

"Fine, way over the minimum." Xia Xiqing slides down to the carpet and starts eating. "You're alright, just not as handsome as me." He drinks a mouthful of soup before he continues, "Your family has a good chef."

Zhou Ziheng is about to correct him and say that it's his mom's cooking, but then he thinks better of it. It wouldn't be a very tactful comment to make in front of Xia Xiqing.

After gulping down the last spoonful of soup, Xia Xiqing feels warm all over; slightly sweaty, even. He unfastens two of the buttons at his shirt collar, arms resting on his propped-up knees. He looks like a cat settling down in a patch of sunlight.

Zhou Ziheng suddenly has the overwhelming urge to buy a cat.

Feeling content and relaxed, Xia Xiqing checks his Weibo. There, he is met with the unwelcome surprise of seeing Zhou Ziheng's "Thank you taitai" post.

"What the hell? Are you crazy? Why would you call me that?"

"Wait, is it a big deal?" Zhou Ziheng does his best to look dumbfounded.

"You..." Xia Xiqing inhales deeply, biting back his uncomplimentary words. "You delete that post right now."

"You know I can't do that." Zhou Ziheng sips at his drink. "If I delete it, it'll be guaranteed a spot in the trending searches."

"Fine! You win!" Even though he's furious, he knows Zhou Ziheng is right. He has to focus on something else, or he'll lose his mind. "I've seen this guy a lot on TV recently."

"You fishing for gossip?" Zhou Ziheng asks, bumping Xia Xiqing's shoulder with his knee. He doesn't feel comfortable talking about other guys with Xia Xiqing, but he doesn't want him to be mad at him either.

"Is there any?" Xia Xiqing says, looking up at him.

The hand placed on Zhou Ziheng's knee distracts him a little. He's sitting on the couch, seeing pretty much everything underneath Xia Xiqing's loose T-shirt without even trying. He flits his eyes back at the TV.

"Truth is, I don't usually have much gossip to tell. I tend not to know about a lot of the stuff that goes on in the industry until the paparazzi get to it."

Xia Xiqing believes him.

"But we had a work dinner with a sponsor tonight. He's kind of...off the books about the way he does things, and it made the conversation feel pretty awkward. He only got a few cups in before he started nagging Director Kun about adding a character."

"For him?" Xia Xiqing points at the guy on TV.

Zhou Ziheng nods. "That sponsor kept talking about him, saying he's good-looking and has high potential... We tried to change the subject, but he was too persistent."

It makes sense. Xia Xiqing chuckles. "What happened then?"

"Director Kun said he'd think about it. The script isn't set in stone yet." Zhou Ziheng then quickly adds, "That guy also kept toasting Writer Xu, trying to get him drunk, you know? But Director Kun and I stopped it from getting too far."

"What the fuck?" Xia Xiqing exclaims, a defensive edge in his voice.

Seeing Xia Xiqing's reaction, Zhou Ziheng feels a bit

irked. "It's okay. He didn't touch his glass at all. He didn't even talk much."

Xia Xiqing sneers. He knows that Xu Qichen is more stubborn than he looks. "I can't believe that bastard tried to do that to our Chen-Chen[6]. Heavens forbid *that one* finds out about this, or things may get out of hand."

Hearing Xia Xiqing refer to Writer Xu as "Chen-Chen," Zhou Ziheng feels even more annoyed. He tries to think of a good way to ask about it, but before he can say anything, Xia Xiqing volunteers an answer.

"Xu Qichen is my friend from high school. Oh, that kid... I bet he's the most heartbreaking kid you'd ever know."

The term "kid" doesn't help Zhou Ziheng lower his guard, either.

Xia Xiqing continues, "He had a happy family life at first, but just after he graduated junior high, his parents took him on a road trip. They got into an accident, and both his parents passed away. He became an overnight orphan." He huffs. "He was super withdrawn in high school. If it wasn't for that idiot always hanging all over him, I don't even want to think about what he might have done..."

Zhou Ziheng honestly didn't expect to hear such a horrible story about that kind, polite screenwriter he knows. "What happened next?"

"Well, things got better. But after a while, there were rumors about him being gay, and that he was involved with a teacher. He was forced to change schools." Xia Xiqing shoots him a glare. "I bet you want to know if he's actually gay, hmm? Well, he'd gotten a crush on that idiot who was always hanging around him, but he never confessed. And in reality

---

6 In Chinese, this method of reduplicating characters is often affectionately used to make diminutive nicknames.

that idiot also liked him a lot, but neither of them knew, so they just secretly pined after one another for a solid decade. And because of those rumors, they even lost contact with each other for several years.

"With experiences like his, it'd be pretty understandable if he'd turned out bitter and mean, but he didn't. He's always been very kind, and he only ever lets himself get hurt. It's all because he's always liked that one guy, and he doesn't want him to see him be unkind."

Zhou Ziheng feels the emotion inside Xia Xiqing's voice.

Xia Xiqing tilts his chin up, voice contemptuous. "I'm different. If someone hurts me, I'll make them pay the price for it no matter what. If I can't be happy, no one can. And they can all go to the hell I'm already in. There's also nobody in this entire world that I care enough about to stop me from being unkind. No matter how mean I get, it won't matter."

It really won't matter.

When he was a kid, he'd felt invisible to his parents, who spent most of their time fighting each other and ignoring him. When he brought home medals or the highest graded homework in his class, he didn't get the slightest reaction. When he found out that picking fights, skipping class, drinking, or getting low grades made them angry enough to actually talk to him, he was happy to do it for attention.

How ironic.

Zhou Ziheng runs a hand through his hair, pulling him into his arms. "I think you got something wrong there."

"What do you mean?" Xia Xiqing asks, confused.

"I said, you got something wrong. He's not the most heartbreaking kid I know," Zhou Ziheng gently replies.

Before the rest of the sentence can be said, Xia Xiqing already starts to get angry. He twists to get his hands on

Zhou Ziheng's shoulders for better pushing leverage, but Zhou Ziheng just wraps his arms even tighter.

"Whoever pushes me is the most heartbreaking kid I know." His voice is tinged with a warm, smiling tone that sounds like a joke, but somehow it instantly soothes Xia Xiqing's anxiety.

Receiving pity from some kid who's five years younger than him is mortifying, so he can't help but blurt, "Whatever. Either way, it's not me."

"Yeah. Not you." Zhou Ziheng sways the both of them back and forth tenderly. He places Xia Xiqing's hand on his own back, changing their position so that they're cuddling, but also so that neither of them can move easily away.

"Then who is it?" Xia Xiqing's tone is hostile, but he also doesn't put down the hand that had been raised into a hugging position.

Zhou Ziheng runs a hand through Xia Xiqing's soft hair, then lowers his head and envelops his entire body in his arms. His voice is soft and warm, like a piece of marshmallow in the shape of a feather, floating down lightly, wavering for a long time before finally floating into Xia Xiqing's hand.

"Right. Who would that be?" he says.

At the end of the rising intonation of his question, he chuckles, lips pressing against Xia Xiqing's ear.

And so Xia Xiqing instantly forgets how to be angry.

C.10

Sinking Deeper

Being cuddled by Zhou Ziheng, Xia Xiqing feels so at ease that he could just go to sleep. But he also feels it's a bit too weird for him to be like this, since Zhou Ziheng is five years younger than him. He'd seemed so childish before, getting angry after so little teasing. How has it come to this?

He's so gentle, and, although Xia Xiqing can't stand it, he also can't push it away.

His anger fading, Xia Xiqing is relaxed and confused. Didn't Zhou Ziheng used to be an angry little lion all the time? Head buried between Zhou Ziheng's head and shoulder, Xia Xiqing tugs on his collar and captures his clavicle between his teeth like a cat; one of those mischievous ones.

"Don't bite." Zhou Ziheng pinches his neck. "I have work."

"Sure thing, big star." Xia Xiqing lifts his head, licking his lower lip. "I suspect you think of me as a child these days."

"Yeah? I don't know about that." Zhou Ziheng bites back on a grin.

"That's your I'm-proud-of-myself smile." Xia Xiqing's fingers trace his face until they land on his lips. "So what are you feeling proud of?" he says, voice soft and fluffy.

Xia Xiqing shifts his gaze to Zhou Ziheng's lips and holds it there, feeling his light breathing.

"Why are you quiet?"

He's just too beautiful, Zhou Ziheng thinks wildly. *The creator must have been very careful when crafting you, giving all the colors in the world to you to draw with, not to mention the talent with which to use them.*

You're the child most favored by God.

"It's just that I have so much to say." Zhou Ziheng runs a hand up and down Xia Xiqing's spine. "But none of it is what you want to hear."

"Then forget it." Xia Xiqing smiles.

Zhou Ziheng kisses him on the nose.

"Hey, who said you could do that?" Xia Xiqing frowns, hands cupping loosely around Zhou Ziheng's neck.

He hates when others kiss his nose, like he's a girl or something. As pretty as his face is, people used to always tease him about it when he was growing up. The insecurity stays with him still—he hates to be feminized.

Xia Xiqing lets go when Zhou Ziheng pretends to choke.

"Drama queen."

"Don't you like what your nose looks like?"

Xia Xiqing rolls his eyes. "Yes, but not the mole. I'll go get it removed tomorrow."

"No way."

"Yes, way. It's mine, so I get to decide." Xia Xiqing puts on his thug face, but soon realizes something. "Oh crap, my legs are numb."

Zhou Ziheng pinches his upper leg, grinning.

"Zhou Ziheng! What the fuck!"

"You just need to move around."

"No, no, no, don't touch me. It's pins and needles."

Zhou Ziheng tries to help him by positioning his leg on the couch behind him. "You'll feel better."

"How is this better?" Xia Xiqing is annoyed because it looks like he's straddling him, so he moves his leg a bit. Immediately, he sucks a breath in through his teeth. "Ouch..."

"It'll pass. Don't move."

"Don't move your mom!"

Zhou Ziheng rubs Xia Xiqing's legs gently. "Here, if I try to massage it away..."

"Fuck. Don't..."

Zhou Ziheng simply ignores Xia Xiqing's complaints. In his mind, numbness won't go away until you massage it.

Xia Xiqing lays his hand over Zhou Ziheng's, slightly out of breath. "I told you to stop. Do you not understand Chinese?"

Finally realizing how intimate they are, Zhou Ziheng finds his palm pressed against Xia Xiqing's thigh, warm and dry. He doesn't dare to move. If he makes a move on Xia Xiqing, he'll probably go along with it. But if he does it right now, that'd be like taking advantage of him, no?

A kiss initiated by Xia Xiqing resolves Zhou Ziheng's internal struggle. Xia Xiqing's tongue is wet and aggressive. Zhou Ziheng's begins to pant.

"So now you stop, hmm?" Xia Xiqing gives him a challenging look.

Zhou Ziheng realizes how naïve he was, thinking he'd ever be able to take advantage of this guy. He responds by rubbing and caressing his skin, but not laying a finger on the one part that Xia Xiqing wants him to touch.

"Zhou Ziheng..."

Zhou Ziheng enjoys the way Xia Xiqing grits his teeth and says his name like that. He kisses his lips, fingers trickling down his spine. Xia Xiqing has to hold back the urge of leaving bite marks on Zhou Ziheng's neck.

Xia Xiqing's happy moans fill the air. Zhou Ziheng feels like they hit right where his heart is—those watery eyes, the pale skin under the lamplight, the warm temperature outside.

Xia Xiqing beams at him, a hint of a tease in his voice. "Don't tell me you have stage fright."

Zhou Ziheng presses his lips against Xia Xiqing's neck and collarbone, more like a gentle rub than a kiss. He breathes into his ear, in a hoarse voice, "I don't, but you don't seem to be able to hold on much longer."

Xia Xiqing is having a mental breakdown. Zhou Ziheng isn't a puppy—he's a wolf, patient and dangerous.

"You're right." Xia Xiqing licks his ear, breathing speeding up. "I want to sleep with you. I want it so bad."

"No, you don't." Zhou Ziheng smiles, his own skin slippery with sweat and burning hot.

"Don't play with me. I can always go to—" Before he finishes his threat, Zhou Ziheng gives him a hard squeeze on his tented crotch. "Oh fuck. Are you kidding me?"

Zhou Ziheng chuckles, hand going soft on him. "Did I do something wrong?"

This is it. This has got to be the biggest trouble Xia Xiqing has encountered in his twenty-five years of life.

Literally the *biggest*.

The two of them make out for over an hour, but in the end Xia Xiqing still doesn't get what he wants. Instead of going home in anger and frustration, he decides to curl up on this couch. It's so comfortable that it makes him sleepy as hell. Zhou Ziheng throws him a long blanket, warm and soft, and then he lays down facing him, tucking him in.

"How many times have I told you to not hold me like this?" Xia Xiqing's muffled voice trickles out from under the blanket.

"But it feels good though, right?" Zhou Ziheng says, amused.

"No, it doesn't." Maybe just a bit, Xia Xiqing admits to himself.

"But I like it. Can I just hold you like this, please?" Zhou Ziheng asks softly, one hand stroking his back.

How a clingy and caring guy like Zhou Ziheng is still single is something Xia Xiqing can't figure out. Xia Xiqing remembers the girl Zhou Ziheng talked about, and struggles a bit inside—he must be really into that girl to not get himself a girlfriend or boyfriend all these years. Maybe he's just too busy juggling work and school, but it doesn't really make sense. Everyone else in his profession manages to have a private life no matter how busy they are. So why not him? Does he like that girl that much?

Wait, what's he doing? Xia Xiqing questions himself and turns around, not wanting to look at Zhou Ziheng's face.

Zhou Ziheng still holds him tightly, like they're two stacked spoons, completely ignorant of what's going on inside Xia Xiqing's head. "If they give me this role, I'll probably have to fly to another city to shoot."

The half-asleep Xia Xiqing opens his eyes. "Where?" He coughs, trying to not sound needy. "How long?"

"I've scheduled four months for this one. I'm not sure yet."

Four months? Almost half a year.

Zhou Ziheng continues, "My role is a guy with AIDS. So

starting this month, I'll need to lose weight, and there are training sessions too. I probably won't come back..."

Xia Xiqing cuts in. "Okay," he says stiffly.

Zhou Ziheng was going to say more, but seeing Xia Xiqing uninterested, he closes his eyes, regretting that he even mentioned it in the first place. They don't have to talk about stuff like this.

His heart drops to his stomach as the seconds go by.

"Do you still hire art designers? I mean, any designer..." Xia Xiqing struggles to find the correct word for what he wants to say. He turns around, looking serious. "I should just invest. Can I do that? Become a sponsor?"

Zhou Ziheng is taken aback. What is he trying to say?

"Hmm, with your background, you don't need a sugar daddy. But I bet there's at least one actor in the film who needs one—" Xia Xiqing rolls his eyes as a finger presses against his lips.

"You want to say that again? Who are you going to sugar daddy for?"

"Fine, only you. Alright?" Xia Xiqing says. Does this guy *want* a sugar daddy or something? "But I don't think they'll allow me to be on set all the time..."

"Why do you want to be on set?" Zhou Ziheng says, unable to hide the joy in his voice.

"You tell me. Can't you recognize all the time and effort I've put into making you want to sleep with me? And now you're telling me that you have to go away for half a year?"

Zhou Ziheng bites back on a grin. "So?"

"Hey! We should just do it tonight." Xia Xiqing rubs Zhou Ziheng's face gently until he frowns again. "Nah; it'll be hard for me if I can't see you for a long time after I get a taste of you..."

Zhou Ziheng finally laughs. "Is this what you think about all the time?"

"Yeah. Want to fuck you. Want to eat you."

"Fine. I'll make a note of that."

That's what they will do.

"It just annoys me. Can I come see you every day? Maybe I can be a producer? Can I?"

"You can, but it's unnecessary." Zhou Ziheng pinches his ear. "I have a way..."

"What?" Xia Xiqing raises his eyebrow, eyes wide.

"Umm. This movie is supposed to have already started filming, but they couldn't find the right female lead. The other day when Director Kun had dinner with us, he told me he watched *Survive and Escape*. I thought he was just being polite, but then he showed me a fanvid..."

"And?"

"Let me tell you the plot first. My role is a thug who contracts AIDS and wants revenge on society for that. He stalks a girl into a dark alley and pins her against the wall—that's an important scene for both characters, but the girls they interviewed couldn't get the moment right. You know?"

Xia Xiqing knows all too well. He recalls when he was pinned against the wall in the study in that first episode of *Survive and Escape*.

"Wait. Don't tell me you guys want me to play the girl."

"No, he didn't suggest cross-dressing." He mutters in a small voice, seemingly to himself, "But you could pull it off." He clears his throat and says, more loudly. "Director Kun asked if you could come to the audition. It depends on you; Writer Xu said he could change up the script a bit."

"Seriously? Xu Qichen said that?" Xia Xiqing rolls his eyes. "What can he do?"

"He said he could drop the love interest angle, and turn it into two male leads. Of course, the girl's background story won't be changed—there's going to be a boy who's autistic and hard of hearing instead of a girl. The theme is two people saving each other, and that doesn't need the deuteragonist to be female."

"Hard of hearing? And autistic?" Xia Xiqing chuckles. "This is hard, man. How come Xu Qichen thinks I can handle the role?"

Zhou Ziheng looks at his face, hesitating on whether to tell him the truth about what Xu Qichen said.

The girl is a victim of domestic violence. She was born into a lower-class family, and her father gambled and always fought with her mother. His beatings were the reason one of her ears became permanently damaged.

When Xu Qichen told him the outline of the script, Zhou Ziheng thought he was being too cruel to his friend.

Yes, it's cruel, but he can't hide from the truth forever.

Zhou Ziheng recalls Xu Qichen's voice, both cold and calm.

Xia Xiqing has been lying to himself his whole life. The only way for him to start loving himself is to accept who he is.

Zhou Ziheng takes a deep breath, thinking it's better not to mention any of that if he wants Xia Xiqing to go to the audition. "He thinks you can, and I bet he has his reasons. Also, he said he can discuss more details with you if you want."

"I've never acted before." Xia Xiqing chuckles without amusement—the truth is, he's been acting for as long as he's lived.

"Well, I think you have talent in acting."

"Are you saying that I'm good at being fake?" Xia Xiqing

sits up, sleepy. "We can talk about it later. Xu Qichen will discuss it with me, I think. I'm going home to sleep."

Zhou Ziheng tugs on his shirt. "Your place is only across the hall. You can stay if you want to."

Xia Xiqing laughs. "Yeah, exactly. It's just two steps away."

"That's not right. It's about fifty feet from this sofa to the front door, then another ten feet to your front door. Even assuming that you'll sleep on your sofa, and also assuming that your stride is a foot and a half, you'd still need to walk at least—"

Scary STEM major. Xia Xiqing interrupts him with a kiss, then lets him go.

"Did you figure it out?"

"I forgot." Zhou Ziheng beams at him.

"But I've got to take a shower."

"You can do it here."

"No pajamas."

"You can wear mine."

"Yours are huge."

"Bigger is better." Zhou Ziheng smirks.

Xia Xiqing slaps him on the head. "What do you know, kid? Size is nothing if you don't know how to use it."

"How can you be so sure that I don't know how to use it?"

"Little virgins don't get to talk about technique."

Zhou Ziheng gives him a hug, his head resting on Xia Xiqing's shoulder. He told himself that he shouldn't let himself sink too deep into this, but it's like he's driving a car with no brake pedal and the edge of a cliff is fast approaching.

No one can save him now.

"Alright, where do I sleep?"

"In my arms."

"Get lost."

The next morning, Zhou Ziheng is gone, leaving Xia Xiqing laying there alone in a set of oversized pajamas. The bed smells like Zhou Ziheng. It's nice.

Xia Xiqing glances at his phone. There are two unread messages.

Moral Role Model: I have a red-carpet event tonight, so I'll be home late. There's a sandwich in the fridge for you.

Xia Xiqing stretches out. The sunlight of early May leaves him feeling quite pleasant. He jumps off the bed and walks to the ledge of the bay window. There, he sees some research papers and personal notes. They're Zhou Ziheng's, and after a brief scan, he realizes that they're all about AIDS, including things like symptoms of its early stages and psychiatric evaluations of victims. It's all very detailed.

Xia Xiqing has to admire Zhou Ziheng's dedication to acting, which is so much greater than most of his peers. He can see that Zhou Ziheng wants to understand his roles as well as he can.

He changes, ready to go home. Before he walks out the door, he suddenly remembers the sandwich and walks to the fridge to get it. Upon closing the fridge door, he sees a bunch of incomprehensible physics equations stuck on with magnets...

Scary STEM major.

When he gets home, he gets a call from his former professor; the one who'd asked him for help with that statue. He's offered a teaching job.

"I think this place is right for you. It's a relaxing environment where you can bring your creations to life."

"Really?" Xia Xiqing laughs politely. "I'm still thinking about my future plans, Professor, but I will definitely take your offer into consideration."

"No matter what you choose to do with your life, don't ever waste your talent."

Talent.

The word carries weight. He's been described as talented for so long. Some say his style is too dark, but controversy isn't necessarily a bad thing in his field. However, he's acutely aware of the dilemma he's facing. When he draws, he doesn't feel like he has a leg to stand on anymore. Darkness has been the only thing he's certain of, but not anymore, and he feels like he's losing the talent that he used to have.

He used to channel his pain into his work, onto a blank piece of paper, which he called art.

How pathetic is that?

Xia Xiqing tilts his head back, trying to pull his thoughts together, when he hears a ring tone.

"Professor..."

"Am I your professor now?" A voice, soft and bright, comes out of the phone.

It's Xu Qichen. Xia Xiqing opens his eyes and chuckles. "Aren't you, though? Professor Xu, Writer Xu."

"Stop that. I was up all night last night, I'm currently running only on caffeine."

Xia Xiqing walks to his balcony and lights a cigarette. "Doing what? Did Xia Zhixu manage to not freak out about you overtaxing yourself?"

"He did nag me a lot last night. So annoying."

The sappiness in his voice is absolutely disgusting, and Xia Xiqing is about to protest when Xu Qichen changes the topic.

"You know I'm the writer for Zhou Ziheng's new film, right?"

As expected, he's calling about the film. "Yeah, I know. So right now you're Writer Xu, no?"

"Ugh. This script has become a pain in the ass. They can't find a female lead."

Xia Xiqing cuts in, "Didn't you have anyone in mind when you wrote that character?"

Xu Qichen blinks. That's how smart Xia Xiqing is—that character had in fact been inspired by Xia Xiqing's awful childhood. But it's not like he can admit that right now.

"Nah. Do I always have to base my characters on real people?"

Xia Xiqing thinks back on his conversation with Zhou Ziheng yesterday. "Hey, Zhou Ziheng told me that you and the director both want me to audition for this role?"

"Yeah, you want to meet up? I have more information to give you."

"Sure. Let's meet at my place."

After dealing with the work he's got on hand, Xu Qichen heads out, arriving at Xia Xiqing's place just after five in the evening.

"The security in your building is incredibly strict..." Xu Qichen hands his backpack over to Xia Xiqing.

"Yeah, because of some people who live here." He slings an arm around Xu Qichen's shoulders. "Hey, how come you always look like a college kid?"

Xu Qichen scratches his head, embarrassed. He looks down at his yellow hoodie. "I didn't have time to change." He glances at the ceiling and living room and exclaims, "This place is huge."

"You like it? You should get Xia Zhixu to buy a unit downstairs so we can see each other every day." Xia Xiqing puts Xu Qichen's backpack on the sofa and walks to the kitchen to get him a glass of juice.

Xu Qichen seems to take his suggestion seriously. "Why downstairs? Wouldn't it be more convenient to be on the same floor? How many are there on this floor?"

Xia Xiqing coughs. "Uh, two."

"And the other one is sold already?"

"Yeah."

"Celebrity?" Xu Qichen looks like he's fishing for gossip.

That intuition... Xia Xiqing nods, groaning inside. "That's right."

"Who is it? Do I know them?"

"Oh, you wouldn't know them." Xia Xiqing presses him bodily down into sitting on the sofa. "You wanna talk about the script?"

Xu Qichen pulls his laptop from his backpack, holding the latest version of his script in his hand. "I don't know how much Zhou Ziheng told you, so I'll just start from the beginning. I'm getting rid of the romance plot completely."

"All of it?"

"Yes. If we're going to have two male leads, making their relationship romantic will only complicate the plot and drive the audience away from the main theme." After pushing his laptop closer to Xia Xiqing, Xu Qichen continues, "So there won't be a girl anymore. Instead, a boy named Jiang Tong."

Xia Xiqing listens carefully.

"Jiang Tong is a high school dropout from a lower-class family. We wanted to make him autistic, but for the sake of the plot, we decided depression would probably work better."

"Depression..." Xia Xiqing scrolls and stops when he sees the plot on the second page.

Xu Qichen pauses for a few seconds and says, "Jiang Tong

is a victim of domestic violence. The relationship between his parents is complicated. One of his ears is deaf from an injury his father gave him."

He watches one side of Xia Xiqing's face and his rising chest, like he's suppressing something inside.

"You must think that I'm being cruel." Xu Qichen lays his hand on Xia Xiqing's knee. "But Xiqing, you can't keep hiding from it."

Xia Xiqing takes a deep breath. If it was anyone else other than Xu Qichen sitting next to him, he'd flip this laptop right this second. But it is him, and Xia Xiqing knows he isn't the type to prod at sore topics for the sake of laughs. He just can't lash out at his best friend.

"Look, if it makes you feel better, you can punch me or yell at me. I don't care." Xu Qichen shifts a bit closer to him. "But the truth is, denying your past won't solve anything. I've been there."

Xia Xiqing grits his teeth, not saying a word.

"I spent a long time on this script, and yes, I was thinking of your past when I wrote that character. I want you to come out of that shadow that's been holding you back for years. I want you to let the pain go. You just have to trust me this once. I think playing this character should be able to help."

"'Should' is the key word there," Xia Xiqing says, unimpressed.

Xu Qichen tries to reassure him, "Even if I know you don't need my help, I still want to help you. It sounds silly, but of all the people in the world, the one person I want to have a chance at happiness is you."

Xia Xiqing feels his heart soften at Xu Qichen's confession. They've been friends for ten years, but this is the first time he's opened up to him like this. He's always been his weakness, and he's trying his best to help Xia Xiqing.

But nevertheless, he doesn't feel comfortable with this film, especially when some of the plot points are based off his actual past experiences. He can't imagine how he would feel playing himself.

Xu Qichen takes Xia Xiqing's silence as rejection. He huffs a sigh. "If you really can't do it, I'll talk to the director. We'll interview some more actors; maybe we can find someone." He closes his laptop. "Zhou Ziheng really likes the plot, and I've heard that his team has rejected an award-winning director to spare our script the filming time. No matter whether you play the role or not, he's going to spend about half a year on this one."

Xia Xiqing feels annoyed at the thought that he won't be able to see Zhou Ziheng for months. "Where are you going to find an actor?"

"Well, there aren't many who qualify. He needs to evoke empathy in the audience and make others feel protective of him. Certainly not a mainstream type of actor... I guess we'll try to find some fresh faces in recent graduates from film schools, or even current students."

Fresh faces? Huh. Young, innocent, pretty...just what Zhou Ziheng needs. All the time and effort that Xia Xiqing has spent working on that man will be for nothing.

Great. Now he's getting pissed. He needs to let go of this topic. "Chen-Chen, you want pizza?"

"Huh?" It takes Xu Qichen a few seconds to register his words. "Okay?"

"Okay. I'll order." Xia Xiqing pulls out his phone. After he orders, he browses the moments section in his WeChat.

Xiao Luo: Sneak peek of Zhou Ziheng at tonight's charity event.

It's Zhou Ziheng's side portrait. His hair has been combed back, leaving all his features exposed under the spotlight. He wears a white suit with a blue tie—it lacks some of the aggressiveness from his previous styling, but it has the added benefit of elegance.

He leaves a comment under the update in Xiao-Luo's WeChat moments.

Great look today, very princely.

Not long after his comment, a message pops out.

Moral Role Model: Thanks.

Xia Xiqing chuckles. That wasn't even a comment for his post.

Terrorist: Go walk your red carpet.

Instantly, a reply.

Moral Role Model: It's done. I'm just sitting here watching the show. Can't stay for dinner anyway.

Xia Xiqing recalls what Zhou Ziheng said yesterday about losing weight, so he teases him.

Terrorist: Good timing. I just ordered a pizza. Let me take a picture for you later.

The delivery guy arrives. Xia Xiqing quickly runs downstairs to get the pizza, then he and Xu Qichen just sprawl on the floor eating pizza and drinking Coke.

"Hey, should we maybe invite Chen Fang and Xia Zhixu over too?"

Xu Qichen shakes his head, voice muffled. "Zhixu has been busy lately, and Chen Fang has a girlfriend. He might even be with her right now."

"A girl? Him?" Xia Xiqing says, eyebrows raised. "Who? Is she blind or something?"

Xu Qichen laughs and his body falls to the side. "He said she's an intern at his company. I saw her the other day. She's pretty cute. I think she's called Xiao-Liang?"

Xia Xiqing huffs a long-suffering sigh.

Xu Qichen gives him a light kick on the leg. "It's just you left, buddy."

"Me?" Xia Xiqing flutters his eyelids. "It takes no more than a text or two for me to grab some...company."

"Not that kind. I'm saying a real relationship." Xu Qichen moves closer. "Zhou Ziheng is a good guy. I mean, he's tall, handsome—morally upstanding, too, and aren't you his fan?"

Xia Xiqing squeezes his cheeks affectionately. "Are you my mom?"

"Of course I am." Xu Qichen gives him a smug look, forking a piece of matcha cake into his mouth.

Their meal stretches out for well over an hour, during which Xia Xiqing carefully evades Xu Qichen's questions about him and Zhou Ziheng. He then sends two pictures to Zhou Ziheng, one of the pizza before they ate it, and one of the mess after they finished.

Moral Role Model: Are you a monster?

Xia Xiqing's lips curl into a big grin. He types with one hand, the other one hanging on to his half-finished bowl of borscht.

"Ahh, I'm so full..." Xu Qichen unexpectedly lays his head on Xia Xiqing's shoulder, causing him to spill most of his soup on Xu Qichen's shirt.

"Ah, fuck." Xia Xiqing puts the bowl aside. "How are you going to go home like this?"

Xu Qichen shrugs. "I feel like I'm a bowl of soup."

"Go shower. You can change into my clothes." Xia Xiqing laughs.

Xu Qichen walks to the guest room to take a shower while Xia Xiqing cleans up the mess they made on the floor.

Soon, he's done, but he's completely forgotten about finding suitable clothes for Xu Qichen. Instead, he sits on the sofa, legs crossed with a bottle of Coke in his hand.

His doorbell suddenly rings. Xia Xiqing slurps the last bit of his Coke and walks to the door to look at the security screen.

Zhou Ziheng?

Xia Xiqing presses the speaker. "What are you doing here?"

"I forgot my card key."

"Then call the building manager."

"I'm tired. I just want sit down. Just let me come in for a bit."

"How long?"

"What?"

Xia Xiqing makes his tone purposefully cold as he asks, "How long?"

Zhou Ziheng manages a sad face. "Five minutes?"

"Fine. You can come for five minutes." Xia Xiqing opens the door, holding back a smile.

Only, there's no one outside. He leans out to look, and that's when Zhou Ziheng pulls him out and pins him against the wall, kissing him without another word.

"Mmm... Hey, Zhou Ziheng..." The sudden kiss renders him like an electrical current. "Fuck... What are you—wait, get off..."

Zhou Ziheng cups the back of Xia Xiqing's neck with his hand. Voice deep, he murmurs, "I'm hungry."

"So what? How's that my prob—mmm..."

Zhou Ziheng has really improved his kissing technique over these past couple months. His tongue reaches deftly past Xia Xiqing's teeth, utterly dominating in its force.

"Mmm, sweet."

Xia Xiqing's heart rate starts to pick up. He lays a hand on Zhou Ziheng's tie, breaths shallow. "I just...had Coke..."

Zhou Ziheng presses more kisses onto his face, from the corner of his mouth all the way to his ear. "No," he says with a smile in his voice. "It's all you."

Xia Xiqing feels Zhou Ziheng's words light up something inside him. He wants more, so he leans in and resumes their kiss.

"Xiqing? Can you grab me some clothing?" A voice comes from far away...

"Hello? Xiqing?"

Wait, clothing?

Fuck.

Xia Xiqing pushes Zhou Ziheng away, eyes flashing open. "Wait, wait, wait... I can explain. That's..."

"Xiiiqiiing?"

*Bro, please can you not—*Xia Xiqing covers his face with his hands, avoiding Zhou Ziheng's eyes. Why is it that even though he hasn't done anything wrong, he's still so nervous? "That's Xu Qichen. You know him. Writer Xu. The skinny one. You remember him, right?"

Zhou Ziheng's face remains unimpressed, his arms folded in front of his chest and his stare heavy with accusation. "And?"

"And we were eating, and I spilled food on his shirt, so he went to shower, and then—"

Before he finishes explaining himself, Zhou Ziheng pulls him in for another passionate kiss. His arms squeeze tightly around him.

"I can't... breathe... Ziheng..." He keeps his voice down.

Zhou Ziheng only deepens the kiss, becoming even more

aggressive. When he's gasping for air, Xu Qichen walks out of the bathroom, dripping wet and clad only in a towel. Having heard the noise, he investigates its source.

Thirty seconds later, the breathless Xia Xiqing finally hears Xu Qichen swear for the first time in his life.

"What the fuck..."

When has karma ever spared anyone?

For the first time in twenty-five years of smooth sailing, Xia Xiqing finds his ship capsizing. Moreover, it capsizes right in front of Xu Qichen. Escaping Zhou Ziheng's embrace, he frantically wipes at his mouth.

"This... look, Chen-Chen... I can explain..."

"You're explaining to him?" Zhou Ziheng turns Xia Xiqing around to face him, then points at the bare-chested Xu Qichen. "What about me? Don't you owe me an explanation too?"

Xia Xiqing clears his throat. "You... You can wait..."

"Why do I have to wait?"

Face stamped with distinct displeasure, Zhou Ziheng takes off the tie that Xia Xiqing loosened for him just earlier and puts it on the counter. Like petting a puppy, Xia Xiqing runs a hand from his back down to his waist, trying to calm him down.

Xu Qichen takes an awkward step back, grabbing a blanket on the sofa to cover himself up. "Uh... So, you two are..."

"We're not together!" Xia Xiqing cuts in so fast it's like he's in a reaction contest.

Zhou Ziheng grabs his wrist. "We're not together?!"

"You're really not together?" Xu Qichen looks confused. "Was I in the shower too long? Did I hallucinate you two kissing?"

And that wasn't a normal kiss, either. It was full-on

making out.

This must be his lucky day. Xia Xiqing grits his teeth and forces a smile out. "Hey, didn't you want to come and sit down for a bit?" he asks Zhou Ziheng, then turns to Xu Qichen. "We can talk too. Let's just all sit down."

The three of them sit on the carpet, turning an awkward encounter into an even more awkward meeting.

"So, between you two, what relation—I mean, what exactly is going on?" Xu Qichen asks.

"About that..." Xia Xiqing can't find an answer. "Well, either way, it's not what you think."

Xu Qichen's eyes widen. "What am I thinking?"

Zhou Ziheng cuts in, "It's *exactly* the kind of relationship you're thinking."

"Really? Heavens..."

"It's really not..." Xia Xiqing wants to die on the spot. For all that Xu Qichen is well aware of the types of "relationships" he's had in the past, it's still very difficult to admit to his best friend that he and Zhou Ziheng have a friends with benefits arrangement.

"But just now you were...kissing." The last word trickles out of Xu Qichen's mouth very quietly.

"You know that I've kissed plenty of people before," Xia Xiqing mumbles, eyes darting away. "You can't say everyone I've ever kissed was..."

Zhou Ziheng grasps Xia Xiqing's wrist, once again displeased. "So you mean you still make a habit of kissing other people?"

"No! I haven't been..." Xia Xiqing feels very attacked right now. "How did you derive that conclusion? I don't even have time to go out anymore."

Xu Qichen analyzes the facts: "What you mean is, you

haven't kissed anyone else since you met him? And you're also saying that you two aren't actually 'together'?"

Fuck. Why are these two so concerned with logic?

"Exactly, so that's why I said we're together." Zhou Ziheng looks at Xu Qichen, who nods solemnly in agreement.

"It certainly seems that way."

"Fine. Whatever you two decide." Xia Xiqing puts his hands up in surrender.

"So why are you here?" Xu Qichen asks Zhou Ziheng.

"I..." Zhou Ziheng answers honestly, "He said I could come for five minutes."

Only, the way this kid has phrased it...

"Come—*come* for five minutes?" Xu Qichen stares at him. "How do you even..."

Xia Xiqing is going insane. "Come *sit down* for five minutes! Come. *Sit.*"

Xu Qichen looks suspicious still, but he stays silent. Even though he's waved goodbye to even the scant vestiges of his dignity, Xia Xiqing is still determined to win some of it back. At least it's Xu Qichen, or his reputation would really truly be ruined.

"It's really not what you think, and it's a bit of a long story...so you can pretend you didn't see anything just now."

Xu Qichen gives him an honest look in return. "But I did see it."

"You..."

"Not only did I see it, I'm also going to talk about it."

Xia Xiqing inhales deeply, keenly aware that he might just implode. He holds Xu Qichen's hand in both of his, and wrestles his face into a puppy-dog expression.

"My most precious Chen-Chen, I'm begging you, please don't let other people know about it, especially that one you've got at home. I'd never hear the end of it."

Xia Xiqing calling Xu Qichen "my most precious Chen-Chen" evidently sets Zhou Ziheng off. "Are you really so afraid of people knowing about us?" he asks, his face falling very rapidly, looking quite like an abandoned puppy. "I don't even mind letting people know. Why would you want to keep it from Writer Xu? Am I that much of an embarrassment?"

Xia Xiqing surrenders. He shakes himself out of Zhou Ziheng's hold. "You really do need to start filming again. This drama queen act of yours is getting out of hand."

"Uh. Okay, Ziheng, hear me out," Xu Qichen turns to Zhou Ziheng, eyes genuinely sympathetic. "I know that sometimes Xia Xiqing can come off as a bit of a playboy, but he's not that bad. Okay, maybe he is that bad, but—"

Xia Xiqing covers Xu Qichen's mouth with his palm. "No buts, thank you very much. This conversation is over. It's time to go home. I don't want that rat bastard Xia Zhixu bothering me about keeping you out so long."

Xu Qichen is pulled up into a standing position. "But what would I wear?"

"Up-up-up, let's go to my dressing room, shall we? Everything in there is yours to pick. If you like, you can even take two outfits." Xia Xiqing grabs Xu Qichen's shoulder and leads him upstairs, sending Zhou Ziheng a brief glare.

What a day...

Xia Xiqing's changing room is big. The shirts alone take up two rows, all arranged by color to form a visually arresting gradient. It goes to show how much of an artist Xia Xiqing is—even his strange organizational compulsions are so aesthetic.

But none of the clothing here is really Xu Qichen's style,

so he delves deeper into the racks of clothing and finds a more casual set of clothes: a dark red hoodie and a matching pair of sweatpants. They don't seem to be Xia Xiqing's usual style, but they look comfy.

"Got unopened packs of underwear in the drawers, too." Xia Xiqing's voice comes from outside.

"Okay." Xu Qichen takes the hoodie and sweatpants, and after he's done changing, he walks out. "These are pretty big..."

Xia Xiqing got out a cigarette as he waited, and now, seeing the dark red hoodie that Zhou Ziheng gave him, his hand gives an involuntary jitter. The ash from the cigarette falls onto the sensitive webbing between his thumb and forefinger.

"Wait, no, Chen-Chen, like you said, those are too big. I've got a great collection. You wanna go pick something else?" Xia Xiqing clears his throat and pushes Xu Qichen back into the dressing room. He picks up a white shirt and says, "This would definitely look good on you. I remember Xia Zhixu has the same one, so you two can match."

"Sure, let me try it on," Xu Qichen replies, giving Xia Xiqing a suspicious stare.

Xia Xiqing lets out a small sigh of relief. If Zhou Ziheng saw Xu Qichen walk downstairs in this set of clothes, he'd probably freak out again.

Wait, why does he care what Zhou Ziheng would do?

His thoughts are all muddled, various instincts fighting against each other and leaving him somewhat of a nervous wreck.

"What's taking you two so long?"

Hearing Zhou Ziheng's voice, Xia Xiqing snaps back to reality. "We're just trying a second outfit. The first set didn't work."

Zhou Ziheng smiles, arms wrapping around Xia Xiqing's waist and pulling him in. "Can I get a kiss now?"

Xia Xiqing shivers every time Zhou Ziheng speaks to him this way, with a smile against his ear.

"It's like you got addicted to this." He laughs halfheartedly, then blows a cloud of cigarette smoke into Zhou Ziheng's face. "Of all the times you could act up, why are you choosing to do so now? Once we're alone, I'll show you who's boss..."

"You used to also seduce me in public." Zhou Ziheng lands a finger on Xia Xiqing's collarbone. "You really mind me doing it?"

He then caresses Xia Xiqing's neck for a second before pulling his fingers away. This move of his works on Xia Xiqing even better than full-on kissing.

He can't help but be impressed. How is Zhou Ziheng such a natural at this? He was a shy little boy just a couple months ago, and now he's almost catching up to Xia Xiqing in how well he flirts.

"Behave," he tells Zhou Ziheng.

As he says that, Xu Qichen comes out of the room holding a jacket in hand. "I feel like I might get cold if I only wear a shirt, can I take this jacket, too?"

That's when Xia Xiqing realizes that the jacket is the one he stole from Zhou Ziheng that one time. Fuck. How is Xu Qichen's instinct for trouble so good?

"Ah, maybe not that one." Xia Xiqing lets go of Zhou Ziheng's hand and slings his arm around Xu Qichen's shoulder, leading him back into the dressing room. "It's not that cold out, and I've got a lighter jacket somewhere in here."

"Why bother? That one seems good enough," Zhou Ziheng

suddenly says.

"Oh?" Xu Qichen turns to look at him. "Why's that?"

Xia Xiqing grabs Xu Qichen's wrist. "Ignore—"

"Because it's mine," Zhou Ziheng says, smiling crookedly.

Xu Qichen blinks, letting go of the jacket. Xia Xiqing catches it before it hits the floor.

"And you said you're not together? You liar," Xu Qichen accuses, eyes wide. "He even has clothes at your place!"

Practically written across his face are the words *"you've definitely slept together."*

"As I said, we're in a relationship." Zhou Ziheng smiles.

Xia Xiqing sighs. He literally brought this upon himself. If only he'd thought further ahead when he took Zhou Ziheng's jacket home.

Xu Qichen is smart enough to put two and two together. "Wait, that athleisure outfit I picked out first. That's his too, right?" He takes Xia Xiqing's silence as a "yes" and pushes further, turning to Zhou Ziheng to ask, "Wait, you live across the hall, right?"

Zhou Ziheng tilts his head. "Yup."

"Fuck..." This has truly backfired directly into Xia Xiqing's face.

Xu Qichen gives Xia Xiqing a wounded look. "Xiqing, how long have we known each other? I can't believe you'd lie to me like this..." His bottom lip quivers.

Xia Xiqing feels a headache coming on. "No, but I didn't mean to! It's just such a long story and it's very complicated, so let me explain—"

"No, I don't want to hear it." Xu Qichen pretends to walk away. "I'm going home."

"Come on, I didn't mean to lie like this. Please don't be mad at me."

Xu Qichen stops and turns around. "I'll stop being mad at you if you agree to go to the audition."

Fuck. So that's what it's about. Xia Xiqing feels like he's fallen into a very terrible trap.

"Will you go or not? If you won't, then I'm leaving."

"Wait, wait, wait," Xia Xiqing says, running a hand through his hair. "Let me think about it..."

"Fine. Take your time. If you go, I'm sure I'll figure out a way to forgive you, and I'll even refrain from telling Xia Zhixu, so don't you worry."

Xu Qichen continues down the stairs. At the bottom, he looks back up at Xia Xiqing, standing halfway up the flight, and waves. Then he does the same to Zhou Ziheng, standing on the second floor of the loft. He smiles.

"Bye! I'll leave you two to yourselves."

Zhou Ziheng returns his smile with a wider one.

Xia Xiqing is the only one who doesn't feel like smiling. The moment his front door closes behind Xu Qichen, he flips Zhou Ziheng the bird. Zhou Ziheng starts walking down the steps toward him, reaching up to undo two of his shirt buttons. In this moment, he looks like quite the scoundrel.

As Zhou Ziheng reaches the same step as him, Xia Xiqing turns to glare at him. He doesn't want to let him off the hook so easily after all that mess, and thrusts that troublesome green jacket into Zhou Ziheng's face.

"Take it and get lost."

"Oh, okay..." Zhou Ziheng obeys, seemingly crestfallen.

Ah? But that's not how he's supposed to respond.

"Wait."

At the bottom of the steps, Zhou Ziheng looks back up at Xia Xiqing.

"That jacket is mine." Xia Xiqing doesn't look at him. He

left his cigarette in his hands throughout the earlier conversation, but now he returns it to his mouth and mumbles around it, "It's in my house, so it's mine now." More firmly, he says, "Give it back."

Zhou Ziheng grins and starts climbing the stairs, slowly and steadily. He stops when he stands one step beneath Xia Xiqing. He drapes the jacket over one of Xia Xiqing's shoulders, then plucks the cigarette out of Xia Xiqing's mouth.

Xia Xiqing pulls him into a kiss, and they lose themselves in a cloud of smoke.

"'Come for five minutes'?" Xia Xiqing teases.

"You said it first!" Zhou Ziheng leans back in and gently nips at Xia Xiqing's glistening lips.

Having just been at an event, Zhou Ziheng is wearing more scent than he normally does. Gone is the youthful freshness that Xia Xiqing has come to associate with him, and in its place is the scent of leather and musk.

Xia Xiqing's hands sneak into Zhou Ziheng's black shirt, pressing tightly on his chest. He breathes into Zhou Ziheng's ear. "You changed cologne?"

"Just for today." Zhou Ziheng leans in to resume the kiss, but Xia Xiqing takes a step back.

Xia Xiqing runs a hand on his neck, the corners of his eyes lifted. "What is it called?"

Zhou Ziheng tilts his head, pressing a kiss to Xia Xiqing's wrist. The moment he looks up at him, he reminds Xia Xiqing of a lion hunting for prey.

The name is in English: *Fucking fabulous.*

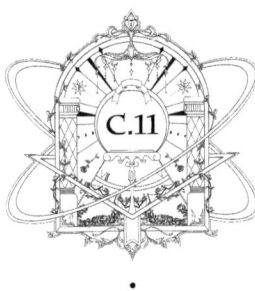

C.11

There Is Exactly One

Xia Xiqing has been plagued with nightmares ever since he promised Xu Qichen he'd think about auditioning. Every time, it's been a dream of his childhood—a childhood that, after all these years, he thought he'd already completely forgotten.

It was only after the first nightmare, when he opened his eyes to find himself covered in sweat, that he realized— he never actually forgot those days. These dark memories have simply been hiding in a corner of his mind, waiting to reemerge and take its chance to strike.

He loathes indignity. He loathes even more that, even as he suffers such indignity, he still cannot bear to face himself.

Unable to fall back asleep, Xia Xiqing grabs his phone to check his social media. And a lucky coincidence is that the first thing he sees is Zhou Ziheng's 2:45 AM update in his WeChat moments.

It's just a picture: a script and some notes—both with

contents blurred out—and a cup of coffee.

Talk about dedication.

Xia Xiqing gives the post a like, then immediately receives a message.

Moral Role Model: Why aren't you asleep yet?

Terrorist: I'm following after my role model.

Phone in hand, he stares at the ceiling, remembering when he was last at Zhou Ziheng's place and those notes he saw in his bedroom. To put so much effort into this, he must really want to do well by his role.

Strangely enough, an image appears in his mind—Zhou Ziheng, dressed in a tuxedo, is standing on a stage and being handed a trophy; meanwhile, he himself is offstage in the audience, similarly dressed up and clapping for him.

He must be sick or something.

But what if the fellow creator clapping offstage were someone else?

Terrorist: Any candidates for the co-lead yet? How about you send me some photos?

He means it as a joke, but, surprisingly, Zhou Ziheng complies.

Moral Role Model: We went scouting in film schools, and these three seem up to snuff. All students of the trade, attractive and skilled enough.

The language Zhou Ziheng uses is already pretty neutral—none of it is particularly complimentary. But still, Xia Xiqing feels a strange sort of pique in response. As always, he finds an excuse for himself: it must be that he's too prideful. But even then, he's still got no clue why he'd compare himself to these three guys Zhou Ziheng has sent him.

Perhaps because Xia Xiqing is taking too long to respond, Zhou Ziheng sends another message.

Moral Role Model: Why do you ask?

Terrorist: Just wondering, curious to see what lucky guy might get the chance to debut with the great Zhou Ziheng.

Xia Xiqing taps on the first photo, and the kid in it looks like he's in his late teens. His features are delicate, his complexion pale, and he's pretty innocent-looking. The subject of the second photo has more or less the same style, just with longer hair.

The boy in the last photo is a bit more eye-catching. His eyes are big and round, and his irises are a lighter brown than most people's; his hair matches the color. He's the type that many girls seem to like nowadays—cute and pure.

Terrorist: Hey, the last kid is pretty cute, he'll probably pair well with you.

But before he hits send, he deletes the last half of the message, sending out only the compliment.

Zhou Ziheng is editing his response to Xia Xiqing's earlier message when he gets this one. He's hesitant to tell Xia Xiqing that he doesn't want to work with anyone else for this project, and before he saw the new message, he'd been repeatedly typing and deleting the few characters necessary to confess this desire.

But then he sees the word *kid*, which is a bit of a trigger for him, not to mention the *cute* that follows it. He deletes the unfinished message he already typed and sends a very different response.

Moral Role Model: What, is he your type?

At this, Xia Xiqing laughs out loud. How has this man still not figured out his type? If he's uncertain, he can always just go take a look in the mirror.

Xia Xiqing looks at the photo again. The boy is smiling very brightly in the photo, and the shape of his eyes is very pleasing. Like a little angel.

Terrorist: I thought that the innocent boy-next-door kind was more your type, no? Wonder if his personality matches his appearance.

Because you wouldn't want another one like me.

This only makes Zhou Ziheng angrier; apparently, Xia Xiqing thinks that the reason he's stuck around is because of that pretty face of his? But Zhou Ziheng has always known what sort of person he is—he was never fooled by his angelic appearance. Frustrated, he sends out one last message before turning off his phone.

Moral Role Model: Yeah, that sure is my type.

Meanwhile, the recipient of the message sits up in bed.

The great Xia Xiqing has always had his choice of bed partners. The names of people waiting around for him to condescend to fuck them could fill lists. And yet here was Zhou Ziheng, telling him to his face that someone else was his type. Xia Xiqing has really been too nice to him of late.

The more he thinks about it, the more vexed he feels, and the more he feels like some sort of sycophant. He lights a cigarette. Not only is he too much of a coward to take on the role Xu Qichen wrote for him in the script, but now he's about to lose to some twenty-year-old kid.

Your type, huh? Too fucking bad. Now I'm gonna make sure you can't work with your type.

It is with this sort of spiteful attitude that, two days later, Xia Xiqing finally agrees to attend the audition. In response, Xu Qichen is astonished.

"Really? You're actually coming? When you first said that you'd consider it, I thought you were just trying to appease me."

Xu Qichen wasn't wrong—Xia Xiqing would never have

considered it if he hadn't wanted to spite Zhou Ziheng.

"Yeah, I'll come. Could you send me the details?"

"Huh? Didn't Ziheng tell you? It's tonight."

"Tonight?" Xia Xiqing blurts, then somewhat regrets the exclamation. Despite living right next door to each other, the two of them haven't talked since that night Zhou Ziheng sent him the pictures, so he didn't know that the auditions are tonight.

"Tonight at seven-thirty. I'll text you the address. Don't drive—take a cab when you come. There're too many reporters around here."

Xia Xiqing makes an agreeable hum and hangs up, only to find that it's already seven o'clock—he's got half an hour. He can't be bothered to clean himself up, so he leaves home in the black coveralls he'd put on for painting at home. Once he gets into a cab, he catches sight of himself in the rear-view mirror and notices that his hair is a bit messy, so he puts it up with a hair tie.

Then he pauses. Why is he in such a rush? He's acting as if he's super eager to work on this film. No, it's just that he wants to thwart Zhou Ziheng. Just thinking about what happened that night makes Xia Xiqing angry all over again.

The cab driver glances over a few times, hesitating before he finally asks, "Are—aren't you that celebrity?"

As always with strangers, Xia Xiqing dons his signature fake smile. "You must be thinking of someone else."

"Uh, I don't think so. I'm pretty sure my little sister has you as her phone background." The driver seems to be about twenty or thirty. "It's you and that actor, that, uh, Zhou Ziheng. Yeah, it's a picture of you two." He casts another quick glance back. "I definitely wouldn't mistake you. You've got long hair, and there's a beauty spot on your nose. My sister really likes you."

For some strange reason, Xia Xiqing feels pleased at this.

After he gets out of the car, the driver reaches out the window with cellphone in hand, trying to take a picture. Though Xia Xiqing notices, he doesn't stop him—how could he, when his sister is a Self-Study fan?

It seems that indulging one's fans is just as satisfying as being indulged by one's idols.

He immediately spots Xu Qichen by the hotel entrance. He's wearing glasses today, looking even more student-like than usual. Xia Xiqing jogs the couple steps it takes to approach.

"Did you wait long?"

"Not at all." Xu Qichen adjusts his glasses and smiles. "The way you came over just now—you looked pretty dreamy."

"You've only just realized that your Xiqing-gege is dreamy?" Xia Xiqing retorts with a wicked grin, putting an arm around Xu Qichen's shoulder. "You know you can always dump Xia Zhixu's ass and give me a chance, right?"

Xu Qichen doesn't respond, just laughs as the two of them walk up the front steps. In the elevator, he gives Xia Xiqing a general rundown of the auditions, then passes him the script of the film with the relevant page dog-eared.

"How many are here today?"

"Including you, four."

"Oh," Xia Xiqing says, remembering the three pictures Zhou Ziheng sent him that night. They must be the other three coming to the audition. "Are there no others?"

Xu Qichen shakes his head. "We already did a first round with other actors, and Director Kun wasn't very happy with most of them. Besides," Xu Qichen lowers his voice, "this film isn't some big production, and Director Kun isn't famous enough to be that much of an attraction, so a lot of the better-off actors aren't very keen on taking this job."

It makes sense. Xia Xiqing knows he's quite similar in some aspects to the character, Jiang Tong, but maybe when Director Kun offered him the audition, he was also thinking about the publicity their shippers can bring to the film. After all, for a longtime director of indie films, a larger audience is probably pretty high on his list of priorities.

Just like artists—even if most of them claim to be free spirits and mavericks, in reality, who doesn't want their work to be known by all? Nothing undiscovered and unseen by an audience can have any true value, any true impact.

"We've finished two already." Xu Qichen pushes the door open. "We're currently on break for discussion. Come in and look through the script—you'll be on after we finish the next one."

Xia Xiqing nods.

Xu Qichen pulls on the wide pant legs of Xia Xiqing's coveralls, eying the paint splattered all over. Laughing, he says, "You're dressed pretty casually today."

Looking down, Xia Xiqing smiles halfheartedly. "Isn't the character supposed to be the withdrawn type? They don't tend to be very fashion-conscious."

They walk into the room using the entrance at the back. They've cleared a space at the front of the room, with both video cameras and lighting set up around this stage area. A man, not too tall, sits at the front, wearing a baseball cap and talking to the man beside him. The other man is wearing a suit, so Xia Xiqing figures that the more casually dressed man must be Director Kun.

But strangely enough, there's also a little girl sitting beside them. Whose kid is that? Or is she a child actress?

The conversation between Director Kun and the suited man ends, and he glances back, noticing Xia Xiqing. He seems somewhat surprised. Xia Xiqing gives a polite smile in return.

"I'm gonna head up, then." Xu Qichen gives Xia Xiqing's shoulder a pat, then walks over to Director Kun.

Xia Xiqing nods, sitting in a corner to read through the script. The dog-eared portion marks a tense scene: Jiang Tong comes home from the hospital and, in the hallway, hears a little girl getting beaten by her family. The family in question have been his downstairs neighbors for two years already, and they beat their kid for the smallest of reasons, so he often heard such sounds.

But today, he'd only just returned from the hospital, and he was reminded of his past when he heard the hoarse cries of a girl through his hearing aid. So, he knocks on their door, louder and louder until he's practically ramming it down, and keeps it up until the girl's father opens the door. Then, he rushes in and embraces the little girl, bodily protecting her from the beating and refusing to let go of her, not even when his hearing aid gets knocked off.

He's only saved when Gao Kun passes by on his way home.

It's a pretty climactic scene, and Xia Xiqing finds it a bit daunting. But fortunately, Jiang Tong is supposed to be hearing impaired—he has relatively few lines despite being such an important character, meaning Xia Xiqing doesn't need to memorize any lines for this scene.

It's strange. The script is very perfunctory in its descriptions, but Xia Xiqing still feels a bit short of breath. He tries to tamp down on his emotions, tries to make himself calm down. There's a benefit to being a longtime artist, which is that he is consistently able to visualize scenes in his mind.

There's no question of whether he can imagine the events as described in the script.

But the question is if he can let go—if he dares to let go.

"Xu Zixi."

He looks up, and sees a young man walking to the stage at the sound of that name.

"Hello, my name is Xu Zixi, a third-year student of acting."

Third year? That'd make him no more than a year older or younger than Zhou Ziheng, who's also in his third year. Xia Xiqing also recognizes his face; he's the one that Zhou Ziheng said is his "type." This kid looks even more attractive in person.

Xia Xiqing watches him walking out of the fake door onstage to the other side. It appears that he wants to start the scene by knocking.

"Ready?" Director Kun asks.

"Yes," Xu Zixi answers outside the door. After thirty seconds, he starts knocking. Weak, at first, and then when he realizes no one is answering, he pounds on the door, a few "ah" sounds slip out of his mouth, like someone who's mute but trying to speak past his disability.

As the pounding comes quicker and louder, an actor pulls the door open, revealing Xu Zixi's terrified face. He raises his hand and puts it down.

This actor doesn't have lines. The little girl beside him also doesn't need to yell or cry. They are merely props helping the audition run smoothly. Xu Zixi stumbles to reach the little girl, kneeling and holding her in his arms. He puts his arms over her head protectively while repeating "D—don't... hit— t..." The words come out stuttered, like he's taking a beating in the meantime.

Xia Xiqing has to admit that this guy is quite good.

At this moment, another guy rushes in through the door and drags Xu Zixi up from the floor. It's Zhou Ziheng. So he's actually here, helping with the audition.

Zhou Ziheng pulls him to the side, and Xu Zixi crouches the moment he lets him go. Tears start streaming down his face almost instantly, and he keeps saying "Don't be afraid" to the little girl. His arms and body are shaking, as if the words have drained him of all his energy. No one makes a sound on the set.

The crying is professional, Xia Xiqing can already feel the weight on his shoulders.

"And, cut."

Xu Zixi quickly comes out of character. He wipes his face free of tears, smiling shyly. He leads the little girl off the stage and speaks to her gently, "Did I scare you?"

The director doesn't say much, but the man in the suit looks satisfied. Xu Zixi turns and bows to Zhou Ziheng, who smiles politely at him and compliments, "Good job."

Most nonprofessionals would probably become too embarrassed to stick around after seeing a performance like that, but Xia Xiqing is both clever and competitive, especially after hearing Zhou Ziheng's compliment.

If he was to play any other character, he wouldn't have the confidence as he does now. But it's Jiang Tong.

Zhou Ziheng turns and sees Xia Xiqing. They lock eyes, and Xia Xiqing's lips curl as he sees the surprise in Zhou Ziheng's gaze.

No, not Jiang Tong. Not really.

It's himself. How can he fail at acting in the role of himself?

Zhou Ziheng didn't expect Xia Xiqing to show up today at all.

Even though he knows how hard Xu Qichen tried to get him to come, he never thought Xia Xiqing would actually expose his deepest fear for the sake of "reclaiming himself" or something like that. Living in a bubble surrounded by his worshippers is easier than loving himself.

The night of their conversation, Zhou Ziheng didn't sleep at all. He regretted what he said right away, and he felt worse thinking that Xia Xiqing might not even care.

About who he works with. About his "type."

Seeing Xia Xiqing here at the audition, Zhou Ziheng feels like he's dreaming. Xia Xiqing walks toward him while letting his hair down from its tie. When he gets there, he turns to Xu Qichen and hands over the script, not looking at Zhou Ziheng.

Xu Zixi has a nervous look on his face. He reaches out a hand. "Hello, I'm Xu Zixi."

Xia Xiqing smiles gently, shaking the proffered hand. "Xia Xiqing." His voice is soothing, like a cloud far, far away. "Your performance was very impressive."

"Thank you, thank you."

Xia Xiqing pulls his hand back, not sparing Zhou Ziheng a glance.

"Then how about we run it through with Xiqing?" Saying that, Director Kun continues, trying to reassure him: "Don't worry. We're just looking at the overall feel of your interpretation."

The crew knows that Xia Xiqing is not an actor, so there's not much expectation. Even if he has the right features for the role, acting skills are still essential.

Xia Xiqing walks to the camera and gives a short introduction. "Good evening, my name is Xia Xiqing."

Then, he takes a deep breath and walks out of the "door" and closes it behind him.

Gazing at the shut door, Xia Xiqing panics. He wonders if this is worth it. He needs to remind himself of all the pain in his life, and for what? His pride? Is that really what he wants to do?

Memories are powerful. They take over his senses once he stops fighting. His eyes start to lose focus, and the door in front of him loses shape and color.

A familiar blue door begins to show itself. He touches the door handle, and his chest tightens.

Breathing becomes difficult. He takes his hand back, trying to convince himself that he's not the one who's locked inside. Not this time.

This time, he's going to save the kid behind that door.

If only you'd never been born, my life wouldn't become like this!

Why do I have a son like you? You're as much of a lunatic as your mother. Why are you still alive?

Xia Xiqing knocks on the door twice, zombie-like. He pauses, and then twice more.

If only there'd been someone who'd saved him.

His hand shakes uncontrollably, and he has to lay his other hand on his wrist to hold it still. He knocks and knocks, each heavier than the last.

The door is pulled open. Xia Xiqing inhales sharply, his lips parted to let the trapped air out slowly.

His whole body is trembling.

Not laying eyes on the father figure, he dashes toward the little girl and pulls her into his arms.

Since Xia Xiqing is an amateur at acting, the other actor there assisting the audition probably thinks he needs a little help to get into character. He grabs Xia Xiqing's arm and yells, "What's your fucking problem?"

Xia Xiqing doesn't look back. He pulls his arm back and carries the girl and walks away, not saying a word. The actor realizes this is Xia Xiqing's approach, so he drags him by the arm. "Hey! What are you doing?! Let her go!"

Xia Xiqing takes a few stumbled steps back. His one hand is above the girl's head the whole time. His limbs are fighting to be freed from the actor. Everyone can see how scared he is. The "father" swears and grabs a chair, moving as if to smash it over Xia Xiqing's head. Xia Xiqing reflexively crouches with the little girl.

Zhou Ziheng feels his heart stutter as he runs to them. The actor is actually keeping his distance—the chair would have never landed on Xia Xiqing, but in his panic, Zhou Ziheng ends up standing too close and gets hit on the arm. He winces at the pain.

He's worried that the actor will break character if he sees him injured, though, so he quickly pulls Xia Xiqing up.

Xia Xiqing keeps his head down as he walks a few steps and puts the girl down.

When he was cursed and yelled at, Xia Xiqing was instantly overwhelmed by his memories. He felt pain, as if he'd been beaten with a golf club. He heard the sound of his parents' yelling, even as he remembered how he himself had been yelling and crying as he tried to get out of the room he'd been locked inside.

Nobody came. Nobody has ever come to rescue him.

Xia Xiqing's unfocused eyes land on the little girl. He kneels and tidies her dress before he runs a gentle hand over her hair, smoothing down the messy flyaway strands. His lips almost curl into a smile. He takes a deep breath and opens his mouth, but nothing comes out. Instead, he picks up her hand, and writes something on her palm.

The message is not only for the kid, but also for himself. Each stroke takes strength and time and a piece of him.

Don't be afraid.

He curls her palm into a fist and puts it inside the pocket of her red sweater. He looks up at the girl, whose face has transformed into the familiar countenance of his youthful self.

Xia Xiqing lowers his gaze, shoulders shaking in fear.

The little actress is too stunned to speak.

Zhou Ziheng can't take it anymore; he no longer cares how the story goes. He squats and puts a firm hand on Xia Xiqing's shoulder. Somehow, Xia Xiqing can hear his own crying, loud and clear, even when everyone is quiet here. The begging, crying for help, sobbing, silence... His tiny body completely out of strength.

Is anyone there? Can someone open the door for me?

It's so dark in here... I'm scared...

It's been so long.

He'd been so scared at the time.

Xia Xiqing looks up. He grits his teeth, eyes refocusing on the girl's face. He gives her a hug, trying to be as gentle as he can, given he's still shaking. He's afraid that he hurt her, afraid that he failed to give her any hope.

Afraid that she's still afraid.

Finally, a tear rolls down his cheek. He closes his eyes.

There's no need to hide anymore. Maybe... maybe it's all over now.

"Cut!"

It's as if everyone in the room has rediscovered their ability to breathe. The crying has been very low-key, but the scene is still very painful to witness.

Xia Xiqing opens his eyes, taking a few breaths before letting go of the little girl. She wipes at the tear tracks on his face.

"Don't cry, gege."

Xia Xiqing laughs. "Gege is only acting. I'm not actually crying." He squishes her cheek. "I'm not sad. Are you sad?"

"Just a little."

Xia Xiqing hugs her, echoing, "Just a little..."

Zhou Ziheng sees fragility in the smile on Xia Xiqing's face.

Xia Xiqing finally lets himself exhale. He turns sideways and grabs Zhou Ziheng's arm, the one that had gotten hit. Zhou Ziheng hisses in pain.

"Where is your professionalism?" Xia Xiqing says coldly.

Zhou Ziheng can't tell what he feels right now. He just wants to hold him, if only he would let him.

Xia Xiqing lets go of his arm and smiles at Director Kun, who stands up and walks to Xia Xiqing with astonishment on his face.

"The skill you showed just now was very professional," he says incredulously. "Are you sure you've never taken any acting classes?"

"No, I'm sure, but I can relate to this character a bit. Maybe that helped." Xia Xiqing tries to put on a smile. "Excuse me. I need to use the washroom."

Kun Cheng nods, watching Xia Xiqing leave the room. Then he sits down and asks the producer beside him, "You also think Xia Xiqing is better, right? That final tear at the end was just brilliant. We'll need a close-up of that."

The producer looks very excited, and he starts chattering about how the scene went down, as well as the angles that they'll want to use.

When he finishes, Kun Cheng shakes his head very slightly.

"He wasn't acting at all."

Kun Cheng noticed that Xia Xiqing hadn't looked the "father" of the story throughout the entire scene, not even once. It was out of fear, a subconscious kind of avoidance. He'd been so scared that he couldn't even look, couldn't resist at all. And it fits—people with depression tend not to show very exaggerated emotions. Maybe Xia Xiqing is familiar with that.

What's more terrifying is that he'd also been too scared to look at the little girl he was protecting.

And when he finally dared to look at the little girl, the scene truly came to life.

That's not acting at all.

At the back of the room, Xu Qichen squeezes the script in his hand, not saying a word. Zhou Ziheng was right about his cruelty. Before he saw Xia Xiqing dissecting himself on stage, he thought he was helping him move on.

Now he's not so sure.

Xia Xiqing splashes his face with water, then leans forward, propping his torso up by holding onto the edge of the counter with his hands. He tries to withdraw himself from the bad memories, but it's not easy.

"Are you okay?"

It's that actor from earlier.

Xia Xiqing instantly puts on his usual smile. He reaches for a piece of paper towel to wipe his hands. "Yes, I'm good." He tosses the paper towel into the garbage bin, eyes landing on Xu Zixi's face.

"I..." Xu Zixi looks hesitant. "I want to know why you interpreted it this way. Like, what's the idea behind it? Because after I got the script, my instinct was that the boy wants to protect the kid, and he's sad..."

Xu Zixi's mumbling, but Xia Xiqing completely understands. He takes a step forward.

"Your method is also good." Xia Xiqing gives Xu Zixi's shoulder a pat, then retrieves his hand and lets it slide into his pocket. "He does want to protect the little girl, but he's afraid, even more so than she is."

Xu Zixi has confusion in his eyes.

Xia Xiqing laughs self-deprecatingly. "It's okay. It's good that you don't understand. You must've had a happy childhood."

Before Xia Xiqing can leave, someone else walks quietly into the washroom. Right this second, Xia Xiqing can put on a smile for anyone in the world—except for him. Every time he sees Zhou Ziheng, he wants to peel off his own skin and show the ugliest side of him.

It's an instinct for self-sabotage. There's no actual logic behind it.

"Zixi, I need a moment alone with him." Zhou Ziheng walks toward them, asking politely, "If you'll excuse us?"

Xu Zixi nods and starts to retreat. "Sure. Thank you, Xiqing-ge! I'll leave you two alone."

Xia Xiqing doesn't say anything. He leans on the counter, eyes lowered. Zhou Ziheng pulls him into the innermost stall and closes the door.

Xia Xiqing feels like he's about to explode. The tight space just makes him feel worse, and he's inexplicably upset that Zhou Ziheng called the new guy "Zixi" and called him, "him."

But being upset is unbecoming.

Xia Xiqing licks his lips, looking at Zhou Ziheng with

false nonchalance. Then, quite passive aggressively, he asks, "Don't I have a name?"

Zhou Ziheng freezes for a moment, but then comprehension dawns on him. He tries to explain, "I just thought it'd be too solemn to call him by his full name, that he'd mistake it for me trying to haze him..."

"And?" Xia Xiqing repeats, "Don't I have a name?"

Being stared down like this, Zhou Ziheng feels quite self-conscious. He wants to call him "Xiqing," or even something more intimate, but what right does he have to that?

"So you've dragged me in here, but you refuse to talk?" Xia Xiqing folds his arms in front of his chest. "Is it because you want to do something else?" He's not sure why he's saying such vulgar things, but he also can't help himself. He has to hide his hurt behind aggressiveness.

"Did you think I did well out there?" His face is still wet from when he splashed it with water. "Did I look good, crying like that? Does it make you feel protective?"

Zhou Ziheng's heart has dropped to his stomach, and Xia Xiqing feels a sense of victory at having talked him into a corner like this.

He continues with a sneer, "Do you find me pitiable? Is that why you've hidden us away in here to do unspeakable things to me?" Xia Xiqing leans closer. "Can't I at least get a kiss first?"

Zhou Ziheng pins him against the wall. Xia Xiqing's eyes are as cold as ice, but the frigidity of his eyes melt into confusion when he's pulled into a warm embrace.

"I am very angry right now." Zhou Ziheng's voice trembles. "But I'll be fine in a second."

Xia Xiqing's voice is weak and uncertain. "Why...why are you hugging me if you're angry?"

"Because then you'd run away, and I know I'd regret it if I let you leave. I don't want to be regretful." Zhou Ziheng's arms tighten around him.

After a moment of silence, Zhou Ziheng takes a deep breath and loosens his grip. "I'm good now." The hand moves up slowly until Xia Xiqing can feel the warmth of that palm massaging his scalp.

It takes both courage and patience to hug a rose.

I know that the thorns will get stuck in my skin, that they'll insert themselves into my veins, but it's okay. Just give me a minute. I'll pull them back out. These pains are only temporary.

But I still want to hug that rose.

Then, in between kisses to the top of Xia Xiqing's head, Zhou Ziheng finally says the words that he's been wanting to say all this time.

"Xiqing, don't be afraid.

"I'm here."

C.12

:

Peach Cigarette

Xia Xiqing is starting to think that Zhou Ziheng might know something.

But how? Did Xu Qichen tell him? They don't seem that close to each other.

His mind is very messy, his thoughts jumping one by one to the surface. He no longer wants to think about any irrelevant details. He doesn't know how, but Zhou Ziheng's hug has some sort of a mystifying power to heal him, able to rapidly smooth over the cracks in his emotions.

He lifts his hand, previously hanging by his side, up to wrap his arm slowly around Zhou Ziheng, returning the hug. His chilled palm presses against the wide expanse of Zhou Ziheng's back, leeching warmth from his slightly jutting shoulder blade.

Zhou Ziheng didn't expect his hug to be returned. Some part of his heart softens, sinking in slightly as if someone has quietly sat himself upon it. Xia Xiqing's fingers are clasping the edges of his shoulder blade, and his forehead is also resting against his shoulder like he's given up.

Does this count as some sort of trust? Zhou Ziheng wonders as he smooths his hand from the nape of Xia Xiqing's neck downward, following the knobs of his spine.

"It's like you're stroking a cat or something." Xia Xiqing's sulky voice is muffled by Zhou Ziheng's shoulder.

Zhou Ziheng laughs. "Are you saying that you're my cat?"

Unable to think of a retort, Xia Xiqing feels his anger reigniting. He lets go of the hug and raises his head, but just as he places his palms against Zhou Ziheng's chest, the latter catches him, entwining their fingers together.

"You've pushed me away too many times." Zhou Ziheng holds his gaze. "I'm constantly on guard against being pushed away by you."

But I know it can't be that you truly don't need me, so it's become reflex for me to prevent you from pushing me away.

Hearing Zhou Ziheng's words, Xia Xiqing feels his ears flush hot. He looks down, avoiding eye contact, but he doesn't try to take back his hands. Suddenly, he feels a press of warmth against his forehead, unbelievably soft.

When he realizes that it's a kiss, he looks up, only to reflexively close his eyes as Zhou Ziheng's lips brush against his eyelashes before kissing him on his eyelid. Then his cheek is cupped, fingertips pressing against the tender spot right behind his ear, and another kiss lands on his nose.

He feels flustered to the point of upset. He suddenly finds that he's really very pathetic, to have never been treated with such tenderness before, to the point of being convinced that he doesn't deserve this.

To the point of, upon given even the smallest modicum of gentleness, feeling so utterly shaken.

His nose sours with unshed tears, but it's too embarrassing to cry right now. With effort, he holds it back, furrowing his brow and opening his eyes very wide. Zhou Ziheng places their foreheads together, rubbing the tips of their noses. His voice is soft, like it's enveloped in ocean mist.

"I know you think we're simply different types of people, that I'm too much of an idealist." Zhou Ziheng's voice is low, and his fingers stroke softly along Xia Xiqing's jawline. "But I promise you, I don't actually go around trying to protect everyone I see."

"You don't?" It's strange, how weak Xia Xiqing's retort sounds.

"I don't... It only happens sometimes, like when I see a stray cat curled up by the side of the road and I get the urge to take him home."

Xia Xiqing scoffs coldly. "And you think he'll just let you do that? You'll get scratched."

"That's alright; I'm willing to pay the necessary price." Zhou Ziheng's lips form a gentle curve, and he taps his forehead against Xia Xiqing's before continuing. "Or like when I see a beautiful rose stuck in a thorny bush, I also want to protect him, to save him."

"Is it good for a rose to leave its bush?" Xia Xiqing looks up through a blur of undispersed tears.

"It's because he wants to leave, that's why I'm trying to save him."

"How do you know?"

"I just do." Zhou Ziheng's smile reaches his eyes, gleefully curving them.

Zhou Ziheng's logic is always strange, yet always persuasive. Xia Xiqing is at a loss for retorts, so he asks, "What else?"

"No more. As a STEM major, this is the extent of my meager capacity for metaphor."

Zhou Ziheng tilts his head, pressing another kiss to the tiny beauty mark on Xia Xiqing's nose. His eyes are bright, and, as if afraid that his smile might seem too childish, his expression becomes more serious, more earnest.

"There is exactly one person who makes me feel protective, and he is Xia Xiqing."

The words are light, so light that Xia Xiqing can't catch them. But then they suddenly become heavy, crashing relentlessly into his heart, burrowing in so deeply that he can't dig them back out.

Stray cats fear humans. Roses fear the hand that seeks to pick them.

Xia Xiqing fears kindness.

Because kindness is the only weapon in the entire world that will never lose a fight.

"Can I kiss you? Now?"

The question too is so earnest, and Xia Xiqing feels defeated by it. He laughs a bit helplessly. "So you *do* want to kiss."

"Yes," but then Zhou Ziheng shakes his head. "No, it's not what you think. I just want to—"

Sound comes from just outside the washroom, but before Zhou Ziheng can cut off his own words, Xia Xiqing seals up his mouth with a kiss.

"Hey, the public restrooms here are actually pretty cushy."

It's a stranger's voice.

"Why do you care so much?" Men's bathroom humor always trends toward dirty jokes. "Do you seek out some sort of *excitement* in places like these?"

Their fingers, already intertwined, lock more tightly

together. Chest pressing against chest, they enter some sort of a give-and-take in terms of exerted force. But his eyes are soft, filled with a gentle light.

Those eyes hold such intense implications that Zhou Ziheng can't help but be the same as all those victims that came before him, convinced that Xia Xiqing really does feel some sort of romance, some sort of love. Even though he knows this is all pretense.

"Hotel restrooms have nothing on night club restrooms. Last time I got drunk and went to the washroom at a night club, the sounds coming from the neighboring stall... Fuck, with how loud they were, it was practically an X-rated livestream."

Hearing this conversation, Xia Xiqing's hands start wandering, fingers wiggling into Zhou Ziheng's black shirt. Their supposedly comforting kiss intensifies too. A sound almost escapes their lips.

The stranger laughs. "How exciting. I should try that next time, too."

Zhou Ziheng's brow is furrowed with intent. Xia Xiqing pulls off of his lips reluctantly, looking into his eyes and raising an eyebrow. Silently, he mouths, *Wanna try?*

"Try? Who would you do it with?"

Zhou Ziheng has been teased to the point of desperation, hanging tightly onto Xia Xiqing and kissing him so aggressively that he almost loses balance.

"Anyone will do. You know how easy girls are to pick up these days—"

A bang coming from the stalls interrupts the guys outside, who stop their conversation to turn around in alarm, but no more sounds appear.

Xia Xiqing is also a little alarmed—just now he was trying

to keep his balance, so grabbed onto the side of the stall, but he used more force than he'd intended.

"What was that? It scared me shitless."

"Something probably dropped, you wuss. You sure you're brave enough to pick up girls? Or is it the girls who pick you up?"

As they bicker, Zhou Ziheng holds Xia Xiqing's lower lip between his teeth, pulling slightly before releasing it. It's his turn to mouth, *I'll pick you up.*

There's another loud bang, and the guys outside hurriedly run off: "What the hell? This place is haunted!"

As their voices disappear, Xia Xiqing, who just now slapped the side of the stall, begins to snicker.

"You've scared them out of bringing dates to the restroom for the rest of their lives," Zhou Ziheng says in a low voice.

Xia Xiqing breathes into his ear, "You say that as if you'd dare to, Mr. Big Shot."

"Do you gain any benefit from provoking me like this?"

"Of course." Xia Xiqing reaches out to smooth over Zhou Ziheng's wrinkled shirt, helping him tuck it into his waistband, then taps his belt. "It's so that I can get in these once you're desperate enough to let me."

Zhou Ziheng smiles helplessly. "Why can't it be that, when I'm desperate enough, I'll get into your pants?"

Xia Xiqing quirks his mouth, unable to find anything wrong with Zhou Ziheng's comment. But he still refutes it. "No, it's better that I top."

"When are you gonna give up on that?" Seeing his persistence, Zhou Ziheng finds it both adorable and laughable.

"It's important, as part of the human condition, for a man to have dreams." Xia Xiqing has on his serious face. "This year, mine is to help you find your awakening—on your back."

"Don't come crying to me when your dream goes up in smoke."

"Mine will be the joyful tears of success."

"That would be better for you." Zhou Ziheng kisses his cheek. Xia Xiqing pretends to be offended, wiping his face where he was kissed, then he remembers Zhou Ziheng's injury and grabs his wrist to look. It's still red, and it looks like it's turning into a bruise.

Zhou Ziheng speaks first. "It's fine."

Xia Xiqing rolls his eyes at him. "Who cares?" He lets go of his wrist. "You brought it on yourself. You deserved it."

"Yeah, I deserved it."

"Don't mock me."

"I'm not. I really think I deserved it." Zhou Ziheng gives Xia Xiqing a bear hug. Then he releases him and holds onto his shoulders, smiling and saying, "You look good today."

Xia Xiqing is used to compliments on his appearance, but ones as genuine as Zhou Ziheng's? He really hasn't received that many. He gets a sudden competitive urge, uncaring that he might seem petty.

"But who looks better? Me or Zixi?" Xia Xiqing looks up at Zhou Ziheng and strokes along his ear.

Zhou Ziheng frowns in confusion. "Why would you compare yourself to him?"

Even though he really is just confused, Xia Xiqing misunderstands and pulls his ear in response. Zhou Ziheng winces.

"Wait, I just meant, does he even count as attractive? In the context of this industry, isn't he pretty average?"

Xia Xiqing wants to play it cool, but his lips betray him by curling up. "Oh? Am I not average, then?"

Zhou Ziheng's frown deepens. He turns Xia Xiqing's face

to the left, and then to the right.

"There is exactly one."

Here he goes again with the uniqueness quantification... Xia Xiqing's heart flutters. He licks his lips, trying to sound casually disparaging as he says, "STEM major."

"It's a pity I can only draw force diagrams. Otherwise, I will be drawing you every day."

Xia Xiqing's heart feels like it'll jump right out of his chest. He covers Zhou Ziheng's mouth with his hand. "Shut up. We should go. It's too stuffy in here."

So stuffy that he can no longer think straight.

Zhou Ziheng smiles and kisses his palm.

This guy... Xia Xiqing pulls his hand back. He suddenly remembers those cheesy nicknames that the Zhou Ziheng fandom likes to give him, stuff like Heart Arsonist and Heart Sniper. Xia Xiqing himself even used them at some point. They actually seem pretty fitting? Well, except that Xia Xiqing has no heart available for sniping.

To avoid suspicion, the two of them leave the washroom separately. When Zhou Ziheng gets to the room, Kun Cheng is talking to the studio manager.

"Kun-ge, Zhou Ziheng is here," the assistant director says.

"Oh, finally. Where have you been all this time?" Kun Cheng asks offhandedly.

Zhou Ziheng sits down beside him. "Had a phone call."

"Is it okay?" Kun Cheng glances at his arm.

Feeling a little awkward, Zhou Ziheng rubs at it. "It's fine. It's nothing serious."

Kun Cheng laughs. "What were you thinking? They were just acting."

Zhou Ziheng takes the ribbing in good humor, not bothering to retort.

"But the way you ran up to block it felt a lot like Gao Kun." Then, shaking his head, Kun Cheng corrects himself. "You *were* Gao Kun."

"Xu Zixi did a good job too. He's got potential." Kun Cheng sighs. "But compared to Xia Xiqing, it becomes clear that he was just acting." He eyes Zhou Ziheng. "You'd also rather partner with Xia Xiqing, right?"

Afraid that Kun Cheng might see through them, Zhou Ziheng tries to dissemble. "I'd of course want to pair with the better actor."

"Oh, come off it." Kun Cheng pats his shoulder. "You're free to go for the day. We'll discuss it more without you and come to a decision within the next couple days. Also, have you seen Xia Xiqing?"

"I think I saw him by the restrooms," he lies smoothly. With excellent timing, Xia Xiqing arrives. "And there he is."

The building is surrounded by reporters, so it may not be a good idea to go back with Xia Xiqing, Zhou Ziheng thinks. He asks Xiao-Luo to drive him back first.

"Zhou Ziheng, you're trending again today."

Zhou Ziheng takes off his mask after getting into the car. "What? Did the company buy that for me?"

"No." Xiao-Luo sounds like he's laughing. "It's the show's trailer for the upcoming episode."

Zhou Ziheng has completely forgotten about that. Now that he thinks about it...the show's director did ask him to promote the trailer on Weibo. He logs onto Weibo and finds that it has already trended with more than forty thousand shares. He clicks on the video, which starts with a close-up shot of a radio. There's static, and then a voice.

It's Xia Xiqing's voice. "The moment I met you was the Big Bang. Every particle left me and flew toward you. After that smallest instant, the universe was truly born."

There's the image of an exploding nebula, its pieces forming into multiple identical nebulae. They tremble, then reform into the original before slowly shrinking and shrinking until the screen shows only the page of a book.

Ruan Xiao's voice asks, "If we're the same person, shouldn't the chain of events be identical?"

Xia Xiqing's voice replies, "What if you're girlfriends from different timelines?"

Then, Zhou Ziheng's voice asks, "So you're the version that went back in time to save the girl? Then why is her death documented in the journal?"

Shang Sirui's voice says, "In my timeline, the girlfriend attempts to save the boyfriend. She goes back to the boyfriend who locked himself in the house with the gas turned on, trying to kill himself."

The voice of the only girl in the episode says, "Xia Xiqing is the original cause of the tragedy. If it weren't for him, none of it would've happened."

Finally, in a voice that sounds like it's hiding laughter, Xia Xiqing says, "Then I should just kill you right now to hide my secret."

The screen goes black. Even the background music, which had been picking up in tempo, dissolves into radio static.

It's brilliant editing. Zhou Ziheng laughs. Now everyone's attention will be shifted to Xia Xiqing.

His own voice comes last: "She thinks you're the Killer."

Then a response, "Why should I believe you?"

In the darkness, a blue butterfly flutters its wings, leaving a glimmering trail of particles that slowly illuminate the surrounding scene. There's a man dressed in dark blue, facing away from the screen. He holds a bookmark in his hands, and that CGI butterfly continues to flutter until it merges into the butterfly in the bookmark.

"Xiqing?"

Xia Xiqing turns around.

The screen is split in half. Xia Xiqing is on the left and Zhou Ziheng is on the right. Even though they're in separate rooms, it looks like they're talking directly to each other.

"If you don't want to give me a chance, then I have nothing else to say."

Now, the screen splits into four vertical slices. The four players' faces quickly flash into being, one by one until it's dark again, and there's only the sound of heavy breathing.

Zhou Ziheng feels a pang in his chest, for he recognizes the sound—it's Xia Xiqing.

The door opens, and a ray of light shines through. A person walks out very slowly.

Ruan Xiao's voice overlays the scene: "Did the boyfriend leave his house that day?"

Xia Xiqing's ashen face gradually emerges from the dark.

Shang Sirui's voice overlays it: "If I leave, the door will close and I won't be able to return."

A smile appears on Xia Xiqing's face.

"I'm going out."

Like an old television shutting down, the screen converges into a single horizontal line at the center before everything fades to black. The title card of *Survive and Escape* appears; then a blue butterfly flies by, leaving the subtitle: "The Butterfly Effect."

Zhou Ziheng expects it to end there, but then comes an Easter egg: the screen is back to four vertical slices. Shang Sirui shows up first. He squats in front of the radio, turning the knobs one by one, first from left to right, then from right to left.

Suddenly, Ruan Xiao's voice emerges from the radio: "Hello?"

Shang Sirui is so startled that he falls into a seat right there on the floor. Beside his strip of video, it shows Ruan Xiao's room, where she's sporting a very hesitant look.

Then their two slices of video darken, the other two strips light up. Xia Xiqing stands in front of a door, his hand reaching out. Beside him, Zhou Ziheng's hand is also reaching out. From the way it's been cut, it looks like they're reaching toward each other.

Through the white line separating the frames of their video clips, they touch.

"Don't you think you might be too biased?"

"Of course I'm biased."

The video ends.

Zhou Ziheng is baffled at how the production team is able to use the fragmented scenes to put together a seemingly romantic story without spoiling any details regarding the truth.

"You're finished?" Xiao-Luo laughs. "Do you know what the trending terms are right now?"

"What?"

Xiao-Luo laughs. "See for yourself."

Huh. Zhou Ziheng looks through the list of trending topics. The first two are about him.

Romantic Zhou Ziheng

Gentle Alpha Zhou Ziheng

Pfft.

He takes a screenshot and sends it over WeChat.

Moral Role Model: Which one would you pick?

Xia Xiqing just got into the elevator with Xu Qichen. He

looks down at his phone and laughs. He doesn't know how, but he can totally imagine the self-satisfied look on Zhou Ziheng's face right now.

"What is it?"

"Nothing." Xia Xiqing answers. He quickly types a response.

Zhou Ziheng receives his answer a few seconds later from Xia Xiqing. The message is completely in English.

Terrorist: *Kids make choices, adults make love.*

When Xia Xiqing walks out of the elevator, he sees a few girls standing not far away on the street. Maybe they're fans, he thinks. As soon as he approaches the hotel's revolving door, the girls all run toward them in excitement.

"Do you have another mask in your bag?" Xia Xiqing nudges Xu Qichen who's covered his face with a mask.

"Nah, just this one."

Xia Xiqing makes an annoyed sound. "You're always so prepared."

But he can only blame himself for not being prepared, so he just braces himself for meeting his fans. The girls outside scream Xia Xiqing's name, all holding their phones up.

"Xiqing-gege, what are you doing here?"

"Just for fun."

The girls laugh. Xia Xiqing finds it curious. How did they know his private schedule?

"How did you all find me?"

One of them says, "Gege, you're trending right now. We were shopping nearby when we saw, so we came over."

"Trending?" Xia Xiqing moves to stand out of the way of passers-by. Xu Qichen leaves him alone with the girls to go fetch his car.

"Yeah! Someone recognized you and it got leaked. And

also the new trailer for your show just came out!"

The other girls begin to squeal, and Xia Xiqing feels like he's surrounded by a herd of chittering groundhogs.

Xia Xiqing laughs. "What about it?"

"Oh, you should go check it out. It's super sweet!"

Sweet? Isn't the show supposed to be suspenseful?

"Xiqing-gege, did you win in the last episode? Can you give us any spoilers?"

"Xiqing-gege, who's the killer?"

"Xiqing-gege, when are you going to film the next one?"

"Well, you'll just have to wait and see." Xu Qichen's car arrives, to which he sighs in relief. "I'm going home now. It's getting dark, so you girls should get going too."

"Xiqing-gege is so nice."

The girls push a bag of snacks into his hand. They keep waving at him until his car drives away. Xia Xiqing puts his gifts down and takes a deep breath to calm himself.

"You're very popular now," Xu Qichen teases him.

"You're laughing now. Bet that they'll figure out who you are soon enough."

"I'm okay with that." Xu Qichen turns the steering wheel. "Even if they find the pseudonym I use for writing BL, all that'll happen is you'll be asked to play a role in a *danmei*[7] dramatization."

"Ugh. No thanks. I'll leave that kind of sappiness to you and that boyfriend of yours."

"Actually, someone wanted to produce a film based on one of my novels. I showed it to you before, remember? The one set in Nice."

"*Nanke's Dream*—I remember." Xia Xiqing rests his head

---

7 A genre of Chinese webnovels that depicts romantic and/or sexual relationships between men.

against the window. "Did you sell it?"

"No. I didn't think anyone fit the role of Yu Ning in my head." Xu Qichen suddenly smiles. "Well, now that I think about it, maybe you and Zhou Ziheng can do it. He can be the 'optimistic and outgoing top who's pretending to be a scumbag,' and you can be the 'depressed and perverted bottom who's also a notorious playboy.'"

"You're the bottom. I'm a playboy top, thank you very much."

"Fine, fine, fine. Pretty-boy top. But seriously, your face is too distinctive. You need a hat and a mask next time."

Xia Xiqing huffs. "Yeah, I know. I can't even go clubbing nowadays."

"It's not a good place for you anyway." Xu Qichen deftly changes the subject: "Besides, what club-goers would be as hot as Zhou Ziheng?"

Xia Xiqing scoffs quietly in response and doesn't say much else out loud. Internally, however, he thinks, *It's pretty difficult to find celebrities worthy of being compared to Zhou Ziheng, let alone random men in clubs.*

Coincidentally, a message comes in from the man himself.

Moral Role Model: Are you done?

Terrorist: What do you want?

"It's late." Xu Qichen checks his watch. "You wanna eat dinner at my place? I'll cook."

Xia Xiqing nods. "I want sweet and sour ribs."

"You got it. I'll ask Zhixu to buy some ribs. Oh right, I forgot to call him back." Xu Qichen dials Xia Zhixu's number, and Xia Xiqing turns on his PDA filter.

Terrorist: I'm going to Chen-Chen's place for dinner. His sweet and sour ribs are to die for.

Zhou Ziheng is in the middle of replying to the previous

message when he sees this one, and he can't help but feel a little jealous of the intimacy between Xia Xiqing and Xu Qichen. He doesn't have a high school buddy like that... How different was Xia Xiqing as a fifteen-year-old? He wants to see it.

As he's thinking about how cute Xia Xiqing must have been back then, a thought hits him: he himself would've only been ten years old at the time, still in elementary school... Well, he feels worse now. All this time between them, and there was never really any way of getting it back.

Meanwhile, Xia Xiqing listens to the sweet nothings being exchanged between the happy couple, letting it enter one ear and exit the other. They're off in their own little world, and he's been left alone like so much chopped liver. But then again, it's been like this since high school, so he's used to it.

Moral Role Model: I can make you sweet and sour ribs too. You should come to my place.

Xia Xiqing sees this and laughs so hard that even Xu Qichen notices.

Terrorist: How do I know if your cooking is any good?

Moral Role Model: That's why you gotta try it.

It's Zhou Ziheng's weird logic again.

Xia Xiqing waits for Xu Qichen to hang up. Finally, he ventures, "Uh, I probably can't go to your place tonight."

"What's the matter? You got other plans?"

"Sort of..." Xia Xiqing realizes this isn't the first time he's flaked on Xu Qichen, and feels quite guilty. "Can I take a rain check? I'll leave you and your boyfriend to yourselves tonight."

Xu Qichen isn't the prying type, so he drives Xia Xiqing home without asking any more questions.

"I think Director Kun will contact you directly about the

role." Xu Qichen scrolls down the window, looking at Xia Xiqing. "If you don't feel like doing it, I promise I won't push you. You should do what you want."

"I know." Xia Xiqing reaches out to tweak Xu Qichen's chin. "Now go home. Drive safe."

Xia Xiqing checks his phone as he heads upstairs. The first two topics on the trending list are still Zhou Ziheng's, but the forth one is "running into Xia Xiqing" and the fifth one is "Easter egg in *Survive and Escape* trailer."

He clicks on the former and he sees a photo of himself. He recognizes it as the one that the cab driver took.

@AGirlWhoLovesSelfStudy: My brother drove Xia Xiqing today! He even took a picture of him for me!

The comments are mostly from Self-Study girls.

@Stacyxx: Omg Xia Xiqing's outfit is so stunning! He even makes coveralls look cool.

@MyArtistLover: His hair! So adorable!

@MelonMelon: He looks amazing without photo editing, like he came straight out of an anime.

@Sweety: Wow. His legs are so long. He doesn't look like a bottom at all, he's got that "perfect boyfriend" vibe to him.

Who's a bottom? I've been a top for twenty-five years.

@CelebrateEverydayforSelfStudy: Xia Xiqing is tall. He just looks short next to Zhou Ziheng. You know what they call Zhou Ziheng, the alpha of all or something?

Alpha? More like a nerdy virgin.

Xia Xiqing steps out of the elevator and rings Zhou Ziheng's doorbell, and Zhou Ziheng opens the door in a white hoodie. It looks like he just came out of the shower, as his hair is still damp. With his black-rimmed glasses, he's full of boyish charm.

He leans in close to press a kiss to Xia Xiqing's lips. It's done so smoothly, like it's the natural order of things. Xia Xiqing freezes in response, a little stunned.

"Come on in."

The intimacy between them has gone beyond the definition of their relationship. Besides confusion, Xia Xiqing feels something else deep down. That something else is foreign to him, making him want to panic.

He nods, closing the door behind him, and spots a pair of blue slippers waiting for him. They're not the ones from last time. This pair fits him perfectly.

Xia Xiqing feels surrounded by Zhou Ziheng's affection like a frog in a pot of warm water. He's finally realized what's happening, but it's already too late for him.

He wasn't given a chance to fight back.

"Sit right there. It'll be ready soon." Zhou Ziheng's voice comes from far away. Xia Xiqing follows the delicious smell of food into the kitchen, finding Zhou Ziheng's back facing him. His heart feels warm. It's a feeling he's never felt before, not even when he watches Xu Qichen cook for him.

Like this entire person belongs to him.

His heart is completely out of his control. Where did this horrible idea come from even? That man is Zhou Ziheng. He's not the kind of person who'd be so simply claimed as anyone else's property. He was going to make fun of Zhou Ziheng for the comments he saw earlier, about the alpha thing, but now that thought has vanished.

Xia Xiqing walks over and finds Zhou Ziheng chopping a tomato. He leans closer. "Do you want any help?"

"No." Zhou Ziheng's lips curl, but he stays focused. "I don't entirely trust your cooking."

Xia Xiqing kicks his leg but Zhou Ziheng just smiles and throws the sliced tomato into a pot.

Xia Xiqing glances at a bowl of cherry tomatoes and throws a few into his mouth. He then walks toward another boiling pot and asks, "What's this?"

"Tomato and fish soup." Zhou Ziheng wipes away the red tomato juice on Xia Xiqing's lips and opens the lid of another pot. Hot steam and the distinct smell of sweet and sour ribs trickles out.

"Mmm, it smells so good..." Xia Xiqing wasn't that hungry before he came, but he is now. "How long before it's ready?"

"It still needs a few minutes." Zhou Ziheng tosses the ribs around a couple times, then covers the pot back up.

"When did you even get the time to learn all this?" Xia Xiqing is very curious, since he knows Zhou Ziheng's acting career started so early.

Zhou Ziheng thinks for a few seconds. "I learned pretty early on. I've always liked cooking and I find it soothing. Besides, there was one time when I had to star as a cook in a show, and I was trained for a month for that. All those cooking scenes were me and not my double."

Amazing; an actor and a cook. Xia Xiqing feels great. He's definitely invested in the right person. He plays with the drawstrings of Zhou Ziheng's hoodie, pulling one out really far. Zhou Ziheng laughs and tells him to stop, but Xia Xiqing doesn't have a particularly obedient nature. The more he's told to stop, the more fun he has playing with the drawstrings.

Zhou Ziheng sighs and gives up on words. Instead, puts an arm around Xia Xiqing's waist and pulls him into an embrace. "Are you done yet?"

Xia Xiqing leans back against the counter, finger still wrapping the drawstring slowly around it, loop by loop all the way up to Zhou Ziheng's neck, at which point he tweaks the spot right behind Zhou Ziheng's ear, very lightly, as if to tickle.

This is torture via gentleness. Zhou Ziheng catches hold of Xia Xiqing's restless finger. "Do you just enjoy bothering me when I'm busy?"

Classic feline behavior.

Xia Xiqing looks up innocently. "What? No. I'm not trying to bother you."

"You're not?" Zhou Ziheng raises an eyebrow.

Xia Xiqing's chin lifts, and he pulls harshly on Zhou Ziheng's collar, the glint in his eyes sharpening instantaneously from innocent to thuggish. The distance between them shortens so much that their lips almost touch.

"How am I bothering you when I haven't even kissed you?"

Zhou Ziheng's breath comes out hot. He's defeated. He just wants to kiss him right now. Xia Xiqing pulls back slightly when Zhou Ziheng leans in, pushing him away in laughter.

"This is what it means to be bothersome."

Zhou Ziheng shakes his head slightly, laughing a little. He stirs the soup and watches the vortex in the middle, heartbeat fluttering.

Xia Xiqing leaves the kitchen and finds himself standing in front of a big window wall in the living room. The buildings outside look brighter through this window than they do in his own apartment. What's funny is, a little distance away, there's an enormous back-lit billboard showing a phone commercial featuring Zhou Ziheng.

Amused, he turns to look at the wall upon which the television has been hung, only to find beside it a bunch of unfamiliar photos. He walks closer to examine them. One of them features Zhou Ziheng's younger self in a group photo on the set of some drama or another. Truth be told, Xia Xiqing only became a fan after he saw those basketball photos of Zhou Ziheng, after the kid had been crowned "Walking Hormones." He used to not care about the entertainment industry at all. He still doesn't, and has no real interest in learning about Zhou Ziheng's movies and shows, especially the ones from his childhood.

But...Xia Xiqing approaches the photos on that wall. The little Zhou Ziheng is so cute, almost girlishly so, with big wide eyes and a little pink face. He can only imagine how much attention and hugs Zhou Ziheng must've gotten from relatives and strangers alike.

Time is the devil. Now that cute little kid has become the giant in front of him. But the weird thing is, Xia Xiqing can't shake off the feeling that he knows this kid from somewhere. It's probably just his mind playing tricks on him—all cute kids have similarities in their features, don't they?

Maybe he should catch up on some of Zhou Ziheng's older shows. The little guy is just too adorable. His fingertip brushes against the cute little face in the photos.

"What are you doing?"

Xia Xiqing pulls his hand back, almost shuddering in shock. He turns to face Zhou Ziheng. "Nothing."

He feels caught out, even though he hadn't been doing anything wrong. It's just a tinier past version of Zhou Ziheng. It's just a kiss from Zhou Ziheng. Maybe he understands. Maybe he doesn't.

All the disturbances to his mental and emotional states have the same source. He doesn't want to admit it, but he's no longer only attracted to Zhou Ziheng's character design.

Xia Xiqing looks around, noticing a rather small dining table in a big dining room. The table seems to fit at most six. It's got an azure blue table cloth and has been laid out with simple white porcelain. There's a deep brown vase at its center, in which is a bouquet of artificial white flowers.

No, not just regular artificial flowers. He plucks one out. It's a white origami rose made of specially-treated crepe paper. He sniffs the petals, which smell of roses too. He frowns. The rose seems so strangely familiar.

He vaguely remembers making these when he was little.

When Zhou Ziheng brings over their final course, a salad, he sees Xia Xiqing in the midst of contemplation, holding a paper rose. The scene is quite picturesque.

"What they say is true; you do look beautiful." Zhou Ziheng puts down the plate and sits across from Xia Xiqing. "Only when you don't talk, though."

"Piss off."

The word "beautiful" is almost taboo to Xia Xiqing, specifically when applied to himself, but Zhou Ziheng doesn't know that. He only knows that Xia Xiqing looks beautiful to him. It's not like the word is only supposed to be used by girls.

"I'm trying to compliment you. Why are you being so mean?"

Xia Xiqing rolls his eyes, putting the rose back in its vase. "Wait till we're in bed." He smirks. "You can compliment me all you want then."

Zhou Ziheng lets out a deep laugh. "Sure, no problem."

"Your dining table is too small." Xia Xiqing stretches his arms out, almost touching the edges on both sides. "But I like the decorations. Good taste."

"I had a bigger one, but I live by myself and spend most of my time on set." Zhou Ziheng passes a bowl of tomato and fish soup to Xia Xiqing, along with a napkin. "It felt kinda wasteful, so I changed to a smaller one."

"But you live in such a big apartment. Isn't *that* wasteful?" Xia Xiqing doesn't understand his logic.

"Well, maybe you wanna move in and use up some of this space?" Zhou Ziheng jokes, but instantly worries it might be too much—he wants to treat Xia Xiqing well, not push him away. Xia Xiqing blinks, but before he can form a response, Zhou Ziheng says, "Just kidding. Houses and dining tables feel different, though. Basically, for me, eating by myself is lonely, especially when there are just two plates on such a big table. I feel sad for myself."

Xia Xiqing doesn't know what to say. Zhou Ziheng has literally just described his entire life. That's why he likes to have dinner at Xu Qichen's place, and why he also likes to have dinner with his various dates even when he isn't spending the night with them.

It seems less lonely that way.

He looks down. His soup smells delicious. He takes a sip, tasting the freshness of the fish and the sour-sweetness of the tomatoes. One sip and he already feels warm inside.

Zhou Ziheng looks nervous. "How does it taste?"

Xia Xiqing is quiet. He downs the rest of the tiny bowl in one go, then passes the empty bowl over. "I want another bowl, and a piece of fish, please."

Seeing how happy Zhou Ziheng is to fill his empty bowl and pick out the fish bones for him, he feels a lot of emotions piling up. He rubs his nose and eats a bite of the sweet and sour ribs.

"Don't drink too fast. You might get too full for actual food."

"I'm not a little girl." Xia Xiqing chews on the ribs. "How did you make it crispy? It's not the kind Xu Qichen makes."

"Well, I fried it." Zhou Ziheng hands him a bowl of rice, only to see Xia Xiqing dumping it in his soup. "That's not good for your stomach."

"Well, yeah, if you eat like this every day." Xia Xiqing scoops. "I haven't eaten rice and soup together like this for ages. This is good."

Zhou Ziheng asks, trying not to sound intrusive, "You mean you used to eat a lot when you're little? Your mom..."

"My mom didn't cook, of course. Her hands were destined for art only." Xia Xiqing's tone is cold. "She was collector of oil paintings. I mean, before she fell sick."

He smiles and lifts his hand up to move his finger in a circle over his temple. Zhou Ziheng has no intention of pursuing this further, even if he is curious. He's already pleasantly surprised that Xia Xiqing's opened up about it.

Xia Xiqing pulls the conversation back on track. "When I was in elementary school, my nanny would make fish soup a lot. We lived in Wuhan by the Yangtze River, so we had fish all the time. But I was a picky eater as a kid, so she had to trick me into eating my rice by pouring soup over it. She picked out the fish bones too, then put it in with the rice."

"And?"

"And nothing." Xia Xiqing chews on the rice. "She quit when she had her own kid."

Zhou Ziheng puts a hand on Xia Xiqing's head and strokes his hair. "Whenever you want to eat this, just let me know."

Xia Xiqing grabs Zhou Ziheng's wrist. "I'm not a kid," he warns.

"No, I just meant..." Zhou Ziheng gently touches one side of Xia Xiqing's face with his outstretched hand. "Since I don't like eating alone, and you don't like it either, we could just keep each other company."

He's lying about his intentions, but it's only because he doesn't want to seem too eager. Cats tend to spook in the face of eagerness.

Xia Xiqing lets go of Zhou Ziheng's wrist. He wants to say no, since the implication of them doing couple-like things is odd and boring, but Zhou Ziheng is such a good cook. He might regret it later if he rejects his proposition right away. He needs to leave himself some breathing room.

After a slow dinner, Xia Xiqing offers to clean the dishes since he didn't help with the cooking. He doesn't mention that he's never done this sort of thing; doing the dishes can't be as difficult as cooking.

Zhou Ziheng rejects his offer. "I have a dishwasher," he says. "Besides, an artist's hands shouldn't be used on cleaning plates. It would be a waste."

With great effort, Xia Xiqing suppresses a pleased smile. He has to give it to Zhou Ziheng; the little virgin seems to be a natural romantic. It's a shame that Xia Xiqing is a high-level player in this game. But then again, an easy happy ending is just a fairy tale for kids. Dancing with words is one of the perks of being an adult.

The night deepens, and Xia Xiqing makes his excuses, saying that he's due for a shower. But upon stepping out of the aforementioned shower, he finds a pair of new messages:

Moral Role Model: You finished yet? Wanna watch a movie?

Moral Role Model: I bought a projector a long time ago, just tested it.

Xia Xiqing dries his hair with a towel and throws it aside. Before he can type a reply, a call comes in. It's his uncle, to whom he hasn't spoken in ages.

"What is it?" Xia Xiqing has no beef with Xi Hui, his

mother's brother, but he also doesn't owe him any favors. He remembers this uncle of his as a pretty nice guy, so he's willing to give him the metaphorical time-of-day for now.

"Xiqing, it's been a while. I know you don't like small talk, so I'll just cut to the chase. Two things. First, your grandfather hasn't been doing too well lately, and he wants to see you. I think you should go, but it's up to you."

"And the second thing?" Xia Xiqing feels the urge to smoke suddenly overcome him, and he pats himself down for one. It takes him a good once-over before he realizes that he's wearing pajamas—of course he wouldn't have a cigarette in his pajamas.

"Alright. As you know, your mother's Pulito Art Gallery finished renovations last month, so it's ready to reopen. And a couple of days ago, I got an invitation to an event that'll have a bunch of big shots from the relevant circles. The gallery is yours, and you're also more familiar with the artist community than I am, so I think you should go. There'll be plenty of businesspeople too, of course, so you could also scout some potential business partners."

It's a nice speech, seamlessly constructed, which is typical of Xi Hui. But Xia Xiqing is well aware that the only reason he wants him to go is Xia Xiqing's reputation—it certainly saves them cash in the marketing department. Xia Xiqing hates to be used, but he also has mixed feelings about the businesses he's inherited from his mother—or rather, his mother herself. It's a terrible mixture of loathing and pity.

"You know, your mom built Pulito to commemorate your birth."

Yeah, that seems about right. The gallery was even named after him. "*Pulito*" is an Italian word, and it correlates to his personal name, "*qing*"—both words mean "clean; clear." In the end, she also destroyed that place. Almost as if it was destiny.

"Xiqing?"

"I heard you. I'll go, but I make no promises." Xia Xiqing's tone is mild. "You know how artists are; we're the most incompetent people around. Don't count on me for anything."

What seems to be a sigh of relief emerges from the other end. "I'll text you the address. Take care of yourself out there." Xi Hui pauses, then emphasizes, "Really, there's shady dealings going on in the entertainment industry. You should be careful when you hang around those circles."

"Not nearly as shady as the circles I grew up in."

Then he hangs up and completely forgets about replying to Zhou Ziheng. He thinks about Pulito reopening—maybe he should take his paintings there. But then again, what kind of proprietor would that make him? Hanging his own artwork in his own gallery? How gauche.

The thing with people's perception is that they always think the most valuable art comes from the most tormented artists. Who would think a trust-fund baby like him capable of anything decent? It's why he never talks about his family fortune to his fellow artists, and why he never talks about his line of work with the people he hangs out with. Mixing the two just feels cheap.

He digs around and finally finds a pack of "Marlboro fusion blast 5" stuck under the seat of his sofa. He stares at it, pretty sure it's the one he got from Xia Zhixu the last time that guy was forced to quit smoking. It's not his favorite, but it'll have to do for satisfying his current craving. It'll be like a dessert. He lights one up, and only has the chance to take one draw through the thin cigarette before his phone starts to ring. Seeing that it's Zhou Ziheng, he finally remembers that he never responded to those messages.

The cigarette has two flavor beads inside. He crushes the outer one and revels in the burst of mint that suffuses his respiratory tract. He leaves the other one, peach flavored, alone for now. Just the mint makes him feel like his head is buzzing, as if someone just pulled on all of his nerve endings. Immediately afterward, he feels himself loosening, relaxing so completely that it feels like his pores have opened.

"Hey."

Zhou Ziheng finds Xia Xiqing's voice softer than usual. He clears his throat. "Have you finished your shower yet? What're you doing right now?"

"Getting high."

"..."

"I'm joking," Xia Xiqing laughs lazily. He sinks into his sofa, then remembers Zhou Ziheng's invitation. He's not really interested in a movie right now. Something else, maybe.

"I'll pass on the movie, but do you have any of your old TV series? I want to watch those."

Zhou Ziheng coughs, startled. "Why those? They're not even good..."

"But I want to watch them." Xia Xiqing puffs out a smoke circle. He tries to grab it, only to have the pale smoke slip through his fingers.

It seems like a century passes before Zhou Ziheng admits defeat. When Xia Xiqing shows up at Zhou Ziheng's doorstep in the slippers he bought for him and a cigarette between his lips, Zhou Ziheng opens the door looking a bit ill at ease. Xia Xiqing puts on a wider grin and runs a hand over Zhou Ziheng's ear, giving it a gentle tweak.

"I'm ready to see a mini Zhou Ziheng!"

"Shut up."

What Xia Xiqing didn't realize is that the projector is in Zhou Ziheng's bedroom. If it had been anyone else asking, Xia Xiqing would probably assume ulterior motives. But since it's Zhou Ziheng, it's probably exactly what he said it would be—watching a movie together.

His bed faces a big white wall. Zhou Ziheng brings out an old box with a few hard drives in it.

"I've never even watched them myself." Zhou Ziheng sounds like a bullied little kid.

Xia Xiqing squats with him and pats his head. "Come on, it's perfect. We can both rewind the wheels of time and see your cute little face."

It's only when Zhou Ziheng looks darkly at him that Xia Xiqing takes the hint and shuts up. He quickly climbs into bed.

"Is it okay to turn off the light?" Zhou Ziheng looks at the dim glow of the projector, worried.

"Yeah, it's okay." Xia Xiqing seems calm.

The darkness sneaks in. The projector casts colorful and flowing shadows on Zhou Ziheng's body, making Xia Xiqing's heart flutter a little.

If only that body could be his canvas...

Zhou Ziheng sits with him on the other side of the bed.

"Why invite me over?" Xia Xiqing turns his head, studying the way light glances off of Zhou Ziheng's eyelashes.

"Once I start filming, I won't have much free time anymore. I found a foreign film whose protagonist has AIDS. I want to learn more, but watching it alone is just depressing." Zhou Ziheng leans back. "Watching with you helps."

He's rambling a little. The truth is far simpler—he just wants to spend more time with him.

Xia Xiqing nods. A little kid has just appeared on the

screen. He laughs almost instantly. "When was this?"

Zhou Ziheng squints. "Six, I think. It was my first year acting."

"Aww, cute." Xia Xiqing stares at Zhou Ziheng, then looks back to the kid, trying to spot all the similarities between them.

Embarrassed, Zhou Ziheng turns Xia Xiqing's head away from his face. "Just watch your show, will you?"

"You mean, your show." Xia Xiqing grins.

Zhou Ziheng thinks he smells fruit, which is not what he expects from Xia Xiqing. "Did you change your shampoo or something?"

"No." Xia Xiqing quickly realizes what he means. "It's my cigarette, probably." His eyes haven't moved away from the kid on the screen, who's running upstairs yelling "Gege! Gege!" in excited abandon. He likes mini-Zhou Ziheng.

"You're saying that the peachy smell is coming from a cigarette?"

Zhou Ziheng, the world's most sheltered man. Xia Xiqing plucks the cigarette from between his lips and hands it to him. "Wanna try?"

"I don't smoke."

"Pah." Xia Xiqing's attention is back on the real Zhou Ziheng next to him. "What a goody-two-shoes."

He's always had a habit of teasing people like that. He likes to corrupt the well-behaved.

"I don't like addictive things. They're usually bad for your body, too," Zhou Ziheng explains, to which Xia Xiqing responds by pressing his shoulders into the mattress and straddling him.

Xia Xiqing takes the cigarette out of his mouth and puffs a smoke ring into Zhou Ziheng's frowning face. Then, holding Zhou Ziheng still, he leans in and kisses him. The fruity smoke passes into Zhou Ziheng's mouth.

Peach, mint, cigarette.

"Look me in the eyes and say it again."

Their lips rub against one another with palpable desire.

"Do you like addictive things?"

Do you like it or not?

He doesn't get a verbal response from Zhou Ziheng, only a physical one. Zhou Ziheng's arms tighten around his back, and his chest heaves as they resume their aggressive kissing.

Xia Xiqing likes being needed; he just needs to feel that with his senses. But he's afraid of Zhou Ziheng actually saying it aloud.

To him, everything falls at its peak. The realization of one's love is the peak, and it only has one direction to go. Like a projectile, the higher the peak, the harder the fall.

Now is good; he needs it. He needs Zhou Ziheng, just like Zhou Ziheng needs him. He doesn't care if they can't define their relationship.

Zhou Ziheng doesn't kiss with skill, just pure instinct wrapped in hot breath, but it makes Xia Xiqing feel like a reaper is coming for his soul.

Zhou Ziheng can't say his feelings out loud, he can only show them using his body. He used to have a rule to stay clear of anything addictive, whether it's cigarettes or alcohol; he likes to be self-aware at all times.

But then Xia Xiqing pierced through his defenses. He knew from the beginning that he was dealing with a liar, that he was handling dangerous goods. He knew that better than anyone else. He had to constantly remind himself to stay away.

"You hot?" Xia Xiqing's voice is misty and deep. His

fingers draw on the end of Zhou Ziheng's hoodie, pulling it up. "Wanna take it off?"

Zhou Ziheng closes the distance between them with a kiss, then takes off his hoodie on his own. The breaking point between two men is always unpredictable. He's fully aware of Xia Xiqing's expectations of him, but it's too bad.

Even if he's the one who got seduced into this...he's going to be the winner.

Xia Xiqing feels his senses burning away as he's kissed so intensively, his skin is slick with sweat. His consciousness and his body seem to not agree with each other—the more heat his body feels, the looser his mind is, tamed like a clingy kitten.

Zhou Ziheng finds a chance to roll them over and reverse the pin Xia Xiqing had on him. A drop of sweat falls down from his face to the corner of Xia Xiqing's lips, and Xia Xiqing just smiles at him and licks it away.

"Salty."

But you're too sweet. Zhou Ziheng's mind completely gives up.

The projector is still on. Xia Xiqing doesn't forget to tease him as they hear the kid's voice in the show. "Well, this... is not at all... PG..." The rest of his words are swallowed shakily with his next indrawn breath. This is actually a very interesting experience, hearing the kid's voice while making out with the adult version of that child.

Zhou Ziheng licks at those swollen red lips. Simultaneously, the kid in the show says "Gege!" in a rather loud voice. Xia Xiqing laughs.

"Gege," Xia Xiqing imitates. He smooths Zhou Ziheng's furrowed brow. Zhou Ziheng bites him hard, feeling his pride wounded.

"You were such a nice kid... Why are you so angry?" Xia Xiqing kisses him, amiably. "You should say that again... Let me hear the difference...between the way you used to say it... and now..."

Xia Xiqing is only joking—he knows Zhou Ziheng has a thing against fulfilling this wish of his. But to his surprise, Zhou Ziheng leans in against his ear, voice low and deep, and complies.

"Gege." Another kiss on Xia Xiqing's earlobe. "Are you satisfied, Xiqing-gege?"

Xia Xiqing can hear the bell ringing in the Florence Cathedral, pounding on his soul and crushing it until every bit of it returns to the cosmos.

The afternoon audition already drained Xia Xiqing of all his strength. No matter how he coaxes him, Zhou Ziheng refuses to let him get his way. Eventually, after who knows how much back-and-forth, he passes out.

He's not in deep sleep, but can't seem to wake up either. He feels someone touching his forehead and his cheeks, so lightly that he can't tell if it's an illusion or if it's real. He wakes up in the early morning in dire thirst, whereupon he goes to the kitchen to get a bottle of iced water.

Summer is so close, but the nighttime draft is still chilly. He walks back to the room, realizing the projector is still playing in silence.

He thinks he should go home. After all, this isn't his place.

Xia Xiqing squats beside the bed, watching the sleeping person's side profile. He lays a finger on his hand first, and after seeing that Zhou Ziheng is indeed still asleep, he grabs his hand. Zhou Ziheng's fingers are long and his palm is wide and dry.

Like playing with a puppy's paws, he spreads out his fingers one by one and puts his own fingers in between them, locking them together.

If only he existed for Xia Xiqing and Xia Xiqing alone...

I built this gallery for you; did you know that?

The image of his mother having a breakdown in the gallery invades his mind. Unease makes him let go of Zhou Ziheng's hand.

When he looks down, he sees a pen on the floor—it's probably what Zhou Ziheng uses to take notes.

Xia Xiqing never believed he'd ever be truly loved. They love his pretty face, they love his talent, they love his family's fortune. But underneath all that, the his bitter true self scares them all away. He's a self-centered materialist, a two-faced compulsive liar, a notoriously flighty playboy.

He used to find Zhou Ziheng stupid for not wanting him. He's always been wanted so much by everyone else. But at this point, no matter how much he doesn't want to admit it, he knows the truth now—he's the one who's not good enough for Zhou Ziheng.

The next afternoon, Zhou Ziheng is woken up by a series of calls from Jiang Yin. He totally forgot that he still has a commercial to shoot. His head is dizzy from last night's dreams. It could be because he watched his old shows, but he was dreaming all night about his childhood, remembering that little *jiejie*[8] who gave him a white origami rose.

Every time he looked up, the girl would disappear. He'd run around in the park and search for her, but he was mute

---

8 "Jie(jie)" is an honorific title or suffix that is used any girl or woman of the same nominal generation as the speaker, occasionally even for those who are slightly younger than the speaker, especially if they have some other form of seniority over the speaker. Literally, it means "older sister," but it is used regardless of familial relation and also sometimes regardless of relative age.

and he couldn't call out for her.

Then he heard the sound of his own name, and turned to see Xia Xiqing holding a dark red rose and smiling at him. He approached, but the rose instantly withered. Xia Xiqing's face looked sad, but he didn't cry.

You don't like me, do you?

At that, he opened his eyes in a cold sweat. He's been left alone in the bed, and the projector is off. His sleeping self couldn't have asked Xia Xiqing to stay, so Xia Xiqing being gone doesn't come as a surprise to him.

He always prepares himself for the worst.

"Okay, I'll head over immediately." Zhou Ziheng sits up, but he slouches, head hanging listlessly. "No, I wasn't drinking. Just tired. I went to sleep a little late last night."

As he puts the phone on his knees, he notices something on his ring finger on the patch of skin right above his palm. He squints, then brings his palm closer to his face.

It's a drawing done in black ink. A tiny rose, growing at the base of his finger.

He laughs slightly. Jiang Yin asks after him from the other end of the call.

"It's nothing."

Just a cute trick that brings him joy.

He has piles of work to do before he goes to shoot the new movie. Magazines, commercials... He needs to get everything done before he can focus on his new role.

Unlike Xia Xiqing, who has all the time in the world.

In the end, after a private meeting with Director Kun, Xia Xiqing agrees to take up the role. The director said something during that meeting that reminded Xia Xiqing of the show in which Zhou Ziheng had debuted, which he'd seen that night he was over at his place a couple days ago.

In this world where everything is uncertain, the one thing that lingers is the work we do. Being yourself an artist, I'm sure you understand what I'm trying to get at.

Over the past two days, he realized that he needs something to tell their story to the world. The world might not understand, but he and Zhou Ziheng will always remember this as a product of their entanglement—and that's enough for him. He doesn't want to be forgotten. Even if the mention of this movie disgusts Zhou Ziheng someday, he'll still feel like he achieved something.

"You free tonight?" Xia Xiqing sends Zhou Ziheng a voice message on his way home.

"I have an event, so I'll be getting home pretty late."

Xia Xiqing sends him an "okay" in regular text. He was originally thinking of asking Zhou Ziheng to go with him to that art event tonight, but now he thinks that's a bit too naïve. With Zhou Ziheng's status, it's probably better that he stays away from private events—especially as anyone's plus-one. Honestly, what was he even thinking?

Zhou Ziheng sends him a text response.

Moral Role Model: Do you have plans tonight?

Terrorist: Yeah, an event. I'll probably also get home pretty late.

Xia Xiqing isn't very detailed in his explanation, and Zhou Ziheng doesn't get a chance to press him for more. Xiao-Luo rushes him into the car, so he has to put his phone away.

The art event is hosted by a prestigious collector: a man named Zhong Henan, who's quite well-known in relevant circles. The venue is his own estate, but for all that the event has been held in his name, Mr. Zhong is nearly ninety years old. In reality, everything has been organized by his son, Zhong Chi, and he's invited many renowned collectors and well-known artists. Unlike his father, Chi is very business-minded, so a good number of businessmen are also present.

If there hadn't been businesspeople there, Xia Xiqing might have wanted to go. It's no small deal for an art salon like this to be held in China, but now the elegance of it has been utterly tainted by the scent of money. Xia Xiqing is similarly less inclined to enjoy himself.

But he's got a competitive nature, and since he's going he'll need to impress—else, it'll be his own people he's letting down. With the good name of Pulito at risk, he picks out a tailored gray suit and navy tie. He also ties his hair half-up, making himself look a bit less casual than usual.

When he's asked to show his invitation at the gate, it seems all eyes are on him; like they know him personally. Nowadays, he knows more and more of the difficulties of being a celebrity. It feels like he's a peacock at the zoo.

The grand hall looks nearly fantastical. Paintings fill the walls, with decorative lilies in between each piece. A few circles of people have formed, all chatting about artwork. To be honest, this part is Xia Xiqing's least favorite of being an artist—the part where they over-analyze each other's work.

He's not that familiar a face in these circles, having been abroad this whole time, and it gives him the space he needs. A pretty lady musters up the courage to approach him for a chat.

"So you prefer oil paintings, huh?"

Xia Xiqing smiles at her, but his gaze passes her to fall onto a young man standing not too far away. He's not really his type, but the guy keeps peeping at him as if he wouldn't notice. He wonders where the confidence comes from.

"Yes, oil paintings." Xia Xiqing loosens his tie a bit. "Ah, excuse me. I think I'm in need of the beverage table."

He walks over to that area, picking up and sipping at a drink. Suddenly, he hears someone call his name and turns his head. It's a guy in a velvet suit who looks vaguely familiar.

"Hey, you're Xia Xiqing, right?" The man raises his hand in an overly familiar manner. "I'm Wei Min."

He can't remember faces too well, but this time he scrounges it up from his memory banks. It's that rich guy he saw outside Xia Xiuze's birthday party, the investor for Director Kun's film. Xia Xiqing turns, but before he does anything, he sees the young man who's been peeping at him startle and turn around.

What's happening today? Why are all these weirdos here?

What he doesn't know is, the young man who just turned around is typing a message.

Zhao Ke: Heng-ge, guess who I just saw here!

Zhao Ke: Never mind I'll just tell you.

Zhao Ke: It's your pairing!

An hour ago, Zhou Ziheng and Zhao Ke were chatting, and Zhao Ke wanted him to come to this party.

"I mean, I've heard lots of artists are going." He sounded super excited over the phone. "There could be some beautiful lady artists."

That reminded Zhou Ziheng of a very particular artist he knew.

"Since when were you into artists?" Zhou Ziheng had his headphones on, eyes closed for his makeup. He's attending a foreign and domestic indie movie conference tonight, and would be the youngest actor there amongst a crowd of older and more acclaimed actors. It was a pretty big deal for him.

Zhao Ke teased, "Well, if you have to ask... I saw your ship with Xia Xiqing on the trending list a few days ago, so I dug deeper into the guy. There's just something about him; I figure it might be an artist thing, you know? I dunno, like in the way they carry themselves. Anyways, he really does look prettier than most girls, even. Actually, does he have any sisters? Do they look like him? Can you introduce me?"

Zhou Ziheng frowned. "You can fuck right off."

"Just kidding. I just wish there was a girl version of him..." Zhao Ke changed the subject. "Hey, I don't think you've mentioned your childhood crush at all lately. Something's off. Are you okay?"

Having been accurately targeted, Zhou Ziheng felt a bit defensive. "Why would I mention her...?"

"No, but really. I haven't heard anything about her for a long time," Zhao Ke teased. "Wait, are you into someone else now?" Getting no response from Zhou Ziheng, he asked, "Hey... You still there? Are you okay?"

It was another while before Zhou Ziheng spoke. "Okay, let me ask you something. If you knew that someone's a bit of a liar, a bit manipulative, and a bit prone to abandoning people who get overly attached, and you knew all of this right off the bat, do you think you could eventually learn to like this person?"

"What kind of 'like' do you mean?" Zhao Ke knew that Zhou Ziheng liked girls, but from the description of things, he thought that this might be about a guy—a friend, maybe. "You mean those typical rich kids who like to party and all that? It doesn't mean you can't be friends with them; they make good friends, actually, even though you might not agree with everything else they do."

Zhou Ziheng realized Zhao Ke hadn't quite understood

his question. He wasn't surprised—honestly, he didn't even know why he asked him. He just was lost and helpless in this "relationship" of theirs. The thought of wanting more was driving him crazy.

Why couldn't Xia Xiqing fall in love with him?

Why was this crazy need growing inside of him?

Zhou Ziheng loses his confidence whenever he thinks about Xia Xiqing's past relationship history; so many others before him who hadn't managed to make Xia Xiqing stay. Why would he be any different this time around? He wasn't special.

He'd lost the war. He was just pretending that he hadn't.

Xia Xiqing would abandon him without hesitation once he knew... If he couldn't escape that ending, then the least he could do was hold on to whatever they had in the moment.

"Yeah, you're right," Zhou Ziheng said absentmindedly.

"But then again, you're such an upstanding guy. You probably don't want to fool around with them anyways. I know your type: kind and amiable, right?"

Zhou Ziheng didn't know what to say. Zhao Ke had just described the opposite of his current life. Not only did he fool around with that kind of person, he also fell in love with them.

"So are you coming or not? We can go together."

"I have a conference. I'm about to get my hair done right now."

The stylist got to work, and thus the call ended.

One hour later, Zhou Ziheng receives Zhao Ke's messages as he sits listening to an Italian director's speech. He's surprised that Zhao Ke's art salon has turned out to be the same thing as Xia Xiqing's art event.

But then again, an art salon sounds right up Xia Xiqing's alley. Now he regrets that he didn't go. He was invited, but he was worried that his profession or his family would draw too much attention to himself. Besides, he has other plans.

He still regrets it.

Zhao Ke's phone beeps.

Heng-Heng: Is he alone?

Zhao Ke: Seems so. He came by himself, but with that face of his, he's got loads of admirers on his ass. He's barely gotten any time to himself.

The last half of the message sets fire to Zhou Ziheng's brain as soon as he sees it. He can almost imagine Xia Xiqing talking and laughing with his admirers.

Only those with a certain appreciation for arts would go to that event. Would Xia Xiqing hit it off with them?

His heart feels all twisted up.

Heng-Heng: Who's there? Anyone I know?

Zhao Ke doesn't over-analyze the question. He glances over the crowd as he types.

Zhao Ke: Most are familiar faces. Zhong Chi invited a lot of rich kids. The cars outside are just unbelievable... And I brought my most low-key one, too. I was afraid I might get reported and cause a scandal for my dad or my brother. Evidently, it's better to be born to money than to politics. Those kids can just drive whatever they want. Ugh.

Zhou Ziheng gets more irritated as the subject veers away from Xia Xiqing. He doesn't know how to ask him to keep an eye on Xia Xiqing without seeming suspicious, but with Zhao Ke's social awareness, he doubts a more circuitous request would get through that thick skull of his.

Heng-Heng: Xia Xiqing is kinda sheltered, you know? He doesn't know much besides art. Can you keep an eye on him? Call me if anything comes up.

Zhao Ke laughs. What could "come up" with Xia Xiqing? Besides, what good would it do to tell Zhou Ziheng about it when he's miles away? He's no Superman. But he knows Zhou Ziheng has always wanted to protect his friends, and Xia Xiqing does fit his description of "sheltered."

Fine, he can be a knight in shining armor tonight, and save the damsel—wait, no, the lad in distress.

Tucking away his phone, Zhao Ke looks up and finds Xia Xiqing gone, along with the guy chatting with him. Zhao Ke panics. He didn't expect his promise to catch him off-guard so quickly.

"Oh fuck, where is he...?" Zhao Ke turns and bumps into a girl in a black velvet dress. He apologizes to her; she looks a little familiar. "Sorry! Sorry! Are you..." His mind goes blank. The name is at the tip of his tongue.

She laughs. "Trust me, it's not just you. I've been having this happen to me all night."

Her voice makes Zhao Ke remember. "You're Ruan Xiao! Am I right?"

On TV, Ruan Xiao's aesthetic was always cute and sweet. Now, with her brown hair dyed black and her lips colored a deep red, she looks completely different to the undiscerning straight-male gaze of Zhao Ke.

"So what brought you here?"

Ruan Xiao gestures to her right. "I came with my father."

Zhao Ke follows her gesture to see a circle of businessmen, and he immediately understands. "You're Ruan Zhengting's daughter?"

She shrugs. "And you're the son of Chief Zhao."

"No, no, no." Zhao Ke is most afraid of that title. Then, he suddenly remembers Zhou Ziheng's request. "Oh right, did you see Xia Xiqing?"

"Xia Xiqing?" Ruan Xiao looks surprised. "The Xia Xiqing I worked with on the show?"

"Yeah." Zhao Ke takes another quick glance over. "I saw him here just now. I don't know. Maybe he got invited because he's an artist? He was just drinking by the tables, but then he got chatted up by a guy in a dark red suit. Now I've lost him."

Ruan Xiao's face turns stern. "Dark red suit. A guy who's our age?"

"Yeah. Nobody else here is dressed nearly as flashy as him. And his cologne! Ugh."

Someone walks by, and Ruan Xiao wraps her arms around Zhao Ke in false intimacy. She lowers her voice and tells him, "You probably don't know him. His name is Wei Min, and he's got a seriously messed up reputation in our circles."

Zhao Ke flushes hotly. He doesn't quite understand what she said. Ruan Xiao drags him into a corner.

"His personal life is really messy—he's into both guys and girls, and he likes to, uh, 'sponsor' celebrities and internet influencers."

This clears things up for him. He frowns. "But...there's nothing he can do if Xia Xiqing rejects him, right?"

"That's what I'm worried about." She looks serious. "He tends to force his way into his 'sponsorships.' I've heard bad things about the guy's methods."

"Fuck; then I need to find Xia Xiqing immediately."

"I'll come with you."

Zhao Ke is a bit of a dolt. He doesn't ask how Ruan Xiao knows him, nor why she's not curious about why he needs to find Xia Xiqing. He just follows her around, searching through the estate, from the gardens outside to the upper floors inside.

Xia Xiqing wants to use his excuse of "getting a cigarette" to leave, but Wei Min won't give up and takes out two cigars.

For all that Xia Xiqing was born into money, he's rarely showed himself at these events due to various family issues. Most people don't know that he's the son of Xia Yunkai.

"Look, you're one talented painter. I saw your work." Wei Min hands him a drink. "And I admire talented people."

All he talks about is paintings; he probably thinks Xia Xiqing got invited because he's a painter. Xia Xiqing shakes his head with a courteous smile, not taking the blue cocktail from his hand.

"So you don't like cocktails; my bad. These ones taste like sugar anyways; awful." He puts down the drink and hands him a cigar. "But you've got to try this. It was privately shipped from the Dominican Republic via jet."

What kind of gaudy expenditure is this? Xia Xiqing doesn't say a word, just keeps smiling. He takes the cigar though, tired of saying no so much. He even lets the guy light it for him.

"I've heard from Director Kun that you're the co-lead in his new movie." Wei Min smiles. "You probably don't know this because you weren't there at the dinner, but I'm one of their sponsors..."

"So?" Xia Xiqing raises his eyes, tempting and contemptuous through the smoke.

Wei Min pauses, not expecting that response. "So, I mean, I don't know if you're free later tonight? I want to set up a mural at home. And I want to know if the great artist, Xia Xiqing, would deign to offer consultation on the prospect." He smiles, slinging an arm over Xia Xiqing's shoulders. "And if you would offer your own handiwork, then I'd be even more honored."

Zhao Ke and Ruan Xiao finally find Xia Xiqing on the third floor, but before they can walk close, they see Wei Min's arm land on Xia Xiqing's shoulder. They look intimate from behind, and Zhao Ke hesitates. Ruan Xiao drags him behind a glass door.

"Why are we hiding?"

"My family is trying to rush me into getting married soon." Ruan Xiao pouts. "I can't be seen with Wei Min. If someone sees us together and thinks that setting us up would be a good idea..."

But aren't we...? Zhao Ke looks at the way Ruan Xiao is grabbing his arm, then decides not to mention anything about it. They've got other priorities. "Look, they're kind of... intimate. Do you think Xia Xiqing might be into that guy?"

"No, can't be. Xiqing's not that kind of guy."

Ruan Xiao watches through the glass door. Still, it's true that Xia Xiqing hasn't pushed Wei Min away yet. She hears the click of a shutter and turns to see Zhao Ke holding up his phone.

"What are you doing?" she asks.

"Zhou Ziheng would want to see this."

"Why's that?" Ruan Xiao asks the most important question.

Zhao Ke blinks. "Yeah, about that..."

Silence falls upon them for two seconds before, simultaneously, they ask, "Do you ship Self-Study?"

Wow. They share a fandom. Ruan Xiao pats Zhao Ke on the shoulder. "Okay. That makes us friends."

Strange developments all around... Zhao Ke's phone vibrates. It's from Zhou Ziheng.

Heng-Heng: What the hell?

Heng-Heng: Who's the guy holding him?

Heng-Heng: Didn't I ask you to keep an eye on him for me?

Zhao Ke types furiously.

Zhao Ke: Hey, I AM keeping an eye out for you. It's just that Xia Xiqing hasn't been forced into it. Am I going to be the guy who comes up and pulls that guy away and yells "Go away, this guy is important to my buddy"? Oh, wait. How is he important to you again? What exactly is he to you?

Zhao Ke's message sends Zhou Ziheng into a daze.

That's right. What exactly is Xia Xiqing to Zhou Ziheng? There isn't really an answer to that question.

It's not like he could do anything even if he were there. If Xia Xiqing wants attention from someone else, who is he to stop that?

Upon getting no reply from Zhou Ziheng, Zhao Ke starts to get nervous. Was he too harsh? It's just that he really doesn't understand why Zhou Ziheng is so concerned about it; Xia Xiqing is a full-grown man who can make his own decisions.

But then, a flash of clarity strikes the chaos of his mind.

Fuck.

Fuck. Fuck. Fuck.

He looks at Ruan Xiao.

"Hey... Do you think maybe our ship might have already sailed?"

The cigar is disgusting.

Or maybe it's the guy in front of him who's disgusting. Xia Xiqing can't take it anymore. He pushes the hand off his shoulder and sticks the cigar in that blue cocktail.

"You can't afford me." Xia Xiqing's voice is cold.

At this rejection, Wei Min's expression twists quite suddenly into anger. But Xia Xiqing truly is his type—he's known that since he saw him at that restaurant. Wei Min doesn't want to just let this opportunity pass him by.

He adjusts his collar. "Mr. Xia, I think you should ask around; figure who exactly I am in the context of Beijing. You don't even know how many people I have to turn down every day. I like you; I want to be your friend. Get rid of that idiotic artist attitude of yours and be a little grateful."

Xia Xiqing laughs coldly. "Friends?"

His expression also cools.

"You're not worthy."

Xia Xiqing turns and walks off the balcony.

Seeing him about to leave, Zhao Ke starts to panic, afraid that he'll be found out, but Ruan Xiao stays calm. She manhandles Zhao Ke by his jacket and turns him around, getting his back to Xia Xiqing and also using his bulk to block herself from sight, pretending to be a trysting couple.

"Should we go?" Ruan Xiao lets go, her gaze following Xia Xiqing. Zhao Ke is unresponsive. She turns, finding him looking quite dazed. "Hey!"

"Yes. Let's go. We need to go. Now. Yes!" Zhao Ke begins to babble, and Ruan Xiao laughs in response.

"Good. Let's go."

Xia Xiqing still feels revolted, to the extent that he feels quite dizzy as he walks downstairs. He saw Ruan Xiao just now; she was with the guy who's been watching him all night. He wanted to say hello, but it looked like she was hiding from him. So he just left, pretending that he didn't see her. He was planning to go to the washroom next, then act like he's seeing her for the first time on his way out. Then he'll just go home after that.

This event is an utter disgrace to the name of art.

Xia Xiqing spots a washroom in a corner of the second floor. He doesn't know if it's the weather or something else, but he feels rather hot.

He goes inside the washroom, but something feels wrong as soon as he closes the door. The nausea has passed. Now he just feels like he's burning everywhere.

He leans back against the door. After a deep breath, he walks to the faucet and splashes some water onto his face. He looks at his flushed neck in the mirror. It feels like someone has set fire to his insides; he can even taste the smoke in his throat. He looks down at his hand to see his fingers shaking.

He's been drugged.

For all that it seems impossible, these aberrations in his behavior can only mean one thing: someone has screwed with him.

When he was abroad for post-secondary, he knew some of his peers would occasionally use drugs like these when they went clubbing. Sometimes it was pills, other times it was liquid; their effects tended to vary wildly. Scumbag though he is, he's never even considered using the stuff—let alone imagined he might ever be on the receiving end of it.

Fuck.

His legs feel shaky. He leans against the counter, chest burning, sweating. He thinks back to that cigar. It must've been in the cigar. He stumbles, feeling boneless. The next moment, he thinks of Zhou Ziheng. He searches in his pocket for his phone, but after he gets it out, he sees there's no signal.

Fuck. Xia Xiqing's back is soaked in sweat. The effects are fully kicking in now. His throat is as dry as a fire.

He's completely lost control.

Ruan Xiao. Look for Ruan Xiao.

Xia Xiqing's fingers grasp at the edges of the counter, barely pulling himself up. After a few more heavy steps, he feels a sharp pain at the back of his neck, then feels as if he's been lifted bodily by two forces on either side of him. He's lost his sense of vision, so he can't be sure what's happening.

In the final moment before he passes out, there is only one thing on his mind.

Zhou Ziheng.

He must've gone insane.

C.13

Heaven and Hell

Ruan Xiao and Zhao Ke see Xia Xiqing walk into the washroom after they follow him downstairs, and they stand a ways away and talk to pass the time. Unexpectedly, after a few minutes, two men in black suits carry Xia Xiqing out by the arms.

"Is this shit really happening under the Zhong family's watch?"

Zhao Ke runs after them, but they get to the elevator first. He immediately decides to descend the stairs in a chase, calling Zhou Ziheng at the same time. Ruan Xiao takes off her heels and runs with him.

"The Zhong family won't do anything about it. I've heard that the two families are planning a real estate collaboration."

"Oh, fuck. Come on. Pick up." Zhao Ke is drowning in nervous sweat. After three attempts, the other side finally picks up.

"Ugh. Finally. Where are you right now?"

"Driving. I'm almost at the Zhong estate."

Not realizing how upset Zhou Ziheng sounds, Zhao Ke starts babbling, "Okay, so, I think Xia Xiqing was sort of kidnapped by two guys. He passed out. I saw him walk into the washroom just fine, but...I don't know what went on in there." Then it occurs to him. "Wait, maybe he was drugged?"

Zhou Ziheng's nerves snap. He presses the accelerator pedal to the floor.

"Block him off!" Zhou Ziheng grits his teeth.

Zhao Ke has never seen his long-time friend behave this way before. He can't ignore Zhou Ziheng's request.

"My driver said they just got into a car and drove away." Ruan Xiao texts the photo she just received to Zhou Ziheng. "I told my driver to follow them. Did you drive here?"

Zhao Ke nods and grabs Ruan Xiao's wrist. "Let's follow that car. Ask your driver to turn on his GPS." He still looks like he's in shock. "I'm afraid Zhou Ziheng might do something dangerous, something irreversible."

"What? No way. Zhou Ziheng..."

Zhao Ke starts the car. "You don't know him." He sees Ruan Xiao's seat belt unfastened, so he quickly rolls over to fasten it for her and passes her his jacket. "I just hope he's not coming with a sniper rifle."

They follow via GPS for a full five minutes before Zhao Ke finally spots Wei Min's car. It's almost eleven at night, and there's just one red race car on the empty roads.

"What should we do now?"

Ruan Xiao says, with a clear mind, "We either cut him off or keep following." She glances over. "Can you confront him? I mean, if something happens, would Chief Zhao...?"

"Ugh. I hate these second-gen rich kids," Zhao Ke curses,

but then realizes that Ruan Xiao is one too. "Sorry. I lose my filter when I get nervous. Present company excluded."

"It's alright. I feel the same way."

As they talk, a black car in the opposite lane pulls a sudden turn and stops on the road, blocking the red race car.

"Fuck." Zhao Ke brakes. Incredulously, he says, "Zhou Ziheng is here."

He's right. A man in a black tuxedo walks out of the car, holding something that looks like a baseball bat in his hand. He slams the door so hard the entire car shudders.

That can only be Zhou Ziheng.

He must be hallucinating, but Zhao Ke could swear that Zhou Ziheng's eyes are balls of fire.

Thumping one foot against the front of the red car, Zhou Ziheng glares at the person sitting inside.

"Open the door."

Wei Min was originally cussing out the black car's driver for being an idiot, but then he realized that it's Zhou Ziheng. Now he's a bit scared. Sure, Zhou Ziheng is kind of untouchable with his family background; he knows that. But what the fuck is his damage? Why does he care?

"What are you doing?" Wei Min pretends to be calm. "You want to make the news, find someone else. Get the fuck away from me!"

Face blank, Zhou Ziheng lifts and points the baseball bat at the windshield.

"Open the door."

"Did you fucking listen to what I…"

Before Wei Min can finish, Zhou Ziheng smashes the windshield. Some shards of glass fly at him and cut through his arm savagely, but he looks like he doesn't even feel it. He walks to the passenger side, raises the bat, and smashes the window there. He then grabs Wei Min's collar and drags his head outside the car, holding his neck just an inch away from the jagged glass edge.

Crazy. This guy must be insane.

Zhao Ke is also shocked. He barely recognizes this version of Zhou Ziheng. He hurriedly unfastens his seatbelt and gets out of his car. "Don't come out. Wait in the car!" he says to Ruan Xiao.

Wei Min is terrified; he's being threatened by someone who's lost his mind. He dares not move a single inch, fearing quite legitimately for his precious neck. Very carefully, he presses the button that unlocks the car doors.

"Okay, okay! It's open! Can you let me go now?"

Zhou Ziheng lets go of him and walks to the back seat, heart thumping. When he sees Xia Xiqing sleeping in the back seat with his shirt torn most of the way open, he feels the last bit of his rationality evaporate.

"Ziheng!" Zhao Ke runs to him, eyes on Xia Xiqing. "Take him away; you'll get caught on video if you hang around any longer. I'll take care of this son of a bitch." He lowers his voice. "Things have been sensitive lately. You can't risk much more scandal."

Zhou Ziheng shoots a glance at Zhao Ke, who trembles; wondering if it's the right decision to let him take Xia Xiqing away.

"Ask him what drug he gave him," Zhou Ziheng says coldly, then carries Xia Xiqing back toward his black Lexus.

The streetlight follows. Zhou Ziheng can see the red flush covering Xia Xiqing's neck and chest, yet he can barely smell any trace of alcohol. The heat radiates past Xia Xiqing's white shirt, casting a heated glow onto Zhou Ziheng. He wants nothing more than to beat Wei Min to death right now.

Morals be damned, he just wants to kill him. Kill everyone who would do this to Xia Xiqing.

He pulls the passenger door open and gently sets Xia Xiqing down. He looks like a fish drowning in air; his chest heaves violently. Zhou Ziheng gets into the driver seat, noticing how shaky his hands are. It's not just because of anger—there's also fear and regret.

What if he hadn't made it in time? What if Zhao Ke never went to the salon?

He can't let himself think of the what ifs.

This must be the fastest he's driven in his life; he feels like he's one second away from exploding.

Zhou Ziheng's phone rings, and he picks it up.

"Zhou Ziheng, he squealed. It's...not simple. I looked it up; the drug is foreign. It's illegal even in the States. It's really strong, and the effects go beyond lost consciousness..." Zhao Ke trails off, but Zhou Ziheng understands him perfectly.

"Is it very harmful to the body?" Zhou Ziheng doesn't notice his lips are trembling.

"There might be lingering effects, it might cause blackouts even after it wears off," Zhao Ke says, also furious. "What's more, this scumbag put it in a cigar. Inhalation means people go under more quickly than if they just took it normally. He must have prepared it long ago—must have other victims in mind. But he saw Xia Xiqing first and he just..."

Zhou Ziheng can't bear to hear any more. Before he hangs up, Zhao Ke says, "Ziheng, there's no antidote. It's probably designed for straight guys who have no experience in...those aspects. You...maybe you can find someone for him and..."

This is an embarrassing topic for Zhao Ke, so he murmurs everything in a low voice, trying to keep Ruan Xiao from hearing. But Zhou Ziheng simply hangs up on him. This has really become such a messy situation...

Xia Xiqing finally wakes up from the blunt pain when they arrive in the parking lot. His vision is still blurry, but he sees Zhou Ziheng's face when he turns his head.

"Zhou Ziheng..."

Something is wrong with his voice. He moans. It's out of his control.

Xia Xiqing comes back to bleary consciousness as Zhou Ziheng drives into the parking garage. He still can't see very well, his vision refusing to focus, but as he turns his head, he sees Zhou Ziheng's side profile.

"Zhou Ziheng..."

His voice is weird: hoarse yet somehow sticky, uncontrollably so. Zhou Ziheng stops the car and catches hold of his hand, then tests his brow for his temperature.

It's really him. It's Zhou Ziheng.

Xia Xiqing huffs a sigh. But soon, his remaining sanity tells him to run so Zhou Ziheng won't see this undignified side of him.

Seeing Xia Xiqing turning his face away, ears unusually red, Zhou Ziheng decides to carry him out of the car.

"You... Let go of me..."

Zhou Ziheng ignores him and walks toward the elevator in large steps. Xia Xiqing pretends to be normal, pushing against his chest with his weak arms.

"Let go."

It feels quiet and narrow in the elevator. Xia Xiqing's breathing sounds extremely distinct, his scent overwhelming Zhou Ziheng just as Zhou Ziheng's scent overwhelms him. Xia Xiqing feels like he's been captured by an indestructible web, and the only part of him that escaped was his desire, like sticky honey dripping through.

But he has nowhere to run.

His eyes are burning in pain. Seeing that they're close to Zhou Ziheng's place, the blunt knife carving at his sanity has touched a spot so deep that he starts to beg.

"I need to go home." His hand clutches Zhou Ziheng's shirt. His voice is shaky. "I...I was drugged... Let me go..."

"I know."

Zhou Ziheng opens the door to his apartment. Without another word, he puts Xia Xiqing down on his sofa. He knows Zhao Ke said all those things for his sake. It's not as if he's never thought of going further with Xia Xiqing—but not like this, never like this. If he does what Zhao Ke suggested, he'd lose his mind in an instant. Too much negative energy has built up in his body, and the thought of Xia Xiqing leaving him torments him day and night. Every touch and every kiss feels like someone is gouging at his heart.

Small beads of sweat appear on Xia Xiqing's forehead. His lips are dry and red, slightly parted. His chest lifting, he lifts a hand to cover his eyes, like he doesn't want to see himself like this.

Zhou Ziheng fetches Xia Xiqing a bottle of water from the fridge. He pries the lid open and passes the bottle to his mouth. "Here, drink this."

Desperately thirsty, Xia Xiqing turns his head, grasping Zhou Ziheng's hand with his burning one. Icy water spills out and washes over his collar. Zhou Ziheng recognizes the shirt Xia Xiqing is wearing as the one he wore when they first met.

Xia Xiqing quickly gulps down the bottle of water. His symptoms are hardly any better, though he's recovered a bit of strength. He attempts to sit up, but his hands slip and he falls off the edge, landing right in Zhou Ziheng's arms. His lips press against Zhou Ziheng's neck.

Like it's a reflex, Xia Xiqing shivers. He violently pushes against the other body, but he lacks strength. He feels like he's dying slowly.

"Let go of me... Zhou Ziheng..." It's like there are two of him in a tug-of-war inside his body. One side has succumbed to lust, and the other side is afraid to be seen by Zhou Ziheng.

"It's okay, Xiqing." Zhou Ziheng kisses Xia Xiqing's brow, circling him with his arms. "I'll think of something. You'll be okay."

The two halves of Xia Xiqing fight over the control of his body. The rope they hold between them is actually a saw, and it starts grinding at his heart.

"It's too hot..."

Xia Xiqing's breaths fall on Zhou Ziheng's chest. As time passes, the side of desire has gained absolute control. His consciousness is fading.

Zhou Ziheng feels the body twitch in his arms like a caged beast. Xia Xiqing whimpers, making all sorts of sounds; some unrecognizable, but others clearly Zhou Ziheng's name. Recklessly, he licks at Zhou Ziheng's throat—from neck to his chin, eventually landing a kiss on his lips and trailing off in a satisfied moan.

"Xiqing, Xiqing..." Zhou Ziheng pulls him away and stands almost cruelly, trying to pull Xia Xiqing up as well. "Let me take you to the shower. You're not yourself right now."

The effects of the drug have reached their peak. Xia Xiqing collapses on the floor, looking like a snake roasting in the sun. He squeezes the fabric of Zhou Ziheng's pants.

"Ziheng, can you..."

"No," Zhou Ziheng answers with certainty, not sure if he's rejecting Xia Xiqing for losing control, or if he's rejecting himself for wanting to take advantage of the situation.

Xia Xiqing lets go. He turns over on his back, eyes half-lidded and fixed on the ceiling. He gasps for air, unable to produce a complete sentence. He truly wants, like he always does, to talk to Zhou Ziheng in his usual indifferent or even scornful tone, but he can't. He feels like he's truly starving; starving so bad that he can no longer be picky about what he must eat to subsist.

"Then I... I'll go find...others... I don't want to...to see you... anyway..."

They can all see this ugly side of me, but you're not allowed.

You've seen too much already, and you're too good.

"I'm going to..." Xia Xiqing sticks a hand into his pocket like he's searching for a phone.

Zhou Ziheng has finally had it. He clutches Xia Xiqing's collar, eyes entirely red, and every word that comes out after seems to be ground through his teeth.

"How *dare* you.

"Xia Xiqing. I've said this before, and I'll say it again. I will kill you if you mess around with other people." Zhou Ziheng has lost control of his trembling hands. The only thing left in his head is Xia Xiqing's earlier words. "You only have me. Do you get it? No matter if you want to see me or not, you only have me."

He has completely lost track of what's pouring from his mouth. The vicious thoughts seem to have taken control of his body, raging and growling in his veins.

"What is there between us?" Xia Xiqing's eyes are red too. He feels stranded, unable to breathe. "Zhou Ziheng... What is there between us?"

The knife is finally going to gouge out his heart.

"Who are you to me...?" Xia Xiqing feels needled. "Weren't we just playing for fun...? Now, I..." His brows furrow. The fire has already burnt him out. "I'm done with you now... Let go of me..."

Play...

"No. Xia Xiqing, I'm the only person you will ever have for the rest of your life."

I love you so much that I don't dare to touch you.

"Look at me." Zhou Ziheng grips his chin. "I don't care who you think I am to you. You are mine."

Hearing this, Xia Xiqing sneers, weak and cruel. "Is that so...?"

All of Zhou Ziheng's morality is shattered by this smile. He closes in and kisses Xia Xiqing like a wild animal tearing up prey. Xia Xiqing has no strength to resist. His bones are almost squashed in Zhou Ziheng's embrace.

This is alright. If he can melt into Zhou Ziheng's skin, his veins, he doesn't need to fight anymore. Neither of them can fight anymore.

Xia Xiqing feels like his soul is being pushed out of his body by the intensity of their kisses, but it's stuck hanging in midair because of the drug. No way in and no way out. Every push from Zhou Ziheng feels vengeful, and he feels the irresistible lust that has invaded him. Every time he breathes out, Zhou Ziheng's name is shaped on his lips.

"Ziheng... Ziheng..."

His hands grab weakly at Zhou Ziheng's chest, his fingers losing dexterity. Xia Xiqing's scratching is torturous. Zhou Ziheng frowns, catching the restless fingers and leading them to his own waist.

"Hold tight." Zhou Ziheng hears his own panting breaths. He lowers his head and kisses Xia Xiqing's neck. Each touch feels like he's dancing with fire. He's standing in between heaven and hell. *Just jump. We can die in each other's arms.*

"Hot... Ziheng... Zhou Ziheng..."

Xia Xiqing's sticky mumbling overcomes what remains of Zhou Ziheng's self-control. He pushes his index and middle fingers into Xia Xiqing's mouth, letting them get thoroughly wet and warm as his right hand unbuttons his shirt. Xia Xiqing's pale skin is stained a lustful red, looking almost juicy as it glistens with sweat.

He leans in, greedily licking and biting at his throat and collarbone, slowly moving all the way down until he reaches his nipples, where he begins to suck.

"Unn..." The fingers make Xia Xiqing unable to moan normally, yet all his sensations feel somehow amplified, unable to be ignored. He shivers, placing his hands on Zhou Ziheng's head. He wants to pinch his neck, but his enervated fingers fumble into an invitation.

Zhou Ziheng raises his head, pulling Xia Xiqing's fingers out. The saliva stretches to Xia Xiqing's chin; his mouth is still parted and the pink tip of his tongue can be vaguely seen. Zhou Ziheng's lips close their distance while pinching his nipples with his wet fingers.

"Emm..."

After Zhou Ziheng releases him from the kiss, Xia Xiqing finally has the chance to breathe. He circles Zhou Ziheng's neck, pushing himself against the man. Two long legs circle Zhou Ziheng's waist.

"I want to do it... Zhou Ziheng..." Xia Xiqing absentmindedly licks at Zhou Ziheng's cheeks as he begs breathlessly, "Stop torturing me..."

Who exactly is torturing who?

Zhou Ziheng props Xia Xiqing's arms around his neck. "Hold on." He pulls Xia Xiqing up by his legs, and the sudden weightlessness doesn't even awaken him. On their way to the bathroom, he keeps licking and kissing Zhou Ziheng's neck and chin, moaning against him, until he's stripped and placed into the bathtub.

The warm water gradually submerges his body.

"Zhou Ziheng... I feel sick..."

When Zhou Ziheng pulls down his pants, he notices that Xia Xiqing has already come once, but doesn't look much better. He might actually look worse.

Zhao Ke was telling the truth. This drug was designed to allow for inexperienced people to be penetrated.

But how can he...

Zhou Ziheng's head's a mess. He takes a small purple bottle from a cabinet. Ever since their first time together, he's been doing his homework online. Even though he knew perfectly well that they might not come to this, he still wanted him to feel good in case it happened.

And now it is.

He squeezes some lubricant into his hand as he walks to the bathtub. He pulls Xia Xiqing up and facing him even as he kisses his lips.

"Xiqing, I..." He hesitates. The lubricant drips slowly from his palm. He's still struggling, but Xia Xiqing seems to have lost himself completely, showing his needs by pressing more tightly against Zhou Ziheng.

Maybe he should just do it. Once is better than nothing.

Zhou Ziheng feels sorry for himself.

"Look at me. Who am I?"

Xia Xiqing clutches onto Zhou Ziheng's belt, voice soft

but anxious. "Zhou Ziheng..."

"You..."

Do you like me?

Are you doing this because you like me?

He grits his teeth, stretching his arms to wrap around Xia Xiqing's waist and make him lean against his shoulder. His lubricated fingers reach for his entrance, but he feels strong resistance as soon as his finger probes into him. Xia Xiqing's lost rationality comes back as if he were experiencing terminal lucidity.

"No! Let me go..."

Fear reverses the flow of his blood, sending it back up to his brain. Xia Xiqing fails to push him away, but Zhou Ziheng backs off the moment he hears a rejection.

"Okay..." Zhou Ziheng strokes down Xia Xiqing's back. "Okay... I won't... I won't..."

But then, hearing that, Xia Xiqing freaks out. He feels terrible right now; he feels like he's dying. "But how can you not do anything... You can't do nothing... I'll die..."

"But you..." Zhou Ziheng cups a hand behind Xia Xiqing's head. "What *should* I do? I'm going crazy here."

The hardships of desire have always been mutual.

Wave after wave of poisonous lust overcomes Xia Xiqing, drowning him in it. He clings to Zhou Ziheng's arms. He's never felt like this before, never felt this urge to be owned. It's strange, but he really wants to hear Zhou Ziheng confess his love to him, just like all those people who've come before him. If only Zhou Ziheng would give him his heart—wouldn't that be nice?

Scenes and pictures flash through his agitated mind. The paper flower in his profile, the paper roses on his dining table, the girl he'd talked about during that drinking game.

All these pieces form a coherent string, and Xia Xiqing feels numb. His heart thumps painfully.

"Do it." Xia Xiqing exhales tiredly against Zhou Ziheng's shoulder. "You can do it...you can put it in."

Zhou Ziheng is stunned.

"Just," Xia Xiqing says, his eyes suddenly welling with tears. He looks down, trying to hide it from Zhou Ziheng. "Just remember who I am."

I'm Xia Xiqing. Not the white rose of your heart.

I can sacrifice myself, but I won't allow myself to be someone else's replacement.

"I know. I know."

Zhou Ziheng presses kisses on Xia Xiqing's neck, sending pleasant shivers through him. With one hand, he circles Xia Xiqing's entrance. With the other, he strokes up and down his spine. Finally, when Xia Xiqing relaxes enough, Zhou Ziheng tries to probe deeper with his fingers. Xia Xiqing is still in great discomfort, but there's no way for him to release the tension, so he bites down on Zhou Ziheng's shoulder.

"Don't be afraid, Xiqing." Zhou Ziheng turns his head to kiss his ear. "I'm here."

Zhou Ziheng's movements are gentle as his fingertips rub and curl inside him, and the initial discomfort has grown into a sense of frightening need. He wants to be with Zhou Ziheng so bad. He doesn't care how. As long as he can have him.

The prep is successful in stretching him out. Zhou Ziheng slips in one more finger and begins to thrust slowly. He worries that Xia Xiqing will catch a cold, so he sets him back into the warm water and wades into the bathtub himself, kneeling while holding up Xia Xiqing's legs. Luckily, Xia Xiqing isn't easily ashamed; he stretches out his arms to hold onto Zhou Ziheng. Zhou Ziheng understands what he wants, so he leans in and kisses his lips as he pushes his fingers in deeper. Probably due to lowered friction and a better angle, it works better this time.

"Mmm... Too fast... Ah..."

"Does it hurt?" Zhou Ziheng's voice slips into Xia Xiqing's ear.

"No. Doesn't hurt... But I'm still..." Xia Xiqing tugs at Zhou Ziheng's belt. "I don't want your hand..."

Zhou Ziheng seals whatever Xia Xiqing wanted to say with a kiss. He unclasps his belt, then undoes his pants. His swollen dick pops out upon its release, jutting against Xia Xiqing's belly. Moaning, Xia Xiqing grabs Zhou Ziheng's dick and gives it a few strokes in his fist. Zhou Ziheng reaches for the bottle of lubricant and squeezes some onto Xia Xiqing's palm.

"Put it on."

Xia Xiqing leans back, head dizzy, his fingers sliding over the hefty shaft and slick head of Zhou Ziheng's cock. The sound of splashing water increases. He grabs the dick, as if ready to force it into himself.

"Come on."

Zhou Ziheng can't endure any more. He wraps a hand around his cock at its base and presses it against Xia Xiqing's hole, but they're both so well-lubricated that his cock slips between his legs instead.

"Quick..." Xia Xiqing grasps his hand. "I need it."

Zhou Ziheng feels an unhealthy sort of satisfaction rising from the bottom of his stomach in response to Xia Xiqing's words. He gives Xia Xiqing a wet kiss with copious tongue as he massages his ass. When Xia Xiqing is fully immersed in the kiss, he feels him open for him, and so he slides into his tight entrance.

"Ah!" Xia Xiqing gasps, and it sounds like he's calling for help. Zhou Ziheng releases him from the kiss and notices his furrowed brow. "Ow... It hurts..."

Zhou Ziheng is too afraid to move. He can only kiss him on the cheek. "I'm sorry, I'm sorry. It's all my fault..."

"Slowly..." Though it hurts, Xia Xiqing doesn't want it to end. He kisses Zhou Ziheng in return. "You're too big."

That was definitely encouragement. Zhou Ziheng seals their mouths in a kiss and props one of Xia Xiqing's legs on his shoulder, hooking the other around his waist.

He starts slow, pushing in and out in a restricted rhythm, grinding as slowly and gently as possible. But after a while, it starts to feels more and more like punishment to Xia Xiqing.

"Faster, faster... Ahh... Ziheng..."

Zhou Ziheng's hips tighten. He pumps faster, harder, deeper, losing control over the force behind his movements. Xia Xiqing bites his lower lip, climbing the cliff of pleasure. The effect of the drug works alongside the rapid thrusting, making Xia Xiqing lose his mind until he has to bite his own lips in order to not make sound. Zhou Ziheng sees and leans in for a kiss.

"If you want to bite someone, bite me."

Xia Xiqing unclenches his teeth and sucks on Zhou Ziheng's lips instead. Even if he's drowning in waves of pleasure, he still won't bite him. Instead, he inhales and exhales in shaky breaths.

Xia Xiqing is finally his, Zhou Ziheng thinks. After all this time, they have finally become whole.

The more Xia Xiqing bites down on his moans, the harder Zhou Ziheng fucks him, splashing through the warm water in the bathtub. As they continue, he sees tears well in his eyes as his abdominal muscles begin to spasm.

"Let me hear it, Xiqing." Zhou Ziheng shoves deeper inside.

"Ah...wait... It's too much...ahh!" Xia Xiqing's fingers curl subconsciously, wanting to hold him. "Ziheng, hold me..."

Zhou Ziheng's arms clutch Xia Xiqing's waist, hauling him in. Xia Xiqing's erection grinds against the fabric of Zhou Ziheng's shirt. Between that sensation and the pleasure of getting fucked, Xia Xiqing feels like he's being tortured with pleasure.

The sound of splashing water echoes in the room, and the temperature rises. The two of them look like two pieces of chocolate melting into one. Xia Xiqing leans back, neck bent and outstretched. Zhou Ziheng sucks on his nipples while thrusting nice and slow, feeling the person in his arms shake.

"I'm...coming... Ziheng... Ziheng!"

The panic in Xia Xiqing's voice only makes Zhou Ziheng go harder, drawing out more shivers from him until he comes on Zhou Ziheng's belly with a cry. Xia Xiqing's head jerks back, and Zhou Ziheng's hand is there to safely catch him, propping him against his shoulder.

Zhou Ziheng moves his hips slightly. When he's about to pull out, Xia Xiqing mumbles a few unrecognizable words and clutches Zhou Ziheng's back. Still, he pulls out and carries Xia Xiqing to the upstairs bedroom. He takes off his soaked clothes, climbs into bed, and cuddles him. The heat on his body hasn't faded yet. Xia Xiqing rubs himself against Zhou Ziheng's thigh.

"Again... Zhou Ziheng..."

"You'll get hurt," Zhou Ziheng says against Xia Xiqing's mouth. "Next time, alright?"

Xia Xiqing shakes his head, eyes filling with tears. He

can't quite produce a full sentence. The incoherent wounded sounds drive Zhou Ziheng mad, and he hugs him from behind as he slides in slowly.

"Ah... so good..." Xia Xiqing's leg is slightly raised as he grinds back against Zhou Ziheng's thrusting hips, each time harder than the last. "I can't... I'll die..."

More absentminded words are drawn out of Xia Xiqing, most incomprehensible. The dominant side of Zhou Ziheng has finally won. He bites down on Xia Xiqing's earlobe, pumping his hips at an unbearably fast pace. "Fucking others or getting fucked by me—which one you like better?"

"Ah! Too deep... Not there... Ah! Aaah!"

"Answer me."

Xia Xiqing turns his head with a kiss. "You fucking me... feels better..."

Satisfied, Zhou Ziheng returns the kiss and wraps his hand around Xia Xiqing's chin. "You can only be mine. Understand?"

Xia Xiqing feels like his mind is being fucked out of his body; he's going to pass out. He repeats Zhou Ziheng's words, sounding like he's begging, "Only... Only yours..."

"You like getting fucked by me?"

Zhou Ziheng is like an unrestrained beast, his hips flush against Xia Xiqing's ass, biting and kissing until Xia Xiqing comes again with loud cries. This time, the fluid that emerges is much clearer, and it drips out much more slowly than previous. He does not release him, though—instead, he flips him over and plunges even deeper. Xia Xiqing bears the storm, tightly clutching Zhou Ziheng's shoulders.

"Ah, ah..." Xia Xiqing's mumbling makes even less sense now, his mind blurred and fried.

The hunger in Zhou Ziheng's body is not lessened. He

thrusts his hips up desperately, feeling like he could thrust through his entire body.

Xia Xiqing has lost all ability to resist, but he really wants to kiss him. He props himself up against the rhythm of the thrusting, but his lips find only Zhou Ziheng's chin. When he tilts in response to an unexpected thrust, his lips brush Zhou Ziheng's ear.

He's definitely dying. He's about to die thanks to him.

Zhou Ziheng's mind is clouded with lust, and he's unable to hear what Xia Xiqing just said. "What did you say? Tell me."

Xia Xiqing pants. "Like...I...like..."

Before the full sentence leaves his mouth, he passes out against Zhou Ziheng's chest. At that moment, Zhou Ziheng climaxes. He couldn't hold back; couldn't pull out. He finishes completely inside Xia Xiqing.

Those two words are too scary. Too heavy. They're enough for his nerves to snap.

Everything that happens after is a blur. Each time Xia Xiqing wakes up, they continue until he's completely drained again. At dawn, Zhou Ziheng hugs him tight, afraid that he'll disappear right before his eyes.

He didn't expect to love him so much; to love him to the point of guilt and regret, to the point of losing himself.

Zhou Ziheng falls into an uneasy sleep. He's been so busy with work lately that he's only been sleeping for three to four hours every night. He's exhausted, to say the least, yet his mind won't let him slide into the deep. He feels like a raft drifting on the sea, unable to come ashore.

He closes his eyes and sees Xia Xiqing's face—his taunting expression, his sly expression, his fragile expression, his desirous expression. Each version flashes by, becoming less and less distinct until they all disappear.

It turns out the raft isn't moving toward the shore, nor even drifting on the sea—instead, it's drifting closer and closer to the precipice of a waterfall. The rapid current washes away his breath, and he falls to the abyss.

When he opens his eyes again, he feels the corners of his eyes slightly cold. Wet. Like the water in his dream.

Xia Xiqing is sleeping beside him, facing him. Zhou Ziheng extends a hand to brush against a lock of hair on his forehead, then his cheek. His heartbeat normalizes. Zhou Ziheng simply watches, neither talking nor touching. His gaze shifts from his brow, his nose, to the contours of his face.

He happens to catch a glimpse of the bruises on his neck: the marks he made last night. He lifts the blanket and sees love bites all over his body—on his neck, his collarbones, his chest, even on his back. There are bruises at Xia Xiqing's waist, too; he'd grasped him too tightly. He recalls that they both lost control last night. By the end, Zhou Ziheng himself had completely succumbed to his lust.

After he tucks Xia Xiqing in, the guilt begins to eat at him. He was not supposed to do that. It was wrong. But his heart breaks into pieces when he thinks about how Xia Xiqing wanted someone else to help instead of him. He didn't intend to get so angry; he tried to control it, but he seems to always lose his mind when it comes to Xia Xiqing.

When they fell into the bed together, exhausted, he even wished that the world would end. It was the only way he could be sure that Xia Xiqing wouldn't leave him and that they would die together.

Just horrible.

He raises a finger and gently brushes Xia Xiqing's hand.

Xia Xiqing will probably be very angry when he wakes up, considering how proud he is as a person. Maybe this is truly the end for them.

Zhou Ziheng... What is there between us?

Weren't we just playing for fun?

I'm done with you now.

He's not capable of guessing how Xia Xiqing felt when he said those words, but surely, his sentiments were similar to his scorn for his past admirers. They've probably all heard these words; maybe even something worse.

Zhou Ziheng extends a finger, poking the tiny mole at the tip of Xia Xiqing's nose. He leans in to kiss his forehead.

Why is he obsessed with someone so cruel?

Xia Xiqing doesn't know how long he's slept, but when he wakes up, his head screams at him. The view isn't as bright as he thought it'd be. Though his consciousness hasn't fully returned to his body, his first instinct is to reach out.

But there's no one else there; it's just him.

Xia Xiqing scoffs at himself. What was he thinking? What else did he expect? It was only sex; he only got fucked by Zhou Ziheng. Beyond their shared physicality, what else could there have been?

He changes into a clean set of clothes. The bed doesn't seem too messy, but Xia Xiqing just feels sad. Should he be grateful that the person last night was Zhou Ziheng? At least his heart is kind and pure, and he cares about him enough to not embarrass him.

Feeling thirsty, he pulls himself up. His joints crack, and he's sore all over. He looks down and sees his chest covered with bruises. He can't even bring himself up to remember that night. Zhou Ziheng became a different person.

He just kept repeating that one sentence: *You only have me.*

But that's just untrue. If he wanted, he could have so many other people. He could have so many; could have countless numbers of people.

His headache worsens. He wants to go home. The bed smells like Zhou Ziheng, making him dizzy. He pulls himself up into a painful seated position, his legs quivering.

He still can't believe that he got fucked by another guy, and that he begged for it. His self-esteem is crushed by the weight of this knowledge. He doesn't want to remember the events of that night; he was so disgustingly weak.

After taking a long moment to calm himself, he leans against the wall and slowly makes his body move downstairs. Every step takes effort. He mentally curses Zhou Ziheng.

Fuck. Twenty-year-olds are too fucking eager; Zhou Ziheng definitely had too much energy. Xia Xiqing seems to have completely forgotten that he'd been the one begging him to continue.

He tries to not let his expectations grow, but he still wonders if Zhou Ziheng is downstairs—maybe sitting on the sofa or something. He wonders how he'll face him. He doesn't want to look like some girl who just survived an assault; he needs to toughen up.

But Zhou Ziheng is nowhere to be found. Xia Xiqing sees the clothes he wore last night folded neatly on the sofa, and a glass of previously heated milk that has since cooled.

Come on, he's a celebrity. This is more than kind. Be more grateful, he tells himself.

After a simple clean-up in the bathroom, he walks out and sits on the sofa, wondering why he wasn't even left with a note this time. He also understands that Zhou Ziheng hasn't always been into guys. Maybe now that he's properly tried it out, he decided that he really is straight after all.

He puts his clothes back on slowly. They've been washed and left with the scent of grapefruit detergent.

He's so thirsty. He lays his pajamas over the armrest of the sofa and tastes the milk, readying himself to go home. Except why does he feel so aggrieved?

Xia Xiqing doesn't realize this change of attitude. If he was still his old self, he'd surely be plotting to kill the son of a bitch who did this to him, but all he can think of right now is Zhou Ziheng. Even as he wonders where he's gone, he feels trepidation at the thought of seeing him again.

The muscles on his back and waist hurt so much that he can't bend over for his shoes—he has to sit for them. Staring at the slippers, he feels more uncomfortable. He just wants to leave this place that Zhou Ziheng lives in and go drinking with...with other people...

The image of an angry Zhou Ziheng floats to the forefront of his mind.

Xia Xiqing exhales and places a hand on the doorknob. Suddenly, the door opens from the outside, and he's stunned to see Zhou Ziheng standing in front of him.

Zhou Ziheng is wearing all black; a black T-shirt and black jeans, black baseball hat and black mask. He even has a black sleeve on his right arm, like the type worn as protection for some sports. His face looks cold, slightly hostile— probably due to the outfit.

There are two shopping bags hanging from his arms. His eyes light up with happy surprise when he sees Xia Xiqing, but they quickly dim again. Zhou Ziheng lowers his masked face.

"Won't you eat before you go? It won't take long."

Despite saying that, Zhou Ziheng doesn't close the door. If

Xia Xiqing wants to leave, he won't stop him.

Seeing Zhou Ziheng walk through the door, Xia Xiqing spaces out for a second. So he only left to go to the grocery store?

Xia Xiqing stands there, not sure what he was about to do. Hearing Zhou Ziheng putting away the groceries, he shuts the open door before he even realizes what he's doing.

The door slams loudly, and the sound startles Xia Xiqing. It's too late to change his decision now. He walks into the living room nonchalantly, and before he can sit, Zhou Ziheng walks toward him holding something in his hand.

"What's that?"

Perhaps he shouldn't have spoken. His voice sounds wrecked. Zhou Ziheng circles behind him and begins to untuck his white shirt from his waistband.

"Hey! What are you..."

Xia Xiqing feels two medicated patches smoothed against his waist. Zhou Ziheng then lets go of his shirt.

"You drank the milk."

Zhou Ziheng's eyebrows furrow. The milk must've gone cold while he was out; knowing Xia Xiqing, he probably drank it cold without reheating it. However, Xia Xiqing misinterprets his comment, thinking maybe he wasn't supposed to drink it at all.

So he insists, "No."

"Really?"

Zhou Ziheng swipes a finger through the trace of milk that remains around Xia Xiqing's lips, then walks silently to the kitchen. Xia Xiqing wipes his lips clean with the back of his hand, his heartbeat quickening. He's not sure why, but he feels there's something off about Zhou Ziheng.

The medicated patches at his waist start to heat up,

working their magic on his muscles. Just as Xia Xiqing is about to head into the kitchen, his phone chimes. He opens his WeChat and finds a friend request. Their profile image is the character *ke,* made using matchsticks. Xia Xiqing doesn't think he knows anyone with that character in their name.

There are a bunch of missed phone calls as well. Some are from Xia Xiuze and Xu Qichen, and at least four from an unknown number. He checks the number; it matches the WeChat friend request.

Who is this guy? Why is he looking for him?

Xia Xiqing isn't bothered enough to overthink it. Instead, he just puts his phone away and heads into the dining room, sitting down at the tiny dining table. He looks at the bouquet of origami roses.

They're not real roses. They're not alive, so neither will they ever fade or wither. Always blooming in his heart, always in beautiful florescence.

Xia Xiqing stands suddenly and calls toward the kitchen to Zhou Ziheng, "I'm not hungry right now. I'll be off."

Zhou Ziheng walks out, hovering at the door. He still has his mask on, which is a bit eccentric. His voice is frosty as he says, "You were unconscious for two days. You need to eat something."

How is that your business? Xia Xiqing frowns and opens his mouth, but the words don't come out. They're too harsh; he can't say something like that when he's awake and coherent. Besides, Zhou Ziheng doesn't look like he's in the mood to argue.

He returns to the table. A message from Ruan Xiao comes in.

Ruan Xiao: Xiqing, are you awake?

Ruan Xiao: Are you feeling better now? We're all worried about you.

Ruan Xiao: Also, the guy who was with me that night we rescued you is Zhou Ziheng's childhood friend. He wanted to ask you about something. You should add him on WeChat.

Ah, mystery solved—it's that guy who kept watching him during the salon. Xia Xiqing accepts his friend request, and a message pops up.

Zhao Ke: Xia Xiqing, you're awake? Are you okay?

Xia Xiqing: More or less. Thank you for helping out that night.

Zhao Ke: No worries. Have you seen Heng-Heng? Did he contact you?

Heng-Heng? How intimate. A little girl to crush on, and a long-time best friend. What a happy childhood. Xia Xiqing walks blithely to the kitchen and takes a picture of Zhou Ziheng to send to Zhao Ke.

Xia Xiqing: Your Heng-Heng is making me dinner.

What kind of malicious PDA is this? Zhao Ke is a little indignant that Xia Xiqing feels the need to show off their domestic relationship. *But I ship Self-Study*, he cries to himself. Immediately after, he screenshots his conversation with Xia Xiqing and sends it to Ruan Xiao. After all, as fellow Self-Study shippers, it's only polite to share content.

Xia Xiqing is kind of exasperated. Why does this guy have to go through him to find his "Heng-Heng"? They're obviously close enough that he has Zhou Ziheng's contact information. At this thought, he becomes a bit sullen. He backs out of the conversation, then notices the entry for his conversation with Zhou Ziheng in the chat menu .

He taps Zhou Ziheng's profile picture and looks at that little paper rose.

Being upset is a vicious cycle. Xia Xiqing turns off

WeChat, hoping to remove any more triggers for potentially upsetting thoughts. He returns to the table and covers the paper flowers with a blue napkin that he pulls from under an adjacent place setting.

Zhou Ziheng comes out with a plate of pesto spaghetti and spots the covered flowers instantly. He sets the plate in front of Xia Xiqing, sits in the seat across from him, then reaches forward to lift the napkin. Before Xia Xiqing can protest, he pulls the bouquet out and throws the paper roses into a nearby garbage bin. Xia Xiqing sits, unmoving. This is the last thing he expected Zhou Ziheng to do.

"Hey... What did you just do...?"

Zhou Ziheng walks back to the kitchen, returns with salad and juice, then sits again.

"You don't like them, so I threw them out."

But don't you like them? Xia Xiqing doesn't get it. He thought those flowers were special to Zhou Ziheng. "But you had those paper flowers specially made, no? And your profile picture... Why would you just throw them away?"

Xia Xiqing moves to fetch the flowers from their ignoble fate, but Zhou Ziheng stops them.

"I made each and every one of them. But now I feel like they've lost their meaning."

Why? Perplexed, Xia Xiqing sits back awkwardly.

What he doesn't know is that Zhou Ziheng remembers everything Xia Xiqing said during that night, including *"Remember who I am."*

Zhou Ziheng immediately understood that Xia Xiqing must think he considers him a substitute for that girl from so long ago. It's a bit shameful to think about, but his feelings really have wavered. Now, the only person for whom he has feelings is Xia Xiqing. Even though he lacks the courage to verbally express this fact, he also can't just stand by and watch Xia Xiqing continue to harbor this misconception.

"You should eat. You must be starving."

Xia Xiqing notices that he's been keeping his head down. "Why are you still wearing your hat and mask? Aren't you hot?" To ease the tension, he tries to joke. "Hey, don't tell me you're embarrassed. Was it you or me getting dicked down that night? Look, I'm not even being awkward about it! What excuse have you got?"

Zhou Ziheng takes off his mask, but his gaze remains fixed on the table before him.

"Or are you feeling bad about it?" Xia Xiqing asks dubiously.

There's no reason for Zhou Ziheng to feel sorry. For all that the resulting dynamic between them wasn't quite how he'd previously expected things would pan out, Zhou Ziheng still got his explicit verbal consent before doing anything.

He forces out a dry laugh. "Don't act like I'm like some poor girl you took advantage of. Sure, I was drugged, but we were both willing and you were trying to help me. I might be a jerk, but I'm a reasonable one.

"Besides, we're both guys. I promise I won't hold you at gunpoint and ask you to take responsibility." He twirls the spaghetti onto his fork. "If you really feel bad about it, just let me return the favor next time. Anyway, this has always been our arrangement, right?"

Yeah. This was always the arrangement. Saying it aloud makes him feel lighter, as if it was some burden that he'd been carrying. Besides, it's really not his style to feel embarrassed after sex.

Zhou Ziheng finally looks up, wearing a conflicted expression. He seems to want to say something, but he never does.

Xia Xiqing realizes that a corner of Zhou Ziheng's mouth is bruised, like he's been in a fight. "Hey, what happened to your face?"

Zhou Ziheng remains unresponsive. He glances down at his watch. Head still lowered, he says, "Eat first. And eat lots." He fetches the shopping bags and starts unpacking. "This is for the bruising, apply twice a day. This is for the swelling down there. I've been applying it for you these past couple days, but you should keep using it for at least two more days.

"The drug that bastard gave you has side effects. You slept for two days straight, and you haven't eaten all throughout. You're probably fairly weak right now, so you'll need these vitamins and supplements—take them home with you. I know you'll probably ignore this next bit, but I still have to say it: you should stay away from spicy food for these next couple days, and you shouldn't even think about drinking or smoking. I'm not sure if the drug has left your system completely, so the side effects may still present themselves. You need to take care of yourself, okay?"

Zhou Ziheng rambles on with these reminders, like he's about to go on holiday or something. Xia Xiqing is a bit confused.

"Even if I slept for two days straight, we still have time before we start shooting for that movie. Are you going on another trip in the meantime?" His gaze falls on Zhou Ziheng's hands and he notices bruising on his knuckles. "And what exactly did you do?"

"Nothing important." Zhou Ziheng pushes a bowl of pumpkin soup toward Xia Xiqing and changes the subject. "Director Kun said you agreed to take on this gig, meaning I'll see you on set. Unless you've changed your mind since."

"On set?" Xia Xiqing frowns. "Where will you be the next couple days?"

"Busy. I'll have to fly around a bit, too, so I probably won't be at the apartment much, if at all." Zhou Ziheng busies himself with his portion of spaghetti, and Xia Xiqing notices something off about the way he's holding his fork.

"Oh? You won't be coming home the next few days?"

Zhou Ziheng meets his gaze. Thinking that Xia Xiqing might doubt the truth of what he just said, he takes out his key card and pushes it over. "If you need anything, feel free to take it."

"What could I need from here? You make it sound like I don't have my own place or something." Xia Xiqing laughs, then returns to his spaghetti.

Meanwhile, Zhou Ziheng gets up and takes his own plate—still mostly full—back to the kitchen. Xia Xiqing's phone rings. It's that unknown number again. He picks up.

"Zhao Ke?"

"Yeah, it's me. Why did you respond to my messages? Is Ziheng still at your place?"

Xia Xiqing takes the final bite of his spaghetti, then says, "Technically, I'm the one at his place."

"Sure, sure. How is he? Is he hurt?"

"Why not call him yourself if you care so much?" Xia Xiqing demands, voice still hoarse. He leans back against his chair in irritation.

This seems to aggravate Zhao Ke. "If I could reach him myself, why would I be talking to you? He scared the shit outta me. I was still in class when the group chat went crazy. They said he went by himself to Wei Min's place and beat him up real bad—that guy's in the hospital now. Fuck, if his brother didn't take it upon himself to deal with all this and quiet everyone down, Zhou Ziheng would definitely be trending right now!"

What...?

"He was alone?" Xia Xiqing asks slowly.

"Yeah, he didn't even tell me. I was the *last* to know. Fuck. I'm so mad right now." Zhao Ke throws in another few swears, but then stops, feeling a bit sorry for his friend. "It's a delicate time for my family right now, so he must've been worried he'd bring us trouble if he told me about it and I got involved. He went there alone—took down the driver, the guards, and then went straight for Wei Min and beat him half to death. From what I've heard from Wei Min's neighbor, Zhou Ziheng went totally nuts; like he was seeing red or something. He didn't stop even when Wei Min started begging. In the end it was the neighbor who stopped them. He was afraid Wei Min would die."

Xia Xiqing is so stunned that he can't quite bring himself to respond.

"He must've told you about it, right? I mean, I'm almost impressed. This kid beats a guy into the hospital, gets himself injured, then turns right around to go home and make you dinner." Zhao Ke sighs. "For all that the media hasn't gotten a hold of it, our circles are gossiping like mad about it. His dad is furious. All these years and Zhou Ziheng has never stepped a toe out of line. He's never so much as quarreled with people, let alone fought someone, and now this? His dad told him to apologize, but he straight up refused—said he'd rather die, that he didn't do anything wrong... And you don't even know how strict his family is...

"I don't know what he'll do now...

"I called his brother before I called you, who said their dad is putting him on house arrest back at his parents' place.

They've already taken his phone, and apparently they're not gonna let him out until it's time for him to start filming. But he told his brother that he had to go home to fetch something very important, and that he'd head over without a fight right after. Anyway, that's why I'm trying to check up on him. To see what his injuries are and make sure they're not too bad..."

Having heard enough, Xia Xiqing hangs up on Zhao Ke before he finishes speaking. Immediately afterward, he dials Zhou Ziheng's number. As expected, it goes straight to voicemail.

He leaves the table and walks solemnly toward the kitchen. Zhou Ziheng is standing at the counter, pouring honey into a jar of lemon slices. Hearing Xia Xiqing's footsteps, he screws on the lid and says, "Your throat is very badly damaged, so you need to take care of it. This is good for that. Keep it in the fridge or it'll go bad." He can't stop worrying. "Or maybe I can bring all these to your place. I'm afraid you won't remember what I—"

"Zhou Ziheng, what's your damage?" Xia Xiqing says, his voice trembling slightly on top of its hoarseness.

"Huh?" Zhou Ziheng doesn't understand. "Do you mean the stuff I'm giving you? It's no big deal." He lowers his head and takes a deep breath, looking like a kid who's done something wrong. "I'm sorry."

"You—"

"I truly am. I was invited to the art salon too, and I should have gone. Then all the bad things wouldn't have happened. But what I actually need to apologize for is what happened afterward, for what I did to you. Even if you said there's no responsibility for me to take, I know how proud you are as a person. I know how hard it must be for you to accept what happened. I don't know how I can make up for that. Maybe when we start filming—"

"Zhou Ziheng." Xia Xiqing moves closer, reaching out to take off the black sleeve and reveal bloody medical gauze beneath. "Before you apologize, can you explain this?"

The wound had actually come from the broken glass when Zhou Ziheng smashed the window of Wei Min's car. He hadn't properly treated it before he went off picking fights, so it ended up reopening.

"It looks worse than it is. It'll heal in a couple of days," he mumbles as he lets Xia Xiqing grab his hand. It's nice to know that he cares about him. His tone is as genuine as it can be as he says, "I'm sorry. I was mad and lashed out at you. I said stupid things I didn't mean... Anyway, I shouldn't have said all that. I was an asshole."

Xia Xiqing recalls what Zhou Ziheng said to him then, and frowns without quite realizing what he's doing.

You only have me.

"So what you're saying is, you didn't mean anything you said that night?"

Zhou Ziheng's eyes widen. He opens his mouth. "I..."

How can he tell Xia Xiqing that those were his real thoughts at the time? He really wanted to kill anyone who so much as had an impure thought about Xia Xiqing. To kill the part of Xia Xiqing that wanted to seek out other people.

"I..."

Zhou Ziheng is interrupted by a sudden phone call. Xia Xiqing takes a deep breath and says, "Go ahead."

Zhou Ziheng takes the phone out of his pocket. Xia Xiqing sees immediately that it's not the same one he uses on a day-to-day basis. The caller ID says "Zhou Zijing." The caller's voice is cold and deep.

"Underground parking. Two minutes. Be there."

Zhou Ziheng hums in assent, then hangs up. His expression betrays his turmoil. He wants to explain the things that have happened over the past couple days, but he doesn't know how. He wants to describe how he rushed back, mad with worry that Xia Xiqing might have already left. Describe that despite knowing how likely it was that Xia Xiqing had already escaped, he'd still gone and bought food and medication just in case he stayed.

And he made it back. He made it home before Xia Xiqing walked out his door.

Too many words are stuck in his throat, and he doesn't know where to begin. Compared to Wei Min, he's rather more concerned about Xia Xiqing's health.

"I need to go to work now." Zhou Ziheng hangs his head and clenches his fist. His voice is crestfallen. "Take care of yourself, and..." He pauses for a moment. "Can I hug—"

The rest of his words are sealed inside an intimate kiss and Xia Xiqing closes the gap between them. The sweetness of the kiss is tinged by the smallest thread of metallic blood. His arms twine tightly behind Zhou Ziheng's back, and then, having barely tested the waters, the kiss stops. His hand slips into the back pocket of Zhou Ziheng's trousers, and he presses their foreheads together, touching their noses to each other.

"When you don't have enough time..."

The only thing Zhou Ziheng can see in those beautiful eyes is his own reflection.

"Shut up and kiss me."

Zhou Ziheng still ends up handing over his key card before leaving.

No reason can be found for handing it over, and no reason can be found to accept it, but for some reason Xia Xiqing still ends up taking it.

For the first time, Xia Xiqing feels that this enormous apartment unit is a bit oversized; that it's so big it feels empty. Objectively, this is strange, since his own place is literally just as big. Still, he plants himself on Zhou Ziheng's sofa and follows his instructions with the various medications and supplements. Perhaps as a side of effect of one of the many things affecting his body, he beings to feel drowsy. Yet he can't be bothered to go home, so he spends another night at Zhou Ziheng's place, crashing in the main bedroom.

The next morning, Xia Xiqing wakes early. He's about to go home when he remembers Zhou Ziheng's instructions. He hesitates, then goes to the kitchen and obediently breaks his fast, making sure to eat plenty of fruit. When he's in the shower, he finds that he feels much better. Whatever medications Zhou Ziheng gave him, they work well.

It's just... He looks at his back in the mirror. How is he supposed to put the medicinal balm on the love bites there when he can't reach them?

He goes on WeChat, ready to complain to Zhou Ziheng, but then he remembers that the poor kid has essentially been grounded.

Boring.

He feels his spirit must have gone with Zhou Ziheng; he can't find the motivation to do anything. Right now, revenge is the only thing interesting enough for him.

For all that he doesn't expect Ruan Xiao to call him, he can guess a little at why she wants to. He already realized her family background that night at the salon; after all, there's only one man named Ruan that runs around their circles.

"Xiqing, I heard that Ziheng beat Wei Min into the hospital?"

Xia Xiqing hums in confirmation as he carefully buttons his shirt.

"The Wei family is looking to make some trouble, and since Zhou Ziheng is a public figure, this affair works well enough as leverage. Even if the Zhou family is powerful enough to not be seriously affected, this could still rock the boat quite a bit." Ruan Xiao seems to be walking somewhere or another. On her end, someone else greets her, and she politely responds. "Also, Zhong and Wei are in collaboration on a project right now. They're pretty much bound together."

"What kind of project?" Xia Xiqing has fastened his shirt up to its the topmost button, yet still the marks on his neck are blatantly showing.

"A shopping mall. I don't know the specifics since it's not related to what my family does." Ruan Xiao sighs. "If only there was another real estate company that could buy Wei out. Like, 'pour money on old Mr. Zhong's head' kind of buyout. He wouldn't be able to resist."

Xia Xiqing chuckles. Ruan Xiao is about to ask him what he's laughing for when he says, "Yeah, there's a company that fits your description."

"What?" Ruan Xiao is confused. Is Xia Xiqing thinking of asking Zhou Ziheng's brother? But isn't that company more into finance?

"Huanya."

Ruan Xiao is startled. Huanya? "But Huanya is run by Xia Yunkai... Xia... You're Xia Yunkai's..."

"Yes. I don't want to admit it, but I'm *his* son. And other than the man himself, I'm also the largest shareholder in the company."

Ruan Xiao remains silent for a prolonged moment. She's previously noticed that Xia Xiqing never seemed to be in need of any money, but he's always been too low-key, and he never talked about his family either. Add his artist's demeanor to all that, and it becomes practically impossible for anyone to clock him as coming from the same circles as she does.

"I thought your family was middle class... But now that I think about it, you do look pretty similar to Xia-shushu..."

Xia Xiqing frowns. "Don't. I'm not like him at all. He thinks I'm a disgrace to the family because I study art, so he never talks about me in public. The only child of his anyone in society has ever seen is his younger son."

Ruan Xiao sighs. She's seen just as many messy family situations as Xia Xiqing. Anyhow, now that he's shared with her the card that he's been keeping up his sleeve, she can rest easy knowing that Wei Min is completely doomed. "God, if only Wei Min knew it was Xia Yunkai's son that he drugged; he might start crying in fear. For all that everyone is certain that the Zhong and Wei families are collaborating for this project, I looked into it and nothing has actually been contracted out yet. Just work your way in when the time is right with your offer, and I'll be over on my end playing support. The Zhong family will be the first to drop this hot potato while they still can."

Xia Xiqing agrees with Ruan Xiao one hundred percent. He mentally rearranges his schedule; he'll need to pay a visit to that company he's never previously visited and set this plan into motion. Even if he's never been proud of being called Xia Yunkai's son, it'd be a waste to not use the title of the person who's never been a father to him.

At first, Xia Xiqing plans to use his flashiest vehicle—a

yellow race car—but then changes his mind. After all, he's more or less a public figure at this point, and he'll need to film a movie with Zhou Ziheng afterward. The less trouble to be had, the better.

The Huanya building isn't far from his apartment—it's the tallest building he sees if he looks out the window. Sporting a pair of sunglasses and wearing clothes far trendier than he typically wears, he throws his car keys to the attendant by the door and, hands in pockets, walks brashly to the prettiest receptionist at the front desk.

"Hello. Is there anything you need, sir?" The girl smiles warmly, studying him with a pair of measuring eyes that have probably already recognized him.

"I'm here to see Xia Yunkai."

"Xia..." Slightly frightened by the name of the CEO, she stutters a little. "Then...do you have an appointment, sir?"

"No." Xia Xiqing taps the marble counter, looking quite nonchalant.

The receptionist puts on an apologetic smile. "I'm sorry, sir, but our CEO is a very busy man. Appointments must be prearranged before any meetings can happen." She takes out a pen and a memo pad, politely handing them to Xia Xiqing. "How about this—if you leave your contact information the reason for your visit, we'll deliver your request and notify you as soon as a spot opens up in his schedule."

"Really?" Xia Xiqing chuckles, playing with the pen. "It's just that he didn't make any appointments with me back when he prearranged my birth."

He lifts his sunglasses up to his forehead, revealing his exquisite eyes, then starts scribbling on the memo as if to test the pen for ink. Seeing the receptionist frozen in shock, he points his chin at telephone for the internal line. "How about you give him a ring? You can tell him that his son is here to make trouble for him."

The girl nods nervously. She dials a number and, as she waits, continues to glance searchingly at Xia Xiqing. The CEO's assistant seems to think that she's being silly, since there's a bit of scolding coming from the other end. But when the girl gives a description of Xia Xiqing, the other end finally quiets down.

After a few seconds, the other end says, "Invite him up."

The receptionist hangs up, then lets out a sigh of relief.

"Uh, Mr...Mr. Xia, our CEO would like to invite you to the twenty-eighth floor. There will be someone by the elevator to serve as a guide."

Xia Xiqing smiles at her gently, then gives a soft thanks before letting his sunglasses fall back down over his eyes. He turns, but then turns back as if he forgot something. "Oh right. You're a very dedicated employee, and you deserve praise for the work you've done today." He lowers his voice. "But please don't post on social media that you saw Xia Xiqing. Consider this a bribe." He smiles and tears off the top piece of paper from the memo pad, then pushes it toward the girl with a single finger.

"Deal?"

With that, Xia Xiqing leaves the front desk and heads straight for the elevator.

The girl looks down at the piece of paper. On it is a quick stylized sketch of a girl with the same hair and outfit as herself. It's super cute. He really is that artist from online! And he's the son of the CEO?!

The girl squeezes the paper in joy, her ensuing happy daze lasting her the entire morning.

Xia Xiqing comes out on the uppermost floor of the building. A solemn-faced woman waits by the elevator, posture politely subservient.

"Hello, young Mr. Xia. I'm Angelica, assistant to the CEO. Please follow me."

Xia Xiqing doesn't bother responding, silently following her to Xia Yunkai's office. Angelica pushes the door open and announces his arrival as he walks inside. Xia Yunkai is standing at the window, gazing outside, but he turns around at the announcement and smiles kindly at Xia Xiqing, who is utterly appalled.

"I'll skip the crap. Between you and me, there's really no need to play the father-and-son act." Xia Xiqing sits on the spinning chair across from Xia Yunkai's office chair, then puts his feet up on the desk. "I want Huanya to participate in the project that the Zhong and Wei families are planning."

Xia Yunkai frowns. "Zhong Chi's project?"

"Correct." Xia Xiqing takes off his sunglasses and twirls them as he looks up and smiles. "Actually, not quite. I don't want Huanya to merely participate; I want Huanya to take Wei Min's place and kick his team off the project."

Hearing Wei Min's name, Xia Yunkai walks over to the desk and sits across from him. "The younger son of the Zhou family beat someone up recently. Do you have anything to do with that? Are you trying to help him out?"

Xia Xiqing stops playing with his sunglasses and chuckles darkly. "Actually, he was helping me out when he put that son of a bitch Wei Min into the hospital." He takes a long look around the spacious office. "Every day you spend your time in this beautiful office. You probably don't even know that your son got drugged and almost raped, do you?"

Xia Yunkai visibly reacts to this bombshell, and Xia

Xiqing chuckles. "Relax, I said 'almost.' I haven't become *that* much of an embarrassment to your name yet. The youngest Mr. Zhou helped me out, and I'm pretty grateful to him for it. But..." He starts playing with his sunglasses again. "When dealing with this kind of vermin, a mere beating is far from enough."

Xia Yunkai thinks for a moment, then says, "About this project, I'll find someone to look into—"

"Do you think I came here to negotiate?" Xia Xiqing's tone has gone suddenly gelid. He stands and looms over the desk. "You owe me so much, and I've just given you a way to make it up to me." He smiles, and his beautiful eyes, so similar to his mother's, gaze coldly at Xia Yunkai. "Dad, shouldn't you value this opportunity?"

Xia Yunkai has gone from astonished to placatory, and Xia Xiqing laughs. He glances at the golf club propped against the corner of the office and clicks his tongue in disapproval.

"If you ask me, Zhou Ziheng was simply too inexperienced. Fists are no good for beating people up—you'll only hurt yourself doing that..." Xia Xiqing's eyes return to Xia Yunkai. "He should have used a golf club. All it really takes is a good swing at the head."

The way Xia Yunkai evades his gaze is a little bit too obvious, and Xia Xiqing feels quite accomplished—not only has he gotten started on his revenge against Wei Min, but he's also managed gain the upper hand in a conversation against his father. He manages to get the contact information of the project manager before he leaves.

Wei Min's company is a subsidiary of the company owned by his father, Wei Cheng. But not even Wei Cheng's company plays at the same level as Huanya. Zhong Chi should be smart; smart enough to accept the olive branch that Huanya is offering for this project.

Days later, Xia Xiqing watches a representative from the Zhong family sign the contract with Huanya. Once it's done, he catches a ride with Xia Yunkai's assistant over to the private hospital where Wei Min is staying. This hospital specializes in a specific clientele—put bluntly, they only treat those with the right backgrounds and connections.

Quite serendipitously, Huanya is also a shareholder here. The manager might not know who Xia Xiqing is, but he recognizes Angelica readily enough.

"We would like to visit the young Mr. Wei. May I know which room he is in?"

The manager nods and smiles widely. "Of course, this way please."

He glances at the person following behind Angelica, a young man in a black suit and dark sunglasses, holding a bouquet of white chrysanthemums. He looks familiar in a way that's difficult to describe.

"Here we are." He leads the two to the comfortable sickroom. "Should I announce your arrival?"

"No need." Angelica shows a professional smile. "Mr. Wu, I'm also here to discuss some further investments. Should we take this somewhere else?"

The manager doesn't dare to decline. He nods and watches as the young man with the flowers walks into the sickroom and closes the door behind him. It's only after they walk out of the VIP zone that he finally realizes what was bothering him—those fresh, beautiful white chrysanthemums looked more suitable for a funeral than a sickroom visitation.

He's overcome with nervous sweat, but he's too afraid to say anything to these powerful investors. The most he can do is offer the young Mr. Wei a silent blessing from afar. But then again, that young Mr. Wei isn't really anyone deserving of well-wishes, anyway.

When Xia Xiqing enters the room, Wei Min is watching a movie, seemingly content. Without looking up, he yells, "Hey, what's wrong with you? Come here and adjust my bed higher. Don't you see I'm watching a movie here? You idiot. If you don't know how to do your job, get the fuck out."

Xia Xiqing walks to the other side of the room, to his bedside. The arrogant idiot doesn't even look at him. He takes off his sunglasses and presses a button to raise the bed.

"Is this height okay?"

"A bit too high..." Wei Min trails off as he realizes that the voice is unexpected. He's in a neck brace, so it's difficult for him to turn his head. Instead, he strains his eyes in a side glance.

Xia Xiqing sets the chrysanthemums on the bedside table, then very considerately leans into view, reaching up to grip Wei Min's chin in hand. "Do you see me now? You like what you see?"

"Xi—Xi—Xia—Xia Xiqing?!" Wei Min looks like he's seeing a ghost. He stutters fearfully, "How—how did you get in here?"

"Huh? Don't you like me anymore?" Xia Xiqing smiles, his eyes curving gently along with his lips. "But I thought Mr. Wei liked how I looked..."

Xia Xiqing lets go of Wei Min's chin. His gaze lands on a peeling knife on the bedside table. "I've come all this way, but I forgot to bring Mr. Wei a fruit basket... How's this? Let me peel an apple for you."

He picks the prettiest apple and sits on the bed, carefully starting to peel. The skin comes off in a long spiral, falling into a pile on the bed. As he peels, he gives Wei Min a once over. His arm is in a cast, and his leg hangs suspended on a strap. His face is even worse off, all swollen and bruised and revolting. He clicks his tongue.

"Zhou Ziheng was a little too harsh, no? I really didn't think he had it in him. He's always been such a good boy when he's with me."

"You... I knew it! You've been screwing!" Wei Min sounds both afraid and angry. "Did he let you in? I'm telling you, if you do something to me, I'll make Zhou Ziheng pay. I'll find some reporters and ruin his life!"

The perfect spiral of apple peel is suddenly broken. Xia Xiqing scowls. "Wanna try?"

The confidence in his voice shocks Wei Min to silence. For all that he's scared, Wei Min figures that, as powerful as the Zhou family might be, they're not exactly capable of getting away with murder. And what does Xia Xiqing count as? How dare a poor artist act so arrogantly?

"I'm not only going to try. I *will* ruin his reputation. His disgustingly perfect character design will be revealed to all as a mere sham! I'll fucking tear—AHH!"

Wei Min's speech ends with a cry. His eyes are dilated with terror, gaze fixed upon the peeling knife held in Xia Xiqing's hand.

"You, you..."

Blood wells up through the comforter. Xia Xiqing pulls the knife out swiftly. He takes a look at Wei Min's horrified face and says, "You know, your tastes are certainly unique. Of the hundred or so guests at the salon, why did you prey on the son of Xia Yunkai?"

"Xia...Xia Yunkai?" Wei Min is stunned beyond pain. "How can you be... You're..."

Xia Xiqing presses hard on the bloody wound through the

comforter. Wei Min screams some more.

"As an artist, I'm pretty familiar with anatomy. Next time, I'll make sure I poke somewhere a lot less gentle than your thigh."

Xia Xiqing drops the bloodied knife on the table with a crisp clatter, then wipes his hands clean with his handkerchief.

"If you're still too dumb to realize you can't ever touch Zhou Ziheng," Xia Xiqing says, patting Wei Min's putrid face while presenting him with a beautifully cruel smile, "then it's no matter whether it's your project, your money, or that thing you have down there...

"I will make it disappear completely."

C.14

:

Clandestine Romance

Summer is almost here. It's Xia Xiqing's least favorite sea-son—sticky sweat, ceaseless cicadas, and the scorching sun. Even cool shade in which to escape the heat becomes a luxury.

He keeps thinking about Zhou Ziheng's swimming pool. On the first night that he's gone, he finally jumps in for a nighttime swim. This kind of entry without permission is as fun and exciting as sneaking into a classroom at night. At one point, he pulls back his hair, and with his top half still bare, he takes a selfie and sends it to Zhou Ziheng.

Oh right. He hasn't got a phone right now. He can't see it.

What a pity.

He spends the entirety of the next night reading the finalized script that Xu Qichen sends over. Once he finishes, his feelings are complicated. Still, if the movie can capture the spirit of the script, then it'll definitely be exceptional.

"You were pretty biased when you wrote this. I can tell

how gay it'll be just by reading the script." Xia Xiqing takes a gulp of his beer. "I can already imagine the fangirls' reactions."

But Xu Qichen sounds unconcerned, saying, "It's alright. I feel I've only written them to have a codependent relationship. As for the nature of their feelings for each other, I haven't made up my mind yet. It'll largely depend on how you two portray your characters, and how the audience interprets it."

"Interpret?" Xia Xiqing chuckles soundlessly. "You know what the Self-Study girls are like. They can read so far into a simple meeting of our eyes that they'll be certain we've slept together."

Xia Zhixu says something in the background, and Xia Xiqing glances at the clock. It's almost eleven at night—not the most appropriate time to be calling, so he excuses himself and hangs up. Unable to sleep, he checks Weibo, then finds a strange topic in the trending section: Dongming Corporation Tax Evasion.

Isn't Dongming the name of Wei Min's little guild? How fun. Xia Xiqing clicks into the topic. The first few results are all articles from the official accounts of things like various daily news agencies and financial news agencies. They're all using the same phrasing: "Dongming Corporation Found Evading ¥120 Million in Taxes, CEO Wei Faces Subpoena."

He reads the article aloud to himself. "According to Mr. Wei's lawyer, Mr. Wei is...experiencing health issues and is currently hospitalized. He will cooperate fully with local authorities on the investigation as soon as he recovers—"

Xia Xiqing dissolves into laughter. Wei Min must be guilty; otherwise, he'd just deny it instead of making such an ambiguous announcement. He must be afraid he can't clean up this mess. But he's a pretty deal around these parts, and he's got his father looking out for him. Who would have the power to expose him like this?

Thinking Ruan Xiao must know something, he asks her to meet up tomorrow for coffee. When she shows up for their meeting, a guy is with her.

"So, are you gonna explain?" Xia Xiqing says, smiling, then sips at his coffee while maintaining his gaze on the two of them. "Why are you here together?"

"I know why you wanted to see me, so I brought the perpetrator here," Ruan Xiao replies, making the young man she brought give her a sidelong glance.

Xia Xiqing studies the guy. He's in a hoodie and black-rimmed glasses, and his face is strangely familiar. His fashion aesthetic is strangely similar to Zhou Ziheng's. That's when he realizes: this is the guy who stalked him at the salon.

"You're Zhao Ke?"

Zhao Ke nods, pushing up his glasses. "You...you're better now?" he asks a bit awkwardly.

His accent is immediately recognizable as heavily local, and Xia Xiqing can't help but wonder why Zhou Ziheng doesn't have a Beijing accent like Zhao Ke does. Is it because he started acting early on?

When Xia Xiqing processes the question, he almost chokes on his coffee. "Hey, how about we never bring this up again?"

He'd just put it behind him, but here it comes again.

"Anyways—so you wanted to ask me about the tax evasion thing with Wei Min?" Ruan Xiao plays with a strand of her hair, a sneaky smile on her face. "That's him."

"Him?"

Xia Xiqing comes to the realization that Zhao Ke is Zhou Ziheng's childhood friend. Though he's not sure how high up the Zhou family is in terms of politics, Zhao Ke probably comes from similar background. The Zhao family must be pretty important.

Ruan Xiao gestures for Xia Xiqing to lean in. When he does, she whispers, "He's Chief Zhao's son."

As soon as Xia Xiqing hears, Zhao Ke tugs Ruan Xiao back into her seat. He even tugs up the collar of her T-shirt, which has a wide neckline that's meant to hang off a shoulder.

"Your back was showing."

"You're being over-dramatic—that's the design."

Ruan Xiao silently mouths something to Xia Xiqing, who soon realizes it's the name of the department that Zhao Ke's father is in charge of. No wonder Wei Min got exposed at such an opportune time: it's because of Zhao Ke.

"How did you convince your father to go after him?" Xia Xiqing asks.

Zhao Ke scratches his head. "Well, about that. I just sort of mentioned it over dinner. My dad didn't even know anyone in the bureau had dealings with Wei Min. Pure luck that there's been increasing friction between him and his second in command. Since he's pretty close to a promotion out of the bureau, he decided to teach him a lesson before he leaves." He stirs his iced Americano. "Wei Min was that lesson."

Huh. Wei Min thinks he's the boss, while everyone else sees him as just a pawn. How ironic.

Xia Xiqing finds himself a bit amused at the three of them sitting at the table. "What a small world. Turns out all three of us are second-gen *something*."

Ruan Xiao is tapping her finger gently against the side of her cup. "We've all hidden it well, too. I for one never clocked you as having so many connections," she says, mostly to Xia Xiqing. She turns to Zhao Ke and asks, "So, Zhou Ziheng's family is like yours?"

"No, no, no. Very different," Zhao Ke objects. "My family is full of bureaucrats. His family is military. Ministers are not generals. He's the third generation down from a proper revolutionary, and his older brother is a finance giant. They can't even write stuff like this in television dramas—not realistic enough."

Ruan Xiao looks confused. "Then what's he doing in the entertainment industry?"

"His sister-in-law is a very successful agent. Yin-jie. Maybe you've heard of her?"

"Jiang Yin?" Xia Xiqing definitely hadn't imagined this. "She's his sister-in-law?"

"Oh, so you know her." Zhao Ke continues, "Anyway, she's been Ziheng's manager ever since he set foot in the industry. Don't you guys ever wonder how he gets so much company resources and yet no gossip? Well, other than with you."

Xia Xiqing is still in shock.

"But he's only staying in this business for two reasons. One, he wants to use his influence to draw more attention to minority groups—you know, do some good with his life. And second..."

Ruan Xiao has to urge him for more before he continues, "He had a crush on a girl when he was little. He said she encouraged him when he was at his lowest point of fear, and that's why he got to stand in front of the camera. He doesn't want to disappoint her, so he hopes that one day the girl will recognize him." Zhao Ke sighs. "Even though I think she must be married with kids by now."

"Wow. Love at first sight... What a fairy tale. I never

would have thought that Zhou Ziheng would be so pure."

They don't notice that Xia Xiqing has fallen quiet. For some strange reason, he gets inexplicably angry whenever that girl is mentioned. He keeps his head down and plays on his phone, hopping back and forth between WeChat and Weibo in attempts to distract himself from this sort of negative emotion.

"But he seems to have had a change of heart," Zhao Ke says, sending a glance to Xia Xiqing. "He hasn't mentioned her for a while. Now he keeps talking about someone else."

"Oh? Who's that?" Ruan Xiao's playful tone betrays her teasing.

"Whoever it is knows full well who I'm talking about."

Xia Xiqing ignores the childish duet, but then he notices a change in the trending list on Weibo. The QingSi ship has overtaken Self-Study on the trending list.

"Hey, has the latest episode of *Survive and Escape* aired yet?" Xia Xiqing asks.

Ruan Xiao checks her phone for the date. "Oh, yeah. Oh no—I'm gonna get so much hate for this episode."

"Why is that?" Zhao Ke asks.

"I almost voted Xiqing out. It was Ziheng who saved him. Honestly, that man... He managed to win the Killer lottery, but he had to keep helping Xiqing. And look where it got him—it would have been an easy win otherwise."

Xia Xiqing feels all warm and fuzzy at this, but he pretends not to hear and instead enters the QingSi topic page. The first one is BNF of the ship's fandom posting a screenshot of Shang Sirui's Weibo. The post shown is the selfie Xia Xiqing took with him back when they just finished filming; the one he'd taken to mess with Zhou Ziheng, where he's leaning his head against Shang Sirui's shoulder.

@SanSanQingQingMarriageNow: Look at this hidden gem! So the "suicidal player" was talking about Xiqing? I didn't realize it was a spoiler until I watched this episode. The friendly teasing is just too cute!

@33Tops: They've always been sweet together, no doubt about that! And fans of certain other ships keep acting all overconfident over nothing... Has their pairing even held hands during the show?

Xia Xiqing doesn't know what to say. It does seem like they haven't held hands during the show, but in private...

@GoGoLetsGoLetsGoSelfStudy: What part of "ship and let ship" do you not understand? You just had to extol your jealousy for all to see, hmm? What future could two bottoms have, anyway?

Okay, girl. You might be a Self-Study girl, but what did you just say about me? Who's a bottom?!

@BestSiqing: It's like some fandoms don't know how to say anything other than "two bottoms no future lol." Stay in your lane pls.

@SelfStudyMyBeloved: Hey, we didn't start it.

Thus begins a ship war. It quickly escalates as the solo-fans of the three people involved join the fight, and the situation gets out of control. What Xia Xiqing can't figure out is why, in the end, his stans and Zhou Ziheng's stans are stuck in the worst cat-fight. He now understands how awkward idols feel when their fandoms start arguing.

He thinks of sharing the news with Zhou Ziheng, but then remembers that he's still grounded, so he decides to go for the second best.

Xiqing: Ship wars are terrifying.

As an idol, Shang Sirui should theoretically be pretty busy, but he responds near-instantly.

Sirui: I'm used to it lmao

Xiqing: I'm still puzzled as to how it turned into a cat-fight between my fans and Zhou Ziheng's fans.

Sirui: I hate you, you hate me. This way our idols can kiss and make up

Pfft.

Fondly exasperated, Xia Xiqing returns to his Weibo page, making sure he hasn't accidentally left any likes behind while scrolling. That might start the battle anew if he was unlucky.

"What? Zhou Ziheng posted on Weibo!" Ruan Xiao exclaims.

"No way! He doesn't even have a phone. Wait, did he ask Xiao-Luo to post for him?" Zhao Ke pulls out his phone too. "What the hell? Seriously?"

Before Xia Xiqing can check out this mysterious post from Zhou Ziheng, he sees Zhao Ke and Ruan Xiao staring at him, wearing the exact same smile...the smile of shippers watching their ship set sail.

"The selfie you two took last time! He posted it!" Ruan Xiao slides her phone to Xia Xiqing even as she brags to Zhao Ke. "I was there personally when they took that. See that red sleeve in the left corner? That's me!"

Xia Xiqing stares down at the phone. Nothing written in the post, just a photo, in which is Xia Xiqing staring a bit cluelessly at the camera, head pressed down into leaning on Zhou Ziheng's shoulder by the man himself.

That idiot.

Still, he can't help but wonder how Zhou Ziheng managed to post that without a phone.

"Okay, guys. Mystery solved. Xiao-Luo posted it." Zhao Ke presents his WeChat page. "He brought Zhou Ziheng his script today, and while they were talking, the ship war thing just slipped out. Zhou Ziheng asked him to log onto his Weibo and send out a draft he saved."

Draft? Xia Xiqing squints at the chat history.

Xiao Luo: I don't know what's gotten into him today. He insisted I had to send it out right away. The only thing in his drafts folder was a draft he made half a month ago, and it was a group selfie with Xiqing. I was so confused, but when I hesitated he just looked at me like he was gonna fight me if I didn't.

The wide grins on their faces get even bigger. Xia Xiqing is somehow still confused about the whole thing. *What was Zhou Ziheng trying to do? Did he think the ship war wasn't heated enough?*

After he finally recollects himself, Zhao Ke says, "Xiao-Luo said Zhou Ziheng has lost a lot of weight these past couple days. What are the chances that he's gone on a hunger strike there?"

"No way..." Xia Xiqing scoffs, then lowers his head to take a sip of his coffee. It's gone completely cold.

"Yes way. I'm telling you—I've known him since we were toddlers. It's been almost two decades and I've never seen him angrier than he was that night. You were unconscious, but we saw everything. He almost gave me a heart attack." Zhao Ke nudges Ruan Xiao. "Right? How Zhou Ziheng smashed that windshield? You saw it."

Ruan Xiao nods. "It's true."

Xia Xiqing props his chin in his hand, eying the foam floating on the surface of his coffee. "He's a very upstanding person. Isn't it normal for him to play brave Samaritan?"

Zhao Ke shakes his head. "Come on, really? Back in grade nine I got into a fight with a bunch of delinquents from a neighboring junior high, and he didn't even try to help. Just sat back and called the cops. After my dad almost killed me over the whole thing, he had the audacity to lecture me about using violence!"

Xia Xiqing recalls Zhou Ziheng's look from that night. He has a good guess of how he rescued him from Wei Min, but Zhao Ke's words are a bit to blatant for him to know how to respond.

Watching Xia Xiqing stay silent, Zhao Ke has to ask more directly, "Do you want to come with us on a jail visit?"

Xia Xiqing frowns at the two excited faces. "Jail visit?"

These past couple of days have felt like a punishment on Zhou Ziheng's body and soul. To physically get into the role, his sister-in-law has regulated his meals with help from a nutritionist, so he's been limited to the disgusting diet meals that he's been prescribed.

Unfortunately, his father also just so happened to be on paid leave, which means he has plenty of time to scold him. Whatever the arguments made, the conclusions are the same: apologize to his victim, Wei Min.

"Explain this: when I asked you to practice martial arts and footwork alongside the troops, was it so that you could beat people up? Hmm? It was so you could help the weak! So you could resolve any trouble you come across!"

Zhou Ziheng, kneeling on the floor, had responded with frustration, "The only people I meet are fans. What trouble could I come across?"

"Are you talking back to me? You beat a guy up! It's utterly unacceptable! I'll drag you there myself to apologize if I have to. Zijing, go get the car ready."

Zhou Zijing had just finished up his teleconference and was on his way downstairs when he heard his dad's order, at which he turned right around and walked back upstairs as if he hadn't heard anything.

"I won't apologize, Dad. He deserved it. Not only did I want to beat him up, I wanted to—"

Lao-Zhou[9] leveled a kick at his waist. "You wanted to do what? Give me an aneurysm?"

"He's really not a good person!"

On the third day, bored to the point of skipping rope while watching daytime television, Zhou Ziheng's attention caught on a familiar name in a news segment. He ran to Lao-Zhou's room and shook him awake from his nap.

"Dad! See, I told you Wei Min's not a good person! He owes a hundred million in taxes! Don't you think he deserves to get beaten up?"

Zhou Ziheng turned on the news.

"One hundred million? How is it even possible?"

"I know, right? Should have killed him that day!"

Lao-Zhou sighed. "Young people these days...so impulsive."

At least it put an end to any mentions of apologizing. Zhou Ziheng was feeling good until Xiao-Luo came over and he learned about the ship war. The day the selfie had been taken, Xia Xiqing's provocations had actually made him delete it—but later that same night, Xia Xiqing had an emotional breakdown. Afterward, Zhou Ziheng recovered it from the trash folder. He'd wanted to post it, but in the end he just kept it in his draft folder.

"Xiao-Luo, you need to send it for me. Please don't forget!"

"But why?"

---

9 "Lao-" is a prefix used for making nicknames. It is most often used for older men, as its literal meaning is "old." This method of address often conveys a certain sense of familiarity.

"It's just...for promoting the new episode!"

The ship war is a fire in his back yard, and he doesn't even have a cell phone with which to put it out. Zhou Ziheng is too angry to even continue eating his dinner. He picks up a piece of broccoli with his chopsticks, staring blankly at it.

"Xia Xiqing absolutely hates this; he won't even touch it," Zhou Ziheng mumbles to himself before stuffing it into his mouth, chewing without tasting anything. "He also hates carrots...and celery. He spits that stuff out half the time..."

He glares at the plate of veggies in front of him. Then, annoyed, he looks up at the ceiling.

How is Xia Xiqing such a picky eater?

Xia Xiqing must have gone out drinking these past few days that he's been stuck at his parents'. He might have even gone out with those shady friends of his. With how attractive he is, who wouldn't hit on him? And with Zhou Ziheng locked up here, who would be there to keep him safe?

It's all so frustrating.

Suddenly, there's the sound of something hitting the window. Zhou Ziheng glances over, but seeing nothing, he looks back to the ceiling.

Clack!

Again, the same sound.

Must be some kid playing a prank, but what neighborhood brat would misbehave like this?

Zhou Ziheng stands. The glass doors to his balcony are locked from the outside, so he can only stand there and peer out at his balcony. But nobody's there.

Okay, that's not weird at all. He shuts his curtains swiftly and walks to his washroom. He must be going crazy, obsessing so much over Xia Xiqing. He should take a shower to distract himself.

But when Zhou Ziheng walks out of the shower wearing only a towel around his waist, he sees the silhouette of some-one crouching on his balcony behind the curtains. He picks up his baseball bat and slowly approaches the glass doors.

The shadow sits right at the seam between the two halves of his curtains. Zhou Ziheng holds his breath, then suddenly yanks the curtains open.

He stares down in disbelief.

The person he's been obsessing over—Xia Xiqing himself—is on one knee on his balcony, hands clutching the lock hanging outside the glass doors. He also seems startled, lifting his eyes to meet Zhou Ziheng's on the other side. He even has a rose, glistening with condensation, held hori-zontally between his teeth. It must have been freshly picked from Zhou family's garden.

Zhou Ziheng loses the grip on his baseball bat.

"You... What are you doing here?"

Xia Xiqing can't hear the exact words through the thick door, but can guess. He stands, tucks the rose behind his ear, and huffs on the glass before starting to draw in the mist.

Zhou Ziheng takes a step forward to distinguish the words.

Breaking and entering.

Xia Xiqing even waggles his eyebrow after he's done. This guy... Zhou Ziheng's face breaks into a smile.

He copies Xia Xiqing, breathing on the glass and writing his response. The sentence is quite long, leaving Xia Xiqing squinting curiously at the glass. The expression, with the crimson rose blooming at his ear, is immensely endearing.

Mouthing the words silently to himself as he deciphers the sentence from the other side of the glass, Xia Xiqing finally understands.

I only have this. Do you want it?

Eyes on the question mark, Xia Xiqing is about to ask, but then Zhou Ziheng moves again. This time he draws a shaky little heart on the glass. It's a bit ugly and very asymmetrical, but it's very cute.

Zhou Ziheng's smile is warm and bright on the other side. There seems to be a lake full of stars in his eyes.

This isn't the first time that Xia Xiqing has sneaked onto private property. As a teenager, he used to sneak off campus during study hall and sneak back when it was over to avoid attention. It wasn't anything sinister—he just wanted some alone time. Sometimes, all he did was watch the stars on clear nights.

But this *is* the first time that he's climbed over a wall for someone else.

Zhao Ke has mastered the art of persuasion. At first it was his comment about hunger strikes, but then it was his vivid descriptions of the strict Zhou patriarch and of corporal punishment administered via batons. Xia Xiqing was only partially convinced, but then he remembered that he was the reason that Zhou Ziheng has been grounded, and that he ought to do something.

Just a visit. Not big deal. It'd be like a day trip.

"Your car can't go in. I'll drive you."

It was eight in the evening and the sky was getting dark. Zhao Ke drove them to the Western Hills. There's a saying about Old Beijing that's been around since the end of the Qing dynasty: the wealthy in the east and the noble in the west. The "west" in the saying refers to these exact Western Hills. Even Xia Xiqing hasn't been this way before, only heard rumors. And the rumors didn't lie—this place really was well-guarded.

"Zhou Ziheng's family lives down the road. See the house with a red rooftop?" Zhao Ke said as they came to another gated intersection. At the gesture of the man standing guard, he slowed down obediently and rolled down the window with a smile. "It's me. Good evening, Wang-ge. I see it's your shift again tonight."

"Oh, Ke-zi[10], it's you." The guard smiled back before he looked into the car. "You've brought friends?"

"Hello, I'm Ke-zi's girlfriend." Ruan Xiao casually wrapped her arms around Zhao Ke, who almost jumped.

"Wow. How did you get yourself such a beautiful girl? Good for you!" This security guard that Zhao Ke had called Wang-ge passed the visitor booklet to him. "Whatever your secret is, you should teach our Heng-Heng."

Zhao Ke's eyes flicker to the rear-view mirror. The person in the back smirks back lazily.

Also noticing the gaze of the security guard, Ruan Xiao explained, "That's my brother. We're all here to visit Ziheng today."

"Of course." Wang-ge took back the booklet. "It's been a while since Ke-zi has visited. Plenty of people around tonight—Zijing is also here. You might even have enough people for two tables of mahjong."

Seeing that they were almost home free, Zhao Ke smiled. "If we don't, we'll come find you."

After passing this final gate, Zhao Ke let out a long sigh of relief. Then he remembered what Ruan Xiao had said to Wang-ge, and he started flushing at the memory. He glanced nervously at her.

Few people were more clever than Ruan Xiao, who caught

---

10 In this context, "-zi" is being used to make a diminutive nickname.

on immediately. She met his gaze, asking, "What are you looking at?"

Intrigued, Xia Xiqing leaned in, arms resting on the front headrests. He reached out a finger to tweak Zhao Ke's ear. "Yeah, what are you looking at?"

Zhao Ke shivered, making the car swerve slightly. "No, I wasn't. It's nothing."

Ruan Xiao leaned in closer with a tiny smile. "You were clearly looking at me."

Xia Xiqing pulled on Zhao Ke's ear and echoed, "Yeah, you were clearly looking at her."

Zhao Ke's ears were so red they looked like they'd been cooked. "No, you two... You..."

"I'm just trying to help my sister." Having done enough teasing, Xia Xiqing leaned back with a sigh. "Ruan Xiao, I think you should just tell him. He's not gonna figure it out on his own."

"Wh—what?"

"Do you think you still need to woo her? Or are you thinking that you should keep your relationship 'ambiguous' for a while longer?" Xia Xiqing's voice was very amused. "She's dropped so many hints, outright flirted so many times. She's done everything short of confessing outright. Use your thick head and think."

Seeing how confused Zhao Ke remained, Xia Xiqing turned to Ruan Xiao. "So, last time at the art salon, did you attend because you knew Zhao Ke would be there? Did you try to chat him up, then realize this guy was on a stakeout for his friend?"

Ruan Xiao huffs. "That's right. I even dyed my hair back, since I heard he prefers it." She twirls a lock of hair around a finger. "But then there was that scumbag Wei Min, and my plans got completely derailed. I even told him that my family was rushing me to get married."

Xia Xiqing couldn't stop laughing, but then he remembered something. "Was he also why you went on the show? You knew that he's Zhou Ziheng's friend?"

"Of course." Ruan Xiao had a look like she'd done nothing wrong. "When he's not at school, he's at home. I had to think of something." She pinched his cheek. "And according to rumors, he doesn't like second gen rich kids."

"I don't...I mean, how could you think that...?" Zhao Ke forced out a tight laugh. There were two second gen rich kids staring at him right there in the car. However, he was still confused. Ruan Xiao was beautiful and smart; she must have plenty of options. "But why are you interested in me? Have we met before?"

Zhao Ke stopped the car in front of Zhou Ziheng's house and waited for an answer. Ruan Xiao puffed up her cheeks, then opened the car door on her own.

"When you have time, go check your family's photo albums. See if you can't find a sad little girl in a red dress."

Xia Xiqing clicked his tongue. Childhood love at first sight—talk about fairytale romance. He had to nudge the spaced out Zhao Ke for him to snap out of it, at which point he explained his plan.

"The three of us go in, then Ruan Xiao and I will ring the front door while you circle to the back of the house. It's so dark and their rose garden is pretty tall; no one will see you. Zhou Ziheng's balcony is right beside the pagoda tree—it's really easy to climb. We'll be in the living room to stall for you. Zhou Ziheng's parents will definitely stop us to chat."

For all that it didn't sound like much of a plan in theory, it worked out pretty well in practice. Xia Xiqing just so happened to know how to climb a tree, too, thanks to his wild adolescent years.

When he landed on the balcony, Xia Xiqing was pretty pleased with himself. He even prepared a rose like a true Romeo. But then he discovered that Zhou Ziheng's parents had locked the door from the outside...

First the show made him unlock doors, and now he also needed to do it in real life? He never wanted to see another lock in his life.

After a brief bout of hesitation, he finally got a length of wire from the railing and got to work. Again, thanks to a history of adolescent misbehavior, this type of lock wasn't actually too difficult for him. But before he could even finish jiggling the second pin, the curtains behind the glass doors were thrown apart.

Zhou Ziheng stood on the other side, half-naked with a wound on his arm.

Xia Xiqing's heart was beating fast, partially due to shock, but he needed to keep his cool. So, he stood up and tried to seduce Zhou Ziheng, but he wound up seducing him instead.

That foggy heart is too adorable. It's so lovely, and makes him feel so soft that he no longer cares about seduction.

The two of them crouch on either side. Zhou Ziheng's staring distracts Xia Xiqing's lockpicking. He begins to worry about failing to unlock the door, or worse, about Zhou Ziheng's parents catching him in the act. But it seems that even the heavens are helping him seduce men.

"Done." Xia Xiqing takes a slow deep breath and puts padlock aside. Zhou Ziheng pulls open the door and gives him a hug. "Hey..."

Xia Xiqing's face is pressed against Zhou Ziheng's shoulder; he drowns in the scent of mint shampoo.

"You smell good." Zhou Ziheng clings to him like a giant puppy.

Xia Xiqing retorts, "I was just in the tree."

"No." Zhou Ziheng picks out some pagoda blossoms from his hair. "I smell you."

Okay, it was clearly Xia Xiqing who initiated the romantic gesture of a secret rendezvous, but why does he feel like he's the one getting seduced? Zhou Ziheng shuts the door and the curtains like he's an old hand at secret affairs. Xia Xiqing thinks he likes Zhou Ziheng better when he's less confident.

"Are you trying to seduce me?" Xia Xiqing's fingers slide down Zhou Ziheng's waist, grinning at him like he's ready to pull on that towel.

Zhou Ziheng simply licks his lips and confesses, "I am."

At a loss for words, Xia Xiqing finds himself pinned against the wall, and a deep voice sneaks into his ear.

"How am I doing so far?"

Xia Xiqing blinks. He grabs Zhou Ziheng's chin, and their eyes meet. "Who did you learn that from?"

"Who else?" Zhou Ziheng looks into his eyes.

"Oh," Xia Xiqing says, voice as soft as a cloud. "So now you don't need a teacher anymore."

"That depends..." Zhou Ziheng presses his left hand on Xia Xiqing's waist, their noses touch. "On how you think I'm doing," he adds.

Okay, Zhou Ziheng has a talent for this, but Xia Xiqing doesn't want any more foreplay. His fingers trace along Zhou Ziheng's lips. "Haven't seen you for quite some time. Let me teach you."

The moment they kiss, the rose stuck behind Xia Xiqing's ear gently brushes Zhou Ziheng's wet hair. Its scent grows stronger as the kiss deepens. He's not sure if it's the rose or the kiss, but Xia Xiqing feels drunk. He runs a hand into Zhou Ziheng's hair.

Entangled, warm, safe, wet.

He doesn't know how Romeo felt when he crept into Juliet's garden, but the excitement of breaking rules begins to kick in. He wants to pry apart Zhou Ziheng's shelled heart and take that most precious thing away with him.

That heart is utterly honest; it'd be a waste not to steal it.

Despite Xia Xiqing aggressively biting his lips, prodding his territory, Zhou Ziheng is gentle in the process like he's afraid of hurting him. Xia Xiqing feels the hand on his neck rubbing his skin, light and slow, and the heat passes onto his skin through his fingertips.

Like he said, that heart is beating too honestly. He feels like a thief who, after so much effort spent breaking and entering, is too cowardly to do more than just cop a feel of the treasure that he wants.

He can't bear to take it away. Maybe next time. Next time he will.

The sound of his want echoes in the room, painting the night darker than it already is. He feels his heartbeat quickening. He throws his jacket on the floor before his fingers press onto Zhou Ziheng's firm chest, pushing him toward the bed.

"So, Young Master Zhou." Xia Xiqing bites on Zhou Ziheng's lower lip and pins him against the bed, but he's worried about his wounded right hand so he only hovers over him despite the deviant way he's looming. He smirks. "Your bed's pretty big."

He takes the rose from his ear and spins it before he touches it to Zhou Ziheng's ear, trailing the blossom down his cheek, down his throat, until reaching his broad shoulders. He sees a small scratch there.

He closes their distance to kiss that minuscule wound, hair falling across his face.

Zhou Ziheng cracks a smile. Suddenly, he rolls them over, reversing their positions. He leans in, brushing Xia Xiqing's hair away from his forehead. "You're very perceptive."

Xia Xiqing deliberately reveals the love bites under his collar. "Discernment is a virtue."

Seeing his masterpiece, the memories of that night flash by. He kisses his collarbone apologetically, but Xia Xiqing can't bear the slow pace at which they're moving.

He feels like Zhou Ziheng is seconds away from apologizing again.

"Hey... I didn't climb to your window to hear an apology."

"Then why was it?" Zhou Ziheng presses a kiss to the tip of Xia Xiqing's nose.

Xia Xiqing raises an eyebrow. "To fuck you, of course." His eyes are alight. "Debts must be repaid or you won't have the credit for future loans."

What is he... Zhou Ziheng is about to laugh in his face, but then hears someone knock on his door. A few seconds later, his brother's spiritless voice comes from outside.

"Zhou Ziheng, get your ass downstairs. Zhao Ke is here."

Zhou Ziheng quickly gets up, grabs a fluffy comforter to cover Xia Xiqing, and hides Xia Xiqing's shoes and jacket in his closet. Then, he climbs into bed.

"I'm about to sleep."

"At nine? Open the door or I'll have dad come up and check on you."

Hearing his brother, Zhou Ziheng jumps from the bed and unlocks the door before quickly inserting himself under a blanket. He sits up from the bed like Virgin Mary, smiling courteously and appreciatively at his brother, who's carrying a bowl of fruit.

"Mom asked me to bring this up." Zhou Zijing puts the bowl on the nightstand, eyes studying Zhou Ziheng.

"Thanks, big bro. I'll eat it in a second."

Zhou Zijing crosses his arms in front of his chest, not intending to leave. "You wanna talk to me?"

"What is there to talk about?" Zhou Ziheng's smile stills. The guy under the blanket has put his hand somewhere he shouldn't. He feels like his heart is about to jump out.

"I'm just curious. What did Wei Min do that was so bad you had to beat him up?" Zhou Zijing observes him like a state prosecutor.

"I...I just don't like him..."

Zhou Zijing nods slowly, then immediately turns and lazily yells, "Dad—"

"Okay, okay! I'll spill!" Zhou Ziheng makes a shushing motion, then clasps his hands together in a pleading gesture. "Please, brother, I'll tell you."

Xia Xiqing almost barks a laugh; it really does seem like Zhou Ziheng is the type to get bullied no matter where he goes. He playfully huffs a breath at Zhou Ziheng's waist, making the man shiver minutely. Xia Xiqing is pleased beyond measure.

Zhou Zijing raises an eyebrow. "Fine. Tell me."

Under attack from both sides, Zhou Ziheng feels untold pressure. "He..." Taking a deep breath, his voice shrinks. "He messed with one of mine."

This shocks Xia Xiqing to stillness. It's the first time he's heard Zhou Ziheng admit this out loud. Distantly, he hears the sound of a glacier shattering under the force of a warm front.

Zhou Zijing chuckles and spares Zhou Ziheng a slightly derisive look before turning around. Seeing his brother turn away, Zhou Ziheng lets out a sigh of relief, but then Zhou Zijing returns and approaches.

One step, two steps, and he's standing by the bed.

Zhou Ziheng's heart is pounding so hard he wouldn't be surprised if Zhou Zijing can hear it.

Is he going to catch Xia Xiqing? How could he explain this to his dad? What if his dad tries to beat Xia Xiqing up?

He has to protect Xia Xiqing first. *At least he's dressed—he'll have an easier time running outside.* Zhou Ziheng's thoughts run wild.

Please, they're brothers! Zhou Zijing can't do this to him!

Zhou Ziheng closes his eyes and awaits his fate.

Zhou Zijing clicks his tongue.

Zhou Ziheng opens his eyes just enough to see Zhou Zijing picking a rose off the floor. "I didn't think you were this romantic." He throws it onto the bed. "Don't mess around."

When Zhou Zijing shuts the door loudly behind him, as if as a reminder to the person under the covers, Zhou Ziheng huffs a long sigh as he lets Xia Xiqing out. "Are you okay?"

Xia Xiqing has a blank expression on his face, and his neck and cheeks are flushed.

"What's wrong?" Zhou Ziheng cups his face, looking worried. "Your face is burning,"

Xia Xiqing pushes his hand away, eyes flickering. "I... I just need some air."

That's so adorable. Xia Xiqing is a beautiful and dangerous leopard with the way he normally looks and acts, but when his guard is down, he looks more like a kitten.

"I came here to have a laugh at your imprisonment. Now that my job is done, I think I should leave."

Head hung with embarrassment, Xia Xiqing takes a step toward the window, but he's immediately pulled back into bed.

"Did you just get embarrassed?"

"No. You're the one who got embarrassed!" Xia Xiqing lifts his head, wanting to escape Zhou Ziheng's hug, but Zhou Ziheng holds on to him tightly, rubbing his back like he's a kitten.

"Okay, okay, it was me. I was embarrassed."

Xia Xiqing still escapes, refusing to be fooled. "Yeah, you should be. You still haven't put on any clothes."

This is the last trick Zhou Ziheng has up his sleeve: "Ouch! My arm..."

Xia Xiqing runs a hand over Zhou Ziheng's bandaged arm, asking worriedly, "What? I didn't touch it..."

Zhou Ziheng pouts. "But it hurts. It started hurting when I was in the shower. What should I do?"

Xia Xiqing rolls his eyes. "That's thanks to your recklessness."

"How can you say that to someone who saved you?" Zhou Ziheng puts on a frown. "If it wasn't for me trying to get you back..."

Xia Xiqing falls silent. He touches Zhou Ziheng's arm, petting lightly like he's comforting a puppy. He stays silent.

"How do you feel? Did you use the medicine? Did you drink or smoke while I wasn't there?" He leans in close as if to check for the scent of cigarettes.

Xia Xiqing pushes away Zhou Ziheng's worried face. "I'm fine. Don't exaggerate."

"I'm just worried about the side effects."

Xia Xiqing lifts his teasing eyes. "Yeah, I guess there's one side effect. That thing made me..."

He touches Zhou Ziheng's chest with his palm, then straddles him with a somewhat condescending air. He unties his tie, then leans down for a lingering kiss, using that as a chance to leash it around Zhou Ziheng's neck.

"...Really want to top you."

Zhou Ziheng's lips curl into a smile. "So you like to ride, is that it?"

"Oh, I think you're confused, kid." Xia Xiqing loosens his tie, pulls it out, and pinches it between his fingers. He brushes it against Zhou Ziheng's cheek before he ties it on his neck.

"Don't move." Xia Xiqing clutches tighter, taking away Zhou Ziheng's breath a little. "Behave or I'll strangle you."

But his victim doesn't seem like he wants to cave. He looks at Xia Xiqing. "I don't mind if you're on top." He runs his hands on Xia Xiqing's waist. "You'll just have to do a bit more work."

"Very funny." Xia Xiqing is about to show Zhou Ziheng he's serious, one hand reaching down to pull off the towel still wrapped around his waist. But then they hear two knocks on the door.

Fuck. Who is it this time? They hold their breath.

"Why is it so quiet...? Do you think they could've left...?"

"Let's just go in?"

Ruan Xiao and Zhao Ke push the door open and immediately freeze at the sight before them. Xia Xiqing, clothes mussed, straddles Zhou Ziheng, nude but for a towel at his hips. Xia Xiqing has a tie around Zhou Ziheng's neck, and his other hand is reaching back for Zhou Ziheng's unmentionables. Zhou Ziheng has both hands on Xia Xiqing's waist.

Zhao Ke subconsciously raises a hand to cover Ruan Xiao's eyes, but she bats it aside.

"Don't look!"

"I need to! My ship is sailing. This is my dream come true!"

"But you're not allowed to ogle other men!"

"Quit interrupting me! My ship is about to have their wedding night!"

These guys... Xia Xiqing lets go of the tie and gets up off the bed, rearranging his rumpled clothing. Zhou Ziheng coughs awkwardly and pulls his comforter up to better cover himself.

"Eh?" Ruan Xiao looks disappointed. "You're stopping?"

Xia Xiqing smirks and pulls his tie from Zhou Ziheng's neck to re-knot it back at his own collar. "I don't actually mind streaming for you guys, but our Heng-Heng is shy."

Zhao Ke and Ruan Xiao take a look at each other, voice syncing. "Such a dom..."

"Are you guys ready to go?" Xia Xiqing puts on his shoes and takes his jacket from the closet.

"Yeah, we'll go downstairs first. They'll have to walk us out, so you'll have some time to sneak away. You can meet us at the corner—it's a surveillance blind spot."

"Okay." Xia Xiqing waggles his eyebrows at Zhou Ziheng. "Too bad I'll have to leave hungry."

Zhou Ziheng suddenly stands, pulls Xia Xiqing closer, and pulls the jacket over both their heads. He presses a kiss to Xia Xiqing's lips and slides in his tongue. The kiss lasts so long that Xia Xiqing's knees weaken. Finally, Zhou Ziheng drops the jacket and Xia Xiqing's face is revealed. He rearranges the jacket so it lies more smoothly over Xia Xiqing's shoulders, and speaks softly into his ear.

"Heng-Heng is also sad we didn't get to try with you on top."

Xia Xiqing feels like his heart is gripped in someone's fist.

He shivers as Zhou Ziheng's warm breath ghosts over his ear.

"Next time, Xiqing-gege."

Filled with the ecstasy of proof that they hadn't messed up the dynamics of their ship, Zhao Ke and Ruan Xiao slip downstairs. Meanwhile, the slightly piqued Xia Xiqing pushes open the glass doors to the balcony and puts one leg over the railing.

The evening breeze washes away all his previous thoughts until only longing remains.

He turns, the wind blowing his hair against his cheek. Zhou Ziheng tilts his head, smiling at him with the rose in his hand. His smile is illuminated by the moonlight.

Xia Xiqing's heart rate picks up. The little prince imprisoned behind the glass doors, and a Romeo who's a bit of a failure. Who's the true thief in tonight's break-in?

The investigation of Wei Min renders Zhou Ziheng's imprisonment meaningless, but it's rare that they ever get the chance for a full family dinner, so he stays around. That night, the television they're watching during dinner is showing a segment about the gay community's fight for equality.

"Dad, what do you think?"

Lao-Zhou takes a bite of bean sprouts. "Huh? What does that matter? It's their own business."

"But for the big picture..." Zhou Ziheng tries to poke further. "Aren't there bills for marriage equality almost every year? The big guys don't seem very transparent about their stance right now."

"It's complicated. Too many factors need to be taken into account." Lao-Zhou puts his chopsticks down, sighing. "I'm not actually that familiar with this group, but I'm also not orthodox or traditionalist. People like who they like. What does that have to do with us?"

Zhou Ziheng relaxes, then tries to venture, "So—"

Before anything comes out of his mouth, Zhou Zijing steps firmly on his foot under the table. He adds some bitter melon to his plate. "You seem a bit imbalanced of late—too much heat, I think."

Bitter melon is a good cure for heat. Zhou Ziheng understands the implication—he's being a bit too hot-headed right now, so he swallows the rest of his words. He realizes that he really didn't think it through. Even if his parents are okay with this, Xia Xiqing still hasn't agreed to be with him...

But what if Xia Xiqing really does start liking him? He wants to take him home to meet his parents without any underlying conflict. He wants everyone in his family to like him. If there's going to be a fight about him coming out, he doesn't want Xia Xiqing to feel burdened.

However, these are all just hypotheticals.

"So what about your new movie, now that Wei Min is under investigation?"

Zhou Zijing changes the subject smoothly, but Zhou Ziheng is still sullen, thinking about his current situation with Xia Xiqing. Seeing him stuck in his own head, Jiang Yin slides into the conversation.

"We're looking for a new sponsor. I talked to Director Kun yesterday; he's really sorry about the whole situation. Independent films are small productions, not the bestselling kind. Even if we market it right, it still doesn't look as good to potential investors."

"Of course, it's just business." Zhou Zijing puts down his chopsticks. "How about I do it? We'll need a confidentiality clause, though. I don't want the trouble."

Zhou Ziheng raises his eyes, surprised. "You?"

"Yes, so you need to be on your A-game. I want a three hundred million yuan box-office hit. Don't go losing my money."

With the funding organized, Jiang Yin starts to do some marketing.

First, she spreads the information that Zhou Ziheng's new movie will feature him as an AIDS victim. No other information is revealed.

Already an icon of his generation, and now with his skills and intelligence shown in the reality program, Zhou Ziheng's popularity has reached a new height.

This simple piece of information raises plenty of discussion online. Most of it is very positive.

@LoserMe: I like Zhou Ziheng's choices in movies! He always focuses on minority groups.

@Arries: AIDS? Zhou Ziheng is the best!

@WhoSaidIDontLikeYou: Finally, a new movie from Zhou Ziheng! Last time I watched Seagull with my mom, and she got super invested in the character. She even cried at the end. The funny thing is that she didn't even recognize that the character was played by Zhou Ziheng until I told her afterward. [cryinglaughing.jpg] That's what I call good acting.

@123Wood: Yeah, his acting is unquestionable. I hope he takes a trophy home this time.

As hype builds, Jiang Yin begins to spread a half-truth about the Self-Study ship collaborating in the new movie—rumor is that Xia Xiqing will be playing a very minor role.

It spreads like wildfire, but this time the wind shifts direction.

One side is Self-Study girls in celebration, and the other side is the rest of the internet in doubt and suspicion.

@SelfStudyGoGoGo: OMG Are they going to film together? Is it true? I'm going to live in the cinema when it comes out.

@SelfStudyforLife: Please don't let there be romantic development between Zhou Ziheng and the lead female character Mr. Director I'm begging you

@LetsBeFriends: I can't even imagine the sparks between them in a movie... I need more scenes from our little painter Xia Xiqing.

But criticisms start to pile up.

@BlueDressGirl: isn't Xia Xiqing just an artist? Reality shows and now films? Can't he just leave the entertainment circle alone and focus on his career?

@CitrusGreen: Leaving a perfectly good career in art for the entertainment industry. I guess he couldn't resist the money.

@rockbyebaby: The pretty privilege is real. His face alone got him into a show with his idol, and now he gets to be in a film too? I'd be furious if I was Zhou Ziheng's fan—he's clearly being used for clout.

As protest grows, some of Zhou Ziheng's adversaries begin to get involved. This is a rare opportunity for them to attack his reputation—they can't touch Zhou Ziheng due to his background, but they can attack Xia Xiqing. They buy some accounts on social media to target Xia Xiqing for his "impure" motives, thus triggering another war between Self-Study shippers and Zhou Ziheng's solo-fans. From there, they buy some headlines and a spot on the trending page, with which they can sabotage Zhou Ziheng's image by criticizing his inability to control his own fans.

It's standard operation in Jiang Yin's line of business. And it's also exactly what she wants.

Before the war even began, she contacted the BNFs using Zhou Ziheng's official channels, asking them to lead their followers away from the battlefield and to avoid any contact with any adversarial accounts. Meanwhile, they buy adversaries out of spots on trending, replacing them with behind-the-scenes clips of Zhou Ziheng preparing for his new role.

Just when everything is at its peak, *Survive and Escape* releases the bonus content that they asked their guests to record after the episodes. This draws the attention of all viewers. The most important part is the Easter egg at the end: the mysterious scriptwriter appears.

"Hello, everyone. I'm the writer for *Survive and Escape*," a masked young man says in front of a work desk.

He carries on, describing his work process. Sitting before the television, Xia Xiqing is stunned. The sadistic writer that's been tormenting them is none other than Xu Qichen!

"At first, I didn't truly believe that I could accomplish such a difficult task, but your positive reviews gave me the confidence to continue my work and test the limits of our contestants' emotional endurance." Xu Qichen smiles at the camera.

"Watching the show with you guys is a really fun process for me, and I get all these new ideas as I watch our contestants trying to solve the puzzles. Especially in the first episode, the scene where the two guests interact in the dark gave me the inspiration for a new story."

"I thought to myself, what if a boy becomes HIV positive and contracts AIDS? What if, as angry as he is, as wronged as he is, tries to go on the warpath to seek vengeance? And what would happen to the victim of his aggression? The scene in that episode seemed to fit very well with a scene in this potential story."

Xu Qichen walks to a wall covered with storyboards, relationship charts, and other various notes.

"I wrote a new script and was lucky enough to have my ideal candidates act out the resulting film."

What...? Xia Xiqing's mind wreaks havoc on him. He slowly takes out his phone and dials Xu Qichen's number.

Xu Qichen confesses immediately. "Yes, it was me. I honestly thought you'd find out sooner."

Yes, he should have. The plot, the connections between each clue, the knowledge about mathematics and physics, and the whole movie-like plot line. Who else could it be other than Xu Qichen, who can rely on his husband, a STEM graduate of Tsinghua University?

With the release of the bonus video, the top two spots of the trending list are dominated by "Writer of *Survive and Escape*" and "Zhou Ziheng New Movie." Public views also change direction again.

@CountDuck: Hmmm. I have a feeling I'll need to eat my previous words, since it really is a movie from that writer...

@SophHastoWorkHardToday: I'm interested in this plot! I think I'm going to watch it.

@KunLun: Does anyone else find that writer really cute? He's my ideal type.

@Love33: They haven't confirmed if Xia Xiqing is going to be in this movie, but I like the writer. Can't wait.

@rockbyebaby: A good writer doesn't equal a good film. Two different things.

Guessing that the adversaries will turn to focus on Xia Xiqing next, Jiang Yin decides to strike back. She edits Xia Xiqing's official audition clip, then takes a recording of it being played on a screen—as if it's being leaked by someone trying to cover any digital traces. She sends it out on a private account, and various media outlets immediately start sharing and reposting the recording with the title "Zhou

Ziheng New Movie—Xia Xiqing Audition Leaked—Possibly Co-Lead."

These twists have given the audience enough satisfaction, especially Xia Xiqing's touching performance. Incidentally, this also gains him another wave of solo-fans.

@PositiveNegativity: I wasn't interested in him until I saw this performance. The look in his eyes when he avoids looking at the little girl...my heart...How is he so good at everything? I'm glad I ignored the ppl criticizing him without proof.

@WhereIs87Im78: That single tear at the end--so good! And some people were so sure that he couldn't act. This must be a rude awakening for them!

@NotEatingDurian: Well, I did say that I'd rather die than watch his movie...Fine. This is me swallowing my words.

@SelfStudyEveryDay: My lovely Xiqing baby! Don't worry come let me hug you! You were so good in the audition omg <3

@MaybeYouLikeSelfStudy: I need the official trailer like right now.

...

A few days later, the movie gains a lot of publicity and the public is left in full anticipation of Xia Xiqing's acting skill. Watching his sister-in-law orchestrate the whole endeavor, Zhou Ziheng can only sigh in admiration.

"Brilliant. No wonder you're the best manager-slash-producer," he flatters, giving her a shoulder rub. "I was wondering why the writer for *Survive and Escape* was never credited—turns out it was all part of your plan to promote the show and the movie together."

Jiang Yin rolls her eyes. "You're such a kiss-ass. Pack your things; we leave tomorrow for the film location. We need to get you familiar with the setting and get you into character. Don't let my work go to waste."

Zhou Ziheng nods, then hesitates, wanting to ask one more question before he leaves, but his sister-in-law beats him to it.

"Xia Xiqing is going, too. You two need to spend some time together, find your characters, get the feelings going."

Zhou Ziheng maintains composure and makes a small sound of acknowledgment. As he turns, he lets his lips widen fully into a grin.

No need to get the feelings going. They already are.

But he'll be able to see Xia Xiqing tomorrow. Thinking about the good news, he falls into deep sleep.

Zhou Ziheng originally planned on picking up Xia Xiqing from his apartment in the morning to go to the airport together, but Jiang Yin stops him.

"You don't want to be seen together right now. Your fans have finally calmed down after the fight."

Although Zhou Ziheng gives a sullen nod, he wants them to be seen together. He wants everyone to know that they're close. But Jiang Yin is right; they need to go separately.

Xia Xiqing doesn't have a managing company, and he'll need an assistant on set. Jiang Yin picked an experienced PA from her company, though the original male assistant she picked was eventually changed to a female one after Zhou Ziheng's protest.

"Do you know where Xia Xiqing lives? I'll give the address to Xiao-Xiao so she can go pick him up."

Zhou Ziheng almost recites the address, but reconsiders. The fact that they're neighbors wouldn't look nearly as coincidental to the outside world as it really was. He doesn't want to give out any information that might cast aspersions upon Xia Xiqing's person—

—Or so he deludes himself into thinking.

"Uh... You should let Xia Xiqing go to the airport by himself. If your car is followed and some reporter takes a photo of him getting into your company's car, they'll say that he's been signed by you."

Jiang Yin rolls her eyes. "I might as well have him signed. It's no different from what I do now, except right now I'm doing it for free."

Zhou Ziheng keeps sweet-talking his sister-in-law on the way to the airport. Jiang Yin considers his warnings, then asks Xiao-Xiao to go to the airport to meet Xia Xiqing there. Finally, everyone gathers at the airport. Zhou Ziheng caught traffic on the way, so he's the last to arrive. When he's close to the gate, he sees Xia Xiqing surrounded by a group of girls, all yelling his name and asking questions. He tries to surprise Xia Xiqing, but he's spotted by the girls quickly.

"Heng-Heng, the gray hoodie you wear fits you really well!"

"Heng-Heng, looking good today!"

"Zhou Ziheng, you look so alpha!"

Zhou Ziheng nods appreciatively and rejects their gifts politely. With difficulty, he moves toward the eye of another storm of activity. Hearing the noise near him increase, Xia Xiqing takes out his earbuds. He wears a black T-shirt, high-waisted work pants in a dark gray, and a light gray baseball hat. Seeing Zhou Ziheng's face in the crowd, his blank expression turns into a smirk.

"Oh, look at how Xia Xiqing and Zhou Ziheng match today."

"Yeah, you're right! Black and gray, a monochrome couple's outfit."

Zhou Ziheng is a bit surprised. He simply put on whatever he could find at home, and it just happened to match Xia Xiqing's outfit. Is this what people mean when they say two individuals are "in sync"?

Zhou Ziheng suddenly feels he's the hottest guy on earth today, having worn this outfit.

When it comes time to board, the number of fans have increased to the point of the space becoming unwalkable. Zhou Ziheng reaches out to brace Xia Xiqing by his shoulders, afraid that he'll trip. That's when the onlookers finally realize how well-fitted Zhou Ziheng's black T-shirt is.

"Ziheng, are you going to finally do it this time?"

"Do what?" Zhou Ziheng looks confused. "What am I going to do?"

The fans all laugh. "A romantic movie, of course!"

Zhou Ziheng coughs. Xia Xiqing feels the hands on his shoulders gripping him tighter. He smiles warmly at the girls beside him. "Still not a romantic movie this time."

Some fans sigh in disappointment.

"But the two characters do have a complicated relationship. From my understanding of the script, they seem to be more than just friends." Xia Xiqing turns his head to find Zhou Ziheng's face. "What do you think?"

Zhou Ziheng hesitates for one second, falling into Xia Xiqing's beautiful eyes. "Ah. Yeah, I agree."

No, not just more than friends. They're straight up romantically involved. Zhou Ziheng repeats this analysis to himself, over and over again.

The flight isn't long. Xia Xiqing sits diagonally in front of him, and Director Kun is his neighbor. He wants to get some shut-eye like he usually gets on planes, but it seems Director Kun has a lot to share with him.

The whole time, Zhou Ziheng's attention is manipulated

by the passenger at the front, his eyes fixing on the back of that seat and lingering on his neck.

"The final script is quite visual, so that's a big help." Director Kun clicks a folder in his laptop. "We went on location last week with the camera crew. This is what we got."

Zhou Ziheng nods. His gaze shifts from Xia Xiqing's back to Director Kun's laptop. In the photo, there are two rows of buildings that almost reach the sky, both lined with tiny windows. Here and there are various counter-regulation structures. The narrow pathway between the two main buildings is barely six feet wide, dark and muddy, shaded from all sunlight.

Director Kun observes Zhou Ziheng's face. "Isn't this place inspiring?"

Zhou Ziheng nods like he's awakened from a dream. "Yes... exactly."

It's on this pathway that the desperate Gao Kun follows Jiang Tong and pushes him against the tarnished green wall.

"This is in Wuhan?" Zhou Ziheng finds it hard to believe a prosperous city like Wuhan has a place like that.

"Yeah." Director Kun nods. "Writer Xu had this place in mind ever since he started writing. I heard that he's from there, so I'm not surprised. He said it's kind of a village-within-a-city, and that this kind of place has almost gone extinct. I guess we are lucky to find one."

Writer Xu is from Wuhan. So is Xia Xiqing.

Zhou Ziheng lifts his eyes, seeing the sleeping person tilting his head almost to a horizontal level. After some turbulence, he swivels his head back to place.

Will shooting in his hometown bring back bad memories for him? Zhou Ziheng is a bit worried, but he immediately thinks of what Xu Qichen said: Xia Xiqing can't hide from it forever. He needs to face his past.

Zhou Ziheng feels the humidity in the air as soon as they land, like an open sauna in May. This kind of weather is unsettling for a born-and-bred Northerner like him, but Xia Xiqing seems unaffected—except that sleeping during the flight made his neck sore. He stretches it out and listens to Zhou Ziheng and Director Kun talking and laughing behind him. At this, his grumpiness worsens.

But then, almost immediately, a warm, dry palm lands on the back of his neck and starts to massage away his soreness. Xia Xiqing turns his head, finding Zhou Ziheng still facing Director Kun, for all that it's his hand on the back of Xia Xiqing's neck.

Zhou Ziheng says in a loud voice, "Director Kun, are we going to the hotel first or the site? Where's the rest of the crew?"

"Hotel first." Kun Cheng laughs. "We're not officially shooting yet." He looks at Xia Xiqing. "Xia Xiqing, we rented a place for you in Hua'anli to help you get into character. It'll be where Jiang Tong lives in the movie. Zhou Ziheng will stay there with you. Just settle in for a few days and feel out the situation." He smiles apologetically. "It'll be a bit tough— the characters aren't exactly living in the best of conditions."

"It's okay." Xia Xiqing smiles, removing Zhou Ziheng's hand from his neck. "I don't mind harsh conditions."

They're picked up by a car after leaving the airport. The driver is a local guy with a strong Wuhan accent, which Xia Xiqing finds very comforting. The hotel is in Wuchang District. The three of them are in one car, and the assistants are in another.

Kun Cheng sits in the front seat. He knows this driver from the last time he came into the city. The driver casts a glance at the rear-view mirror, smiling.

"Oh, I know this handsome guy. Big star. My daughter likes you. I'm Yang Fei, by the way, but call me Lao-Yang."

"How about Fei-ge?" Zhou Ziheng smiles in a friendly way.

Fei-ge's gaze lands on Xia Xiqing. "This handsome guy doesn't look much like a Northerner. Skin's too fair, haha."

Xia Xiqing smiles. He pulls on the brim of his hat. "I'm from Wuhan."

This is the first time Zhou Ziheng hears Xia Xiqing speak in his native dialect. Unlike many southerners, Xia Xiqing has always spoken Mandarin with a very standard accent, maybe even with a bit of a northern tinge. Few people can identify his place of origin from his accent alone. But when he speaks in his native dialect, his voice deepens and his tone livens up with a bit of a drawl. Zhou Ziheng thinks he sounds adorable and cool at the same time.

"Oh! You're a local. No wonder." The driver also falls back into local dialect. "I was thinking you look pretty local."

Xia Xiqing spares Zhou Ziheng an amused look, only to find their gazes meet. He murmurs an amused question, "Did you understand what Fei-ge said?"

Zhou Ziheng blinks. "Huh? Uhh... He said you're handsome, too."

What? Xia Xiqing laughs. "Keep up the pretense."

He plants himself deeper into the seat, letting his hat hide his face in shadow. Xia Xiqing looks outside at the office buildings, the blue construction fences, the overpass near the train station... Everything is filtered through a gray lens, like it's an old black-and-white movie that he's watched too many times.

Every scene is familiar, yet each time he's able to find

something new.

Zhou Ziheng imitates him, trying to sink into the seat, but there's no more space for his legs. He stretches out one leg, sticking that foot in between Xia Xiqing's feet, pretending that was his intention all along. He doesn't want to bother Xia Xiqing, so he sits there quietly.

The scenery changes dramatically after a while on the road. Buildings are older, with peeling walls looking like they're from the 80s. The most distinct one says "Friendly General Goods" at the top, surrounded by other similar but smaller buildings, with various signs for hardware and grocery stores.

"They can't tear these buildings down. Too close to the river," Xia Xiqing suddenly says. "Lots of old structures in this area. This place used to be a central district."

"I can tell." Zhou Ziheng is surprised that Xia Xiqing has initiated a conversation—pleasantly so.

Not long after, they're on the Yangtze River Bridge. Zhou Ziheng's view has suddenly broadened. The river is covered with the golden glitter of sunset. He sees ferries on the river, hears the long horns, and watches the stained red clouds in the evening sky illuminated by the fiery light of the sun.

This is different from the scenes of the Yangtze River in Jiangnan. Here, the river is broad, unreserved, dashing in a way reminiscent of old wuxia stories.

A bit like Xia Xiqing—seemingly soft, but actually very lively upon contact.

"This is amazing," Zhou Ziheng sighs. He's reminded of a line from a Song dynasty poem: *"The evening clouds hang heavy over the vast heavens of the state of Chu."*

Xia Xiqing chuckles. "Not bad for a physicist."

They don't rest or eat after checking into the hotel; instead getting right back in the car. Xia Xiqing doesn't know where they're going, so he asks, "Director, where will the filming take place?"

"Hua'anli."

"Hua'anli?" He's surprised, but soon recovers. "Can't believe you guys managed to find that place."

Director Kun laughs. "Writer Xu told me about it. He said he even returned for a visit while writing the script."

"Oh, yeah. I almost forgot." Xia Xiqing stares out the window. "Few Wuhan locals ever go there. Hua'anli has practically been excluded from the city."

"Oh..." Director Kun looks at Xia Xiqing. "I heard you and Writer Xu were schoolmates? You guys must've known each other for quite some time."

"Yeah, we've known each other since high school. He was pretty amazing even then; he kept writing for essay contests and the like. His articles were great." Xia Xiqing's face softens as he mentions their high school years together. "He was super introverted back then. Never talked to anyone."

Xia Xiqing feels his wrist gripped by another hand. Surprised, he turns to find Zhou Ziheng has covered their joined hands with his backpack. He tries to pull his hand away, but Zhou Ziheng's grip is too tight, and he even forcefully uncurls Xia Xiqing's fist and intertwines their fingers.

Xia Xiqing mouths a questioning *what* to him, but Zhou Ziheng just smiles wordlessly, hanging onto his hand. He likes when Xia Xiqing reveals his soft side, but he doesn't like it when the reason isn't himself.

"Well, Writer Xu still doesn't talk much. But he's easy to talk to when he does, and he's always kind to everyone."

"Ah? Yeah... That sure is him," Xia Xiqing replies halfheartedly, afraid of being caught by Director Kun.

Zhou Ziheng, on the other hand, asks Xia Xiqing, "What about you?"

"Me? What about me?"

"What were you like in high school?"

Xia Xiqing senses a hint of regret in Zhou Ziheng's question; it's as if he thinks he missed something important. Not wanting to see the sincerity in Zhou Ziheng's eyes, he lowers his head. "Sort of like who I am now."

"Xiqing must have been popular back then," Director Kun cuts in, half-teasing. "Must have been the most eligible boy in the entire school."

"That's right!" Fei-ge is interested, too. "It must've been hard to find someone as handsome as Xiqing."

Finding Zhou Ziheng's hand squeezing him tighter, he realizes that this is not the right time to gloat. Xia Xiqing is about to turn and give him a glare when Zhou Ziheng leans in first, grinning widely.

"Yeah, you don't say. He's so very handsome."

The sarcasm in his tone is a bit too obvious.

"So?" Xia Xiqing's eyebrows lift.

Zhou Ziheng scans him with care and impure intent. Their joined hands emit untold amounts of heat.

"I'm just curious. Are you more experienced in pursuing others or being pursued?"

Xia Xiqing laughs silently. His gently rubs a finger over the back of Zhou Ziheng's hand. He eventually responds, but it's not an answer. "I'm hard to pursue."

His whisper falls on Zhou Ziheng's heart like a half-burnt feather, landing softly upon Zhou Ziheng's heart-of-hearts, scorching its way through his veins. Nonchalant, he rubs the side of Xia Xiqing's index finger with his thumb.

"I guessed you would be."

After they pass the river and the more prosperous parts of the city, the landscape starts to become more sparse, less urban. Zhou Ziheng pokes Xia Xiqing's feet with his own. "Are we close yet?"

"I don't know." Xia Xiqing doesn't seem to have given his answer much thought.

"Aren't you from here?"

"Yeah, but not many locals can say they've been to every part of Wuhan," Xia Xiqing says, almost sounding like a sigh. Only Zhou Ziheng has noticed.

Fei-ge is in a talkative mood, adding, "Yeah, he's right. Not even drivers like me."

Xia Xiqing casts a look at Zhou Ziheng, whose attention is focused on the tiny mole on his nose. "You know the saying, right? The 'three towns of Wuhan'?" Seeing Zhou Ziheng nod, he continues, "Well, they're more like three cities. They're all really big. My family lived in Hankou. I liked to go sketching at the University of Wuhan during high school. It took two hours by transit." The memories have brought out the softness in him. "Theoretically it was enough time to take a full nap, but the drivers here are aggressive, so you really can't."

Zhou Ziheng wants to hold him and listen to him talk through the night.

"You've got enough time. There's still a week until we start filming." Director Kun smiles. "Xiqing, you can take Ziheng to have a look around the city. Help him get into character."

Xia Xiqing nods. His clutched hand is a bit sore, so he gives Zhou Ziheng a look, who instantly gets the message and lets go, thinking that he hurt him. Xia Xiqing, however, chooses not to take his hand back, so Zhou Ziheng gently puts his hand on top of his.

Not long after, they reach their destination. This is the infamous "village in a city," the most un-Wuhan-like part of the city. The roads are narrow and the crowds are tightly packed. Passersby are forced to brush shoulders. With some difficulty, Fei-ge drives the car into the Hua'anli Tunnel.

The tunnel is more like a pathway through Hua'anli. The two walls beside them are painted green, and the ceiling is concrete. The entire thing is about sixteen feet wide, and it's responsible for moving hundreds of thousands of people in and out of Hua'anli every day.

Fei-ge honks at a dirty van in front of them. "We're in luck today. If there'd been any cars going in the opposite direction, we might have gotten stuck head-to-head."

Finally, the boxy van in front of them moves forward, like a senior citizen walking across the street. They, too, have to move slowly. As it gets darker inside the tunnel, Zhou Ziheng subconsciously grabs Xia Xiqing's hand. When he looks in Xia Xiqing's direction, he finds him staring at the view outside.

At least he didn't reject me, Zhou Ziheng comforts himself.

It seems there's been a lot of rain lately; the roads are all muddy. There's a woman carrying two grocery bags walking past their car. After she gets a few mud stains on her clothes from the wheels, she curses them in the local dialect, albeit an accented version thereof.

As an actor, Zhou Ziheng actually likes places with normal everyday folks. Everyone is a storybook, written in their expressions and their body language.

Finally, they get to a point where the car can no longer advance, so they get out and start walking. Fei-ge guides them toward the house that Director Kun rented. Zhou

Ziheng and Xia Xiqing walk at the back, their shoulders brushing together in the hot, humid air.

The four of them arrive at the place in the photo. The high-rises are similar to "living cubicles" in Hong Kong, but not quite the same. The upper floors were clearly added on top of the original apartments at a later date. The lower half of the walls is dark gray, drenched in oil and smoke, and the upper half is light blue, looking a bit purple in the rosy dusk.

"The conditions here are harsh." Fei-ge lights a cigarette, and even the smoke seems sticky. "Too many people living in such a tiny place. Can't expand, so they have to build higher."

Before Zhou Ziheng can look up, he feels a hand pressing on the back of his head. After he moves forward a step and turns, he sees a wire exposed above his head. Xia Xiqing has already put his hands in his pockets.

"You need to keep your head down a little." Xia Xiqing's voice sounds bright and clear in such a humid environment. "Who knows what they fed you as a kid; your height is unnatural."

Fei-ge adds, "Yeah, how did you get so long, Ziheng?"

"Long?" The puzzled Zhou Ziheng sends a look to Xia Xiqing in hopes he'll be rescued.

Xia Xiqing chuckles. "In the Wuhan dialect, we don't say people are tall, especially kids. For example, if I were your uncle..." He touches Zhou Ziheng's hat, imitating the tone of an older guy and saying in the local dialect, "Heng-Heng, how long you've grown in this last half a year!" Then he recovers. "You know?"

Zhou Ziheng smiles.

"Xiqing's Wuhan dialect is pretty authentic," Fei-ge compliments, laughing with Director Kun.

Director Kun is also pleased. "Writer Xu is amazing. He's

even saved me the money of hiring an accent coach. Xiqing, you can just do a Wuhan accent for your character."

"Aren't I playing someone hard of hearing?"

The road ahead is so muddy that Xia Xiqing has to lift up his pant legs to continue the walk. Zhou Ziheng spaces out for a second when he sees Xia Xiqing's ankles and the exposed skin. His mind goes back to the night when Xia Xiqing's ankles had been propped on his shoulders. His eyes had looked just like the humid atmosphere of this city.

"Oh, yes, you're right. Jiang Tong has a slight communication disability." Director Kun taps himself on the forehead in remembrance. "You won't have many lines, and the disability will get in the way of the accent. I guess you can teach Zhou Ziheng, then."

Fei-ge says, "But Zhou Ziheng's character isn't a Wuhan local, is he?"

"Then he'll need an inauthentic Wuhan accent." Director Kun laughs.

Xia Xiqing takes off his hat and scratches his head. The weather has finally gotten to him. Before he can put his hat back on, Zhou Ziheng pulls him over and whispers something in his ear.

"I agree. I am pretty long."

Xia Xiqing frowns and gazes up, his hair soaked in sweat and glued to his cheeks. His angry expression comes off more seductive than anything else.

Zhou Ziheng whispers against his ear, "You even said that I could reach deepest."

This pervert! Xia Xiqing is trying to not let his anger show. He won't give Zhou Ziheng the satisfaction of getting under his skin. He takes a deep breath. Is this karma? Is he being punished by the universe?

With his newly adjusted facial expression, he turns to Zhou Ziheng and says, "Length is not important. Experience is."

To Zhou Ziheng, this is clearly flirting.

He nods, grabbing Xia Xiqing's shoulder. Director Kun happens to turn around and is relieved to find his actors talking to each other. After all, they'll need to have a certain level of friendship to be able to work long hours together.

"Experience requires continuous work." Zhou Ziheng's eyes land back on Xia Xiqing. His words are plainly submissive, but the way he says them is strangely dominant. "Won't gege teach me?"

Flushed to his ears, Xia Xiqing pushes him away. "Hot," he says. Zhou Ziheng doesn't know if it's the Wuhan accent or something else, but the way he said it seems to have a coquettish effect.

Despite being pushed away, Zhou Ziheng is happy. It's dinner time, and there's a delicious smell of lotus root and pork ribs soup in the air, making him feel utterly contented with life as he looks at Xia Xiqing walking in front of him.

As long as he's here with him.

They walk into a building. The stairs are narrow and dark. After a few steps, Xia Xiqing finds his hand locked again with Zhou Ziheng's. He's too lazy to resist and the light is so dim the two people in front of them can't possibly find out, so he just lets it be.

They get to the fourth floor. Fei-ge takes a key from his pocket and opens the door, lit by the flashlight on his phone.

"Here it is." Fei-ge steps in. "Come on in. It's really kind of tiny."

It's actually in better shape than Xia Xiqing expected. He assumed the place would be old and dirty, when in fact, it's just small. It's a very standard one-bedroom apartment, but it feels crowded with four people standing in it. Everything in this place has been designed for one person only. The only source of light is a small window in the bedroom with a cactus pot beneath it.

The stuffy feeling is like a cling film, transparent but airtight, cloaking Zhou Ziheng's senses. He pulls on his collar a few times in attempts to air out his shirt.

"So, this is it. The owner of this place keeps it pretty clean. It's a young man who works around here." Director Kun laughs. "He's a good kid. I said I could pay him more because we needed to redecorate this place, but he wouldn't take it. We did pay him more in the end, though. He was so thrilled he wouldn't stop thanking me."

Xia Xiqing tries to link this place to Jiang Tong. It's a unique feeling, like he's remodeling himself to be someone else. He sits on the sofa and turns on the small dusty fan in the corner. The airflow is slow, but still better than nothing.

Zhou Ziheng's eyes are fixed on Xia Xiqing, watching the heated air blow through his hair, his outstretched neck as he leans closer to the draft. There's a lock of hair stuck at the corner of his lips, which he fixes.

It's an incredibly sexy look.

"Oh right, time to go. I have a meeting with the crew later. We'll go shoot some night scenes. Are you guys staying here or going back to the hotel?"

Zhou Ziheng jumps into the conversation before Xia Xiqing can respond. "I'll stay. I want to run some lines here, find my character." Then he sits beside Xia Xiqing, grabbing his shoulder. "Xia Xiqing will stay too. I'll call Xiao-Luo to pick us up once we're done."

Fei-ge tosses him the key. "Okay, this is yours then. My

wife is rushing me to pick up the kid from tutoring."

"No problem. Thank you, Fei-ge. I'll ask my assistant to come later." Zhou Ziheng's fingers tap Xia Xiqing's shoulder. "Don't worry. Xiqing is sort of a local. We'll be fine."

Persuaded, the two older men leave the place. As the sound of them walking downstairs gradually disappears, Zhou Ziheng closes the door. He's pinned against it as soon as he turns around.

"What are you planning on doing?" Xia Xiqing tosses his hat onto the green sofa.

Zhou Ziheng feels his heart has been branded by Xia Xiqing's palm on his chest. "You," he answers.

Xia Xiqing lowers his head, removing Zhou Ziheng's grip on him. "In your dreams." He walks toward the bathroom, voice echoing in the room. "I'm going for a quick rinse. It's too hot. You should call Xiao-Luo and ask him to bring us some food. I'm hungry."

When he goes inside and tries to lock the door, he finds that the rusted latch won't even move. A hand tugs on the door frame. Xia Xiqing lifts his gaze, finding Zhou Ziheng smirking down at him.

"I'm hungry too."

After that, Zhou Ziheng slides inside, crowding the already cramped bathroom. Xia Xiqing already turned on the water, and the humidity inside the room gradually increases.

The sticky atmosphere warms the bed for their desire.

"Two people don't fit in here." Xia Xiqing pulls his shirt off.

Zhou Ziheng takes a step closer, almost touching him. "Not if we stand closer."

Xia Xiqing's flushed lips part slightly. His face seems amused, but his words are harsh. "Why are you so clingy?"

Zhou Ziheng takes the black T-shirt from his hand and tosses it outside the bathroom. He pushes Xia Xiqing backward until he stands under the showerhead's main trajectory. The warm water cascades over him.

"Better than you. Hard to pursue, hard to get with."

"Fuck." Xia Xiqing looks down at his drenched pants. "How am I supposed to go out later? I'm fucking drenched."

Zhou Ziheng kisses his cheek. "There are clothes in the wardrobe. I saw them."

"Are we allowed to wear them?" Xia Xiqing stretches his neck and the water flows down his chin.

"I'm good with not getting permission." Zhou Ziheng licks the piece of skin under his ear. "Yours, for example."

Xia Xiqing pretends to not understand. Zhou Ziheng holds his hand and leads it down to the part that needs action.

"Don't you want it?" He continues kissing his ear. The splash of water echoes in the room. "I've been wanting to do this since I saw you at the airport."

Xia Xiqing is never a shy person when it comes to sex. He's good at it, but he needs to be in control right now. "I want to, but let me top."

He pulls his hand from Zhou Ziheng's grip, but Zhou Ziheng seems uncaring of what he said and pins him against the slippery wall while groping for his groin. His touch is rough and forceful, and a moan slips helplessly out of Xia Xiqing's mouth.

Encouraged, Zhou Ziheng presses their lips together. He yanks down Xia Xiqing's fly, reaches into his pants, and starts rubbing him through his underwear. The hot steam has filled up the entire room, making Xia Xiqing's head spin in pleasure. Zhou Ziheng's tongue invades his mouth, almost suffocating. It elicits a strangled moan from him. He feels like a wet circuit board, like he could explode any second.

"Are you...in heat?" Xia Xiqing finally escapes those lips.

He lifts Zhou Ziheng by the neck and leans against the wall, gasping. Zhou Ziheng's hands haven't been stopped, and he grabs Xia Xiqing's leaking cock and gives it a few slow strokes.

"Yes." He kisses his forehead. "I've been wanting to do it with you. I want to do it while you're sober."

Xia Xiqing can hardly keep himself together. They've been playing for so long, and there has always been an itch he can't scratch. It's built up so strong that he has no strength to resist anymore, but he still wants to be on top. He doesn't even know why he's still struggling. He's struggling for the sake of struggling.

Zhou Ziheng feels his body trembling, so he holds him and kisses him gently.

"Come on. Let me top once, this is only... hnn... fair." Xia Xiqing snaps his head back, enduring Zhou Ziheng's hands.

"Sure." Zhou Ziheng gives his nipple a light squeeze before he leans in and licks it. "If you have the strength."

"Fuck..."

Before Xia Xiqing can retaliate, Zhou Ziheng is suddenly on his knees with his lips wrapped around Xia Xiqing's cock, with both his hands on his waist pinning him to the wall. This is a big surprise to Xia Xiqing, but it's so good that he can't help but put his hands on Zhou Ziheng's head.

"Ah... Less teeth... Yes, suck more...hnn..."

Zhou Ziheng is a good student in every sense of the word. He wraps a hand around the base and jacks him off while his mouth swallows the head in and out, and he smooths his other hand over Xia Xiqing's ass.

"Oh, I'm gonna come... Get off..."

Even Xia Xiqing's tone is different, with each word coming out wrapped in hot steam. Zhou Ziheng releases him as requested, but he immediately squeezes his hand around the base of Xia Xiqing's shaft, staving off the orgasm.

"Ah..." Xia Xiqing shivers. "Let... let go."

"If you let me fuck you." Zhou Ziheng is clearly very sober as he begins to bargain.

Xia Xiqing frowns, eyes watery. "You're a jerk."

"But Xiqing-gege, you were the one who seduced me first." Zhou Ziheng kisses his lips, voice softer. "Please, I'll make you feel so good." Seeing that Xia Xiqing has calmed down a little, he gives him a few strokes, then immediately tightens his grip around the base of the shaft.

"You fucking...deviant..." Xia Xiqing bites Zhou Ziheng's shoulder. "Let me come."

"If you agree to my terms."

Xia Xiqing is at his wit's end. His hands hold onto Zhou Ziheng's back, and his voice is almost inaudible. "Okay..."

"Really?" Zhou Ziheng is utterly shocked.

"Fuck..." Xia Xiqing gasps, but then trails off in a moan as Zhou Ziheng starts stroking again.

Zhou Ziheng puts Xia Xiqing down on the toilet lid. After taking a condom from his pocket, he quickly removes his pants. His sizable erection juts out.

"Are you out of your mind...?" Xia Xiqing leans back. "What if that fell from your pocket? You're a public figure..."

"It was in my backpack."

Zhou Ziheng tears the wrapper open with his teeth. He squeezes excess lubricant onto his hand and reaches behind Xia Xiqing, rubbing his fingers insistently at his entrance. Having stretched him rather crudely last time, Zhou Ziheng tries to be more patient. Xia Xiqing is quiet at first, but starts to moan louder. When his two fingers poke a very particular place, Xia Xiqing suddenly bites down on his shoulder.

"Is it good?" Zhou Ziheng presses again and again at that same place, feeling Xia Xiqing trembling ceaselessly. He's trying to hold back his moans, but occasional sounds leak through.

Upon fully stretching him, Zhou Ziheng strokes Xia Xiqing's softening cock back to full hardness, then hands him the condom. "Put it on me."

Xia Xiqing slumps to the side, gasping a little. "Then come here."

Zhou Ziheng walks closer, his erection almost poking Xia Xiqing in the face. He puts his hand on Zhou Ziheng's cock, who takes a deep breath. Against all expectations, Xia Xiqing puts the condom in his mouth. His tongue pokes cutely out the center of the ring of latex, then retracts. And just like that, he begins to swallow Zhou Ziheng's length.

He's rolling the condom down with his mouth!

Zhou Ziheng tries very hard to control his reaction. Gritting his teeth, he reaches down and pulls up Xia Xiqing's legs, holding him by the knees and spreading him wide. They both curse as he slides in all the way.

After a few thrusts in this position, Zhou Ziheng feels that it's not quite good enough, so he pulls out. Xia Xiqing's neck is flushed and beaded with sweat. He turns his head to the wall, gasping. "Do you even know how to fuck...? If you don't, then you should let me..."

Zhou Ziheng leans down and thrusts his tongue into his parted lips, trying to suck the breath out of him. "Look at the state you're in. Would you even have the strength to fuck me?" He pulls him up to a standing position, lifting one leg by the knee and leaving the other standing. The position is too embarrassing, and Xia Xiqing feels the urge to escape, but he's backed against the wall.

"Oh...ahh...hnn..."

Zhou Ziheng starts to thrust, each in-stroke harder than the last. The bottom of his shirt is getting in the way, but he has no time to take it off. Instead, he picks up the hem and holds it between his teeth. Xia Xiqing feels a rush of pleasure shiver down his spine as he looks at him—as he looks at how sexy he is when he focuses entirely on fucking him.

"Ah... faster...ahh! Too deep..." He wraps his arms around Zhou Ziheng's waist, watching his cock disappear and reappear as he fucks in and out in an almost bestial manner. His own cock slaps against Zhou Ziheng's abs. He feels like he's being electrocuted. "Fuck...good...ahh!"

Xia Xiqing's face contorts, and his entire body shudders. Zhou Ziheng knows he's hit the right spot. He thrusts in harder and faster, and Xia Xiqing moans in response, his nails almost ripping into Zhou Ziheng's skin. "Ahh...wait... aaaah, wait! Wait...ah! Ah..."

Zhou Ziheng lets go of his shirt and starts to suck along Xia Xiqing's throat. "Do you like getting fucked by me?"

"Ahh..." Xia Xiqing is climbing that peak, and his thoughts are scattered and fleeting. He mumbles, "Mmm...yes...yes, I do..."

"More specific." Zhou Ziheng grinds against that spot.

"Yes...I like...I like getting fucked by you..." Xia Xiqing is so close. He just wants to come. "Fuck me...faster...ah! Ah..."

He's completely fucked open, and the orgasm drags on for so long, sweeping its way from his groin through to the rest of his body, sparks of ecstasy electrifying him from head to toe. He shudders, and Zhou Ziheng turns him around and thrusts a few more times.

Xia Xiqing sobs, feeling completely liquefied. Zhou Ziheng's hips move faster and press harder, until he feels he's on the edge. He pulls out, peels off the condom, and rocks into his own fist until he comes all over Xia Xiqing's ass.

Seeing Xia Xiqing slipping down along the wall, Zhou Ziheng picks him up and sits him back on the toilet lid, kissing gently at his nose and cheeks.

"You good?"

Xia Xiqing rests his head lazily against the crook of Zhou Ziheng's neck, sleepy but still sharp-tongued. "No."

Zhou Ziheng beams at him. "Want more?"

"Fuck off. My bones are coming apart."

"A hug? A cuddle?" Zhou Ziheng pats him on the back. "It's a good position."

"Fuck off."

"Lets go again?"

"You dare..."

C.15

A Smoldering Heatwave

Tired and spaced out, Xia Xiqing lets Zhou Ziheng shower him from head to toe, then watches as he does the same to himself. Xia Xiqing, sitting on the toilet, pops the occasional bubbles that splash onto his arms and continues to admire Zhou Ziheng from this angle.

They look just like an ordinary couple doing couple-like things in this small corner of the city.

Except it's not real. Xia Xiqing gathers his soaked hair behind his head and collects himself.

"What are you thinking about?" Zhou Ziheng walks up to him, running a hand over his face. He hasn't even dried off yet.

Xia Xiqing bites down on Zhou Ziheng's thumb. "I was just thinking how perverted we are," he says, raising his head at these words.

"True." Zhou Ziheng's thumb rubs gently on his teeth. "And I used to be so innocent."

Xia Xiqing lets out a snorting chuckle. "After messing around with me, you're no longer allowed to use that word." The afterglow hasn't faded completely from his face. "Who would've guessed that the set would be first used for this? It's not like we're doing porn."

Zhou Ziheng pulls his thumb out a bit, drawing on Xia Xiqing's soft lower lip. The smile on him looks incredibly sexy.

"I wouldn't mind if it was with you." Zhou Ziheng looks childish again. "To complete my acting career."

Xia Xiqing slaps his hand away and rolls his eyes. "Stop it." He leans back and says, "It's so stuffy in here."

At this, Zhou Ziheng immediately says, "I'll go out for a bit." He stands and walks out of the bathroom to fetch clean underwear, a white cotton T-shirt, and a pair of dark blue sports shorts from his backpack. After a moment of hesitation, he leaves them there and walks into the bedroom.

Staring at the half-empty closet, he struggles for a bit, but eventually feels too guilty to touch anything. He walks back to the living room, puts on his clothes, grabs his mask, and leaves in his drenched sneakers.

Xia Xiqing hears the sound of Zhou Ziheng moving around, but is unsure what he's doing. Ten minutes later, he steps into the bathroom in a pair of blue slippers, holding clothes, a towel, and another pair of slippers.

"You went out?"

"Yeah. I went to buy some stuff." He places the clothes on the washing machine in the bathroom, then starts rinsing out the new towel before wringing it out. He then uses it to wipe down Xia Xiqing. At this, Xia Xiqing feels all warm and fuzzy inside.

You don't have to, is what he wants to say. Those words have come out of his mouth so many times before, but somehow, he can't do it with Zhou Ziheng. It's still true. People like him don't deserve the tenderness Zhou Ziheng has shown.

"Okay. Raise your arms." Zhou Ziheng helps him get into the white T-shirt he wore when he went out. Meanwhile, he's wearing the black T-shirt he bought downstairs for thirty yuan.

After getting Xia Xiqing dressed, Zhou Ziheng lays out a pair of blue slippers, same as his own, and personally puts them onto Xia Xiqing's feet.

"Better?" Zhou Ziheng drags him standing, then sneaks a hand around Xia Xiqing's waist only for him to bat it aside.

"I'm fine." Xia Xiqing escapes Zhou Ziheng's grip and walks out of the bathroom in his fitting slippers. Wiping his hair dry, he feels utterly refreshed.

It's completely dark outside, and only a dim lamp engulfs the room in yellow light.

"What's wrong?" Xia Xiqing asks as he sees Zhou Ziheng turning his head, trying to check something on his back.

"The tag makes my neck itch."

"Go sit on the sofa." Xia Xiqing looks around and his gaze lands on an old pair of scissors on the shelf. He walks over and picks them up. They feel well-used in his hand—the rubber is so aged that it's started to peel off. "Where did you buy that cheap shirt? Night market?" he asks while walking toward Zhou Ziheng.

Zhou Ziheng pats his legs suggestively and gives Xia Xiqing a toothy grin. "Bingo. How did you guess?"

He sure is the least picky celebrity I know. Incapable of resisting that smile, Xia Xiqing walks over and straddles the proffered leg while reaching for the tag on his back.

"Don't move. I'm not responsible for cutting you if you

do."

"Uh-huh."

Zhou Ziheng couldn't be happier. His arms circle Xia Xiqing's waist loosely, head leaning on the crook of his neck. This time, Xia Xiqing smells only like mint shampoo. To him, the ebb and flow of the passion and the calmness after the storm are both incredibly satisfying.

Xia Xiqing cuts the last thread and removes the tag. Despite being careful, he still did some damage to the collar.

"Done."

Zhou Ziheng playfully refuses to raise his head. "Just a little longer."

"Are you some kind of puppy?"

"No." Zhou Ziheng looks up at him, his eyes full of longing. "Let me kiss you."

Seeing Xia Xiqing unmoved, he repeats his request. Despite looking unimpressed, Xia Xiqing eventually leans in and kisses him.

"Are you satisfied now?"

"No." Zhou Ziheng pulls him forward and deepens the kiss.

"I'll use these." Xia Xiqing threatens him with the scissors.

"I don't think so." Zhou Ziheng's lips fall on his neck. Holding Xia Xiqing's hand with his own, he moves it toward his chest. "Do it then."

Xia Xiqing has had many pursuers in his life, and they all promised him the world. But frankly, he couldn't feel anything. Deep down, he knew they wouldn't love him if they truly knew him. But Zhou Ziheng is something else. His affection is like blue lava—although it looks as calm as the ocean, once you let it touch your skin, it will swallow and melt you.

Xia Xiqing can only let go of the scissors. He presses their lips harder together. When has he ever been so dull and indecisive? As long as Zhou Ziheng won't break the balance between them... Still, Xia Xiqing wonders if he's too narcissistic. Maybe Zhou Ziheng is just playing with him. Maybe he's trying to simulate love like he's doing an audition—that wouldn't be too bad either.

Summer sends its breeze through the windows, cloaking their eyes. This kind of loving and tender kiss rarely happens to Xia Xiqing, who always chooses to conquer rather than allow himself to be conquered.

Suddenly, Zhou Ziheng's stomach growls. The two of them have to break the sweet entanglement.

"I guess you're truly hungry this time." Xia Xiqing laughs and gets off of him. He glances at the hanging clock and says, "Let's go. I'll take you to eat."

The humidity is still overwhelming, but it's a cool evening. They walk downstairs side-by-side. When they stand on the street, they see lots of market stalls around them. Each one sells different things, from clothes to plants to electronics.

"You've never been to a night market, have you?" Xia Xiqing pushes Zhou Ziheng's baseball hat down.

Zhou Ziheng also adjusts his glasses. "No. These stalls have gone extinct in Beijing."

"Of course. That was for the city's image." Xia Xiqing drags him to the pedestrian side of the road. He reminds Zhou Ziheng after he adjusts his mask, "Be careful of your phone. I've lost three of mine to night markets."

Zhou Ziheng smiles, relaxed, his arms wrapping loosely around Xia Xiqing's shoulder.

"You're not afraid of people photographing us?"

"Let them." Zhou Ziheng leans closer. "It's good for celebrities to show how personable they are by condescending to be in this sort of place."

But then Xia Xiqing feels the hand on his shoulder lift. He turns and sees that Zhou Ziheng has caught a cart that had been about to tip over.

"Thank you, young man. You just saved my day's work!" The speaker is an old lady with gray hair.

Zhou Ziheng doesn't understand, as she spoke in the local dialect, but he still listens carefully with a smile after he puts the cart back in place.

"Please be careful," he says, then squats. He takes a napkin from his pocket, folds it, and places it under the short leg of the trolley. "Here. Now you're good."

As he raises his head, his gaze meets with Xia Xiqing's. Seeing Zhou Ziheng smile, Xia Xiqing thinks he must be hallucinating. He sees a pair of glowing wings on Zhou Ziheng's back.

Why would someone as kind as Zhou Ziheng hang out with him?

He walks to them, glancing at the insulated barrel and sliced fruits, then says to the old lady in the local dialect, "Ma'am, could I have a cup of mung bean ice slush and a *biqi* skewer?"

After getting the snack and drink, Xia Xiqing walks on ahead.

"I want to eat too," Zhou Ziheng says, chasing after.

"Go buy some yourself."

"But I want yours."

Xia Xiqing suddenly turns, making Zhou Ziheng come to a hasty stop and take a quick step back. Xia Xiqing hands him the drink. "Don't drink it yet," he says. He takes a fruit off the skewer and thrusts it forward. "Try this. It's probably not considered fruit where you're from."

Zhou Ziheng, however, bends down and eats the peeled fruit directly from Xia Xiqing's hand. It tastes crunchy, juicy, and sweet.

"Yummy." His eyes light up. "Another!"

Xia Xiqing laughs too. He takes the mung bean slush back and turns around. "Buy it yourself."

"Come on! Can I have one more please?"

"This is water chestnut."

"Really? I think we only use water chestnut for dumplings or meatballs. We don't usually eat them raw. Plus, ours aren't so crisp." Zhou Ziheng puts his arm around Xia Xiqing's shoulders again. "It's better here. You have stalls selling all kinds of fruits. And they're affordable too."

It's always a pleasure to hear compliments about one's hometown.

There's a food court near the center of the night market, and all the food stalls get good business. Xia Xiqing leads Zhou Ziheng to sit at a corner table, then orders four plates of kebabs. The smell of cumin and chopped green onions on the sizzling meat is extraordinary. He walks to a stall next to them to order some braised snacks and soup dumplings with tomato filling. Soon, the table is covered in food.

"Try them."

Zhou Ziheng takes one bite of the chicken knuckles and instantly feels the heat exploding in his mouth. He takes a gulp of Xia Xiqing's slush.

"Wow! This is spicy!"

Seeing Zhou Ziheng huffing air in through his mouth like a golden retriever, Xia Xiqing laughs so hard that he almost chokes. "I asked for mild."

"You can't eat anything as spicy as this. You've only just—"

Xia Xiqing kicks his knee, hard. "Shut up or I'll leave you here."

With a wild grin on his face, Zhou Ziheng reaches for Xia Xiqing's hand and gently strokes it, trying to comfort him, However, Xia Xiqing he pulls his hand back and picks up a knotted piece of braised seaweed to put on Zhou Ziheng's plate.

"Try this. My favorite."

Without hesitation, Zhou Ziheng puts it in his mouth. It's soft and savory after hours of braising. "Hmm, I like this!" And then the spiciness hits. He sticks out his tongue. "Wow, it's spicy too."

Xia Xiqing clicks his tongue and shakes his head, finishing his skewer of green peppers. "Almost everything here is spicy."

In the end, Zhou Ziheng polishes off the two tiers of soup dumplings by himself. Then, having not had enough, he orders two more tiers.

"Here you go, young man." An older guy puts the food on their table. At this point, Xia Xiqing has already put his mask back on. The guy seems to be the owner of the stall, and he casts a look at Xia Xiqing's tied-up hair before he says, his Mandarin accented so heavily that it might as well be the local dialect, "Wow. You're blessed to be playing around with such a pretty girl."

Zhou Ziheng only understands a little. He smiles, thinking the owner was praising how good-looking Xia Xiqing is, so he starts smiling in response. Before he can reply, Xia Xiqing takes off his mask and says, quite soberly, "I'm a man."

"Ah?" The owner takes a more careful look, then realizes how wrong he was. He smiles apologetically. "My bad! Sorry, please excuse me. My wife told me there was a really tall, really pretty girl who ordered two tiers of dumplings, and I thought that was you. Sorry."

Xia Xiqing gives a superficial smile and says that it's okay. The owner apologizes again, then backs away.

"Was he saying that you're good-looking?" Zhou Ziheng asks him after the owner leaves. He's just curious why Xia Xiqing had to explain he's a guy. Then he recalls—play? "What does 'playing around' mean?"

Xia Xiqing has just taken a bite out of a soup dumpling, and, hearing this question, he burns his tongue on the hot broth that spurts from the bite. It splashes to his plate.

From a table next to them, a half-drunk middle-aged man also hears Zhou Ziheng's question, and he taps him on the back. "You a Northerner? Tourist?"

Zhou Ziheng subconsciously adjusts his glasses a bit. It doesn't seem that he's been recognized, so he replies, "Yeah."

Laughing, the guy explains with accented words, "Playing with someone means going out, dating, that you're a couple. Got it?"

A—a couple? So the owner thought Xia Xiqing was his girlfriend?

Tongue burnt, Xia Xiqing buries himself in his almost empty slush like it's the most important thing in the world.

After their midnight snack, they walk along side-by-side. The noisy traffic and people seem to disappear as they walk further away from the central area. A train passes by, and they feel their hearts trembling in its wake.

Zhou Ziheng's mind is still occupied by the stall owner's words, and he contemplates how Xia Xiqing is a perfect representative of this city—free, adventurous, and bold—this city that calls romance "playing around."

"Do you think..." Zhou Ziheng begins with a small voice.

Xia Xiqing walks past him and throws the empty cup into a garbage bin like shooting basketball.

"Do we count as play—" The sound of another train coming their way submerges the rest of his words, like a monster eating away the silence of a summer night.

After the world falls quiet again, Xia Xiqing turns with his fingers curled into a half-fist.

"What did you just say?"

Xia Xiqing is very smart man. Zhou Ziheng watches that flawless face under the moonlight.

A short silence follows.

"Nothing," is his response.

How many times does he have to warn himself? It's not time yet.

They practice the script against each other in the hotel for the rest of the week. In the screenplay, there are many confrontations and flashbacks. Since Gao Kun must go through each stage of a disease—from HIV-positive all the way to AIDS—Zhou Ziheng's appearance will be dramatically different in the later stages of Gao Kun's life.

"I think you should wear an ear stud," Xia Xiqing suddenly raises his head and talks to Zhou Ziheng after going over the script for twenty minutes in silence. "And dye your hair too."

Zhou Ziheng scratches the hair that he purposefully left long for filming. "You sure?"

"Of course." Xia Xiqing picks up his phone and sends a message to the creator's group.

Xia Xiqing: Director Kun, I have an idea. We can get Gao Kun to dye his hair or wear an ear stud to make him look more thuggish.

There are only four people in this group: two actors, one

director, and one screenwriter. Soon, Kun Cheng answers.

Kun Cheng: I agree. As a kid who's been hanging with the wrong crowd for three years, he's probably dyed his hair already.

Xu Qichen: Yeah, and the hair will add contrast between his and Jiang Tong's visuals.

Kun Cheng: Good to have a fine arts major on our team! Maybe Xiqing can even do a sketch for the major characters.

Kun Cheng: Just joking lol

Not a hard task, Xia Xiqing thinks, but he only has the energy to do one or two. Hesitating on his response, he sees a new message.

Zhou Ziheng: I think his plate is full enough with memorizing his script haha. Anyways, what color should I go for?

Xia Xiqing feels the warmth spreading through his chest at the sight of Zhou Ziheng excusing him from additional work.

Kun Cheng: Blond, maybe? The rustically lurid kind. Super brassy, super cheap.

Xu Qichen: Hmm... Seconded.

Almost laughing out loud at the thuggish, yellow-haired image, Xia Xiqing's eyes flit over Zhou Ziheng, who is sitting with his legs crossed as he texts. Xia Xiqing turns Zhou Ziheng's head in his direction and stares at him with shifty eyes, then picks up a tablet and stylus next to him.

"Are you going to draw me?"

"Shush..."

Zhou Ziheng lowers his head and sees the message he's about to send—*"You guys are serious? I guess if you all think yellow is the way to go, I'll do it. An artistic sacrifice."*

He deletes it and types a new one after seeing Xia Xiqing start to draw him.

Zhou Ziheng: Hair color is a big deal! I need at least three minutes to think about it.

Kun Cheng: You just don't want to.

Xu Qichen: [laughing.jpg]

Soon, Xia Xiqing sends a screenshot to the group.

Xia Xiqing: What do you guys think?

Zhou Ziheng doesn't click open the attachment. Instead, he moves closer to Xia Xiqing and looks at the digital sketch with his chin resting on Xia Xiqing's shoulder. He sees a tall figure, a blurry face, a dark red buzz cut, and a black stud on his right ear like a mole. He wears a black vest, blue jeans, and old sneakers. There are tattoos on his left arm and a cigarette between his fingers.

"What do you think? Does it work?" Xia Xiqing asks Zhou Ziheng.

"Hmm, I don't think so," Zhou Ziheng answers, lips pursed.

Xia Xiqing slightly frowns, eyes fixed on the drawing. "Where do you think the problem is?" He purses his lips, back straightened. He says in a small voice, like mumbling, "That's my impression of him, anyway."

Zhou Ziheng chuckles, running a hand through Xia Xiqing's hair. Then he sends a message to the group.

Zhou Ziheng: Kun-ge's design is settled, then.

Kun Cheng: Kudos to Xiqing. Well done! I've sent it to our styling team lead.

Xu Qichen: That's my impression of the early-stage Gao Kun too. Thanks, Xiqing!

Seeing all the messages, Xia Xiqing kicks Zhou Ziheng on the waist. "Can you not say good things about me to my fucking face?"

"I was trying to tease you!" Zhou Ziheng laughs and grabs

hold of Xia Xiqing's ankle, then he rolls down Xia Xiqing's rolled-up pants—the AC in the room has made it too cold.

"You're not wrong, though. He's too handsome." Xia Xiqing isn't a fussy person, but when it comes to his art, he can be extremely strict with himself. "Maybe darker skin? What about a scar?" After a few unsatisfactory changes to the sketch, he rolls over and pinches Zhou Ziheng's face. "This isn't my fault; if anything, it's on you. I should ruin your flawless face."

Zhou Ziheng's head falls back after being jumped by Xia Xiqing, but his hand is still on Xia Xiqing's back. He teases, "Fine by me. But do you have the heart to do it?"

The words come out without much thought. He wonders if he's being too self-centered. When he sees Xia Xiqing's hand still in the air, he immediately adds, "I thought you liked my face."

"Well, I like your body too." Xia Xiqing lets go of him. "But you'll be one skinny kid by the end of the film."

"And?" Zhou Ziheng quickly sits up, looking a bit sullen.

Patting Zhou Ziheng's head, Xia Xiqing comforts him, "Don't worry. Beauty is in the eye of the beholder." He kisses him loudly on the lips. "A painting won't lose its artistic value just because the canvas fades."

Such a sweet talker. The corners of Zhou Ziheng's lips lift. He pokes the tip of Xia Xiqing's nose with his index finger, feeling satisfied. "Can't argue with someone who knows art."

Baffled and slightly embarrassed, Xia Xiqing says in his usual defensive tone, "Don't touch my nose like that again, or I'll surgically remove that mole you like." He runs a hand into Zhou Ziheng's collar, smirking. "I can do more than art."

Zhou Ziheng grabs that hand. "Oh really, you want me to show you how to do it again?"

"Stop gloating. One day, it'll be me on top."

"I didn't even stop you last time. You were the one gave inmmph?! Don't block my mouth just because I'm saying something you don't like!"

"I'll be doing you next time!"

"Be my guest."

The two of them snuggle for a while until Xiao-Luo knocks on the door to deliver the itinerary for opening ceremony. To the public, Zhou Ziheng's golden manager is the producer of his film, which is not an uncommon practice. However, to Xia Xiqing, things start to look funny.

"Huh. This is like your family's own movie, isn't it? You act, your brother invests, and your sister-in-law produces."

Zhou Ziheng shrugs. *Not only that, the guy I'm into is my co-lead, and his friend is the screenwriter.*

The opening ceremony is rather simple, as a few supporting actors haven't arrived yet. The director just leads his pair of lead actors in burning the ceremonial incense. To avoid spoilers, they don't even do it in costume, everyone undergoing the ceremony in casual clothing.

In a thirty-minute press conference, Xia Xiqing and Zhou Ziheng take on the responsibility of answering most of the questions, since Kun Cheng isn't good with this kind of stuff. After the conference ends, the shooting officially begins and the stylists work their magic on the actors. Xia Xiqing is relatively easy to dress, as Jiang Tong was originally based on him—even their skin tones are the same kind of pale. He has his hair cut, he changes into a different set of clothes, and then he's done. But Zhou Ziheng is another story—he needs a different hair color, an ear stud, and a tattoo.

On the first day, Xia Xiqing has only one scene to shoot, which will happen in a few hours at sunset. In this scene,

Gao Kun beats up some guys who are asking Jiang Tong for protection fees. This is the first time the two meet each other after the first "stalking" incident. The dialogue is very important.

Their studio is temporarily set up in an apartment in Hua'anli. After Xia Xiqing's makeup is done, he walks from the makeup room to the styling room, where he sees a guy with tanned skin and an energetic look standing at the door.

The guy greets Xia Xiqing, "Hello."

During their handshake, Xia Xiqing finds his face familiar. *Maybe this guy was in a TV show? Or I browsed his profile on Weibo? Probably not a A-list actor.* Xia Xiqing offers a friendly smile. "Hello. My name is Xia Xiqing."

"I know. I watched your show. Loved it." The boy laughs nervously. Probably thinking he's being too casual, he lets go of Xia Xiqing's hand and scratches his head. "My name is Yang Bo. Uh... I play *A-Long*[11]."

Oh. Xia Xiqing realizes he's playing the blood dealer guy who indirectly caused Gao Kun to contract AIDS. "Nice to meet you! You're doing the first scene, right? Are you nervous?"

"Yup, a little nervous." Despite looking quite average, Yang Bo's facial expressions are so vivid that you know he is in the right business.

The makeup artist, Su-jie, who'd just done Xia Xiqing's face, catches up to them. Seeing the two chatting by the door, she nudges Xia Xiqing. "Come on. Let's go inside. You guys can talk when you sit."

Once the door is pushed open, Xia Xiqing instantly spots Zhou Ziheng. He sits in front of the mirror with his hair

---

11 "A-" is a prefix used for making diminutive nicknames, often used affectionately or to show casualness. It has no particular meaning.

covered in a wrap—probably waiting for the dye to set in. There's also a guy sticking a temporary tattoo on his left arm. Zhou Ziheng's gaze shifts from his arm to the door when he hears them. Seeing Xia Xiqing come in with another guy, he greets, "Xiqing!"

When they're together, they rarely call each other's names, so Xia Xiqing isn't very used to hearing it come from Zhou Ziheng's mouth. He smiles back at him.

Yang Bo doesn't notice Xia Xiqing's focus has changed, and he asks, "Are you still going on the reality show while filming for this?"

Xia Xiqing returns his gaze to Yang Bo. "Probably not right now, they've found other contestants."

Not getting the attention he deserves, Zhou Ziheng is slightly unhappy. But there are a lot of people in this room, so he can only endure.

"Done. Don't move." The tattoo guy takes out a hand fan to dry the tattoo, which makes for a funny scene—a big tough guy with tattoos from head to toe swinging a small pink hand fan.

"Ge, how many copies of this sleeve did you make?"

Embarrassed, Zhou Ziheng takes the hand fan to dry himself. The contents of the tattoo include fire, branches, and upon close investigation, an old woman's face. She's supposed to be Gao Kun's grandmother. Gao Kun's father worked in Guangzhou, and his mother abandoned her family after he was born, so his grandmother was the closest family he ever had.

"About a hundred? If that's not enough, we can always print more."

Staring at the tattoo, Zhou Ziheng spaces out a little. After looking at his own hand, he asks, "Ge, a real tattoo wouldn't take all that long either, right?"

"That depends on the design and surface area." The tattoo guy laughs. "Are you thinking of getting one?"

"No, just curious." Zhou Ziheng shakes his head. "Can't do it with my profession. And my father wouldn't approve."

"Makes sense. You'd need to have it pixelated if you go on television."

Zhou Ziheng's hair and tattoo are both finished around the same time. The hair stylist, A-Jie, takes him to wash his hair while carefully avoiding his arm.

Xia Xiqing and Yang Bo talk about the script on the sofa. Yang Bo is from Harbin, and he fits the easygoing stereotype of Northeasterners to a tee. He talks to Xia Xiqing casually, as if they're blood brothers. Their topic has also shifted from the script to their styling.

Xia Xiqing pinches a lock of the brassy yellow hair on Yang Bo's head, smiling. "You know, the director told Zhou Ziheng to dye his hair yellow too, at first."

"Yeah?" Yang Bo laughs. "He'd probably look better than me. Oh right, you guys must be pretty close thanks to the reality show and this film?"

Xia Xiqing's eyes flick to the side. "We're okay, I guess."

It's kind of embarrassing to say that, because the distance between them could probably be described as "negative."

Zhou Ziheng has been glancing over at the corner where Xia Xiqing is. Seeing him touch that guy's hair and laugh, Zhou Ziheng feels increasingly agitated.

"Done." A-Jie puts both her hands on Zhou Ziheng's shoulders. "This is a good color on you, Ziheng."

Zhou Ziheng takes a look in the mirror. *You don't say.* This is exactly how he feels inside, like there's fire blasting out of his head.

No. He takes another look at the corner.

His hair should be green, with how jealous Xia Xiqing is making him.

In reality, Xia Xiqing has been checking in Zhou Ziheng's direction every so often. Seeing that the dark red color has turned out exactly as he imagined, he stands and walks to him.

"Well, you look good."

"Good?" Zhou Ziheng raises his eyebrow.

"Handsome." Xia Xiqing would pinch his face if no one was here. He compliments instead, "Incredibly handsome."

Zhou Ziheng's sharpened contour and his un-groomed brows give him a wild thug look. Seeing the black ear stud, Xia Xiqing touches his earlobe gently. "I mean, you are the most handsome guy on this street."

Zhou Ziheng finds the corners of his lips uncontrollably lifted, but he bites back on the grin.

Even A-Jie starts to joke, "Too bad our director won't give him a pretty girl. You know, the prettiest girl for the most handsome guy."

No, no, no. Zhou Ziheng objects internally. *This handsome guy is going to chase another handsome guy.* He notices how short Xia Xiqing's hair is now. He used to have hair to his shoulders, now it's only to his chin. Just like the first time they met.

"Nice haircut."

"Of course. They're professionals," Xia Xiqing says, placing one hand on Zhou Ziheng's shoulder fondly but not intimately enough to raise suspicion. "But not you. If you give me a bad haircut, you're dead."

Xia Xiqing is talking about the scene where Gao Kun gives Jiang Tong a haircut.

"It's fine. Even without hair, your beauty won't be affected," Zhou Ziheng teases him.

"Go away."

At this time, the assistant director walks into the room. He wipes the sweat from his hairless head before he says in a heavy Beijing accent, "Are we ready to go?"

The guys look at each other and laugh childishly. The assistant director scratches his head again, looking puzzled.

The first scene is between Zhou Ziheng and Yang Bo. The setup is in A-Long's broke-ass apartment—a place the production team only rented for a day, which is why this scene needs to be done first.

In this scene, Gao Kun confronts A-Long about AIDS, and they argue through the security door. Beginning with a confrontation is hard on actors; since Zhou Ziheng is more experienced in acting, Kun Cheng is more worried about Yang Bo.

"Let's do a take first. Don't worry too much—we still have time before dusk."

Xia Xiqing and Zhou Ziheng will be doing the next scene immediately after. The time constraint is real, as they have to wrap up this scene in under two or three hours. Xia Xiqing is supposedly free in this period, but he still stands from afar to watch and learn.

A camera assistant holds a clapperboard in view of the camera and says loudly, "*Stalking*, scene one, take one, first try. Action!"

With a clap, Zhou Ziheng immediately gets into character under a two-camera setup. This side of Zhou Ziheng is unfamiliar to Xia Xiqing.

Gao Kun lowers his eyelids, grits his teeth, and pounds repeatedly on the steel security door. The banging quickly sucks Xia Xiqing into the story.

"Who is it? What the hell?" The inner door opens. A-Long narrows his eyes. The hair on his head is like withered grass. He frowns in disgust. "Are you freaking insane? Do you still want to keep making money or not? Huh?"

Gao Kun clenches his fist, lips pressed together in a tight line.

"Talk! Are you deaf?" A-Long scratches his head and his hand falls on the doorknob. "I don't owe you money, so what's your problem?"

Bang! Gao Kun swings his fist against the door, eyes wide and reddish, like a caged animal in the zoo.

"Fuck you...your..." Gao Kun hisses in a strangled voice. "It was your needle..."

A-Long is baffled, but he soon regains his posture. Gao Kun is just a walking blood bag to him. What's there to be afraid of?

"My what? Are you so poor you've gone insane?"

"I've got AIDS," Gao Kun says.

First, he's calm, like he's talking about someone else's life. But a few seconds later, he begins to bang on the steel door repeatedly, like what's inside that door is the only hope of saving his life.

"AIDS! Do you understand? AIDS!"

A-Long falls into a long silence.

Xia Xiqing is captivated by the story. Silently, A-Long takes a few steps back, looking like he's trying to say something. Gao Kun keeps striking the door like a vengeful ghost.

"It's you. You made me into this! I'm going to kill you! Open the door!"

Xia Xiqing's eyes land on A-Long. Something's wrong, and Gao Kun is trying to save the moment.

"Cut! A-Long forgot his lines." Director Kun makes a gesture to tell them to stop. "A-Long, take a minute. It's okay. We'll do the close-up on Gao Kun first."

Yang Bo has a regretful look on his face and he apologizes repeatedly while bowing. "I'm sorry. Sorry. I was kinda scared by Ziheng."

Xia Xiqing smiles. Growing up acting does have its advantages. Zhou Ziheng got into character really quickly.

After having the sweat wiped from his face by a makeup artist, Zhou Ziheng asks Yang Bo to open the door for him so they can talk about the feelings of their characters in the scene.

"It's okay." Zhou Ziheng pats his shoulder. "I had trouble with conflict-heavy scenes too when I was new to acting. It just takes time."

Yang Bo didn't expect Zhou Ziheng, a brilliant actor with an aggressive look and physique, to be so gentle and patient with him. He's really grateful in return.

"Are we ready? Let's do Gao Kun's close-up. Gao Kun, get ready." Director Kun's eyes land on Yang Bo. "A-Long, stand behind the camera. Get used to his expressions so he won't scare you anymore."

"Am I that scary?" Zhou Ziheng's teases. His exaggerated tone amuses everyone. Even Yang Bo feels more relaxed.

You do look scary when you are angry. Xia Xiqing thinks of the night he was drugged.

"*Stalking*, scene one, take two, first try. Action!"

It starts again. Yang Bo observes Zhou Ziheng while reading his lines behind the camera. This time, Zhou Ziheng immerses himself deeper into Gao Kun. The transition of emotions from his initial confusion and disbelief, to his enormous anger, and then to his pain and helplessness, is smooth and natural. There seem to be tears prickling at the back of his eyes.

"Come out! I'm going to kill you!" Gao Kun pounds and kicks. He even picks up an old mop from a corner as his weapon. "Out! You will die with me!"

But the strength in him seems to be slowly sucked from his body as time goes by. He waves the mop, he pounds, but eventually he stops. He lowers his head, his jaw muscles flickering. He seems to be making a great effort not to let his body shiver.

"I'm nineteen years old..."

Xia Xiqing's chest tightens. It's a heartbreaking line.

A-Long's voice is heard. "Y—you...this isn't funny. I—I don't know anything. You can't put this on me. You can't! I've given you your money. This is on someone else, not me."

"Who am I supposed to get revenge on?" Gao Kun strikes the door again. "Who?"

A-Long's voice shivers. "I—I don't know, okay?! You should look for whoever infected you! I don't have AIDS. It's not me!"

Gao Kun's whole body trembles in anger. He just wants to pull this guy outside and flay him alive. "You come out! Come out! I want you dead! I want you dead!"

"Cut!" Director Kun says. "Good. We'll shoot A-Long next. His lines were well executed this time. A-Long, remember, you're terrified and you want to pass the blame."

Yang Bo nods. Zhou Ziheng is patted on the shoulder by his makeup artist, who powders his face again. To fit his character better, Zhou Ziheng is using a darker skin tone, and it's starting to wear off in the hot Wuhan summer.

As he's being powdered, his eyes flit over to a corner and he spots Xia Xiqing, who's standing off to the side. His eyes suddenly light up—he didn't expect Xia Xiqing to spend his free time here, watching. Xia Xiqing smiles back at him, finding it endearing that, despite all his skill in acting, Zhou Ziheng is so candid with his emotions in real life.

They're on a tight schedule today, so they begin shooting immediately after Zhou Ziheng's face is ready. In the first take, A-Long's expressions are still stiff, especially when he learns about Gao Kun's AIDS.

"You don't have to separate your panic and fear. On one hand, he's completely shocked, and on the other, he's terrified. Not only of Gao Kun, but the disease," Director Kun explains patiently. Eventually, the take is finished on the sixth try.

"Sorry, sorry. I wasted so much time for you guys." Yang Bo apologizes while casting a glance outside. Luckily, the sun is still up.

"It's okay." Zhou Ziheng smiles at him. "You did well for a beginner."

"You knew this was my first film?" Yang Bo didn't expect Zhou Ziheng to know who he was.

"I searched everyone online after the cast list was confirmed. I feel it's better to know these things ahead of time." A bead of sweat dangling from his temple makes Zhou Ziheng look up and smile. "Anyway, I think you're great. I mean, I wasn't able to do what you did in my first film."

Yang Bo wants to embrace Zhou Ziheng. He instantly becomes a fan of this actor who, at twenty, is younger even than he is.

Xia Xiqing walks over. After he recognizes the expression on Zhou Ziheng's face, he compliments him heartily, "Good job!"

Zhou Ziheng smiles with his lips pursed, like a gentleman.

But he needs to find another way to express his joy, so he asks, "Buy me ice cream?"

"Ask Xiao-Luo. I'm not your assistant." Xia Xiqing rolls his eyes. "Ice cream? Are you three years old?"

Whenever these two get together, Yang Bo feels like there's a natural privacy screen that separates them from the rest of the world. He feels the sudden urge to fill the air with romantic bubbles.

Fuck. Wait. Is this what it feels like to have a ship? No wonder their fandom is so big...

Finally, the crew moves the set to an alley behind a hotel before sundown. Since Xia Xiqing's role is an introvert and he's new to acting, Director Kun spends a few minutes explaining the shoot.

As an introvert, Jiang Tong has to communicate with the audience using minute changes in his expressions and more subtle gestures. It'll be difficult to avoid over-acting.

"Are you ready?"

Xia Xiqing nods as he stands just outside the hotel's back entrance. After he hears the clapper, he walks toward a row of bins with two bags in his hands in the alley. He opens the lid of a green bin and dumps the bags into it. After a look at the dirt on his hands, he walks slowly to the sink. He turns the faucet on, then keeps turning it further, but the water still comes out in a thin stream. He puts both of his hands under the faucet and starts washing.

Suddenly, he feels something hit his head. He turns, a little baffled. The sunset paints his face red and he can only see the silhouettes of a few guys walking toward him.

With a beer can in his hand, the leader of that group yells, "Hey cripple, have you been trying to avoid us lately?"

He throws the can at Jiang Tong, who immediately covers

his head. The can ends up hitting his wrist, spilling a few drops on his shirt. Jiang Tong has just finished his shift at the hotel, and he's in a shabby white work uniform with an apron. His lips move, but there's no sound.

Those guys circle him. "Where's your money? If you cooperate, we'll let you go today unharmed."

Jiang Tong nervously makes a hand gesture, but what he feels next is a kick in the stomach from the group's leader.

"Are you an idiot? Talk!"

"I don't...don't have money." Jiang Tong falls to the ground with his back leaning against the wall. He pulls his pockets inside-out. "I...I don't..."

"You don't? Are you picking a fight with me?"

"Cut!" Director Kun says. "Jiang Tong's expression is too rigid. You need to show more fear."

Xia Xiqing stands. He was worried that his fall wasn't smooth enough when he was fake-kicked; he didn't expect the problem would've been his expression.

"Jiang Tong has been beaten up constantly by these thugs. Fear of them should be in his nature. You were too calm before." Director Kun is very easy-tempered, a rare quality among directors. "It's okay. Let's do it again. Xia Xiqing, try to think like him."

As everyone prepares for the next take, Xia Xiqing says, "Director Kun, I think something's wrong."

The lead thug makes eye contact with Xia Xiqing and gestures. In this business, directors have the ultimate say in film-making, and actors don't have the autonomy to reject their suggestions. They risk their careers when doing so. But Xia Xiqing doesn't have a career to protect, so he's unafraid to speak his mind.

"Jiang Tong isn't a coward. He'd be dead if he was. He's

used to being beaten up by his gambler of a father. As a prostitute, his mother wound up beaten to death when entertaining a client at home. He's managed to come so far working all these low-skill jobs, when anyone else would've killed themselves already if they went through what he has."

Xia Xiqing's tone is steady, but Zhou Ziheng feels an ache in his chest.

"He's not afraid. He just needs to get through this horrible day, and because he's powerless to defend himself, enduring is his only choice. Like you said, he's used to the beatings. Maybe acting cold and unfeeling is closer to the truth."

No other crew member contributes to this discussion. They all know that Kun Cheng is a good-tempered director, but he's also a stubborn one.

"I agree." Zhou Ziheng's voice breaks the silence. "In fact, Jiang Tong, who seems weaker, has more courage than Gao Kun, who's the one that's truly afraid."

Director Kun's brows are furrowed as he looks at the ground, and then Xia Xiqing. At this moment, the determined look on Xia Xiqing makes him look like he's the real Jiang Tong.

"Okay. Point to you." Kun Cheng shrugs, pulling on his hair with a smile. "The Jiang Tong you described is closer to the script. Excellent." He can feel a fire rising from the pit of his stomach. All he wants is for his audience to feel the core of this script under his direction. "Yes. We'll do it this way." He then repeats with more excitement, "We'll shoot this way!"

Xia Xiqing smiles. Kun Cheng's facial expression is utterly familiar to him: it's the craving for artistic perfection.

From then on, Kun Cheng gives Xia Xiqing his unconditional trust in character judgment. It's a risky move—the worst outcome is that the entire movie is ruined. Despite Kun Cheng having absolute authority over his crew, not everyone is convinced by the new actor, which is obvious to Xia Xiqing. The only thing he can do is to act to the best of his ability. But what kind of ability does he have, to be honest?

The determination to dissect himself is all he has.

"Action!"

Jiang Tong gets down on his knees, then on his stomach, but there's not a trace of surrender in his eyes despite being the subject of bullying. No matter how many fists land on him, or how they insult him, his words are unchanged.

He doesn't have money. It's the truth. Most of his salary was used to pay rent, and he used what's left to buy some groceries and painting materials—the only hobby he has. He doesn't even have the money to repair his bicycle.

"No money? I'll show you who's boss."

The leader has lost his patience. He pulls Jiang Tong up and smashes him into a wall. Jiang Tong feels like his insides have tied into a knot, and all his strength is used to fight the sharp pain. Seeing a punch about to land on his face, all he can do is shut his eyes. This isn't new to him, anyway. All this pain will go away as long as he can live through it.

He waits for the incoming fist, but instead of the pain, he hears a loud scream and feels a few warm drops on his face. His collar is released and he slips from the wall. When he opens his eyes, he freezes. The leader falls to the ground in front of him, blood all over his face. Jiang Tong touches his own face blankly.

His fingers come away dyed with blood.

He sees a baseball bat on the ground that wasn't there before. Did someone use that to hit him?

"Wang-ge? Wang-ge, are you alright?"

The other gang members come up and help their leader stand.

"Who the fuck hit me? He's dead! Fuck, my head..."

They turn around, and Jiang Tong stares blankly in that direction too. There's a tall guy walking toward them from the end of the alley. His hair looks like fire in the sunset, and his face is unrecognizable. The light is his veil.

The intruder walks to them silently.

"Catch him! I want him dead!"

This is a four-on-one fight. Jiang Tong waves frantically at him and says with great difficulty, "Le—Leave!"

That person seems deafer than Jiang Tong himself. He rushes a few steps and kicks the first guy in the chest. But that's when Jiang Tong finally sees his features—especially his eyes.

He shivers and mumbles, "That night...that..."

It's the stalker who almost killed him!

Like someone is squeezing his throat, Jiang Tong falls quiet. His pupils dilate in apprehension.

In the darkness, his mouth had been covered by those hands, and when their gazes met, he'd seen the eyes of a trapped wolf.

The tall man's each and every strike and kick feels like he wants his target dead. Jiang Tong is terrified by the realization that this guy doesn't care if he kills someone. The most dangerous kind of people are those who have nothing to lose.

Soon enough, the thugs fall one by one, until they're all moaning in pain on the ground, too weak to escape.

Panting, the guy turns to look at Jiang Tong. At the same time, Jiang Tong turns his head to avoid eye contact.

Sweat drips from his forehead. It's cold. He's afraid. This is the first time he admits it. He's truly afraid.

He still can't overcome the fear of death from that night.

"Why are you still here?" the guy asks, voice low and out of breath. "Are you waiting for them to beat you to death?"

Jiang Tong's head snaps toward the guy, gazing at his face and at the blood on his lips and eyebrows. How can he say that? As if he isn't the one who tried to kill him that night.

Apparently, he gets to live if he runs away right now. However, for some reason, he can't move. He stares into those eyes.

"You...you are..."

Instead of walking closer like Jiang Tong thought he would, the guy slowly bends down until their eyes are on the same level. He stares at Jiang Tong with a blank expression.

"I was the guy who stalked you that night." The corners of his lips lift, more like a warning than a smile.

"I...I know..."

Jiang Tong's response is strenuous but firm. His back is against the wall and there's no weapon in sight. Even if there was, his chances are slim. Those guys already tried.

He tries to steady his breathing while moving his legs to stand with his back against the wall. The pain in his stomach hasn't lessened. His right leg is injured. Each step takes strength. Yes, he got away from the thugs. But he's more terrified than ever—a shadow follows him, just like that night. He speeds up, and so does the ghostly shadow.

He walks past his bicycle after a split-second of hesitation. He's almost at the end of the tunnel, and his heart is pounding.

"You fear me," the guy says behind him.

Jiang Tong shivers. He can no longer worry about his bicycle. He limps faster toward the light, but with nothing to hold onto, he stumbles and falls to the ground. His shadow stops too.

"You should fear me," he says, sounding desperate. "But not now."

Jiang Tong can't comprehend what he means, and has no intention to. He doesn't turn around. The two of them move onto a quiet street with almost no traffic.

There are parasol trees on each side of the road, so overgrown in the summer that their branches almost brush each other in the middle, like they're trying to cover the entire blue sky—like two beings rooted in different places reaching out to each other. They know it'll all be worth it when their branches touch.

Jiang Tong enjoys these trees in this season. Somehow, this has become one of the rare moments of hope in his hopeless life. He lowers his head and sees the shadow is still there. He's able to lean against a tree every three or four steps, but as the pain grows, each of his steps takes longer than the last...

"Stop."

Startled, Jiang Tong almost trips.

"Turn around."

Jiang Tong obeys, fearing for his life. But he's also stubborn, so he only turns his face to the side.

He thought this natural-born killer would bring him somewhere, torture him, kill him, maybe even cut his dead body to pieces. After all, if not a natural killer, if not for money or pleasure, what kind of person would follow a random guy and try to kill him?

However, the "serial killer" just quietly sits on the sidewalk, staring at him.

What does he want?

Jiang Tong turns around. He doesn't dare to move, but the guy gives him a threatening look and Jiang Tong walks closer to him.

"Don't sit too close to me."

Confused, Jiang Tong chooses not to argue. He bends his knees with much pain and sits. His eyes flicker to the guy's face. The blood on his eyelids has dripped down his cheek. His face is like a sculpture he can't afford to buy for his sketching practice.

Jiang Tong's gaze is fixed on him. Heart beating fast, he swallows nervously and turns his head.

"Cut!"

Kun Cheng stands, unable to hide the surprise on his face. "Bravo! That long shot is very usable."

The previous fight took five or six tries, which is reasonable considering the intensity and the multiple angles they had to do. But what makes Kun Cheng really excited is the long shot of Jiang Tong standing and emerging from the alley with Gao Kun following him.

The chemistry between them is so natural that it's exceeded even his highest expectations. Even Gao Kun's lines after that were executed flawlessly. This time, he has really found a diamond in the rough.

Xia Xiqing huffs a long breath, letting go of the toxic emotions. He feels a bit exhausted and lost, but he's amazed at what actors can do. Without professional training, it must be hard to let go of the negativity during film production.

Xiao-Luo walks over with a small pink fan. Before he can speak, Zhou Ziheng takes the fan from his hand and gives it to Xia Xiqing, who's sitting next to him. "Are you hot? Here, use this."

Xia Xiqing casts a glance at Zhou Ziheng's forehead,

which is covered in sweat. "You seem more bothered by the heat."

"I'm okay." Zhou Ziheng turns off the fan and tosses it into Xia Xiqing's lap.

The makeup artist pats Zhou Ziheng's head, laughing. "Then stop sweating so we won't need to powder you every break. See? Your blood is getting diluted by your sweat."

Zhou Ziheng smiles, slightly embarrassed. Xia Xiqing smiles too, one hand holding the fan. He turns it on and moves closer to Zhou Ziheng, holding the fan between the two of them. Remembering the script, he teases, "I want to sit closer."

Zhou Ziheng notices and moves a bit to the right, repeating Gao Kun's words. "Don't sit too close to me."

"But I want to." Xia Xiqing moves a bit again.

"Stop it, guys. Let me work." The makeup artist laughs at the two childish guys. Xiao-Luo has a scornful look on his face, but he doesn't dare to let Zhou Ziheng see.

"Is it hard for you to play Jiang Tong?"

Xia Xiqing arches a brow, eyes teasing like a thug. He lowers his voice and says, "Making the person who started fights in school play someone who keeps getting bullied..."

Zhou Ziheng lowers his voice too. "You should blame it on your looks."

Xia Xiqing fixes him with an angry stare. Zhou Ziheng immediately apologizes, "I was kidding!" Then, he's amused. "I never picked fights at school."

"I'm not surprised. You were the kid who called the cops."

Zhou Ziheng looks at him in shock. "How do you know?"

Xia Xiqing laughs a bit childishly. "I just do."

Zhou Ziheng falls quiet, the smile fading from his face. He changes the subject. "You...how did you look so afraid of me just now?" He thinks about his phrasing for a second. "I mean, you don't seem to fear anything, not even violence."

After a few seconds, Xia Xiqing replies. "I fear the dark." He chuckles. "I just borrowed that feeling."

His chuckle falls heavily on Zhou Ziheng. Borrowing one's biggest fear shouldn't be so easy.

Suddenly, Xia Xiqing feels his cheek getting wiped.

"Sweat."

Xia Xiqing looks up, seeing Zhou Ziheng smiling apologetically.

"Oops. I think I just made it worse."

"Go away. You're annoying." Xia Xiqing wipes his face while looking down with a smile.

Kun Cheng replays the long shot one more time before he walks toward the two leads with satisfaction on his face. "That shot was brilliant. I was right about shooting from the walking angle." He walks to the head cameraman to talk about the scene.

"Nice job. Long shot for your first scene." After Kun Cheng leaves, Zhou Ziheng starts to tease Xia Xiqing, "What a talented newbie."

"Wasn't that once your title?"

"Me? It's mostly just practice for me." Zhou Ziheng puts a cooling pad against his forehead. "Little by little." He puts his hands on his knees. "I was told by many directors that I was good with big dramatic scenes, but I could never act like a normal average person. I can't act if I don't understand."

He gazes at the street. "I would sit on the sidewalk, just like this, sometimes for a whole afternoon. I was young, in high school, and I didn't have the fame back then. I just watched people passing by, day after day. I finally realized one day that we're all just vessels for our emotions. Our emotions pull on each other to keep us moving and breathing. They grind and grind until our surface becomes smooth and we look calm to the world."

He looks back at Xia Xiqing with a smile on his face. "After that, I realized I have to show that calmness as an actor."

The sunset paints the contours of Zhou Ziheng's face in gold. Xia Xiqing can't move his eyes away. He watches without saying anything. He wants to, but no words in his vocabulary can describe his feelings at this moment. They're wonderful feelings, and he won't ruin them with words. If only he had paint and a canvas right now—he'd draw this amazing and devoted actor.

"What are you looking at?" Zhou Ziheng is a little confused by that gaze.

"You, little handsome guy," Xia Xiqing teases him.

"*Big* handsome guy." Zhou Ziheng taps Xia Xiqing's foot with his own while peeling the cooling pad off his forehead.

The next scene is coming soon. Xia Xiqing pulls himself up and walks back to his original position to wait.

"But you don't have to look calm."

Xia Xiqing stiffens at Zhou Ziheng's voice. He can only stare at his shadow.

"I want to see all of your emotions, the good ones and the bad ones, no matter how complicated and no matter how sharp. Don't let them grind away at each other. Just let them all out."

Zhou Ziheng's words get smaller at the end of his sentence. Now only the two of them can hear.

"I can handle everything you give me."

Via Lactea